THE SIREN SERIES

SiRen's Capture

USA TODAY BESTSELLING AUTHOR
JESSICA CAGE

4

Written by Jessica Cage

Edited by Cynful Monarch
Cover Design by: Solidarity Graphics
Book Design by: Jessica Cage

ISBN-13: **978-1-958295-29-8**

DEDICATION

To the readers who championed this story and asked for more. Syrinada returns because of your love and support.

Thank you,
Jessica

PROLOGUE

The longer I lay there alone, the more aggravated I became. My body vibrated with a reserved energy I had no way of expelling. Each day I waited for him I wanted to kick myself. Here I was, a siren, humming with sexual energy and committed to a man who rarely spent more than two nights at home with me.

I could hear my mother's voice in my head. She warned me that a life like this would be difficult. My chosen path wouldn't be able to sustain my needs. Rhys was a witch, not a merman. Though he was powerful, there was a part of me he couldn't fulfill. I refused to believe her. I loved Rhys, and we would be fine as soon as we could be around each other more often.

This had become a pattern. Me waiting for Rhys to arrive hours after we said we would meet in our fabricated space. We called it Sol. The space, fabricated with a blend of our magic, worked in the same way as the Mates Doorways. Those ancient trees sirens used to connect with their partners when they couldn't physically be together. We weren't able to use them because they were created to keep his kind out. Warlocks.

When the covens went to war with the seas, sirens needed a safe space. We thought if I invited him inside with me it would work, but it didn't. My mother, though she was against our union, was the one to tell us of the world we could create because she'd done it with my father.

I pushed thoughts of my parents out of my head. It was already frustrating enough to be there alone. I didn't need more reason to ruin my mood. The bed was enormous, comfortable, but not so comfortable that I would forget his ass was making me wait. As it was, we were only meeting once a week, and last week he hadn't shown at all. I felt like I was starving.

"Sorry I'm late." Rhys appeared at the foot of the bed.

His hair was a mess, his eyes dark with exhaustion. No need to pretty up for me.

"Again," I huffed and rolled my eyes.

"Yes, Sy." He sighed, ready to give me the same list of excuses as he had before.

Rhys was changing. I didn't know why, but he was. Before, he never called me Sy. Most people used the shortened version of my name, but never him. It was one of the many things I loved about him, and yet he changed that. Every time he said it, my stomach clenched with fear that I was losing something that meant so much to me.

"I don't want to argue about it now, Rhys." Instead of debating his tardiness or examining the growing list of changes in our relationship, I turned up my sex appeal.

All I had to do was call the siren to the surface. After being suppressed for so long, when she awakened, I couldn't care about anything other than my physical appetite. His tardiness could be an argument for another day.

I crawled across the bed and met him where he stood at the foot of it. He was reluctant at first, wanting to talk about things I'd already pushed out of my mind.

"Sy, we really should talk about what's going on between us." Rhys tried to get me to talk, but I refused.

"We have little time here." I got to my knees on the

bed in front of him. "I don't want to waste it arguing. I want to enjoy you." When my hand lowered past his waist, into his pants, and gripped his dick, he dropped the topic altogether. All it took was a little physical coaxing to remind him of the reason for our time in this metaphysical space.

My lips pressed against his neck, and I ran my tongue across that sweet spot. Just beneath his jawline. It always did the trick. As expected, the deep moan slipped through his lips, and his hands grabbed my waist, bringing me closer to him. I released his dick after a few strokes, and he dropped to his knees in front of me and pressed his lips against the bare flesh of my stomach. Hot kisses traveled across my flesh, and a soft moan slipped through my lips, encouraging him to continue.

This sweet foreplay was just what I needed. I held on to him as he removed my bra and let my breasts free. Rhys knew the ways to my body. Our months together, before he left to work with the covens, gave him plenty of time to learn what I liked.

He took my nipple into his mouth as he lifted me from the bed, wrapping my legs around his hips. He carried me around the bed and slowly lowered me until my back hit the soft surface.

"Rhys," I moaned his name beneath a kiss.

"Sy, I've missed you, baby," he responded.

"I missed you, too," I returned.

Rhys carefully slipped my panties from my body. When they were off, he continued kissing me as his fingers played with my lower lips and teased my clit. Alternating between soft flickers and firm strokes, he teased my body, and my pussy responded with a wet release, ready for him to do more.

Inspired by his action, I busied myself and reached into his pants again to stroke the length of him. He was already hard and ready for me. Lifting my hips, I rolled him over onto his back and freed him from his pants.

I hadn't tasted him in so long that my mouth watered at the thought. I lowered to suck his dick, twirling my tongue around the head just enough to tease him. He tensed from the sensation and called out my name as I took all of him into my mouth.

As I sucked, he turned my body so my knees were on either side of his face and pulled my ass to sit on his face. His mouth went to work, licking, sticking, sucking, and drinking from me. I moaned around his dick, and when I neared my first orgasm, I bit his inner thigh and kept stroking his dick with my hand.

When he feared he might come, he pulled me away,

flipping me to my back, and continued his feast. I came on his face three more times before he relented. After my fourth explosion, his fingers joined his tongue, and there was the fifth orgasm.

I was far from satisfied. He knew it. After weeks of waiting, my siren was just getting started. He climbed back up my body, again kissing and licking every curve until we were face to face, and he slowly slid inside of my pulsating pussy.

My hands gripped his shoulders, ready for the ride of my life, but Rhys remained still. He laid between my legs, balls deep inside my pussy, teasing me with a series of pulses along his shaft. I tried to lift my hips and encourage him to do more, but he refused me. Usually, I loved this intimacy. The closeness was refreshing, but I wasn't in control. The siren was, and she was hungry for more.

"Sy," Rhys said my name as he kissed my cheek.

"Yes," I sighed. Of course, he wanted to talk now. I wanted to be railed, and he wanted discourse.

"I love you." His words were a breathy whisper that shocked my oversexed brain, and I paused longer than I should have.

"I love you, too," I finally responded, but my

stomach knotted weirdly.

"I'm so sorry—" he started, but I pressed my finger against his lips to stop him.

I didn't want to hear what he had to say. His apologies would only take my head out of the moment and ruin what little time we had together. We could do all the deep discussion later. Now was the time for him to fuck my brains out and feed that side of me he'd left starving for two weeks.

"Fuck me, Rhys," I ordered and smacked his ass.

Understanding how I felt, he held his comment for later and did as I asked.

He fucked me until I was full, until I came on his dick, his face, and his fingers at least ten more times. We fell asleep wrapped in each other, spent from the night's work.

When my eyes opened, the sound of the waves crashing against the beach reminded me I was once again alone. That I would continue to be alone, and that I had no idea when this solitary existence would end.

CHAPTER
I

I wasn't sure what to expect of my life after my father died. I wanted peace, to feel whole again, but that was not what I got. Instead of feeling like I could take on the world, I felt empty, as if I lost some important part of my soul. Sitting alone in a home I thought I'd be sharing with my chosen mate, all I could do was overthink everything that happened and drive myself insane.

When Rhys asked me how I felt, I lied. Every time he brought it up, I brushed it off and told him I was okay. I was tired or just needed a swim. I didn't want to lie to him, but what was I supposed to say?

Was I supposed to tell him I couldn't sleep at night because of the dreams of my father? Was I supposed to tell him that even though I chose him, a part of me still longed for someone else? That I missed the people who'd been so important to me, but I could no longer be around. There were so many things I needed to talk about, but I couldn't talk to him about them.

Standing in the window overlooking the beach, I wiped tears from my face. This was the third morning I'd awakened with the crushing sadness. It wouldn't go away, no matter what I did. Even a night with Rhys hadn't helped the incoming bought of depression. It felt like my soul was aching and nothing I could do would take that pain away.

"Syrinada?" the soft voice broke through my thoughts and warmed my heart.

I'd waited my entire life to know that voice. Dreamt of it every night of my orphaned childhood, and now it was as familiar to me as my own. There was something good that came out of all the heartache. A second chance to know the woman I thought I'd never be able to.

"Mom?" standing on the beach, hair wet from the seas, was my mother. "What are you doing here?" I called down to her.

"I need to talk to you." She looked up at me with love in her eyes.

"I'll be right there," I called down to her.

I wrapped the robe around my waist and left our open deck to meet my mother on the beach. The sand moved between my toes, and the water called to me. As much as I wanted to dive into the waters and swim away, I couldn't. Not only could I not leave Rhys like that, but I also wasn't welcomed back to the waters yet.

Outside of a quick swim for rejuvenation, I stayed out of the ocean. The sirens who dwelled within still had the jury out on my existence. The covens had accepted me, even if I was still on probation, but the sirens blamed me for the destruction brought on Xylon, the capital of their underwater world.

"Mom." I wrapped my arms around her. "I've missed you."

"I've missed you, too." She hugged me tightly.

"What took so long?" I spoke into her shoulder and inhaled her fresh scent. She just climbed from the ocean but still somehow smelled of a fresh field of flowers. "I thought you would have been back a week ago."

My mother was my twin, and despite her age, she looked only a few years older than I did. She had wide eyes with brown irises that soaked up the sun and glowed with its light. Her skin was lighter than my own but still had that warm undertone that reminded me of a smooth cup of coffee, and her hair, longer than my own, fell past her ass. She had strong middle eastern features, though sirens had no nationality. The only comparable differences in our faces were our noses. I had my father's, which was wider and more prominent than hers.

"That was the plan, but things have changed." She released me and fixed my hair. "There have been some complications."

"What complications?" I frowned because there was a never ending list of complications. It would have been nice to not add to it.

"Let's not discuss it here." She pointed to the house. "Let's go inside, have some tea, and chat."

"Okay." I nodded, understanding that she wanted to get out of earshot of anyone who might have listened within the waters.

Once back inside the house, I started the water for tea and brought the tea set she had gifted us to the small dining room table. It came complete with two infuser cups, a honey pot, and a container for sugar cubes. After the kettle whistled, I retrieved it from the stove and brought it back to join her at the table.

"So, what are the complications you were talking about?" I asked immediately. I never knew how long my mother would hang around and didn't want to waste valuable time.

"There are others like you," she answered directly. "The discovery has led to greater conflicting opinions about the safety of our people and the stability we would risk if accepting you into the siren home."

This was why I was in hiding. The sirens didn't trust me. My mother wanted me to come home and learn the ways of our people, but when she brought it up to the elders, they dismissed her. They were no longer concerned with protecting me but with protecting the people of Deuterio from potential threats. My mother was hard at work trying to make sure I got a fair shot at proving myself trustworthy.

I didn't have the heart to tell her I didn't care if they accepted me. I was fine with not going back to Deuterio. There were other options for me, like staying in the human oceans or on land. As long as it didn't stop me from having a relationship with her, it didn't matter. This was important to her. She wanted me to have access to things I wouldn't be able to experience if I remained outside of their realm.

"What do you mean there are others like me?" I stopped mid-pour.

"Hybrids that were hidden, and when word got out about you, well, they made their presence known." She looked me in the eye and grabbed the hot kettle from my hands.

"Hybrids?" I sat back in the wicker chair and stared out the window for a moment. "There are more people like me. How do you know?"

"They made themselves known, Syrinada. They came forward, and when they did, it worried everyone." She took over my job, adding the tea to the hot water to steep.

"You mean I have other siblings?" I didn't know why it was surprising. After all, I had another sister, one I'd only met for a moment before I had to kill my father.

"No, you don't share a father with them, but there are others, and I fear…" she hesitated.

"What? What is it?"

"I'm afraid you aren't safe anymore." My mother sighed. That usual optimistic look, that expression of hope, faded to something tired and worried.

"How could I not be safe?" I touched her hand. "I have nothing to do with them. Mom, I promise. You just told me about them. It wasn't something I knew about and kept from you. Hell, I know nothing about what's going on outside of these walls now. I've been here, being good, like everyone wants."

"There has been talk that we need to set an example, a precedent to let them know we will not tolerate any misbehavior." Her words hung out in the air between us.

"They want to set an example by coming for me?" I said what my mother couldn't. I was a known threat. Someone with great power, and if they could take me out, punish me for simply existing, who else would think to act out of line?

"Yes." She nodded. "The others aren't as strong as you, but while they are weaker, it doesn't mean they couldn't bring a genuine threat to our world. The people of Deuterio are worried that, if left unchecked, these new beings will bring the wrath of the covens down on us like nothing we have ever seen. We aren't strong enough to take them on, Syrinada. There are only a handful of sirens who even have their full powers now."

"Great, so because I'm strong, I deserve to be killed." The tea that sat in front of me no longer felt appetizing. I watched the swirling steam rise from the cup, and my mind spun again.

"Syrinada," my mother called my focus to her again.

"Yes?" Eyes watering with the threat of tears, I looked her in the eye.

"I know this is a lot to take on. I know your mind is full of worry. Trust me, I have been the same way, but I need to you focus. You need to find your sister."

"My sister?" I shook my head. "What are you talking about?"

"The succubus." She nodded. "The young girl in the field. I know you remember her."

I nodded. I remembered her, and I remembered looking for her after that day and never seeing her again. For all I knew, she was a figment of our collective imaginations. "Why do I need to find her?"

"She is like you. I don't know what it was about your father, but his bloodline made for some powerful offspring." She rubbed the back of my hand with gentle strokes and looked at me with sad eyes. "You need her strength on your side."

"What makes you think she is going to want to help me?"

"Because you are family, and if she doesn't see it that way, convince her to." She returned to preparing her tea, dropping two sugar cubes in the cup before stirring it. "There is nothing saying they will stop with you. If nothing else, she is next on their list."

"Why is this happening?" I stared at the tea in front of me. "I mean, when will it end? It's not bad enough I had to kill my own father, but now I'm being punished for what other people did?"

"I know how you've been feeling lately," she responded, "and I know the emptiness within you, even if you don't talk to your mate about it. I can feel it even in the waters outside of your home, Syrinada. As difficult as this task may be, it could also be good for you. Maybe connecting with your family and building a new bond to replace the one you lost will help fill that hole inside of you."

"What bond did I lose?" I shook my head. There were plenty. Malachi, Demetrius, Aunt Noreen.

"The one with your father," she answered, as if it should have been obvious to me.

"We never had a bond, and I'm not going to pretend as if we did. He used me." I couldn't look at her, so I stared at the ant crossing the floor. "Hell, I only exist because he wanted a weapon he could use against his own people."

"You exist for a lot more reasons than your father's

selfish goals. You exist because I love you, and I wanted you to be here. I know you want to believe there is no connection between you and your father, but there is. There will always be. You are his daughter, and so is she. Connect with her. Hell, bond over how shitty he was, but you have to find a way to move forward. You deserve as much."

"What are you going to do?" I asked. She wasn't coming with me. I could tell by the way she spoke. She wanted me to go by myself to find Imara, my succubus half-sister.

"I'll do everything I can to protect you from their madness. I won't let them make my daughter out to be a villain. Not after you saved the lives of countless people by taking a stand against your father. Hell, if it weren't for you, they wouldn't be making half the progress they are."

"What progress?"

"The coven accepted you, Syrinada, which means they aren't allowed to attack anymore. Not unless we do something terrible to go against them, which we do not plan to do. Our people are free to restore what they took from us so many years ago."

"Does that mean that sirens don't have to complete the Naiad's Walk anymore?" The Naiad's

Walk was an arduous journey that the women of our kind had to complete if they wanted to access their full power. It was one that most never attempted, and few actually completed. It was also another reason the siren people hated me. Because, despite my unconventional upbringing, I completed the test.

I was successful with my journey, but it nearly killed me. My mother was another siren who'd completed the test, another reason both the people of Deuterio and the covens feared me. A powerful warlock father and a fully powered siren mother. It was a potentially deadly combination.

"Oh no, that is still a thing, and if I am honest, I think it's for the best. Power is something that should be earned, but we aren't being attacked like we were before. We're able to aid the other cities and rebuild."

"That's good." I smiled.

"Yes, it is, but it's because of you, Syrinada. They want to act as if you had nothing to do with that change and make an example of you. Hell, I wouldn't be surprised if harming you actually added fuel to the fire."

"You think the witches would go to war over me?" I laughed thinking of the part of my bloodline that had already made it clear they wanted nothing to do with me. If it were up to them, and not the ancestors who cast their judgment on me, I'd already be dead.

"Okay, maybe not, but either way, they should appreciate the progress we've made. They should thank you. Not try to make you some cautionary tale for other hybrids."

"Yeah, if only everyone thought about things as logically as you do."

"Syrinada, promise me you will find your sister and protect yourself. At least until I can confirm you aren't in danger."

"I promise," I nodded. "Maybe you're right. Getting out of this house and reconnecting with life might be good for me."

"Good." She looked around. "I honestly don't know how you've stayed here secluded like this. When will Rhys return?"

"I don't know. He was only supposed to be gone for a few days, and that was two months ago. Every time we talk, he tells me he has to extend his trip more, but we make it work."

"Do you?"

"Yes, I'm managing." I sipped my tea for the first

time, only to continue avoiding eye contact with her. "Do you have to leave right away?"

"No, I can stay for a while." She lifted her own cup to her lips. "It's so good to see you. I hate that I've had to be away all this time."

"I've missed you so much, even before I knew you were still alive." My shoulders relaxed. "I really hope this all ends soon so we can hang out. There is so much about you I want to know. Questions I've never been able to ask. Now that you're here, it seems unfair that I still haven't had the chance."

"I feel the same way, but I'm just glad to have the time we have now." She tapped the side of her cup with the small teaspoon. "Enough sulking. Tell me more about my daughter."

It was interesting, learning about my mother. About how much she loved tea and her sense of humor. I imagined what growing up with her would have been like. Full of laughter and sweet treats. Along with her tea, she ate two pieces of cake and a handful of donut holes. She joked about if not for all the swimming, she would have been a lot heavier.

We talked for hours until the sun dipped from the sky, allowing the moon to take its place. I watched as the dark waves crashed over her tail, accepting her return to the waters. One day we would be able to exist together, swim beneath the seas, mother and daughter. I just had to stop yet another attempt on my life to make that happen.

~*~

Her absence left me alone with my thoughts again. I couldn't avoid the dark circle that usually spiraled in my mind when the sky turned that midnight blue. I needed someone to talk to, but I had no one. It was hard not to end up searching the internet for answers, but what could Google possibly have to say about an emotionally drained and confused mermaid? Were there any psychological studies on a supernatural hybrid rejected by both sides of her family?

I never wanted to be a normal woman more than I did then, to go out into the world and mingle with regular people. Get a drink at the bar, hang out with friends. Latasha, my former best friend and newly changed vampire, would push me toward some cute guy as she tried to snag one of her own. Of course, that was where my night would go left, because I'm a siren who can't afford to get careless around human men. One slip up and a guy could lose his life.

That was what everyone was waiting for. They wanted me to mess up. They wanted me to hurt someone solely so they could make an example out of me. So instead of risking going out onto the beach down to where there were bonfires and drunken locals singing into the night sky, I climbed into my bed, thanked the heavens for Wi-Fi, and started the next episode of the animated vampire series that had me in its clutches for the last two days.

Before my mother left, I promised her again that I would do my best to find my sister. I just wanted time to talk to Rhys first. He was supposed to be home at the end of the week, that was if he didn't extend his visit to Louisiana again. All I would have to do was avoid talking myself out of it before I got to talk to him.

The episode had just ended, and once again, I cursed at the screen. I could have continued the season, but I wanted to make it last. It was so hard to find good content to watch. Instead, I flipped through the streaming services, hoping to find something semi-entertaining to watch until I fell asleep again.

"How long are you going to sit around moping?" The small voice came from every shadow in the room, and my heart stopped.

"Who's there?" I sat up, muted the television, and searched the room for the source of the voice.

"I've only been here a short while and already I'm bored." The soft echo took shape, and at the foot of the bed appeared a hauntingly familiar face.

I screamed and fell off the bed as I scrambled to get away from the apparition before I realized who it was. She was one of the coven's ancestral spirits, a girl with great power who lost her life far too young.

"What the hell!" I clutched my chest as I caught my breath. "What are you doing here?"

"You're a daughter of my coven." Ebon plopped down on the bed and scanned the room with her eyes. "I have every right to check in on you when needed."

"I didn't know ancestral spirits made house calls." I huffed and picked up the fallen bedding from the floor.

"We don't, well, at least not usually, but it appears we have special circumstances here." She watched me closely and smiled.

"We do?" Of course, there were special circumstances. My life was nothing but a running list of special circumstances.

"Yes. You should be aware. Your mother warned you of the changes happening." Ebon's words had some urgency behind them. "The hybrids that were recently discovered."

"She told me about that, but what does that have to do with you?" I shook my head. "Why does everyone keep wanting me to take responsibility for things that have nothing to do with me?"

"It's more of a threat than even she knows." She softened. "Your mother fears the wrath of her people, but what she doesn't know is that you are in danger, and the entity coming for you isn't a simple threat. The ones who will appear are working for a greater power."

"Why come for me? I'm living the most boring existence ever." I waved my hand at the room. "There is no way anyone can think I'm a threat here!"

"Syrinada, whether you choose to live a life of solitude or not, you are still someone with an amazing power that some people fear and others want. Why do you think so many sirens refuse to go on the Naiad's Walk? It's not always fear that they will fail, but they are afraid of succeeding."

"This isn't fair." I ran my hands through my hair. "I wouldn't have even gone on that walk if they hadn't been threatening my life!"

"Very few things in life are." She rounded the corner and put her hand on my shoulder. "Syrinada, we need to go."

"I told my mother I will wait for Rhys to come home. When he gets back, we will go to find my sister together."

"You don't have time for that. You must go now," Ebon urged.

"Now, but Rhys—"

"Will survive without you, but it may not work the other way around." Her finger lifted to point to the large window that opened to the ocean outside.

My heart stopped as I witnessed the quick formation of an enormous wave in the distance. With no warning, beneath the clearest of night skies, it came to a crest high enough to wipe out my entire home.

"Oh, my god."

"Yeah, like I said, it's time to go," Ebon rushed.

She grabbed my wrist, and a searing and feverish light filled the room, carrying us away from the home just as the waters came crashing into the window.

CHAPTER 2

My *chest burned as I gasped for air.* The light faded, and with it, so did the heat around my wrist. I fell forward, stumbling from my bedside into an enormous field of tall grass. Inhaling the earthy smell, I looked around for the crashing waves, but there was nothing.

"Oh." I searched the field and found Ebon standing behind me. "What the hell was that?"

"You're welcome." She raised a brow. "That was me saving your life. Siren or not, a wave like that would have killed you."

"Thank you," I choked out as I gained my footing. "Where are we?"

"Somewhere safe," she spoke as she walked away from me.

Still disoriented, I followed her across the field and waited for an explanation that never came. I was alive. I should be grateful, but how could I not wonder what magic she used to do what she did? Besides, this new place didn't feel real. I couldn't understand it, but the ground beneath my feet, the air that filled my lungs, and the blades of grass that rubbed against my bare legs, all felt oddly manufactured.

It reminded me of being back in Alderic's house. My father was powerful enough to create a living home full of plants and paintings and other artifacts that moved on their own. This world felt like being in those walls. Artificially safe, but the threat of something darker lied beneath its esthetically pleasing surface.

In the distance, sitting in the middle of the field, sat a small shabby house. The slanted roof threatened to fall off. The worn wood looked as if it would disintegrate if touched. Ebon approached it with no fear, while I worried if the thing would fall down on us. All the magic she possessed and yet this place, which I understood now was her home, was a disaster.

On the small porch that barely looked attached to the house, there were two small white chairs and a table in between them. On the table was an intimate set up of tea with two cups. Ebon took the seat on the left, leaving the right open for me. She looked at me expectantly, and I sat down.

"What now?" I asked, looking over the field of tall grass.

"Now we wait. We're a bit early, actually." She poured herself a cup of tea and sipped from it.

"Wait… for what?"

"Have some tea." Ebon filled the cup in front of me. "It's my favorite. Something about it just reminds me of home, you know?"

"Okay." I picked up the cup and inhaled the sweet aroma of lavender and citrus. The smell and taste of the tea worked to calm my frantic mind. There were so many questions, and Ebon clearly would not be providing any answers to them.

"I never got to tell you, but you did a great job." She nodded and held the cup between the palms of her hand. "So many people doubted you, but I always knew what you were capable of."

"What do you mean?" Of course, people doubted I could keep my shit together. That wasn't news. I hadn't considered there would be continued conversation about me in the ghostly realm.

"I mean, how you managed things with your father. I know it had to be difficult, what you went through, but I think you handled yourself well," she repeated the compliment.

"Oh, thank you." I didn't want to think of him. I worked so hard over the months to push thoughts of my father from my mind, and yet in a day, I'd been forced to consider that man by my mother and now her.

"You're struggling with it, though, aren't you?" She placed her cup back on the small table. "It's bad enough that you lived your life thinking they were dead, but to find out both of your parents were alive, and then to have to kill one to save the other. "

"Yeah." Tears threatened to fall, so I focused on the swaying blades of grass, the safest thing my mind could find.

"You're going to have to face that decision, eventually."

"Face it how? I did it. It's done."

"Yes, but there are consequences to every action, Syrinada." I could hear the pity in her voice. "Even if the action was for a good reason. It may not come as you expect, but every action, every choice you make, has a ripple effect."

"Consequence?" I stopped a horrible man

from doing horrible things, and I had to deal with consequences?

"Oh, good." Ebon stood from her seat. "They're here, finally."

"Who?" I searched the field and saw nothing. Just as I turned to ask her again who she was referring to, I saw them. Out in the distance, two figures approached, gliding on the current of the wind.

I recognized one of them. The ancestor who never gave me his name but terrified me when he came to judge me, just as Ebon had. He still wore a three-piece suit, complete with a pocket watch and top hat that sat comfortably on his snow white hair. The other person who accompanied him was smaller, a hooded figure who remained a mystery, even after they neared. Even though I couldn't see their face, they felt familiar to me. I couldn't explain it, but a wave of recognition hit me. I knew this person.

"It's about time you got here," Ebon huffed.

"Oh, don't bore me with feigned impatience." the man whose name I would never know answered her but looked at me. "Is she ready?"

"Does she have a choice but to be at this point?" Ebon answered with a sass that made me wonder what the dynamic of their relationship was. "The good thing is that she is here, ready or not."

"You're right. I don't think any of us have a choice in this anymore," he agreed.

"Besides, the wheels are in motion already. We've seen it," she offered. "They've launched their first attack. I barely got her out of there before it happened."

"Are you going to tell me what's going on?" I asked. The two were talking about me like I wasn't right there. They also talked about potentially horrible events that were apparently outside of even their ghostly control.

"In time," he answered.

"Sounds like we're out of time here," I huffed.

"Child," the man reprimanded me, but Ebon cut him off.

"No, she is right. We don't have time to beat around the bush here. We need to prepare her for what is coming."

"Fine, you explain it." He waved his hand, annoyed with the topic.

How else did he see this going? Was I supposed to

just comply with whatever task they planned to give me with no background information? How was that going to work? They supposedly knew me so well but didn't know I wouldn't simply go along with their plans for me without asking questions. Everything about me went against what they wanted. Why wouldn't this?

Ebon turned, annoyed by the tall man, and headed for the door. Whatever the conversation we needed to have would happen inside the fragile home.

He gestured for me to follow her, and I did, reluctant to turn my back to the ghostly figure. But what did that matter? He could attack me from any position, regardless of if I was paying attention to him. Something told me he wouldn't do it, not with Ebon around. She was smaller than he, but her energy felt stronger.

We entered the small house and found a quaint interior. The home was dated, and the small structure built of wood had three main rooms. A thick curtain split the front room into two, and just beyond it was the doorway to the only bedroom. To the left of where we sat was a small kitchen that smelled of fresh bread. I hoped the inside of the house would have a magical facelift, but it didn't. The furniture was all worn, the floors had gaps in the boards, and every corner held fresh cobwebs.

After we all set down at the table, Ebon served tea

again, and the hooded figure had none. I couldn't help but stare and wonder when the hood would come off. This wasn't just some pet for the tall man. Whoever was under that hood was important, and I could sense they were holding out for a grand revelation.

"So here is where we stand." Ebon began her coverage of events. "Your mother provided a pretty good explanation of things already. There are others out there that are just like you. They are hybrids, the products of mating between two powerful beings, and because of that, they pose a potential threat to the balance of power.

"They exist outside the laws of their ancestors, and some wish to change the current landscape of the world. Now, while your people, the sirens, are determined to make an example out of you, I fear they are missing the bigger picture at hand. Your role in this isn't to be a cautionary tale. Syrinada, you will play a much bigger part in this."

"What part is that?"

"Instead of being a lesson on what happens when rules are broken, you will be the one to enforce those rules," Ebon continued.

"You want me to be an enforcer?" I scoffed. "What does that even mean?"

"Yes. We want you to let these people know that just because they are different, doesn't mean they are above the laws that govern the supernatural realms. In a matter of words, you *are* the law for them," the man spoke with excitement in his eyes.

"And how do you expect me to do that?" I laughed. "Slap on a badge and go police the world for hybrids? You can't be serious."

"Build a team. You said your mother suggested your sister. Find her and work together," Ebon offered.

"You want me to find a sister that I barely know and convince her to be on your supernatural police squad?" I shook my head. "What makes you think she is going to go for that? What gives me the right to ask her to abandon whatever life she has to deal with any of this?"

"You are her sister, and the two of you share a great pain, your father. That gives you the right," he answered. "As I recall, you saved her life when your dear old daddy was going to use her to mess things up, did you not?"

"I will not use the shitty things our father did as some point against her." Neither of us knew the man until he came back into our lives to fuck things up. She deserved the consequences of his actions no more than I did.

"You won't have to, trust me," Ebon spoke before he could say another heartless thing.

"And exactly how do you expect us to do this? Do you know what we are up against? Do you know what kind of powers they have? Is there anything you want to give me besides *go power up and kick ass*?"

"We do. Over the recent months, we've worked to collect as much valuable information as possible, which wasn't exactly easy to do. Being a spirit doesn't mean we don't have limitations." Ebon nodded.

"You will have help." He added something useful to the conversation.

"Great. What help?" I asked. At least they were giving me more than stories and plausibility.

They looked at the hooded figure, and I followed their eyes.

"Wait, you're giving me a ghost?" I pointed to the hooded figure.

"No, we aren't giving you anything. You don't own her," he scoffed as if disgusted with me.

"Her?" Well, at least I knew I'd be working with another woman.

"Well, we've kept the secret long enough." Ebon nodded.

Two gloved hands lifted and moved the hood away from her face. My heart slammed to a halt and then sped up with excitement.

"Hey, bitch!" Maggie smiled, and he scoffed at her language. "Oh, settle down, old man."

"Maggie?" I jumped from my seat and pulled her into a hug.

"Hey, I thought you might miss me." She hugged me back. "When they said you'd need help on this little adventure, of course, I volunteered for the gig."

"Not that anyone else wanted it," he spoke again, and I rolled my eyes.

"I can't believe it's you." My arms still wrapped around my friend, I felt some of the weight lift from my shoulders.

"Yeah, well, you sacrifice your life for the greater good, and you get some perks on the other side, like being able to meet up with old friends."

I tightened my hold on her, afraid she would vanish if I let go. "Oh, I've missed you so much."

"Well, look at how things have changed." Maggie laughed. "Remember when you first met me? You couldn't stand me."

"Yeah, I know, and now I cry every time I think about you." I sniffled. "I wished I could see you again so many times."

"No reason to do that now." She tapped my arm. "You can ease up on the kung-fu grip. I'm not going anywhere."

"Oh, my bad." I let her go with a nervous laugh.

"So, is this sufficient? We gave you aid. Will you do as we ask?" Ebon asked with a small smile.

"Do I really have a choice in the matter?" I rolled my eyes.

"There is always a choice. There is a right choice and a wrong choice. Be careful of the one you make," he said in an ominous tone.

"In other words, no, you do not have a choice, but why would you make any other decision than to be with me?" Maggie boasted. "Hell, as long as we are policing these assholes, I'll be right by your side!"

"I guess you're right." I smiled. "There's one perk

to this."

"Is that a yes?" Ebon asked.

"Yes." I nodded. "I'll do it."

"Excellent." He clapped his hands, and the sound thundered around us. My head rushed with pressure as the space shifted, and it pushed us out of the small home, through the tall fields, and back into another familiar place.

A small apartment in a big city that no one had touched in nearly a year. The single bed against the wall, the thrifted desk covered in random notes and drawings, the large closet still home to a winter coat I wished I had on that cold night. My home. There was a swell of emotions that settled in my throat like a knot as I took in the details of the single apartment that saw me through some of the toughest moments of my life.

"Wow, this place smells horrible." Maggie pinched her nose knocking the emotions from the moment.

I turned ready to explain about how the apartment had been sealed for a year and of course the air was stale. But before I could begin to explain about trash that hadn't been emptied or the moldy fruit in the refrigerator, my mouth fell open. Maggie wasn't at all what I expected. She wasn't an ethereal expression of her formal self. She stood there like the girl I knew before. Whole and human.

"Wait, you aren't a ghost." I poked her arm. "I expected you to be all translucent and floaty."

She looked down at herself. "Well damn, look at that. I guess they thought it would be better if I wasn't floating around scaring everyone."

"Yeah, definitely." I paused. "Does your magic work the same?"

"Let's find out." She lifted her hand, and the window opened, letting a fresh breeze enter the apartment. "Looks like everything's still working."

"Great, we're going to need it." I looked around my apartment. Nothing had changed. Why? "I have questions."

"And those are?" Maggie twirled in the room, patting her body with her hands.

"Why would they send us here, and why the hell has nothing changed? I for sure haven't paid rent in months." I touched the desk where I once sat, drawing the faces of the men who attacked me. "This place should have been emptied by now."

"I don't know."

Moving outside in the hall was a familiar voice. One with sass and more nerve than anyone else I knew.

"Latasha," I spoke the name of my best friend.

I didn't open the door, just looked through the peephole at my friend who entered her apartment with a man following her. I scented the air. He was human. I couldn't help but wonder if he was a friend or food.

"Are you going to go out there?" Maggie asked after Latasha's door closed.

"No, I mean, I don't know if I should." I shrugged. "We haven't spoken since everything went down. I'm actually shocked to see she still lives here."

"Well, like you said, they sent us here for a reason. I don't know if that reason was to sit in your apartment looking at cobwebs. "

"I can't, not right now. Besides, she isn't alone," I pointed out. "I don't want to interrupt whatever she has going on over there."

"Right, okay, so where to, then?"

I leaned against the door, trying to think. My gut

told me what I should do, but my heart refused to listen. I needed help. Help from people who were like me, powerful and unique. There were two people I knew for certain who fit the bill.

"We have to go see the Denalis, don't we?" Maggie read my mind.

"Yes, I think we do."

"Are you up for that?" She sat on the edge of the desk. "I mean, can your heart handle it?"

"No, but again, what choice do I have?" It was refreshing to be honest about what I felt. It helped that Maggie had a way of knowing what I was thinking without me having to say it.

We were careful about leaving the apartment. Music played in Latasha's apartment, but I could never be sure with her. The woman had ears like a wolf. The slightest sound, and she would know I was there. Not only did I have to avoid her but anyone else who might report back to her. The last thing I needed was her learning that I was home and didn't come to speak to her.

CHAPTER 3

As soon as we made it out of the building, we sprinted three blocks away before I slowed my pace. I had to be sure there wasn't a chance of being recognized. Even with the large hoodie I threw on to cover my face, it felt like at any moment Latasha would pop out and scream, "Gotcha!"

As we got further from the building, my mind switched focus from my nosey friend to the Denalis, the mermen brothers who were charged with my protection. Things hadn't ended on the best terms with the brothers. The last I heard, Demetrius threw himself back into his work, and Malachi was missing in action. No one had heard from him since we defeated my father, not even his brother.

"Is the plan to walk to their house?" Maggie asked as she shuffled along beside me.

"No, they live too far." I paused. "Shit, I don't have

money for the train, and I have no idea where my car is. Probably tucked away in some junkyard right now."

"We could use magic, but that might cause attraction, and they kind of want us to keep a low profile." Maggie shrugged.

Just then, a man pulled up in a black sedan. He hopped out of his car, laughing and holding a phone to his ear.

"Hold on." I winked at Maggie then crossed the street to where the man stood laughing about something he saw on television.

"Alright, man, yeah, I just got home. I should be there soon. Just gotta let the dog out before he tears up my couch again." The man who sported a blue hoodie and jeans laughed and flashed a smile that would make a normal woman melt.

Just as he ended the call, I stepped in front of him and quickly captured his dark brown eyes with my own.

"Hello," I spoke, allowing just enough of my siren to surface and entice him.

"H-hi," he stuttered and swallowed air.

"My friend and I could really use a ride." I touched his hand, and he froze. "Do you think you can help us out?"

"A ride?" he asked and looked over at Maggie, but

I pulled his attention back to me.

"Yes, it would really help us out if you could take us to our friend's house." Another wave of my lure washed over him, and I felt him give in.

"Yes, of course." He hit the button on the car to unlock it and stepped to open the back door so I could climb in.

I waved to Maggie to join me, and we piled into the back of the man's car. Without even telling him the address, he took off driving. I relaxed in the back seat of the dark sedan as we pulled away but kept checking my phone for any word from my friends.

If any of Latasha's minions saw me, they would have already blown the whistle. After fifteen minutes, we were on the expressway, and I had heard nothing from Latasha. Part of me wished I had. Even if she would be angry, it would mean I got to get chewed out by my friend one more time. It was sick how I could miss something like that.

Fortunately, the drive was a quick one. On a Friday night, most of the traffic moved in the opposite direction. Most were heading into the city, not away from it. It tempted me to make a quick detour. I'd missed Chicago. Beaches and oceans were nice, but the busy city with its amazing food and culture was home. Instead, we drove an hour in the opposite direction, to Naperville, to the home of the Denali's brothers.

We sat in the dark car outside of the large home for a few moments before Maggie prodded me about getting out. After exiting, I walked around to the driver's window, ran my fingers along the jawline of our mystery driver, and sent him on his way. Dazed look in his eyes, he'd make it home before my spell faded.

"How long are we going to stand out here?" Maggie asked.

We'd been standing on the curb outside the large suburban home for nearly ten minutes while I worked up the nerve to knock on the door. I ran through every excuse possible for turning and running the other way and nothing held up.

"A few more minutes? Maybe an hour?" I laughed.

"No, girl, get it over with." Maggie headed for the door.

Before I caught up with her, she'd already pounded her fist on the door, alerting anyone inside of our presence. We stood there waiting for someone to open the door.

"See, they aren't even—" Just as I considered they might not be home, the door swung open, and the oldest Denali stood there, bare chest and grey sweatpants.

"Syrinada?" his deep voice wrapped around my name, and I had to remind myself that I was with Rhys, and any physical response to the man in front of me had to be squashed immediately.

"Demetrius." I damn near choked at the sound of my name slipping through his lips.

"What are you doing here?" he asked with an expression like he'd seen a ghost. If he'd been looking at Maggie, it would have been justified.

"It's complicated and too crazy to express standing on your stoop. Can we come inside?" I asked.

"Uh, yeah," he hesitated before stepping aside to let us in.

"Hi again!" Maggie bubbled.

"I thought you were—" Demetrius pointed at Maggie.

"Dead, yeah well, I got a temporary pass on that whole mortality thing." Maggie winked and slapped him on the shoulder. Her hand lingered there as she squeezed his muscle admiringly. "I'm here to help."

"Help with what? What's going on?"

"Long story short, a bunch of supernatural hybrids are looking to stir up trouble, and the ghostly powers that be would like for us to stop that from happening," Maggie laid it out as simply as she could.

"Ghostly powers that be?" He scratched his head, shifting the locs that fell around his face and matched his goatee perfectly. "It's been a long day. I'm going to need more than that."

"Our coven ancestors," I clarified while trying to keep my eyes off the dark skin that coated his pecks.

"Right." He looked at me. "And you're here. Why?"

"Are we not welcomed? If so, we can leave." I pointed to the doorway.

"That's not what I said," he backtracked. "I just want to know what you want from me. I assume that's why you're here."

"They sent me back to Chicago. I don't know why, but considering they want me to put together my own little team of avengers, well, you're the only other people I know here that fit the bill." I looked around. "Where is—"

"He isn't here. He never came back," Demetrius answered my question before I could say his brother's name. The look of hurt that flashed in his eyes was enough to tell a story. They weren't on speaking terms.

"Oh," I paused, not sure where to go with the conversation. The smart thing to do would have been to change the topic altogether, but I was lost in my own internal battle.

"I'm sorry." Demetrius softened. "You must have been looking forward to seeing him."

"What do you have to be sorry about?" I shrugged. "It was me who broke his heart. There isn't anything to be sorry about. I had hoped he'd heal, moved on."

"Yeah, he did, away from here. I think being here, where you two were—" Demetrius trailed off, but I knew exactly what he meant.

There held had so many memories for us. It was where we connected, where he told me about who I was. It was where he defended me against werewolves and where we first had sex. I looked at the stairs, where I'd once straddled Malachi, and had to, of course, push the thoughts aside.

"I get it." I held my hand up. "Let's not recount all that right now, okay?"

"Look, I'm here to help you in whatever way I can," Demetrius offered. "It's still my duty to protect you. I'm sorry if that isn't what you wanted. I'm not Malachi, but I'm here."

"I appreciate that." I didn't want to admit it, but he was right. There was a significant part of me that wanted Malachi to be there. That part of me hoped we could reconcile our differences, but there wouldn't be time for that.

"I'm actually making dinner. I'll finish up, and then we can discuss things over a good meal."

"Sounds good to me," Maggie chimed in. "I wonder

if food will taste the same now that I'm undead."

"Does that make you a zombie?" Demetrius asked and turned to the kitchen.

"No, I mean, I don't think so. It's not like I'm craving your flesh right now." She laughed at her own joke. "Though your flesh looks real delicious. Tell me, do you often cook without a shirt on?"

Maggie followed Demetrius into the kitchen, where they laughed and talked as if they were old friends. They continued joking about Maggie's undead status and trying to classify her in one of the standard supernatural terms, but felt nothing fit her specific situation.

I headed in the opposite direction. Finding the sitting room, which still had the tan couch where I once slept with Malachi. It was one of the most intimate moments of my life, and it hurt to remember it. I ran my hand along the couch, and flashes of our encounter ran through my mind. My stomach clenched, and my pussy tightened between my legs.

Shit.

I hadn't had sex in days. Rhys was away, and now I was in the house with Demetrius. I couldn't allow thoughts of past sexual encounters to get me so riled up. It would mean trouble for everyone involved. Especially with Demetrius walking around shirtless and showing off those unreal eight-pack abs.

I found a quiet place to sit and meditate. I learned that meditation was a great way to control those primal urges. Whenever I felt overwhelmed, I just needed to get away from the temptations and push them from my mind. I wasn't worried about attacking Demetrius, but if I didn't take a moment to reel myself in, I couldn't be sure it would remain an innocent visit.

By the time dinner was ready, I felt level-headed again. I entered the kitchen to find Maggie and Demetrius sitting at the counter. Maggie sipped from a glass of wine and moaned.

"How does it taste even better than I remember?" She swirled the glass in her hand before taking another sip.

"Life after death. Maybe you appreciate it more?" I answered.

"Maybe." She turned to the door and winked at me. "I know I'll be drinking as much as I can before they repossess this body!"

"What's for dinner?" I asked, laughing at Maggie.

"Pasta. Luckily, I made enough for everyone. I can never seem to make just one serving. It seems wrong," Demetrius spoke as he stirred the pot of sauce. "I hope that's okay."

"Pasta is perfect." I smiled. "Come to think of it, I don't know when the last time I ate was. It's been at least a few days."

"Well, pull up a seat." Demetrius served the plates.

He was working overtime to make us feel more comfortable. Despite his efforts sitting in that kitchen, at the table where I'd once kissed his brother, the entire thing felt so awkward. All I could think was that soon it would be over. We could talk to him, get him on our side, and move on to the next location.

"So, tell me what's going on," he broke the silence.

"Well, Maggie could probably explain things better, but basically there are other hybrids out there. Ones that are apparently trying to fuck up the balance of things, and of course, that made me the perfect recruit to get them in line because I haven't done enough after killing my own father to protect the world."

"Yeah." Maggie slurped up more pasta and wiped her mouth. "Removing the personal strife from the story, after everyone found out about Syrinada, it caused some issues amongst the seas. First, we found there were others like her. Hybrids of sirens and witches, not as powerful, but still concerning. This led us to do more digging. We wondered if there were other hybrids out there? It wasn't long until we found out there were other warlocks spreading their seeds, and well, seven covens have reported twenty-six hybrids."

"Twenty-six?" Demetrius scoffed.

"Yes, but investigations are still happening. The problem, as I said, is that some of the hybrids we're finding are powerful. Some pose no threat at all. But—" Maggie trailed off and stuffed more food in her mouth.

"But what?" I nudged her arm.

"You." She pointed to me. "You are the strongest we've seen, well, you and your sister. The issue is, we think your father had another child. One that could be just as powerful as you and your sister." She sipped her wine again. "Or more powerful? Who knows?"

Maggie dropped the bomb on my lap and continued shoveling food into her mouth like it was no big deal.

"What?" I suddenly lost my appetite. "What makes you think that? Why would you say that?"

"Calm down, girl." She held her hand up to me. "We don't have confirmation of anything. We found his plans."

"Plans?" I frowned. "He had plans for creating hybrid offspring?"

"Yes, he hoped to breed more of his powerful children, and he had a list of species he thought would be viable mates. After reviewing his notes and deciphering what all the strange symbols meant, we figured there were three successes. A siren, a succubus, and well, that's the problem. We don't really know what the other one is."

"How could you not know?" I asked. "You have his notes. Are you telling me he didn't write down what the other child was?"

"He placed a spell on the pages. The moment we moved them, the information deteriorated. All we know is that the third child was a shifter type."

"A shifter?" I sat back in my seat. "So I possibly have a sibling out there that can turn into a bird or something?"

"Knowing him, it's something more powerful. I'd guess we're looking for something along the lines of a werewolf or a dragon." Demetrius laughed.

"A dragon sister." I scoffed. "Could life get any more insane?"

"Well, they have high speculation that it's a strong shifter, and when we consider shifters, a dragon is pretty damn strong." Maggie nodded.

"It couldn't be a dragon, right?" I asked. "I mean, I thought they were extinct."

"That's what they want us to believe. There are still some on protected lands. Hidden by magic, protected by the covens," Maggie confirmed. "Which would have given him the perfect opportunity to connect with a woman there."

"Great." I picked up my fork and tapped it against

the plate. "So there is an actual chance my father has another child. Someone with the ability to grow wings and burn towns."

My heart hurt. The more I thought about what she said, the more I wanted to scream. It was bad enough knowing my father didn't love me the way I hoped, but to find out I was just one in a laundry list of genetic science experiments that just happened to turn out right made things that much worse.

"What's our plan?" Demetrius drew his eyes from me to Maggie.

"We have to find Imara." Maggie lifted her glass. "We track her down, then we go on the hunt for their mystery sibling."

"And what do we do when if we find them?" I asked.

"We hope like hell they're on our side of this," Demetrius answered. "There is a real possibility they won't be. If everyone is so worried about what unknown hybrids are capable of, that means there's evidence they have or will do something terrible."

"Just like there was evidence that I would be so bad?" I raised a brow.

"You did kill four men, Syrinada," Demetrius pointed out.

"Men who tried to rape and kill me first!" I dropped my fork again, splashing sauce on the table. "Shit, sorry."

"Don't worry." Demetrius handed me a napkin. "Either way, there was evidence that you could lose control. Since then, you've proven yourself capable of being better than that."

"Shouldn't we give them a chance to prove the same thing?" I asked.

"We will." Maggie nodded. "This isn't a witch hunt, Sy. We're just introducing ourselves and letting them know should they step out of line, we'll be there, watching."

"And waiting to drop the hammer?" I rolled my eyes.

"Well, yes. Exactly." She smiled and went back to eating her food. "At least it's not the other way around."

"I just remember what it felt like to be on the other side of this. Hell, I still am on the other side. Not everyone has accepted me, and yet, I'm supposed to be some enforcer for them."

"Sy…" Maggie touched my shoulder. "It's going to be okay."

"No, it's fine. I'm doing it because I have to, right? If I don't, then I'm just another problem to deal with." I pushed back from the table. "I need some air."

CHAPTER 4

I left the two of them sitting together at the kitchen table and headed for the exit. A few minutes later, I found myself in the backyard of their house. Just beyond the back deck was a small blue claw footed bench beneath the cover of trees. While my mind wandered, I sat down, grateful for the momentary silence. They had an amazing garden full of flowers that bloomed and filled the air with their fragrance. I inhaled the smell deeply and tried to clear my mind of the troubling thoughts.

"Are you okay?" Demetrius stood in the sliding doors that led into the house.

"I'm fine." I called back. "Just taking a moment to myself."

"You don't look like you're fine." He shut the door behind him. "Not like Maggie, who is eating the rest of the pasta."

"She's always had a healthy appetite. Me, not so much." I chuckled before the weight returned to my mind. "Difficult to think of food right now, anyway."

"Is it?" he asked and adjusted a chair on the deck.

"How would you feel in my position?" I watched him closely.

"I don't know." He left the chair and walked over to me, stopping just before the bench, and pointing to the space beside me. "Mind if I sit?"

"It's your bench." I shrugged. "Who am I to stop you?"

He stood and waited for confirmation.

"Yes, Demetrius sit." I nodded.

"Thank you." He joined me. "What's really bothering you?"

"Isn't it obvious? I'm being used as a tool for people who were trying to end my life six months ago."

"And?" He raised a brow, as if that wasn't enough to warrant my mood.

"And," I paused. "And I'm tired of being looked at as a weapon. Either to be defended against or used for their purpose. The witches, the sirens, hell, even my own father. Every person I come in contact with has some preconceived notion of who I am and what I will do, and if I don't do what they want, then I deserve to die. Now they want me to do that to other people."

"I may be wrong, but it sounds a bit more complicated than that," Demetrius commented. "There are more layers to this, right?"

"Is it? Because from what I've been told, it's all speculation. The hybrids have done nothing but refuse to abide by laws that they don't feel apply to them."

"Laws are in place for a reason."

"Yes, but who decides the reasons?" I shifted in my seat to look at his face. "Demetrius, you and I both know that being a hybrid changes things. I mean, look at me. Nothing about me goes by the book. My power, my challenge in the Naiad's walk. I couldn't even choose a mate that everyone approved of."

"Rhys, yes, how is he?" Demetrius asked, with only a slight tinge of irritation in his voice.

"Um," I hesitated.

"We don't have to talk about him." He relieved me of the awkward moment.

"No, I just realized I don't have my phone. He could have been trying to reach me all this time," I lied. Yes, that was a concern, but no, it wasn't why I hesitated. I had other ways of communicating with Rhys if necessary.

"I'll get you a new one." He pulled out his phone, typed on the screen, and put it away. "You'll have one soon."

"Just like that, huh?"

"Yes." He shrugged.

"Wait, were you paying my rent all this time?" I thought about my untouched apartment.

"Um, yes, I suppose I have been. We put it on auto-pay when we left to go to New Orleans, wanted you to have a place to come home to when all the dust settled."

"That was really thoughtful of you, thank you." I smiled. It never occurred to me to preserve anything from my former life, but it felt good to know it was there for me if I needed it.

"It was Malachi's idea, but you're welcome."

"Malachi," I repeated the name that flowed so easily from his lips.

"Yes, my little brother." He nodded. "Wherever he is in the world."

"And you still haven't heard from him. It's been months." I looked up at the dark sky as if Malachi would appear there like an angel coming to save the day.

"Nope, I haven't, but I'm sure he is okay. Just taking his time." Demetrius picked a flower from the bush that sat next to the bench. "Everything that happened was hard on him. That level of rejection, it's hard to deal with."

"I'm sorry."

"I told you, don't apologize. Like you said, the rules of the sirens don't apply to you. We shouldn't have just assumed they would. What matters, what's important, is that you're okay now."

"And what about you?" I looked him in the eye. "Are you okay?"

"I'm getting there. A lot happened, Syrinada. You, Malachi, Verena, and—" he stopped, swallowing whatever thought put that haunted expression on his face.

"I can't imagine what you must have been going through. I should have been there for you." There it was… that guilt that often left me choking on my own sorrow.

"It wouldn't have made things easier. Like my brother, you're a reminder of everything I lost. It's not like I raced off to search for Malachi. I was dealing with my own mourning." Demetrius took a deep breath to still himself before he continued. "She was pregnant, Sy. I almost had a child. I didn't realize it, but I wanted that so bad, and within moments of finding out, they took it away from me. It took a lot to move on after you left with Rhys. Being with Verena made it okay because she loved me, and I loved her."

"I know you said not to apologize, but I am sorry for your loss." I placed my hand on his shoulder.

"Thank you, and I'm sorry for yours."

I raised a brow. "My loss?"

"Your father. Syrinada, I know you are trying not to feel anything about it, but he was your father, and as shitty as the relationship might have been, trust me, I know about shitty fathers, you still wanted him to be in your life. He disappointed you and then—"

"Then I had to kill him," I finished his thought.

"Yes. You did."

"Man, how can so much bullshit happen in less than a year?" I sighed. "This time last year I was celebrating my new job. I was excited about the opportunity to build a solid future for myself, and now all that seems so trivial."

"I wish I knew." He chuckled. "But we survived it, and we'll survive this. I think we need to just accept that life will never deal us the easy hand."

"The hand full of luxury vacations and buffets?" I said in a dreamy tone.

"Exactly, so how about we go back inside and finish dinner? It sounds like we are going to need all the fuel we can get, and if we don't go back now, Maggie may eat our food as well."

I followed Demetrius back into the house, and we found Maggie loading her plate with another helping of pasta.

"How are you not full already?" Demetrius asked as he eyed the mountain of food on her plate.

"Hey, the rules don't apply to this ghost-filled body!" she laughed and pointed to the near-empty bottle of wine.

"Go for it. There is more where that came from." Demetrius laughed. "I'll go grab another bottle from the cellar."

Demetrius left us alone, and Maggie wasted about three seconds before she started grilling me.

"What did you two talk about? I thought of going ghost mode and eavesdropping, but it seemed like a private moment, and I didn't want to intrude."

"But asking now is not intrusive?" I frowned.

"No, not at all." She smiled. "You could always tell

me to butt out, but you won't."

"We didn't talk about anything, just how I feel, how he feels. It's all overwhelming right now."

"I can tell." We returned to the table. "I didn't mean to sound insensitive earlier."

"It's okay,"

"No, it's not. I mean, it's different now." She sipped the wine. "While this food and drink taste so much better, everything else is dull."

"What do you mean?"

"I'm detached from human emotions. It's what happens when you die. To me, I was just stating facts, but to you, I was shitting on your entire experience, and that's not okay."

"You didn't mean it. It's okay." I sipped my own glass and sighed. The wine really was amazing. "I'll try to keep in mind that you aren't exactly the Maggie I remember."

"How depressing is that?" she responded. "I want to be the Maggie you remember."

"In most ways, you are. You're just a bit heartless now," I joked.

"Oh, hilarious!" She laughed.

"I'm back," Demetrius announced as he entered the kitchen through the doors that led to the underground wine cellar.

"And with more wine!" Maggie clapped. "Get this man a Purple Heart!"

"A Purple Heart? Really?" I asked.

"Or whatever award is fitting for getting more wine." Maggie shrugged.

"I'll take it." Demetrius laughed and returned to the table where the rest of our food waited.

We finished eating and catching up on all that had happened since we last saw each other. Demetrius tried to look for his brother for a while, but eventually gave up. Malachi covered his tracks. He even stopped using his bank accounts, cell phones, etc. There was no trace of him.

"Hell, I just figured if the man wanted to be lost so bad, I would let him." Demetrius sat back in his seat, lifting the wine to his lips. "Eventually, we will find each other. We always come back together. I think Malachi just needs more time."

"Yeah, in time he will come home. I'm sure," Maggie reassured him.

"And what about you? What have you been up to?" Demetrius asked as she finished the last of the pasta.

"So much for leftovers." He laughed.

"Ha, yeah, sorry." Maggie wiped her mouth with a napkin. "Well, I've been up to all the ghostly things. Hanging out with the ancestors. I haunted a couple of my cousins for a little while. They deserved it, trust me, and then I got recruited into this. Finding out information about the hybrids, building as much knowledge as we could. As soon as they brought up Syrinada, I volunteered to come back to help out, and well, here we are."

"I can't believe you actually haunted your family." I shook my head and smiled.

"Hey, a girl has to have a little fun, even after death. Besides, those heathens tortured me growing up. It's only fair that I get payback."

"Well, you all know what I've been up to. Nothing much at all," I admitted. "As soon as everything was over, I left with Rhys. I wanted to get away, but I didn't think it would last forever. For the past months, I've been living by the sea but not allowed to go into it. My mom hung around for a bit, but then she had to go back to Deuterio.

"About six weeks ago, Rhys was called to return to the coven. With his mom, Roxanne, taking over as the high priestess, he inherited more duties. Unfortunately, I couldn't go with him. Just like with the sirens, I'm not exactly accepted in the coven homes, so I've been alone, taking in a steady diet of tea and Netflix."

"That sounds awful." Maggie gagged.

"I appreciate your honesty." I rolled my eyes.

"I mean…" she turned to me. "You went through so much, Sy, and your reward for proving how badass you really are is a timeout?"

"It's for the best." I bit my lip.

"For who?" Demetrius asked.

Our eyes met, and I had to swallow the lump that formed in my throat. I couldn't answer his question because I didn't know anymore. I was much more in control of myself. Even with the human parties happening on the beach, I kept to myself. Temptation was all around, yet I hurt no one.

"Well," Maggie clapped her hands, interrupting the pregnant pause, "I could use some rest. Funny, I don't sleep in the ghost realm, but I guess this body still needs to catch a few Zs."

"Right, I assume you two will sleep here tonight. Just let me clean up, and then I'll show you to your rooms." Demetrius pulled his eyes away and cleared the table of the dishes.

"You're welcome," Maggie whispered as Demetrius loaded the dishwasher.

"Yeah, thanks." Though she'd avoided my having to answer Demetrius' questions, I couldn't help but think about it. Why was I still punishing myself? What was I so afraid of?

We helped clear the rest of the dishes from the table and wipe things down. Maggie grabbed the last bottle of wine and carried the bottles to the recycling bin. With the kitchen clean and the wine empty, Demetrius led us up the stairs to the second floor, where the bedrooms waited.

He showed Maggie her room first and then ushered me to the room I'd previously used when I stayed with the brothers.

"Ah, this old room." I looked at the door.

Memories of Malachi flooded my mind. Not all were good, but they were all welcome.

"It welcomes you back." Demetrius smiled and pushed the door open to reveal the room, which, besides the bedding, hadn't changed.

"Thank you for not turning us away," I spoke as he stepped away from the door.

"I would never do that, Syrinada. You know that." He smiled.

"Still, thank you. I rarely come with good news, so I appreciate it." I turned to go into the room.

"Syrinada," he spoke my name, and there was something more in the sound. Concern.

"Yes?" I looked back at him.

"Are you really alone on that beach?" he asked.

"Yeah, it's not so bad. Lots of time to meditate and work on me." I smiled.

"Do you ever go in the water?"

"I do. I stay close to the shore. Nothing deep enough to call my tail." I frowned. "I can't. It's not safe. Not yet."

"A siren, by the sea, trapped on the shore." He shook his head. "It makes no sense."

"That's me." All I could muster was a slight lift at the corner of my lips. Anything more, and I would have cried. I didn't need Demetrius to know just how sad his words made me feel.

"That's not the life you should be living. You know that, right?"

"I do." I nodded.

"And what of your other needs?" he asked, and I swore his words wrapped around my neck like a hand pulling me to him.

"My other needs?" I knew what he was asking, but

it felt safer to play dumb.

"You said Rhys is away for weeks at a time. You have more needs than food and shelter." His eyes dropped to the floor, then traced a path back up my body. "Even if you aren't fighting battles, you need restoration."

"We've found ways around that." The nervous smile struggled to take space on my face. "I'm good. I promise."

"Well, goodnight. You know where my room is if you need anything."

My breath caught. If I needed anything. What could I need from him besides something I should only be doing with my mate, Rhys?

CHAPTER 5

While I re-familiarized myself with the room, I heard Maggie and Demetrius talking. They stood outside the door to her assigned room as they joked about different wines and foods that she would need to eat while back in the land of the living. Even though I tried not to eavesdrop, I couldn't help but enjoy the sounds of their voices. It felt good to have other people around me again. It felt nice to not be by myself.

With Rhys on the move all the time, it left me alone so often that I forgot what it meant to have someone there. The voices I typically heard every day were the ones inside my own mind. The ones I created to keep me company.

The dominant voice was the voice of an older version of myself. We often discussed just how much my life had changed over the year. The voice of my siren usually cursed me out for not having more sex. My future self, who I imagined myself becoming, told me to be patient. That everything I was going through was worth it. The voice of reason was the main thing that kept me from going out into the world and finding a man to feed on.

My former self often reminded me of the man I left withered in the gym locker room or the man who never made it from the alley behind that busy club. I didn't want to be like her again, the monster who couldn't control herself.

So instead of going out and doing something I would regret, I made tea, created art, solved puzzles, and sent messages into the sea that I hoped would reach my mother. Glass bottles that floated off into the distance with secrets I always hoped to share with her. Imagining her reading them comforted me, though when I talked to her, she never mentioned them. It felt silly to bring them up, so I didn't.

I sat on the bed when they quieted. Sleep was what I needed. I needed to rest and to see Rhys. On the bed was a cell phone. When Demetrius meant to get things done, he did just that. I turned it on and quickly shot Rhys a text to tell him I was okay and that this was the number he could reach me on. I followed that up with an invitation to join me in our magical realm.

I settled into the bed, ready to shift my mind to our meeting place, but the knock on the door took my thoughts away from my love.

"Syrinada?" Demetrius spoke my name on the other side of the door.

"Yes?" I put the phone back down on the bed.

"Are you okay?"

"Yes, I am." I looked at the door. "You can come in."

The door opened just enough for him to peek his head through. "Sorry, I didn't mean to bother you. I just wanted to say goodnight and check to see if you were okay."

"Yes, I'm good. Thanks for checking. It sounds like you and Maggie hit it off." I pointed to the hall behind him.

"Yeah, she's pretty cool for a dead chick," he joked.

"I heard that!" Maggie called out from her room.

"Thin walls." I smiled.

"Or just ghostly beings who don't apply to the laws of physics." He shrugged.

"That too." It felt good to laugh again. With Maggie around, I knew it would be happening a lot more often.

"Well, you know where I am. Let me know if you need anything." He stepped back to exit the room.

He said it again. What was it he expected me to need from him?

"Thanks, again." I smiled.

When he closed the door, I took a deep breath. The siren stirred, and I heard her song in the back of my mind. Checking the phone once more, I hoped for a response from Rhys, but there was nothing.

I looked at the door, and thoughts of the eldest Denali brother crossed my mind.

"Nope!" I shook my head and hopped up from the bed. "I need a shower."

~*~

The shower was refreshing, but did nothing to stop the way my mind wandered out of the bedroom door, down the hall, and to Demetrius' room. I couldn't understand it. I hadn't thought of him in that way for months, and yet there I was, slowing rubbing the soap over my breasts and imagining it was his hands doing the work instead of my own.

When I got out of the shower, I checked the phone again. A word from Rhys would set my mind right. Just a confirmation text or a missed phone call, something to let me know the man I chose was out in the world thinking about me. How busy could he possibly be?

There was nothing. No text. No call. Nothing from

Rhys. I called his phone, and after a few rings, it went to voicemail. I considered leaving a message but decided against it. The night would be a long one regardless of if I heard from him or not, so I climbed into bed and stared out the window until my mind was quiet enough to allow me to sleep.

When I finally could sleep, though, I hoped I would find myself in a subconscious space with Rhys. What I found was a merman.

"What are you doing here?" I doubled checked my surroundings. I was in the same metaphysical place. The enormous bed and endless surroundings were there, only this time there was the sound of waves crashing against a shore I couldn't see.

"I don't know. Where is here?" Demetrius answered me.

"It's a metaphysical realm, where I meet with Rhys," I explained. "We couldn't use the Mates Doorway, so we had to create our own."

"Ah, Rhys. How is he? You know you haven't talked about him much since you've been here." Demetrius looked around, as if expecting my boyfriend to pop out at him.

"I'm not sure what you want me to say about him." I frowned. What more could I possibly tell him? He already knew Rhys was away and that I was in isolation.

There really wasn't much else to say about it.

"How are you doing? How is the relationship? I know he is away, but are you two still good together? I don't know. It's been a while, and if you two are together, I would think you would want to talk about it."

"There is nothing to talk about," I rejected his theory. "Besides, it's weird to discuss Rhys with you."

"We could always talk about how you haven't had sex." He threw it out there, right in my face.

"What?" I froze. How did he know?

"When was the last time?" He stepped closer to me, and I moved back, but my legs hit the side of the bed, stopping my retreat.

"Demetrius." Suddenly all I could think about was the last time Demetrius and I met in metaphysical space. It was my first encounter with the Mates Doorway, and before it ended, his head was between my thighs.

"It's just a question." He took another step forward, knowing I had nowhere else to go.

"It's intrusive." Instead of falling back on the bed, I slid to the left, removing myself from temptation.

"If you say so, but I can feel it, you know." Eyes darkening with his own desire, he moved closer to me.

"I can taste it in the air, your sex, your passion. You're hungry, and it's not for pasta and wine."

"What are you doing?" I watched him closely.

"I'm not here because I made it happen, Syrinada." He frowned before his lips turned up into a slight smile. "You know that don't you? You called me here."

"I—" I shook my head. There was no way I did what he said. When I went to sleep, my thoughts were of Rhys. I wanted Rhys.

"You want to deny it. I get it." Again, he moved closer, but I didn't retreat. "You don't want to feel guilty. We've been here before. You promising yourself to someone else, and here I am, once again, the object of your desire."

"Demetrius." I took a deep breath as his last step brought him within arm's reach.

"What, Syrinada? What is it?"

"Don't do this. Please." I looked into his eyes, and despite my efforts, my body responded to him. "I can't, not here."

"If you want me to go, make me go." He reached out to touch my face, and I leaned into him. "I didn't bring me here. I can't leave unless you want me to."

"I..."

"You, what?" His voice was a deep caress over my inner thighs. "Tell me."

"I don't want you to go," I admitted, and my stomach twisted into a knot so tight it felt like I would cave in from the pressure.

"As long as you want me here, I'll be here." He pulled me into his arms. "Tell me. What do you want?"

"I want…" I couldn't say it, not there. Not in the place created with the bond of my magic and my mate's. How could I do that to him? "I can't."

"It's okay. I understand." He leaned into me.

"You can't be here. This isn't right." I shook my head.

"Then make me go." Demetrius pressed his lips against my ear. "Do it. You want me gone, say the words, and I'm out of here."

I couldn't do it. Even though I knew it wasn't right, I couldn't make him go. I was tired of being alone, tired of waiting by the phone for Rhys to call or text. I'd come to this place so many times, hoping for time with him, and he never showed. How many more times would that happen? How much longer would I be waiting for him?

My logical mind told me it wasn't that bad. That the wait wasn't as terrible as my body told me it was. I could make it, but there was more to me than the logical mind. There was the primal side, the side that needed more than sparing text messages and a bi-weekly hook-up. Looking into Demetrius's eyes, there was something I hadn't seen in Rhys. Passion.

It had been months, even before Rhys went to help the covens, since he looked at me like that. Now I felt more of a project, another thing for him to check off his to-do list, and it made me feel horrible. Instead of telling him that, I kept it to myself. He was out in the world doing amazing things. How could I complain about wanting more attention?

Demetrius saw the internal turmoil, my fight with my logical mind and my siren side. I was torn between kicking him out and jumping his bones. Neither felt like the right thing to do.

He took the option away from me.

Demetrius pulled me into his arms, lifted my face to his, and planted a kiss on me that reminded me of what it was to be desired. The heat left his lips, slipped between my own, and filled my body with a passionate fire that brought beads of sweat to my forehead.

I should have pulled back. I should have pushed him away and told him that wasn't the time or the place for things like that. That I had a mate, I severed the bond with Demetrius so I could be with Rhys, and I had to honor that. That was what I should have done. It was not what happened.

Instead of pushing the brother away, I leaned into him. I drank in his kiss and returned one of my own so hot and heavy I became lost in the moment. My hands ran across his back, wrapped in the locs that fell from his head, and pulled him closer to me.

Before I knew it, he lifted me into his arms, wrapped my legs around his waist, and held me in the air, kissing me with a fire that fed the growing desire within me. I ground my hips against him as the moisture built between my thighs. How far could I allow this to go?

My head dropped back as he released my lips and kissed my face, jawline, and neck. I felt amazing in his arms. I wanted more of him, and I would have had every bit of him if it was not for the sound that interrupted my thoughts. One last moan slipped from my lips before I realized we weren't alone.

"Sy?" His voice crushed me. My heart slammed to a stop in my chest, and I froze.

Maybe this was a nightmare, something I could wake up from, a cautionary tale of what I shouldn't let happen. I closed my eyes tight and hoped it was the case. Instead of waking up in my bed, he spoke again.

"You've got to be fucking kidding me, right?" There was so much anger in his voice. A level of hurt I knew I couldn't fix.

I pushed away from Demetrius, dropping back to the floor, and straightened myself before turning to see the heartbroken face of my lover.

"Rhys," I breathed.

"What the fuck is this?" He looked from me to the Demetrius and back. "Are you serious right now?"

"I didn't—" I wanted to explain, but what could I possibly say that would make any of what he saw okay?

"You didn't what? Bring him here?" he pointed to Demetrius. "Don't bother lying to me. You asked me to come here, to meet you, and for what? Did you want an audience for your betrayal? Did you want to rub it in my face that you're out here fucking whatever walks by?"

"That is not fair, Rhys," I defended myself. "That's not what this is."

"Then what is it, Sy?" he asked. "You talk about what is fair, but is this fair to me? Is it fair that I get to walk into this space, a space you and I created for us, to find you here with another man? And not just another man, Sy. The man you were mated to. I thought you were over this."

"Rhys, come on. You know I was never really mated to him," I tried to explain what was happening. "There was never anything between us, you know that!"

"Do I? Because right now it looks like there is a hell

of a lot between you two."

"If you would just let me explain," I pleaded.

"I don't want to hear your explanation. I have to go back. I have work to do." He threw his hands up and turned to leave.

"Rhys." I ran after him, but he shifted away from me.

The vision, our space, shook as I tried to keep up with him. The ground split and shattered beneath my feet as I ran, and I fell into the abyss of darkness.

When my eyes opened, I was back in bed, back in the Denali's house. Tears fell down my face because as much as I wanted to believe it was a dream, I knew it wasn't. I looked at my phone. One notification, a text from Rhys. "Be there soon."

I never saw it. He sent it after I fell asleep. There was no way I was getting back to sleep. I stared at the ceiling for the rest of the night, refusing to leave the room. I couldn't see anyone. Yes, I thought of going to Demetrius' room and banging on the door. I wanted to curse him out, but for what? I knew what they said was true. Like it or not, I called Demetrius to that space. All he did was answer the call.

CHAPTER 6

Just as the sun touched the sky, a heavy knock sounded on the door. I stared at it, knowing damn well who was on the other side. Even without his voice to call my name, I could feel his presence on the other side of the door. That strength and power beneath a careful façade. Along with his power was the scent of his sex, his arousal. It called to me. Odds were he'd gotten just as much sleep as I did after what happened.

I didn't answer the door. I knew it was him, and I knew he knew I was awake, but I couldn't face him, not yet. Even though I sat up most of the night planning what I would say. When it came down to it, I didn't know what to do. I was afraid of what he would expect from me after what happened.

Did he think things had changed between us? Did he want to continue what we started and go further? Whatever he expected, I couldn't even consider, not when I still hadn't heard from Rhys. I texted him three times and called him twice, and each time he ignored me. I couldn't blame him. After what he walked in on, I wouldn't want to talk to me either.

After a long pause, his footsteps carried him away from my door, and I sighed. It irritated me how much I wanted him to come back and knock again, to try harder to reach me. I questioned what the hell was wrong with me? There I was, supposed to be focused on getting Rhys to forgive me, but instead, I was longing for the man who broke us up.

I opted for another shower before the sun finished its ascent into the sky. When I came out, I dressed and sat back on the bed, where I remained late into the morning.

A soft tap on the door caught my attention, followed by a voice. "It's me. Maggie," she called from the other side.

With a heavy mind from the lack of sleep, I opened the door. "Hey." I stepped aside, letting her in, and quickly shut the door behind her again.

"How long do you plan on staying locked up in here?" she asked as she looked around the room. "Man, your spot is better than mine. I guess our host has a favorite."

"It's where I stayed last time. I'm sure that's why he put me here this time."

"It's also the furthest from his bedroom." She winked.

"That too." I nodded and wondered if her ghostly abilities allowed her insight into what had happened the night before.

"You going to come out of hiding or not?" she asked.

"I don't know what you mean." I shrugged. "Just been sitting here relaxing."

"I mean, it's eleven o'clock. We're supposed to be working on our super important plan to save the world, and here you are sitting in your room pouting."

"I'm not pouting," I defended myself. "What makes you think I'm pouting?"

"What would you call it?" She tapped her chin with her finger. "Sulking? That has a good ring to it."

"I would call it taking my time in a difficult situation," I clarified. "Things are complicated, more than you know."

"So, you almost mind-banged your ex's brother in your dreams. What's the big deal?" She shrugged. "Worse things have happened."

"First, how the fuck did you know that? Second, it is a big deal because I'm with Rhys," I reminded her.

"You know, the guy I left both the Denali's behind for?"

"Rhys, oh yeah." She nodded. "Almost forgot about him."

"Well, I didn't, and I chose him, so mind fucking someone else, successfully or not, is kind of a big deal."

"Did you really? Choose him?" she asked. "I mean, maybe half of your anatomy is okay with being with Rhys. What about the other half?"

"The other half?" I feigned ignorance.

"Come on, Sy, you're a siren. You have this entire magical sexual beast inside of you. She is probably going ape shit right now after what you described your living situation to be. You're basically on a sex diet."

"Maggie," I huffed.

"No, I'm serious. Answer me this." She sat on the bed and bounced a little before issuing her question. "Does Rhys really do it for you? Does he feed that hunger like those sexy mermen do? Or are you telling yourself he does?"

"Why are you asking these questions?" I crossed my arms and looked out the window because I didn't know how to answer her.

"Because you won't ask them yourself. I can see how you're avoiding the obvious, but hell, someone has to say it. I love Rhys. He's a great guy, really. He's honest, loyal, caring, all the things you want in your bae, but he is only half of what you are, and despite your human attachment to him, you need to ask yourself the hard questions. Is Rhys enough for all of you? Not just the part that fits into his world."

"I don't want to talk to you about this right now." I threw my hand up. "Rhys and I are okay, Maggie."

"Okay, you don't want to talk about it. Do me a favor and tell me when you'll be open to having an actual conversation about this. I will pencil it into my daybook." She raised a brow. "Really, I mean, anytime you're ready. With this whole undead, dead girl thing, my schedule is free and clear!"

"Ha-ha, very funny." I rolled my eyes. "We have more important things to worry about than my relationship mess, anyway."

"I'm glad you bring that up." She clapped. "Because if you won't talk about the rainbow-colored elephant in the room, you can at least get your ass up and come downstairs. Awkward or not, we need to make a move. We have to find that succubus sister of yours. I've been dying to meet her. Well, I'm already dead, but you get what I mean."

~*~

Demetrius stood in the kitchen sipping a hot cup of coffee. The aroma of the fresh brew filled the air, and I made a beeline for the coffeepot. Yes, caffeine, that was just what a girl needed when already on edge and not sure what to do with herself. At least it would make it easier to stay awake during what would be an awkward morning meeting.

"Good morning." Maggie smiled, bouncing into the kitchen after me.

"Morning." Demetrius lifted his cup to her.

"Good morning," I said because I didn't want to be the rude ass in the room who refused to say good morning to everyone else.

"Sleep well?" Maggie asked, and Demetrius smirked.

"Thanks a lot," I whispered smugly, lifting my cup to her. So much for hoping we would ignore what happened.

"Well, hell, someone had to break the tension. I don't know how the two of you think we are going to get through this if you won't even talk to each other. So what, you had a dream? You are a siren, he is a merman. Y'all were attracted to each other before, right? Why would that go away? Now just reel that shit in, and let's get to work," Maggie spoke low enough so he couldn't hear as she poured her own cup of coffee before heading for the table to join Demetrius.

"She's right." Demetrius looked at me, and as much as I wanted to look away, I didn't.

"Yeah, okay." I took a long sip of coffee and let the warm liquid flow down my throat while my thoughts focused. "So, let's start thinking this through."

"The plan is to find Imara, right?" Demetrius asked.

"Yep. We need to find the second sexy sister." Maggie shimmied in her seat.

"Nothing weird about that." I shook my head and sat in the seat next to Maggie.

"Hey, I call it like I see it." She stuck her tongue out at me.

"I have some insight about where she might be." Demetrius avoided the topic of our sexualities.

"Oh yeah, where's that?" I asked. I thought it would be weeks before we knew anything about her. Maybe spend some time scouting Chicago before we would move on. Okay, maybe I was trying to prolong things.

"I'm not sure, but one of my scouts saw her nearby. She was hanging with someone I think you know."

Demetrius leaned back in his seat. "I think you all hung out a lot before you left."

"Who?" I blew on my coffee. There weren't many people I hung out with outside of Malachi and Latasha, and I wasn't on speaking terms with either of them.

"Straught," Demetrius answered.

"The vampire hunk?" Maggie perked up.

"Um, yeah." He frowned. "I thought witches didn't like vampires."

"We aren't supposed to, but if you haven't figured it out yet, I rarely do what I'm supposed to do." Maggie winked. "I play by my own rules."

"I still can't believe Straught is a damn vampire." My nail tapped against the table as I processed the idea again. "I mean, all that time we hung around him, I never would have thought he was different."

"I can't believe you didn't know he was one. I mean, look at the man." Maggie pretended to fan herself with her hand. "No human is that perfect."

"The man is attractive, yes, but aren't vampires supposed to be super alluring?" I shrugged. "I don't get it."

"It's different for you, Syrinada." Demetrius smiled as if happy I didn't find the undead attractive.

"A vampire's power is designed for their food source. Humans. You aren't human. If anything, he would be drawn to you. In this world, you're the predator, not the prey."

"Right." I bit my lip, ignoring the internal reaction to his words. The way he looked at me made me want to run from the room. "So we go see Straught and hope she left a calling card with him?"

"Even if she didn't, your buddy is a lot more powerful than we thought he was, and in vampire land, he has his own set of eyes and ears. Even if Imara was avoiding us, she wouldn't be so weary around vampires."

"Which means he might already know where she is." I chewed my lip.

"Exactly," Demetrius confirmed. "I figure we just ask him where she is. No real reason he wouldn't want to tell us."

"Unless she doesn't want anyone to know where she is," I corrected. "Maybe she's in hiding now."

"I suppose that is a possibility, yes." He nodded.

"Does that mean we get to go partying tonight?" Maggie looked like she would bounce right out of her seat.

"Yeah, I guess it does." Demetrius laughed at her

display.

"Oh, this is going to be fun. I've never been to a club in the city." She grabbed my arm and shook me. "We have to find something to wear."

"For what? It's not like we're going there to have fun. We're going there to find answers and leave." I shook my head.

"Come on." She pouted. "Do it for me, the dead girl who may never get another chance to go out and get picked up by hot guys."

"Oh, you are laying it on thick," I scoffed.

"Hey, I can pour it heavier if that helps."

"No, no, you've done enough."

"There are some shops nearby you guys can go to. There's also a mall," Demetrius suggested.

"Oh yes, a mall!" Maggie grinned. "We need to go shopping. Demetrius can loan us some coin, right?" she asked him with wide eyes.

"Yes, I could do that," Demetrius agreed easily.

"Maggie—" I started.

"Oh, get off it. You know you want this just as much as I do. A girls' day out, shopping, we can get mani-pedis. When was the last time you did anything like this? When do you think you'd ever have another chance to do it again? I mean, after tonight, we're off to hunt down a succubus and a group of potentially deadly hybrids."

"She has a point." Demetrius smiled, and I met his eyes.

My stomach flipped. I could see the concern there. He wanted me to do something nice for myself.

"Okay, okay." I threw my hands up. "I'll go."

"Great!" Maggie jumped up and headed out the door.

"Do I at least get to finish my coffee first?" I called after her.

"I guess not." Demetrius laughed and tossed me a set of keys and his credit card. "Have fun."

CHAPTER 7

I had to admit it. Maggie was right. I needed a day to just be a normal woman. When I didn't have to worry about magic and men and all the mayhem both had brought into my life. I needed to walk through a mall going in and out of stores filled with clothes I would never buy. I needed to stand in line in a fragrance store with so many distinct aromas that the mixture left my head spinning.

I needed to be pampered. The mani-pedi turned into a full spa day, complete with a massage from a woman named Maria who I was sure I would dream about for months to come. Her hands were heavenly. Gentle and yet firm in just the right spots. And when she placed the hot stones on my back, I nearly orgasmed. Yes, I was touch deprived.

"I'm glad you came," Maggie said as we sat next to each other, getting our nails painted.

"I am too." I smiled at her. "Thanks for pushing me to get out."

"Of course. Besides, this is for me just as much as it is for you." She winked. "I never got to do anything like this before. You know, just hang out with a girlfriend. There was always something more important to be done, and now, well, you know, after this is over, it's really not an option for me anymore."

"Do you think you could visit? You know, after you go back?" I peeked at the man who worked on my hands, afraid he would try to decode our conversation.

He was too busy bopping his head and singing to the song that blasted from his headphones.

"I don't know. I mean, the others can, but I'm a newbie, so the rules are different." She shrugged. "I also got into a little trouble after one of my cousins ended up with a short stint in the psych ward."

"You didn't." I gawked. "You made them go crazy?"

"The man threw a bucket of frogs on me when I was sleeping! I was a child. It traumatized me for years. I still get triggered if one of those damn things hops too fast." She scrunched up her nose.

"Such a fun and loving family." I chuckled. "No wonder you're such a handful."

"Yes, it was the best." She laughed.

When we finished with our nails, we stopped at a local sandwich shop and picked up lunch, including food for Demetrius who hadn't bothered us all day. I worried about spending too much money while Maggie swiped the card so freely you'd think she could take her new clothes to the afterlife with her.

We also bought things we could take on our trip. I'd lost everything I owned to the sea, and I preferred having more than one pair of underwear. We pulled up to the house just in time to see a dark SUV drive away.

"Who do you think that was?" Maggie asked as we parked the car.

I stepped out and took a deep breath, catching the last of the scent of the driver. "I don't know, but they're not human."

"No?" she squinted at the disappearing car. "How can you tell?"

"I know that smell, it's wolf." I nodded. "Kinda of woody, a little dirty, and an underlining musk."

"Demetrius is buddy-buddy with wolves?" Her eyes widened. "I would have never guessed."

"He works with a lot of different people." I nodded.

"This man gets more intriguing every day." She grabbed the bags from the back seat. "Good luck with that."

"Thanks," I muttered as she headed for the house.

Every time I got my mind off of things, there was Maggie to bring it slamming back into focus. Waiting inside the house was a man who had been nothing but kind to us since we showed up on his doorstep. I should be grateful to him. Instead, all I could think about was how I wanted to get away from him. Flashes of being in his arms both excited me and broke my heart.

If it weren't for the bag of food in my hand, I would have gotten back in the car and drove off. Unfortunately, there was also a starving ghost in that house who would haunt me for the rest of my life, if for no other reason than to torture me for driving away with the four sandwiches she ordered just for herself.

I made it two steps inside the door before Maggie snatched the bags of food from me and entered the kitchen. I followed her because my stomach was growling, and I didn't want to risk her monstrous appetite getting the best of her and my food disappearing along with hers.

We were already sitting and eating when Demetrius walked in. He wore a look of worry that concerned me, but I thought it best not to ask.

"We got you something too." I pointed to the covered plate on the table across from me.

"Oh, thank you." He shook his head. "I was just

getting coffee, but I should eat. I'm running on an empty tank at this point."

"Everything okay?" I asked.

"Yes, just tying up some loose ends is all." He adjusted the locs that fell around his face. "Business never ends."

"With the wolf?" Maggie asked, and I rolled my eyes.

"Maggie," I warned her to back off.

"No, it's okay." He sat down. "Yes, with the wolf. There was some residual damage here after we left. Witches came through as we suspected, trying to find Syrinada. They moved on, but not before they disrupted things."

"Why would they mess with the wolves?" I asked.

"They know we work with them," he answered.

"Guilty by association," Maggie added. "That's how the covens work. It's such an archaic concept."

"Exactly." Demetrius grabbed a can of soda from the edge of the table and a bag of chips. "The witches swept through here, stirred up shit, and left the balance in our supernatural world out of whack. It's not just the sirens and the wolves. It's the vampires, fairies… hell, they even pissed off a few gnomes."

"Gnomes." I shook my head. "Someday I'll get used to all this."

"Trust me, you won't." Maggie laughed. "I was born into this, lived it every day of my life, and this is the first I'm hearing that gnomes still exist!"

"Yes, they do. There aren't many, but they're out there, and until the coven got here, they were a peaceful part of this territory." He sipped the soda and sighed.

"And now it's your responsibility to fix things?" I asked, the weight of guilt crushing me.

"Don't look like that. This isn't your fault. This was bound to happen. The covens want to control the supernatural system. They won't come out and say it, but that's always been their goal. It's been happening all over. They find a reason to come in and fuck shit up. It would have happened here with or without your involvement."

"Why are they doing this?" I looked at Maggie, who looked just as clueless as I felt.

"Because something is coming, we can all feel it. Something big. I think they're trying to get ahead of it," she explained. "They want to restore order before shit gets worse, but they're going about it the wrong way."

"Great, just a little more drama to add to the list of shit to be concerned with." I bit my sandwich and spoke around the food. "Crazy covens and impending doom. You want to crack open another bottle of that wine? Because this Sprite ain't enough for me right now."

"Yes, we could use a little pregame before we go out!" Maggie cheered, and Demetrius headed for the cellar.

~*~

We arrived outside of the club that stood at the heart of the triangle, a three corner section of Chicago where you could find some of the best party vibes. While the streets were just as lively as I remembered, it felt strange to be there. Not just because we pulled up to the front and had the car parked by a valet service that never existed before, but because I was a different person. The last time I came there, I was unsure of myself. I lacked confidence in my sexuality, and I felt like I had to shrink into the shadows to make sure I wasn't in the way.

When I stepped out of the car, all eyes shot my way. I lived in the attention for a moment, enjoying the desire of the men and the jealousy of the women. Demetrius appeared next to me, and the men's passion shifted to anger. When he touched my arm, I reeled in my pull.

Shielding the world from the siren that lived inside of me, everyone returned to normal. Some looked confused as they tried to return to their conversations, their minds struggling to pick up where they left off.

"Alright, let's get this party started." Maggie skipped around the car and bounced on the spot beside me.

"Again," I shook my head, "we aren't here to party."

"And yet you're standing here in a dress that hugs every curve of your body," she looked behind me at my ass, "and some I didn't realize you had."

"You picked out the dress," I reminded her.

"Yeah, but you didn't *have* to wear it." She winked. "Come on, let me enjoy the little things."

"Fine, but don't forget why we're here." I narrowed my eyes at her. "We're leaving as soon as we get what we need."

"Scout's honor." She pretended to do the girl scouts hand signal but had no idea what she was doing and ended up looking like she was trying to direct a plane to a landing spot.

"Alright, let's head in," Demetrius said when we finished our exchange.

"Oh, no line?" Maggie asked.

"Not when you're walking in with two seductive hybrids." He winked.

"I could get used to this." Maggie lifted her chin and walked ahead.

As expected, the bouncer let us walk right in, ahead of the line of people already waiting. Maggie giggled as the others complained about having to wait while we cut the line.

The inside of the club hadn't changed at all. It was still just as busy, and the DJ was on top of his game. The only thing that was new was the smell. Before, the mix of sweat, cologne, and alcohol would slightly irritate me. Instead of repulsion, I felt arousal. One that I had to quickly put the cap on. While Maggie danced off into the crowd, Demetrius pulled me close to him.

"You okay?" he spoke into my ear as my back met his stomach.

I leaned into him and lifted my chin to better inhale that woody smell of his cologne. For a moment, I lost myself to my desires and imagined him taking me in the middle of the club full of onlookers. Then, as I realized how close I was to creating a very terrible scene, I corrected myself.

"Yeah, I'm good." I cleared my throat.

"You sure?" He gripped my arm, and I had to bite my bottom lip to stop myself from turning and kissing him.

Instead, I assessed the situation. Despite my own excitement, no one around us paid me any mind. There were no lustful men pulling at my clothes or angry women trying to come for my neck. I had it under control.

"Yes, I'm good." I turned to look him in the eye. "Thank you."

"Of course." He nodded. "Just let me know if you need to get away."

"We should look for Straught now. I know Maggie wants to party, but I think we should limit how long we stay here," I admitted. Just because I was fine in that moment didn't mean things couldn't get bad fast.

"I think you're right." He looked away from me, then frowned. "Speaking of Maggie, where is she?"

"Crap." I scanned the moving crowd. "I should have known to keep an eye on her. I'll go find her."

"You sure?" He grabbed my hand as I tried to step away.

Both our eyes dropped to our hands. Where our skin met, it radiated with energy that felt familiar and good, but definitely didn't belong.

"Yes, just try to find Straught." I nodded and slowly pulled my hand from his.

I left Demetrius by the front door and pushed my way through the crowd of people. Maggie couldn't have gotten too far. All I needed to do was find her and get back to Demetrius. I was okay, but the further I got away from him, the more I felt the sexual energy in the room. It was like he worked as a blocker for it.

All around me, men revved up as they found women who turned them on. Women perked up, doing their mating dances, waiting for the right man to press up behind them. I laughed at a particularly enthusiastic dancer, who finally looked back to see an old man with a receding hairline and way too many gold chains around his neck grinding on her ass. The girl nearly fell on her face trying to get away from him.

When I saw her again, she was cursing out her friends.

"Bitch, you let me twerk on the elderly!" she screamed.

"My bad, you looked like you were enjoying it." One of her friends snickered and handed her a drink.

I was completely on her side. Her girls dropped the ball on that one.

At the back of the club, in the new VIP section, I found Maggie sitting on the lap of a man who looked like he could be a body double for The Rock! When she saw me, she squealed and hopped down from his lap.

"See, I told you my friend was amazing." Maggie swayed her hips to the music. "Just look at her!"

"Yeah, you didn't lie." Another equally massive hunk stood behind her. "We could have a lot of fun together."

"Excuse me?" I asked.

"Maggie said you're looking for a party," her guy answered. "We're here to provide one."

"We're not looking for anything." I shot Maggie a stern look. "We're here to get work done and move on."

"Oh, come on, Sy." She pouted. "Have a little fun with me."

"No, that's not going to work this time, Maggie. Have you forgotten what we're here for? Or what will happen if we don't get this done?" I hated sounding like the responsible adult, but someone had to do it.

"Fine," she huffed.

"Your friend is intense." The second guy took a step back. "I like 'em fiery, but I think this one may burn me."

"You're right about that." Maggie rolled her eyes. "Sorry, Zeke baby. I have to go."

"Oh damn, make sure you come back to see me

again." He pulled her close to him and kissed her.

I frowned. If the girl wasn't already dead, I'd be warning her about kissing strange men in dark clubs, but then again, who was I to talk? I once banged a total stranger on the hood of his car. Wonder if he ever got that dent out.

With Maggie in tow, I found my way back across the crowded club where Demetrius stood with two men I didn't recognize. One with platinum braids that hung past his shoulder shook his head, and Demetrius frowned.

"What's wrong?" I asked, keeping my hand tightly gripped around Maggie's wrist so she didn't run off again.

"He isn't here. Hasn't been in for a while, according to the manager." Demetrius nodded to the braided man, who left his side.

"What?" It was unlike Straught not to be at his club. He was a part of the feature, what people came to see. "Do they know where he is?"

"No, but the manager has his address," Demetrius answered with a tight jaw. "He is going to get it for me."

"So, we're leaving?" Maggie pouted.

"Good." I shook my head. "You're going to lose it if we stay in here any longer."

"Okay, Mom!" She stuck her tongue out at me.

"Whatever." I rolled my eyes. "We're not here to party, Maggie."

"I know you have got to be fucking kidding me," the familiar voice sounded off behind me.

"Oh shit." I slowly turned to find my friend and the woman I'd been avoiding standing behind me.

Latasha stood with her best 'get-em-girl' dress on and a scowl on her face.

"Tasha," I said nervously.

"I knew I smelled your scent at the apartment. Thought maybe I was just missing you, but here you are." She rolled her eyes.

"I'm sorry. I just had some things to take care of."

"Are you serious, Sy? You disappear for months and then show up here at our spot like nothing ever happened?" She laughed. "What things did you have to take care of that were so important you couldn't stop by and say hi? I mean, hell, my number hasn't changed. You could have texted me or something."

"I can explain," I started, but she put her hand in my face.

"Why bother? You're just going to go missing again,

right? Not like you plan on hanging around."

"Tasha, don't do that."

"No, just save it, Sy. I really thought we were friends, but I see how little truth was in that. I mean, I fucking flew to New Orleans to help you fight demons, and you just disappeared! And I know that's what you're going to do now. I swear, I miss the woman you were before you figured out this siren shit. She knew how to treat her friends."

She stomped off.

"Well, drama just follows you wherever you go, doesn't it?" Maggie chirped as I turned and headed for the door.

"Not now, Maggie."

CHAPTER
8

I kept quiet during the car ride. It was the first time I saw Latasha in months. I'd thought about that moment for so long and what it would be like to see her and reconnect. I went over in my head just how much I could tell her without the powers that be coming down on my head for spilling the beans.

I beat myself up for not considering that I might run into her there. This was her spot. I'd only found out about it because of her. Of course, she would be there on a Friday night. To her, a Friday night there was like Mardi Gras. She could pick up a man or two, hell, I'd seen her go home with six different potential baes logged in her phone. None of them worked out, but that wasn't the point.

And now, with her own vampire allure, the turnout would be much better for her. No more dragging the unknown siren out to pull in men for her. She could do that all on her own.

Back in the car and headed to the address the manager provided, I texted her from the new phone. Luckily I could log into my cloud for the backup information and get to her phone number because I sure as hell didn't remember it. I hoped she would respond, but I would not hold my breath. Latasha held a grudge like no other.

The drive to Straught's home was fairly quick, considering we were going in the opposite direction of every other driver. Leaving the party scene behind, Maggie leaned out the window and waved to the Chicago skyline.

"This blows." She plopped down in her seat. "We could have stayed a little longer. It wouldn't have hurt anyone."

"We have to stay focused." Demetrius looked at her through the review mirror and winked.

"Yeah whatever," she huffed. "Can you at least turn some music on? As cute as I look, I'll just dance in my seatbelt. Not wasting this outfit!"

Demetrius did as she asked, turning on a playlist that had enough bass to inspire hip thrusts and arm waves from the woman in the back seat. I laughed at her when she got on her knees in the seat and wiggled her ass at the men in the next car.

"This is his house? A little simple for a vampire, isn't it?" I asked as we pulled up to the two story home with the black fence that wrapped the property.

"Yeah, well, apparently he's been avoiding the condo downtown." Demetrius looked over his shoulder at Maggie who'd settled into her seat.

"Why would he need to avoid home?" I asked.

"Bad blood with some other vampires? I don't know, but I sure as hell am going to find out." Demetrius turned off the engine and got out of the car.

Maggie and I followed him. Stepping into the night air, I caught the scent of something familiar. The same one that lingered outside of Demetrius' house earlier that day. Werewolf. It hadn't been long since the shifters left the home. My question was why were werewolves visiting a vampire in his home away from home?

I looked at Demetrius, knowing that he caught the scent, but he said nothing.

"Shall we go in? I don't know what it is about you merpeople standing outside of houses." Maggie nudged my shoulder. "I say we just get the shit over with. Maybe we'll have time to go back to the club."

"I'm sure Zeke has already moved on to his next target of the night," Demetrius said.

"Must you always be so cynical?" Maggie frowned at him.

"Sorry," he said.

"Let's head in," I agreed with Maggie. We needed to get moving, and standing on the curb wasn't going to get us any closer to doing what we needed to do.

Demetrius took the lead and walked up to the door. We were careful to check our surroundings as we moved forward. The street was idle but not empty. Human men hung out on the corner smoking weed and drinking. Across from them were three women who taunted their friend by twerking to music that played from their car.

I expected vampire guards, someone who would be concerned with keeping their leader safe, but while Straught was rich and well connected, he wasn't exactly vampire royalty. Money may have provided him with some comforts, but it didn't guarantee him protection in his world.

The previous guests left the door slightly ajar when they left. Demetrius pushed cautiously, and when it swung open to reveal the cozy interior, the smell of sex and blood came wafting out.

"That can't be good, right?" I swallowed my rapidly activated arousal. This was not the time to lose myself to lust.

"Well, it is a vampire's house, so who knows?" Demetrius shrugged. "I've seen and smelled a lot worse walking into one of their dens. This is actually pretty modest."

"I could always go ghost mode and look inside," Maggie offered. "See what we're up against."

"That's a good idea." I nodded, and Maggie vanished in front of my eyes, shifting to her ethereal form. Her clothes fell to the ground where she stood.

"That's not strange at all." Demetrius smirked as I picked her things up. "Did you know she could do that?"

"Only recently found out." I looked away from him because I didn't want to give away that our ghostly friend had been spying on him.

We stood awkwardly looking out onto the street while Maggie searched the home. It took longer than I would have liked, but after about five minutes, she appeared in her human form standing in the open doorway.

"All clear inside, guys." She waved us forward.

"Thanks," I said, moved to hand her the clothes, but she was fully dressed. Her body resetting to the state it was prior to our spa day.

She looked down at herself and cursed. "Well fuck, my nails." She sighed, looking at her plain fingertips.

"Sorry," I pulled the clothes back. "Guess you won't need these."

"This blows." Maggie stomped her foot, pouting like a toddler. "I just wanted to look pretty, and you're telling me I'm going to keep resetting to this gothic state? It wasn't the only thing I ever wore."

"Well, maybe you just don't go ghost anymore. Then you can look however you want," I offered her comfort.

"Um, ladies, the vampire?" Demetrius reminded us to focus on our mission.

"Oh yeah, he is okay, I think. Upstairs in bed. Bloody but breathing." Maggie waved her hand toward the stairs at the side of the entrance.

"Shouldn't he be down here? I mean vampire hearing and speed?" I asked because it made no sense that Straught wouldn't at least try to figure out who had intruded on his home. "It's not like we tiptoed in here. Something is wrong."

"You're right, let's go." Demetrius again went ahead of us.

Right off the landing at the top of the stairs were three doors. Maggie pointed to the one in the second on the left, claiming that to be the one where she saw the vampire. We entered the room, and it was just as Maggie said. Straught laid across his bed, bloodied and barely breathing.

"Straught?" I rushed to the bedside and knelt

beside the man I once knew as a friend. "Are you okay?"

He lifted his head from the bed, and my heart broke. The handsome man I'd know before was now withered, frail. His brown skin looked paler than I thought possible, and thick veins stretched from his sunken eyes down to his bare chest and lower. Straught was doing bad.

"I will be. Bad blood is all." He looked over my should and found Demetrius. "This again, man? I told your lackey I'd pay up!"

"What?" Demetrius looked behind him as if expecting someone else to be there. "I don't know what he's talking about."

"Are you okay?" I asked Straught again. Clearly, the man was delusional.

"They fucked with my blood supply. I was worse before, so yeah, I'll heal." He threw another angry glare at Demetrius. "What do you want from me, man?"

"We need to know where Imara is," Demetrius answered.

"Why the hell would I tell you that?" Straught tried to sit up but fell back. "You going to send your hellhounds to fuck with her like they did me?"

"What the hell are you talking about? Hell hounds?" Demetrius shook his head. "I don't know what you're talking about."

"Oh, he pretends he doesn't know!" Straught finally made it to an upright position. "You and your people come around here swinging your weight around."

"What is going on?" I asked. "What is he talking about?"

"I don't know." Demetrius shrugged. "How many times do I have to say that?"

"That wolf, the one that was at the house, he was here. I smell him," I pointed out. "You caught that too."

"Yeah, I did." Demetrius nodded and moved to look out the window where the street outside was still silent.

"Of course, you did because you sent him here. Didn't you? Made sure he got the job done," Straught accused Demetrius.

"Again, and for the last time, I don't know what you're talking about." Demetrius was turning hot with anger. "Now, if you want to stop accusing me of shit I didn't do and give us some information that we can actually work with, then maybe we could actually work on figuring this shit out."

"You don't know that your wolf boy has been beating down supernatural doors asking for money or he'll reveal their deep dirty secrets." Straught laughed and blood spilled from his mouth. "Or that they postponed all of our fucking blood supply? You say you want us to keep our hands off the humans, but right now there are hundreds of vampires sick and dying because of this shit. And more who no longer trust the blood we're getting. And for what? Law and order? They are just going to go out there and start feeding on your precious humans again. Better to get the food from the source and avoid any more tampering."

"What?" Demetrius turned back to Straught. "You're lying."

"How could you do that?" I asked.

"Syrinada, are you seriously accusing me of this? I didn't do that. I would never." Demetrius pointed at me. "This is fucked up and only going to lead to more trouble for me."

"Well, someone did." I looked to Straught, who looked like he was moments from losing his everlasting lifespan.

"I'll handle this." Demetrius picked up his phone.

"Who are you calling?"

"I'm checking in with the team."

"Your team?" I asked. "The same ones that betrayed you before. Are we trusting them again?"

"Yes, we are. I've made some serious changes to the roster. They are friends, and I screened them each myself."

"Good, because we don't need another Maurice on our hands," Maggie pointed out. "Did you ever find him after he ran?"

"No. We still don't know where he is." Demetrius' jaw clenched.

"Well, someone should look into that. I mean, he could still be working with the enemy, even if one of them is already dead." Maggie waved her hand up and down her body. "Case and point."

"We are, and when we find him, I'll deal with it." Demetrius clutched the phone so tightly I thought it would break in his palm.

"Looks like another one is on the bad side of things. Not a good track record, if you ask me." Straught spit out blood.

"We'll sort this out, I promise," I said. "I really need to know where my sister is. Please tell me."

"I'll tell you if you promise they won't hurt her."

"We're not here to hurt her," I explained. "I need her help, Straught."

"Are you okay?" he looked at Demetrius, who turned and left the room, phone to his ear.

"Yes, Demetrius would never do anything to hurt me."

"Good." He grunted. "I don't trust that guy, but if you do, then I'll take your word for it. How is Imara supposed to help you? What's going on?"

"I just need her by my side. Something big is coming, something that will hurt us both. We will be stronger if we are together."

"You feel it too, huh?" he wiped the corner of his mouth on the back of his hand and sighed. "Shit has been feeling real heavy lately."

"What?" Maggie stepped forward.

"Oh shit, ghost girl. I didn't see you there." He winked at her. "Good to see you back from the dead."

"Thanks. The afterlife is treating me well. Wish I could say you looked good."

"Well yeah," he brushed her off. "There is something big coming. Like it's waiting in the shadows. We aren't the only ones feeling it. I can promise you that."

"Where is the succubus sister?" Maggie asked.

"She's in Washington. She said she needed to get away from the city. Wanted a fresh start. I have a house there. I told her it was hers as long as she wanted it." He pointed to the book on his nightstand. "Address is in there. I'll give it to you."

"You did that for her?" I grabbed the small leather book and handed it to him.

"Hey, I care about her just as much as you." He smiled. "Maybe more, considering I actually know her. I know I barely talked to you, but I was happy to see you around the club, and I'm glad to see you are okay now, especially after all the shit that went down before."

"Thank you, Straught. For taking care of her." I hugged him, and he coughed more blood onto my shoulder. "Oh, shit, sorry."

"No, it's okay." He took a heavy breath. "And of course I took care of her, just like I did Latasha."

"Sy, we should go." Maggie stood by the window looking out at Demetrius who'd removed himself from the house.

"Yeah, in a minute."

I put my hand on Straught's knee. "I'm going to help you if you're okay with that."

"Shit, if you can take this pain away, go for it!" He nodded.

I used my magic, the same magic that kept my plants alive and healed Rhys, to feed the vampire strength. The veining and the dark circles around his eyes faded. He didn't look perfect, not his sexy self we came to know and love at the club, but he looked a lot better than when we first found him.

"That should help you feel better." I rubbed his shoulder. "I'm not sure how long it will last, though."

"Oh my god, girl." He stood up and stretched. "What the hell do you have in those hands?"

"I've learned a few handy techniques." I smiled.

"I'll say."

"We have to get going now." I looked over at my shoulder at Maggie, who still looked out the window. "You sure you will be okay?"

"After that, yeah, I'll be fine." Straught hugged me again. "Thank you, Sy."

"Great," I said nervously. "You're welcome. Just keep my gift between us, please."

"Of course," Straught agreed, and we left him alone in the room that smelled of death and sex.

"That was nice of you," Maggie said as we headed down the stairs.

"It's the least I could do, really." I shrugged.

There were enough people in the world who thought I was a bad guy. At least maybe I could do some good, help the people I cared about. That was what mattered. Not what others thought about me. Not their misconceptions, but the truth I carried with me.

~*~

Tension filled the car as Demetrius drove us from the north side of the city back to his home in the suburbs. I wanted to say something, but I didn't know what I could say. I understood how he felt, and I would feel the same if the person I laid my life on the line for so many times questioned me when I was being accused of something horrible.

"I'm sorry," I spoke as he pulled onto the expressway.

"What?" He glanced over at me. "What are you apologizing for?"

"I'm sorry for not trusting you back there," I admitted. "It was wrong of me to question you."

"Syrinada." Demetrius ran his free hand down his face.

"This feels like a private moment." Maggie sat forward in the back seat. "I'm just going to meet you two back at the house."

"Maggie," I started, but she held her hand up.

"I promise to go straight home, Mom, no detours to Zeke." She smiled and then vanished.

I looked at the empty back seat for a moment, gathering my thoughts to speak.

"You don't have to apologize for anything, you know that," he spoke before I could figure out what to say.

"Yes, I know, but I want to." I straightened in my seat. "Demetrius, I owe you so much. You and Malachi, you did so much for me, and here I am doubting you. I need to apologize for that."

"How could you think I would do that?" He kept his eyes on the road ahead, but I heard all the pain in his voice. My doubt hurt him.

"With everything going on, I don't know what to think. I never thought my aunt would betray me, or my father, or anyone else. And in the last few days, I've basically been told that even though I supposedly proved myself, it wasn't enough. Nothing is ever what I think it is, so yeah, I doubt a lot." I looked at him. "But I shouldn't doubt you. I know that. Not after everything we've been through."

"We have been through a lot." He smiled.

"Yes, we have," I nodded. "And everything that's happened has shown me who you really are. It showed me your character. You care so much about everyone, including me."

"Especially you," he clarified.

"Don't say that." I stared out the window at the passing lights.

"Why not?"

"Because it's not right. It shouldn't be especially me."

"Look, I know how you feel, and I'm trying to respect that." Demetrius' voice was calm and hid the weight of his words flawlessly. "You don't want what exists between us to be there. I understand that, but it is there. It's there for me, I can't lie about it."

"I understand." I kept my eyes on the lights.

"Syrinada," he started.

"You know, I really like that you use my full name." My heart fluttered, and I had to take a deep breath to calm my racing mind. "Few people do."

"I like the sound of your name. I get why people call you Sy, but to me it's lazy. There is a melody to your name. It's special. I enjoy hearing it, and I enjoy saying it."

My stomach tightened with butterflies, and then the phone buzzed in the handbag. I thought it would be Latasha finally responding to my plea for forgiveness. It wasn't.

We need to talk.

The text from Rhys flashed on the screen. I should have responded, but I didn't. I put the phone back in my bag and focused on the road ahead.

"What's next?" I asked Demetrius, glad he didn't

question my neglect of responding to the message.

"I'm going to reach out to my guys, send some scouts to check on the location Straught gave you, and then check in on the situation with the wolves. If they're working for someone, I need to figure out who it is. I can't have my name being dragged through shit because once again, I can't trust the people I've employed."

"What are you going to do when you find out who it is?" I looked at Demetrius, and his jaw tightened.

"Do you really want to know?" He looked over at me.

"No, I guess not." I looked back at the sky.

I wasn't naïve. I understood there were parts of Demetrius' work I wouldn't be a fan of. He had so much on his plate, more than I ever really understood. If we made it through this alive, I would take the time to learn. I knew Malachi, but at that moment, I realized Demetrius was a stranger to me. Yes, I knew he cared about me and would protect me, but outside of what other people told me about him, I had taken little time to investigate the stoic man myself. I had to rectify that.

We made it to the house, and as soon as we got there, Maggie came out and greeted us.

"Took you guys long enough!" she shouted.

"What can I say?" Demetrius shrugged. "Traffic."

"Well, get in here so we can start planning our trip!" She turned and bounced back into the house.

"Coming," I laughed. The girl talked like we were going on vacation.

"You two go ahead. I'll be there in a minute." Demetrius pulled the phone from his pocket. "I need to make a few phone calls."

Demetrius never came back into the house. We waited for him, but when I went out to find him, his car was gone. I checked my phone.

Got some info. Going to go check it out. See you in the morning.

I chewed my lip before responding. Be careful.

CHAPTER 9

It wasn't until the next morning that I remembered to respond to Rhys' text message, and even then, I didn't know what to say. He wanted to talk. That was a good thing. There was so much we needed to discuss. Some of which I'd rather avoid, but that was the problem. I'd been avoiding the hard topics with him because I feared where they would lead.

Knowing what I needed to do didn't make doing it any easier. Every time I picked up the phone and opened his message to respond, all I could think was nothing I could say would be good enough. He would want an apology, and he deserved one, but any apology I could give him wouldn't be genuine. Yes, I was sorry for hurting him, but that was it. I wouldn't apologize for bringing Demetrius into the space because I didn't do it intentionally. And if I said I was sorry for what happened with Demetrius I would be lying.

I didn't want to admit it, but Maggie was right. Rhys wasn't enough for me. No matter how much I wanted him to be. I loved him, but even when he wasn't away from me, I felt like something was lacking in our relationship.

He'd changed so much in such a short time. It made me wonder if he was ever the man I thought he was, or if he was just a more appealing alternative to the brothers who wanted everything from me. Rhys asked for so little, but maybe he didn't ask for enough. Malachi challenged me to be better. Demetrius inspired me to embrace all sides of myself. While Rhys was encouraging, he was also limiting.

He wanted me to stay put, to keep out of the way, and not cause any trouble. And I did it because I loved him, and I wanted things to work out, but while he was out living an exciting life, I was at home, starving for more than just physical touch.

After staring at the phone for another additional ten minutes, I responded simply; *I agree.*

I waited for his response, but of course, nothing came, so instead of agonizing over what he might say or what he might feel about what I had said or done, I took a shower. I needed to wash away the negative energy I felt building inside of me.

It felt good standing beneath the warm stream. The water running over my flesh, as always, invigorated me. Not only was I upset from my thoughts about my flailing relationship with Rhys, but helping Straught the night before had taken a lot more energy than I expected. Luckily, the water fed my body, restoring everything I'd given to him.

If the Chicago suburb wasn't so far from the ocean, I would have believed the water was pulling its effect from the seas. It felt like it was reaching into the depths of the ocean across the barrier realm to Deuterio and bringing back the magic of my people. Once again, I stood beneath the flow until the water ran cool before I stepped from the tub.

Our girl's shopping trip provided me with a fresh outfit to wear. Jeans, some black booties, and a grey t-shirt that I took from the men's section. I didn't care how much Maggie complained. Men's shirts just felt better on the skin. Once dressed, I checked my phone again and wanted to punch the air when I saw that in all that time, Rhys still hadn't responded to me.

Instead of Maggie knocking on my door and dragging me down the stairs with her, she let the sweet aroma of breakfast do the work. My stomach growled when the smell of bacon reached beneath the door and filled my nostrils. Of course, I couldn't resist it. Water restored my body, but it didn't fill my belly.

I tucked the phone in the back pocket of my jeans and headed downstairs.

My jaw almost hit the floor when I walked through the kitchen door to find Maggie standing over the stove flipping pancakes and singing the latest pop song that played over the speaker on the counter. She was shaking her booty and popping a piece of bacon in her mouth. I couldn't help but laugh at the sight.

Hair wrapped up in a bonnet on her head, the woman was cooking enough food for an army. On a platter that set next to the stove was a mountain of fluffy pancakes. The damn thing had to have at least thirty pancakes stacked in three leaning towers on it, and she still had a bowl full of batter ready to make more.

"You think you made enough food?" I looked at the overloaded plate of bacon and the bowl of eggs that were propped next to the pancakes. "Are we expecting guests I don't know about?"

"Nope, just us!" She twirled and swayed her hips to the rhythm.

"So why the hell are you making so much food, Maggie?" I asked. "I know you don't expect to eat all this by yourself?"

"Hey, we have to carbo-load." Maggie lifted the spatula in the air as if it was a magic wand. "We didn't really get to plan what we're doing to do next, but I assumed we're going to be hitting the road soon, and who knows, we might run into some wolves. What if we get into a big fight and have to kick some furry asses?

We're going to need energy to do that, Sy."

"You mean to tell me you're worried about potentially going up against a pack of werewolves, and you're expecting pancakes and eggs to be the fuel you need to get the job done?"

"That and it's just another thing I missed having been in the land of the dead for the last few months."

"You missed cooking pancakes?" I raised a brow. "Didn't take you to be such a homemaker."

"Yes, I used to do it all the time. I can't explain, it but making pancakes, well cooking in general, relaxes me. I just always used to make pancakes because I could count on the ingredients being in the house."

"Of course, you're as stressed out as I am." My twisting guilt replaced the hunger pangs. "Sorry, I haven't been checking in on you. All this must be so chaotic. I just assumed you were okay."

"I'm good, Sy. It just, like I said before, I don't know how much time I have here, and I'm trying to enjoy everything I can, even stuffing myself full of pancakes. Besides, I'm not the one who's going to be driving, so if this puts me in a food coma, I'll be good. I can sleep all the way to Washington."

"I guess this is as good of a plan as any." I grabbed a plate and then looked at the stack of food. "You do plan on sharing this, right? I mean, you didn't make all of this for you." I laughed.

"And for that, you won't be getting any of my special homemade syrup." Maggie stuck her tongue out at me and pointed to the pantry behind her. "You can just stick with that cheap generic stuff he has in there."

"What?" I snorted.

"I checked," she lowered her voice, looking around to make sure the invisible people couldn't hear her, and said, "I mean, come on… you think the guy would have at least some Aunt Jemima in the house with all the money he got."

"I don't know." I laughed. "Demetrius doesn't really seem to me like the kind of guy who cares about the brand of the syrup he's eating, but you say you made homemade syrup?"

"Yes, with some berries and shit." She smirked.

"Well?" I pouted.

"Oh fine, you can have some. Who could say no to that face?"

"You're amazing. Let me fix a plate now. I swear my stomach feels like it's empty, even though I ate two of those sandwiches last night."

"You used a lot of energy." Maggie watched me carefully before returning to the sizzling griddle.

"Feeding a vampire was a risk."

"But it was worth it if he helps him." I shrugged. "I still can't believe the wolves are in on something so terrible. Poisoning the food supply hardly sounds like a smart thing to do. I hope Demetrius finds out what the hell is going on with that."

"Did he ever come home last night?" Maggie poured more batter out onto the griddle in front of her. "His room was empty when I checked in this morning."

"I don't know. You're the ghost. You mean to tell me you didn't stay up to find out?" I did a double take when the second part of her comment registered. "You checked in on him?"

"Yeah, I'm nosey. What can I say?" She flipped the pancakes. "I tried to stay up, but I just couldn't do it. You know I didn't think I would need sleep anymore. As a ghost, it's not even a thing. You're just awake forever. Some of them pretend to sleep, but it doesn't really work. It's just a thing of habit. This whole being stuck to a body thing really sucks when you've been free of it for so long."

"How does it feel being a ghost? I mean outside of the not having to worry about body maintenance part. What's it really like?"

"It's weird at first. You just feel fuzzy all over. You know, like when your leg falls asleep. And it takes some time to get used to it. Soon you forget what it felt like to be in a body. All of your insecurities and worries melt away, and you find yourself in your purest form. For some, it's an amazing experience. For me, it was absolutely terrifying."

"Why?" Her honesty worried me.

"I realized how little I knew about myself and how I would never get the opportunity to come to those conclusions. That's the great thing about life. It's the discovery. Over time, you get to peel back the layers of yourself. Each one revealing more about who you truly are. That's, of course, if you care to find out. I wanted to know myself outside of the trauma I experienced growing up. I wanted to have a life that wasn't controlled by my mother. I wanted to evolve into this amazing new woman, but I don't get that journey. So, I'm left with this feeling of being incomplete. And yeah, I could do all that in the afterlife, but what's the point now, you know? It's all over. The thrill of discovery."

"I never thought about that, about what it would feel like to not have the opportunity to get to know myself." My friend was pouring batter and flipping pancakes when I looked at her. "I'm sorry, Maggie. I don't know if I ever said that to you, but I am."

"Why are you apologizing to me?"

"Because your life ended so short, and it's because of me, or at least, in some part. Had my father not been plotting to take over the world, you could still be alive and on your journey of discovery."

"You know something else you find out when you die?" She turned off the stove and removed the griddle from the hot eye.

"What's that?" I asked.

"We all have an allotment of time. Regardless of what path we take, it doesn't change the time that's promised to us. My clock ran out, Sy, and it didn't matter if I was making a grand sacrifice to protect the friend I love or sitting at home on the couch ignoring yet another rant from my mother. My time was up. Hell, I'm much happier to have gone out while fighting for a loved one. It gave me an epic ending."

"I'm glad we got to know each other while you were alive." I picked up a piece of bacon.

"I'm glad I get to haunt you now that I'm dead." She laughed.

"You know what, now that I think about it, where is Demetrius?" I walked over to the window and looked out, hoping I could see the front of the house where his car would be, but I couldn't. Just as I was going to head to the front of the house for a better view, the door opened, and the sound of keys jingling rang out.

"D, is that you?" Maggie called out.

"D?" I went to her with wide eyes. Since when did she have a nickname for him?

"Look, I'm sorry, but Demetrius is such a long name. Think about how we call you Sy. Who has the time to be wasting it on all those syllables?" She laughed.

"This from the eternal ghost?" I poked her in the side.

"Yes, it's me. I'll be right there," he called back.

I busied myself filling my plate with food and headed to the table where I could sit and eat.

"You know, it would have been really nice if you'd also put on a pot of coffee when you started cooking. You know, just to be efficient about things." I pointed to the empty coffeepot, and in return, got a finger flip and a mimed punch.

"Well, excuse the hell out of me. I only just slaved over this hot stove, making a beautiful meal for you." She sucked her teeth. "Hell, you want coffee, you make it your damn self. See if I ever cook for you again."

"Ah, come on, Maggie, you know you love me." I poked at her as I headed to the coffeemaker. "You know you're so feisty after a good night of sleep."

"I'll show you feisty if you keep messing with me!" Again, she pretended to throw jabs at me.

Just as the brew filled the carafe, Demetrius walked into the kitchen. I turned around to see him and gasped. There were bruises on his face and arms, and blood still dripped from a fresh cut just beneath his eye.

CHAPTER 10

Forgetting the coffee, I crossed the kitchen to the doorway where Demetrius stood. Suddenly, the food or the sweet, caffeinated beverage didn't matter. I wanted to know that he was okay.

"What happened?" I stopped in front of him, lifting my hand to the scar beneath this eye. "Are you okay?"

Demetrice froze beneath my touch and looked me in the eye. It was as if he was waiting for me to realize what I was doing, and I'd admit; it took a minute. My eyes widened as I understood the intimate nature of the moment. For the first time since I arrived there, I dropped the barrier that existed against him. I didn't want to pull away from his touch.

There I was, all of my guards down and standing as close to him as I could get with my hand on his face, looking deeply into his eyes. I realized after that moment, I wouldn't be able to deny how much I really cared about him. What was even scarier was I didn't want to deny it anymore.

Maggie was right. Life had a limit. We were supposed to discover new things about ourselves. We were supposed to work to understand what made us human. Since I found out about my true identity, I felt like all I'd been doing was trying to prove who I wasn't. No one stopped to consider who I was beneath the labels. Not even me.

Demetrius lifted his hand to cover mine, touching me softly at first, and then leaning into my touch just a little more. The corners of his lips lifted when he realized I would not pull away from him.

"Yes, Syrinada, I am okay." Those dark eyes captured mine, and there was something more there.

I felt something stir inside of me. It wasn't the typical response of my siren. It wasn't a hunger for physical touch, but it felt important. I felt like I had to pay attention to it. I couldn't find the words to speak, though my mind was running at a hundred miles a minute.

"What happened to you?" Maggie asked, interrupting the unexpectedly intimate moment.

She turned off the stove after plating the last of the pancake on her tower. At the sound of her voice, I slowly lowered my hand from his face, never losing eye contact.

"Yeah, what happened?" I asked, taking a small step back from him. "You didn't come home last night, did you?"

"No, I didn't," Demetrius answered. "After making a few calls, it was easy to figure out who was the one behind Straught's accusations. I hate to say it, but he was right. Once again, there are people in my company who I cannot trust.

"I paid a brief visit to my friend Cameron. That's the wolf who visited me yesterday and who you sensed at Straught's home. After I called him out, the fucker attacked me. He turned on me like a damn animal."

"You fought a werewolf?" I gasped. "You can't be serious."

"Three of them, yeah." He nodded. "I'm a little rusty, but I can still handle myself just fine. After some physical convincing, Cameron admitted who he's working for. I gave them a friendly message to relay to their leader and told them to get out of my territory."

"Your territory?" I asked. Now that I knew he was okay, I found myself impressed. Demetrius had his own territory, and he defended it in combat against not one but three wolves. I don't care who you are, that shit was hot.

"Yes, Syrinada. Ultimately, it's my responsibility to keep the peace in this area. Something the witches, and now the wolves, have fucked with, but now that I know who is behind this, I can handle it. I'll admit, it's not the best news, but I'm taking care of it."

"I can't believe you had to fight them," Maggie said around a mouthful of pancake. "That's so badass!"

"It comes with the job. As much as I wish everyone would just act right, sometimes things get a little tough out there, but again, I'm okay," he reassured me, not my wide-eyed friend. "I don't want you worrying about me. Everything is going to be okay."

"You sure about that?" Maggie asked from behind me.

"Yes." He took his eyes off me to address her and then changed the subject to poke fun at Maggie. "Wow, you made all this food? I never would have considered you a homemaker."

"That's what I said!" I laughed.

"Is there enough for me here?" Demetrius pointed to the mountains of food.

"I'm going to need both of you to stop acting like I'm some kind of pig. There's plenty of food to go around, even if I don't want to share it with you now." Maggie laughed and handed Demetrius a plate.

Before either of us could start in on asking more questions about his bruises or what he found out about who the wolves were working for, Demetrius provided information he thought was more important to our current cause.

"I sent some scouts ahead to look into what Straught told us." He popped a piece of bacon in his mouth between loading his plate. "He was telling the truth. They set your sister up in a real nice spot. The mansion used to be a vampire den. It seems the vampires have all moved on, leaving the property up for grabs. It's gonna be a long drive to Washington."

"Did your contact provide any proof that she's there?" Maggie asked. "I mean, not to be skeptical, but you know, their track record is a little shady."

"Yes, I asked for proof. I hate to admit it, but even I don't have the greatest confidence in my men, which is a considerable problem." Demetrius sat down at the table and pulled out a laptop from the bag I hadn't noticed hanging around his shoulder.

He opened his laptop and tapped a few keys, then turned it toward me. Maggie stepped behind me just in time to see the picture of my sister on the screen. She stood outside a massive home, dark skin, and head full of curls that looked longer than the last time I saw her.

I'd only seen her once before, but she felt so familiar already. Our face was the same. Strong features in the nose and frame of the eyes that our father passed on to us.

"Is she alone?" Maggie asked. "Are there others with her?"

"Looks to be a couple, but we can't be sure if they are living there or just visiting. She is a succubus, so it wouldn't surprise me if she has regular visitors. The scout only stayed long enough to snap a few photos, then got out. The lair isn't crawling with vampires, but they are still in the area."

"Smart." I nodded. "No sense stirring up any more drama."

"There's something else," he said in an ominous tone.

"What?" I finally looked up from the photo.

"There is a nearby hotel. They've reported strange activity with their guests. Quite a few people are checking in and forgetting to check out."

"Do you think she is feeding?" Maggie asked.

"What?" I looked at her.

"Hell, you two are similar," she explained herself. "Imara is a succubus and feeds from sexual energy, just like you do. She might be luring the tourist to her new home. Perfect bait. No one would look for them. I'm surprised the hotel management even reported it."

"They wouldn't have, but the visitors left all their belongings in the hotel. Clothes, IDs, money, everything left behind." Demetrius touched my hand, bringing my attention to him. "Don't jump to the conclusion that this is her. We know there is a lot of unusual shit going on right now, and with the vampires being less trusting in their food supply, I would bet my money that they're behind the disappearances. Succubi rarely kill their prey nowadays. Better to let them live, regenerate, and keep an endless supply. Most of their victims live out their lives and die of natural causes."

"I really wanted to this to be simple." I chewed on my lip.

"Yeah, I know you did."

"So, we go there and find her and hope she has killed no one or done anything that might piss off the covens." I shook my head. "What if she's done something bad? They'll be after her. They'll brand her a monster just like they did me."

"Oh, the covens have bigger fish to fry," Maggie muttered. "They're not worried about a succubus feeding on tourists."

"Is that so?" Demetrius raised a brow. "What other catastrophes have their attention now?"

"Yes, and, I um… am not at liberty to speak on it." She smiled. "Ghost honors, there are some things that the living can't know. Messes up the balance and all."

"Uh, huh? Okay." I gave her the side eye.

"How soon can we leave?" Maggie changed the topic.

"Whenever you're ready," he answered. "After last night, I cleared my calendar. Bureaucratic meetings can wait. If we don't get this shit under control soon, it's going to fuck up the entire system. Besides, the wolves are frantically trying to cover their asses and figure out who else in the packs is untrustworthy. That will take some time to figure out."

"Damn, I really didn't think this would have a ripple effect like this." Maggie finally sat down with her own plate of food. "Maybe that means I can stick around longer than I thought. I would love it. I mean, not the whole threat to our way of life thing, but the extra time with real food thing." She stuffed half a pancake in her mouth.

"Of course, the food thing." I laughed.

"And also, you!" She grinned. "I get to hang out with my girl getting pampered at spas." She held up her hands, then frowned. "Fuck, I forgot about my nails."

"Just think of it this way. You get to get them done

all over again."

"Right, and the next time I go ghost mode, they'll be busted again. I know I'm done with the social construct of time, but I would rather not waste another moment on nails that last half a day." Maggie pointed to the counter. "By the way, the coffee you just had to have is going to burn if you leave it sitting there much longer."

"Oh, crap." I hopped up to grab the coffee.

"You know," Maggie spoke to Demetrius, "for a rich guy you really are a cheapskate."

"What?" He laughed around a mouthful of eggs.

"I mean, generic syrup, and that ancient coffee maker." She snapped her fingers in his face. "You know the times have progressed, you can get a coffee maker that won't continue to cook the brew after it's done."

"It's called a warmer," he corrected her. "It's supposed to make sure the coffee doesn't get cold."

"It's called archaic." She stuck her tongue out. "And it clearly doesn't work like it's intended."

"Maybe I like archaic. Archaic things were an indicator of simpler times."

"Right, simple times. Just admit that you're cheap."

I laughed, bringing the carafe, three cups, and the

creamer to the table. Maggie was a character. She was loud, bold, and unfiltered. You had to love her for it.

While we ate, Demetrius went over the plans for our trip. We'd be driving because he was more comfortable on the road than flying. We could have used magic to cover ground, but driving would give him time to work out a plan and get his men in place should we need backup in the area. When he explained his reasoning for the mode of transport, I could feel Maggie's stare piercing into the side of my face.

I ignored her, listening to his plans for where we would stay along the way.

"We'll make two stops to rest. It should take us about two days to get to Washington. We could do it faster, but there are other resources along the way I think would be beneficial if we could tap into," he explained.

"Sounds good to me." I nodded, agreeing with his extended plan, not because it made the most sense, but because it gave me more of the time back that I felt slipping away when he announced how easy it would be to find Imara.

I wanted more time. Time to process what was going on and time to figure out what I would say to Imara. How was one to bond with someone over the commonality of a psycho warlock daddy who only wanted to use them as a weapon in his plot to take over the world? It wasn't exactly a thing that filled you with warm fuzzy feelings.

"Fuck," Demetrius cursed as he pulled the vibrating phone from his pocket. "I have to take this."

"Everything okay?" I asked as he stood from his seat.

"Yeah, I'm sure it will be fine, just more of the bullshit I'll be dealing with for the coming months, I'm sure." He took another piece of bacon from his plate. "You two fuel up for the road."

"On it!" Maggie stuffed her mouth with more food.

"Demetrius," he answered the phone as he disappeared down the hall.

"I wonder what that's about?" I asked when I could no longer hear the mumbles of his conversation.

"You want me to use my ghostly ways to find out?"

"That's right, you can do that." I paused and then waved off the idea. "No, it wouldn't be right."

"Yeah, you're right" Maggie nodded before tip-toeing out of the room. When she crossed the threshold between the kitchen and hall, her body faded from view.

CHAPTER II

Maggie returned to the kitchen defeated *and with no new information to share.* Apparently, Demetrius was careful not to say much before he headed out the door yet again, jumped into his car, and drove off. Just as she was complaining about his stealth, my phone buzzed.

Don't worry, I'll be back soon.

I couldn't help the smile that stretched across my face.

"Is that Rhys? You two make up?" Maggie asked as she cleared the table.

"Um, no." I blushed, then frowned. "I still haven't heard from him."

"Oh, so who has you smiling like that?" She held her hand out for my phone.

"No one." I turned the screen off and stuffed it back into my pocket.

"Oh shit, you're over there cheesing over a text from D?" She skipped across the kitchen to my side and reached for my pocket. "What did he say?"

"Nothing." I ran from her and put my back to the counter so she couldn't get to the pocket.

"Then why are you hiding it from me?" She crossed her arms over her chest. "If it were nothing, you'd be able to share."

"He just said he will be back soon, that's all," I caved and told her what the message said.

"Right, I just bet that's all." She laughed and headed off to clear the table. "Look, I'm not judging. I'm all for you exploring your options."

"I'm not exploring any options." I handed her an empty cup to add to her collection of dishes. "It's just, I've decided not to walk around all guarded anymore. It's exhausting. Like you said, life is about discovery. How much can I really discover if I keep shutting myself from everyone around me?"

"You're right." She returned to the table after loading and starting the dishwasher. "What about Rhys? I know I joke about it, but you love him. What's going on with that?"

"I really wish I knew, Maggie. I'd be lying if I said this is all just because I'm here. It's been happening for a while, this thing that's growing between us. It's not his fault, and I'm understanding now that it's not mine. I just wish we could talk, but so far, it's been a handful of text messages, and that's it. I love him, but the waiting game is wearing on me."

"What do you want to happen between you two?" she asked.

"That's the problem." My shoulders slumped as I considered her question. "I don't know. I used to think I want this normal life with him, to have a relationship, grow together, and see where life takes us, but life is taking him away from me, and I'm left sitting at home alone, hoping he will have time to visit me in a virtual world."

"Sounds like there is a lot for you to consider." Maggie's tone was serious. "And that doesn't mean you just have to run to D, either. I mean, I like the guy, but don't limit yourself to just the men in the closest vicinity. The world is enormous. There are other guys, other mermen, that you've never even met. Maybe these dramatic ass men in your life need some new competition."

"You're insane." I laughed, but the concept was appealing. Maybe when everything was over, I could meet someone new. Someone who wasn't tied to all the chaos. Somehow that didn't seem like where things were going, but a girl could dream.

Demetrius was gone for three hours. In that time, Maggie snooped through half the house, reporting back on all the locked doors that led to nothing. I tried to distract her with tales of the wonders in their basement, but when she returned, she said it was empty. They'd moved all their family heirlooms to a new location.

"It's weird. Why do they have locked doors if the rooms are empty?" Maggie complained. "Just implying mystery where there is none."

"I told you they allow their men to stay here from time to time. Some of them come back regularly and lock their belongings up when they leave." I laughed at the disappointment on her face. "It's not as sinister as you want it to be."

"Well, D needs to get his ass back here so we can get on the road. I need something to do."

"Clearly. Why don't you go catch up on some current events? Watch a movie maybe?" I suggested and pointed to the massive television that hung on the wall behind her head.

"Sad to say, I'm all caught up. One thing I'm not missing out on in the afterlife is TV! I swear it's like being in an old folks' home sometimes."

"Sounds like Demetrius is back." I nodded at the sound of a car door closing.

Maggie ran to the window. "Yes, it's him. About damn time." She turned and ran for the stairs.

"Where are you going?"

"To pack my things. The sooner I get my shit together, the sooner we can get the hell out of this boring ass house."

Moments later, our tired host walked back into the house. He headed straight for the living room and fell onto the couch across from where I sat.

"You look exhausted," I commented when he yawned.

"Long night, no sleep, lots of supernatural bullshit going on." He rubbed his hand across his face. "I would love to sit on a beach right now with a nice whiskey."

"I can't help with the beach part, but I can make you a drink." I got up and headed for the bar in the corner. "Whiskey?"

"Actually, make it a rum and coke, please," he answered. "Thank you."

"No problem." I made his drink and brought it to him, sitting next to him on the couch, closer than I was before.

"We can get on the road as soon as you're ready to go." He sipped the drink and nodded in approval.

"No, we can't." I touched his leg and both our eyes dropped to the point of contact, but I continued speaking. "You look like you're going to pass out, Demetrius. You need to rest first."

"I'll be okay." He swallowed whatever response my touch stirred up. "I've been through worse."

"Are you in some kind of competition with your past self?" I looked from my hand on his leg to his face. "Are you trying to see how hard you can beat your body up before it breaks down on you?"

"No, but every second we sit here is one we lose. We need to work on getting things back in order." Demetrius' words came slowly, intentional.

"From the sound of it, things have been out of order for a lot longer than we thought. A few more hours won't hurt." I gripped his thigh to emphasize my point, then pulled my hand away.

"You may be right." He sipped the drink.

"Are you worried?" I asked. "About all of this, about the changes, the betrayals?"

"Yes." He nodded. "If it were just one thing, no, I wouldn't be worried at all, but it just keeps piling on, you know? I don't know what's happening, but I don't like it at all."

"It shouldn't be, but it's comforting knowing I'm not the only one who feels that way." I relaxed on the couch, and Demetrius handed me his glass. After taking a quick sip, I handed it back to him.

"We're going to get through this. You know that, right?" He turned his head to the side to look at me.

"Yes, we will." I nodded. "We have before, right? What's another fight to save the world when you've already done it once?"

"Right, it's simple." He chuckled. "Find the bad guy, reveal the plan, get creative, save the world."

"Do you trust me?" I asked him.

"Of course, I do. You wouldn't be in my home if I didn't trust you." He frowned. "Why would you ask that?"

I didn't answer his question with words. I pulled his hand into mine, and for the second time in less than twenty-four hours, I fed my energy to someone else. Demetrius' injuries were worse than he let on, and I wanted to help him feel better. This time was different. It was cyclic. Usually when I gave my energy, I felt it leaving me. It was draining, and I got tired. This wasn't like it was with Straught. What left me came back to me.

The energy strengthened as it pushed and pulled

between us. It wasn't just ours anymore. We pulled life from the plants in the room, the trees outside, even the water that flowed in the pipes in the house. I could see the streams of power coming to us from all directions. If Maggie was alive, it would have taken from her as well. With our connection, and the collective pull, came intense and satisfying regeneration.

Demetrius sat his drink on the coffee table before he pulled me into his lap. I sat with my back against his chest and dropped my head back. The connection no longer passed through our hands but our entire bodies. It felt like I would orgasm simply from the touch, but I kept myself in check.

"You're amazing." he whispered in my ear.

"Do you feel better?" I looked back at him.

"I do, yes." He brushed the hair from my face. "Thank you."

"Good." I yawned, slid from his lap to sit next to him, and laid my head on his shoulder.

"Sounds like you're the one who needs a nap now," he spoke between heavy breaths. I wasn't the only one trying to keep myself under control.

"It's strange how I can feel so energized and yet so damn sleepy," I answered as my eyes fluttered beneath the weight of my newfound tiredness.

"I know the feeling." Demetrius brushed my hair with his fingers. "Rest up, little siren."

An hour later, I woke up cuddled on the couch with Demetrius, who sat next to me reading an article on his phone.

"Shit." I straightened. "Sorry."

"You apologize too much, you know that?" He put the phone down on the couch next to him.

"I fell asleep on you." I casually wiped my face, hoping there wasn't any drool, and sighed when I found none. The last thing I needed was to add to my embarrassment.

"Did you hear me complaining?" He smirked. "You're fine."

"No, I guess not." I shrugged.

"Does that happen every time you do that?" he asked.

"What?"

"You helped Straught the same way yesterday, right?" Demetrius got up and grabbed a bottle of water from the bar, then handed it to me before sitting back down.

"Yes," I yawned the confirmation. "I did."

"And it exhausted you after that, and now again today."

"I don't know. It didn't happen before when I would practice or when I used it to help Rhys. I guess I'm just tired." I sipped the water. "Or maybe it's different with you because of what you are."

"Or maybe you're hungry?" Demetrius suggested.

"Hungry, no. I ate plenty of food." I put the bottle back down. "Honestly, I'm still stuffed. I don't know what she put in those pancakes."

"That's not the hunger I'm talking about." He tilted his head. "You know?"

"Oh, well," I hesitated. "Nothing I can do about that now."

"Here." He reached into his bag and handed me a small vial.

"What is that?" I looked at the strange bottle.

"Water from Deuterio. We carry it with us, especially when things are as crazy as they are now. Drink it, and it will help restore you a lot faster and without sex."

"Oh." I carefully grabbed the bottle, making sure not to touch his skin again. "Thank you."

"No problem. I know it's not exactly what your body is craving right now, but it will really help until you can get to Rhys."

"Rhys, yeah." I shrugged. "We'll see."

"Have you talked to him yet?"

"No, he said he wants to, but I haven't heard from him since yesterday. He's real busy with things at home." Making excuses for Rhys' absence was like second nature. I'd been telling them to myself for so long they just rolled off my tongue like water.

"Interesting." He stood from the couch.

"What is?"

"I've never been too busy to answer a call from a beautiful woman, let alone someone I was involved with." He released the ties from his head, letting his locs fall. "Must be some major shit going down in the witchy world for him to not answer you all this time."

"Yeah, I'm sure they just have a lot going on." I got up from the couch and straightened the pillows to avoid looking at him. I didn't want him to see my embarrassment or my insecurities bubbling to the surface. There was something more going on with Rhys. I knew it for a while, and with Maggie and Demetrius calling out their observations, it was getting harder to ignore.

CHAPTER 12

A few hours later, as the sun reached its peak, we were loading up the car with our bags. Maggie looked like she was going to jump out of her skin if we didn't get on the road soon, which for her was very possible.

"You okay over there?" I asked as I put a bag stuffed with clothes into the trunk.

"Yes, just ready to get the hell out of here." She tossed the second bag in the trunk.

"You really that antsy?" I leaned against the side of the car. "Are you okay?"

"I just can't sit here anymore." She shook her arms like she was preparing for a race. "I don't know what it is."

"It has to be strange being back in a physical body,"

I suggested. "Maybe you're just readjusting."

"Readjustment sucks. I need to keep it moving." She sighed. "It's not even like I have to move my body. I just don't want it to be in the same place."

"We'll be on the road soon." I stepped behind her and rubbed her shoulders. "Take a few deep breaths. You'll be okay."

"Yes, we will," Demetrius called out. "Pretty sure this is the last of the bags. Not sure how you two accumulated so much on one shopping trip."

"Hey, us girls need things, girl things," Maggie joked.

"How long of a drive are we looking at?" I asked as Demetrius dropped the bags by the car.

"Collectively thirty hours, but we aren't driving straight there." He adjusted the luggage, clearly unhappy with how we packed it all. "Our first stop will be in Minnesota. There is a hotel we can stay for the night. Then we'll make our second push tomorrow."

"Sounds good to me." Maggie popped her headphones in her ears and jumped into the backseat. "Let's get this show on the road!"

"She's pushy," he grunted with a half smile.

"She just needs to keep moving." I laughed. "The

ghost has ants in her pants."

"I guess we better get going." He closed the trunk. "I'm just going to lock up the house, then we can get out of here."

I climbed in the front passenger seat and looked back at Maggie, who had already zoned out and was bobbing her head to whatever song played through her Bluetooth earbuds. A few minutes later, Demetrius was in the driver's seat, and we were pulling away from his house.

Demetrius turned on some low music, and I tried my best to relax. Despite having become more comfortable with him, there was still tension between us. We'd yet to address what happened between us, and I still hadn't talked to Rhys.

Luckily, he didn't force a conversation. Instead, we rode in silence. The only sound was the random singing from Maggie in the back seat and the hum of the tires on the road. We drove for hours until the sun left the sky, only stopping once for gas. We made it to the hotel that Demetrius chose, and he parked the car in the lot.

"Thank god." Maggie jumped out of the car when we parked.

"What's that about?" I opened my door to get out.

"I thought I would choke on the tension between

you two." She took the earbuds out of her ear. "These things died hours ago, but I just kept them in to avoid having to be a part of that awkwardness."

"It wasn't that bad." I looked over my shoulder at Demetrius, who was heading into the hotel to secure our rooms.

"I'm just saying." She shrugged. "You two could have fucked each other on the dashboard, and it would have been less awkward."

"Since when do you talk like this?" I gasped.

"Since I died." She rolled her eyes. "I can be as filthy as I want to be. They won't take my ghost pass away. Lighten up, Sy." She headed into the hotel.

"Either way, it's a lot more complicated than that," I called after her, and she ignored me.

I had to consider if she was right. Maybe I needed to lighten up. I took a deep breath, rolled my shoulders, and lowered the mental guard I'd been keeping up around myself. Then a man who oozed sex walked by me. My eyes climbed the length of what had to be over six feet of muscle until he stopped, turned, and headed straight for me. I tightened right back up. He shook the fog from his head, nodded awkwardly at me, and went into the hotel. Nope, a relaxed Sy was one that sucked the life out of innocent men.

I stood by the car for a while longer, taking controlled breaths to calm the inner seductress. I watched the clouds in the sky. The puffs had become my peace. On nights when Rhys wasn't around, I stared up and imaged life was different. It was better than allowing my thoughts to run rampant. I drifted mentally on their fluffy backs and let my imagination take me wherever they reached.

As a kid, they were calming. Whenever I felt uneasy or upset about not knowing my mother or father, I could look at the clouds. Some coping mechanisms still worked even after you worked to resolve the initial trauma that made them necessary.

"You coming in or not?" Maggie called from the hotel door. "D got our rooms."

"Yeah, I'll be right there." I took another cleansing breath and headed for the door.

That cleansing breath turned out to be a waste of time because the inside the hotel smelled like stepping into a sex den. The sexual energy was so strong it coated every surface and made my skin tingle. I rolled my neck as a wave of passion washed over me.

"I know." Demetrius grabbed my arm. "We can go somewhere else. I didn't know it would be like this."

"What is this place?" I looked past him. "Where are we?"

"It's the only place within a thirty-mile radius that has availability, and I thought it was far enough off the grid to avoid anything like this happening." Demetrius' frustration with himself had him looking like he would throw me over his shoulder and carry me out to the car.

"It's also a sex den!" Maggie squealed from behind him.

"What?" I looked at my short friend, who was damn near bouncing.

"It's a total sex den!" Maggie grinned. "Finally, something interesting going on!"

"That's *not* a good thing," I corrected her. "This is very dangerous, Maggie."

"Hell, I'm excited." She danced.

"We can go. I didn't realize it was like this here. I chose it because it was off the grid, less traffic here," he repeated himself.

"Well, I understand why!" Maggie peered at the other guests. "The freaks need their privacy."

"Maggie!" I snapped at her.

"My bad." She held her hands up. "I'll chill."

"Syrinada, if you want to leave, we can leave," Demetrius offered again.

"No, that's fine. I can handle this. When I get to my room, I should be okay." I looked around at the couples who stood in corners and sat in chairs all around the lobby. "I'll just have to deadbolt the door."

"Let's go." Demetrius placed his hand on my back, and I jumped from the shiver that shot up my spine. "Sorry, it's just..." He pointed to the outside of the building.

A party bus pulled up, and like a river flowing, a line of sexually charged people poured out of the door. We made a beeline for the elevator. I thought I would be safe, but I wasn't. Before the doors slid shut, the outside doors opened, and the smell of desire flooded the elevator.

I held my breath until the doors closed, and even after, I had to keep my mind clear. The fucking elevator had to be the slowest in all the world. It felt like an hour passed between each floor. Demetrius pressed himself against the wall opposite me as he tried to give me as much space as possible, while Maggie bounced with curious energy.

I knew the second she was away from us, she would go into ghost mode. It was written all over her face. She wanted to see what kinky shit would go down in the hotel. Hey, get your ghostly kicks if you could. I, however, couldn't wait to get to my damn room.

"I got us all single rooms," Demetrius announced

as the doors opened. He handed Maggie the key to her room, and she took it and headed down the hall.

"Sy?" He held the key to my room out to me.

I just stared at him. Completely frozen. I knew what he wanted me to do: take the key, go to my room, and barricade myself inside, but I couldn't do it. My mind flooded with thoughts of sex, of our close encounters we never got to see through.

"I got you. Follow me." He nodded, understanding my reaction. Demetrius grabbed my arm and pulled me from the elevator. He carefully escorted me down the hall.

We moved in the opposite direction from Maggie, and with each step, I realized how much my self-control was slipping. The further from the elevator we got, the more the smell of sex flooded the air. It wasn't just the smell that caused my struggle. Along with the musky aroma came a symphony of passion. I could hear people inside their rooms having sex. Moans, groans, screams of ecstasy rang out around us.

"You okay?" He checked with me, pressing his hand against the small of my back as he ushered me forward.

I nodded tightly, afraid to speak. All I could think was that I would open my mouth and my siren song would come out instead of the affirmation of my limited control. What would that do to the people who were already aroused? Would we have to fight our way out?

At the end of the longest fucking hall I'd ever walked was my room. Great, I would have to go back through that in the morning.

"I'm right across the hall." He opened my door. "I thought it was best. Maggie can handle herself, but if you need me, I'm here."

"Thanks," I said quickly and slammed the door in his face.

As soon as the door closed, I went to the bathroom and turned the shower on. It was right next to the entrance of the room, and the steam would help clear the smell of sex. I took a towel and laid it along the base of the door. Anything to keep the temptation out.

I opened the window, thinking it would help, but was met with the sounds of a couple going at it. Beneath my window was a heart-shaped pool. Inside it, two men were having the time of their lives. I watched like a damn voyeur as the one who looked the size of a bear pounded his smaller companion, making the water slap as they went.

My hands gripped the edge of the window, and I leaned so far forward I could dive into the pool with them. When the third person joined, an Amazonian sized woman with breasts the size of my head, I slammed the window shut and headed for the bathroom. I needed to feel the flow of the water on my body and hoped it would help me calm the hell down.

After an hour in the shower, the water ran cold. I got out. Still agitated, I headed to the bed. Maybe I could sleep through it. Force my brain into an unconscious state, and I wouldn't have to deal with the way my body tingled with untapped energy. Of course, that was unsuccessful. Even with the towel cutting off the fresh flow of air, I could still smell sex. I could hear it. Hell, I could feel it.

I could actually feel people fucking in the surrounding rooms. Hips thrusting, teeth biting, nails clawing at sweaty flesh, I felt it as if I was being pulled into each room. I tossed and turned in the bed and then did the only thing I could do.

I reached out to Rhys. We weren't talking, but I needed him. I needed to meet him in our space. We needed to put aside our difference for one night so I wouldn't feed on everyone in that hotel. I closed my eyes and tried to shift from the physical space to the virtual, but my mind slammed into a wall. First, I was confused, then I was heartbroken.

I remembered then what happened the last time we were there and how angry he'd been. He didn't just leave our place; he destroyed it. It took both of our magic to sustain the space. Rhys' magic was no longer connected to it.

Frustrated, I called his phone, and after two rings, the call went to voicemail. He rejected my call. How could he claim to want to talk and then completely ignore me?

"Dammit, Rhys." I tossed the phone across the bed.

The only thing to do at that point was to force myself to sleep. I'd already tried and failed, but I had to block out the sex. I turned the television on, not caring about what was on the screen, and turned the volume up as loud as it would go. Then, burying my head beneath the pillow, I pretended to be asleep long enough until my mind actually drifted off.

The pounding on the door woke me from a dream of Demetrius. Once again, we'd been unable to complete what we started. Frustrated by the interrupted dream, I sat up to see the door shaking under the impact of a heavy fist.

"What the hell?" I muted the TV and wiped the sleep from my eyes, refocusing on the door to make sure I wasn't dreaming.

"Syrinada," Demetrius called my name. "Open the door."

I hopped from the bed, ran for the door, kicked the

towel to the side, and flung it open.

"What's wrong? What happened?" I asked before I saw the lust in his eyes. "Demetrius? Are you okay?"

He said nothing, lifted me into his arms as he entered the room, and kicked the door shut behind him. In two steps he crossed the room where he tossed me onto the bed and stood in front of me, huffing and puffing like a man on a mission.

"What are you doing?" I asked.

"You," he grunted. "You called to me."

I could see he was struggling, fighting that primal side of himself, but I didn't understand why. Yes, I had been struggling when I last saw him, but I succeeded. It wasn't like I jumped into the pool and fucked the minds out of the unsuspecting humans like I could have. I took my ass to bed. I did nothing wrong, yet he was standing in front of me like I had sucked the sex out of everyone in the building.

"What? I was sleeping. I didn't call you."

"I heard you in my dreams." He looked me in the eye. "Syrinada, I could feel you in my bed."

"I have been here the entire time." In my bed, dreaming about being in his bed, which he apparently felt. A large knot formed in my throat.

"Dammit." He paced the floor. "This isn't supposed to be happening. None of this. You made a choice. Why is this happening now?"

"Demetrius I—" I started, but with the towel away from the door, the smell of sex filled the room, and I lost my train of thought.

"Syrinada," Demetrius called me back to focus.

"Yes?" My breathing matched his. Heavy rises and falls of my chest as I thought about climbing him like a tree.

"Do you want me? Tell me you want me, and I will give you all of me. I cannot unless I hear you say the words." He paced the floor. "I know your siren is different. I know it makes you do things, things you might not want to."

"Demetrius," I said his name, but he continued.

"I will not take advantage of you. I—"

"I want you," I said.

"You—" he stopped pacing and looked me in the eye. "What?"

I took another deep breath of sex, lust, and passion, and it rolled across me in rough waves. "Yes, I want you. Now."

He bit his lip and fell to his knees before me as a hungry grin stretched across his face.

"Finally." Demetrius bowed his head as if giving thanks for what he was about to receive.

My wearing nothing but a t-shirt and panties made his task of undressing me easy. He took the panties off and went to his feast. Demetrius dipped his tongue inside me and spelled his name on my clit repeatedly. I wrapped my hands in his locs and let the first orgasm roll over me.

It wasn't enough. I wanted to taste him. I stood from the bed, pointed for him to take my place, and got on my knees in front of him. My eyes bucked, and my mouth watered when I reached into his boxers and pulled out all of him. Freshly showered and trimmed to perfection. I licked my lips, looked at him, then slowly dragged my tongue across the tip of his head.

He shivered, and his shaft pulsed as I drew circles with my tongue, teasing him. He watched in anticipation for me to do more, to take him in my mouth. I did. One slow pull going as deep as I could until I gagged. Then I worked up and down his dick. Twisting, sucking, stroking with my hands until he was ready to pop. Just as he was about to cum, I stopped.

I stood in front of him.

"Stroke yourself, but don't cum," I ordered. He

nodded, and his hand worked a slow path up and down his dick.

I stepped on the bed, one foot on either side of him.

"Eat."

He grinned, eyes wide, and went to it. Still stroking his dick and with one hand on my ass to add to my stability, Demetrius devoured me. I held on to his head as he brought me to another powerful climax.

"Cum with me," I called out, and he looked up at me. Eyes connected, we came together.

I fell to the bed beside him, and my leg trembled with the ending of my orgasm. Demetrius left me on the bed to go to the bathroom. When he returned, he had a towel. He cleaned the cum from his erect dick as he watched me. He reached down to the pajama pants I'd pulled from his legs and pulled a condom from the pocket. The man was prepared.

Joining me on the bed, protection in place, he pulled me to his lap. I slowly lowered myself onto his dick, feeling my walls stretch as he reached further inside of me. He took my shirt off and pulling my breast in his mouth. While he sucked on one nipple, he teased the other between his fingers.

"Fuck!" I cried. I swore my nipples connected directly to my g-spot.

I rocked my hips slowly, building up a rhythm that had him moaning around my nipple. As the tension built between my legs, I pushed him back on the bed and spun on his dick until my ass faced him. Still riding him, I placed my hands on his knees for support as I bounced my ass on him.

"Yes!" He slapped my ass, then held on to me when I quickened my pace. "Give it to me."

I shifted my hips, moving in a circular motion now, motivated by his moans, grunts, and words of encouragement. I loved a man who was vocal in the bed!

"Dammit, baby!" He slapped my ass hard enough to leave it stinging where his hand contacted my flesh.

"Harder!" I ordered, and he slapped my ass again, making it shake. "Yes!"

Demetrius gripped my waist, lifted his hips, and put me on my knees. He pushed me down so my ass arched up to him and pounded me. I gripped the sheets and bit my lip as I took him in. My pussy dripped with cum as his thumb slid into my asshole.

"Fuck! You feel so fucking good." He slapped my ass again and quickened his pace.

"Harder, yes, oh my god!" I called out. "Please, give it to me." I reached back, pulling him into me harder.

"Oh shit, I'm gonna cum."

"Cum for me, baby!" I thrust my ass back on his, playing with my clit as I did.

"I'm coming," he screamed and slammed into me a final time.

He fell on top of me, and we lay in the bed, heart racing and wrapped in each other until my pulse returned to a normal one. Demetrius was caring afterward. He rubbed my back, kissed my neck and cheek, and brushed my hair from my face.

"You okay?" he asked.

"Yes." I smiled.

"You need anything? Water?" he offered.

"I need a shower," I said.

"Yeah, we do."

"We do?" I looked back at him.

"Yes, I would like to join you, if you don't mind."

"I don't mind," I confirmed.

Demetrius carried me to the bathroom. We showered together. I expected another round of sex beneath the stream, but it wasn't that. It was another level of unexpected intimacy. He washed my hair, scrubbed my back, and kissed me gently, and because he knew I wanted it, fingered me until I came once more, but he didn't fuck me again.

After our shower, Demetrius carried me back to the bed where we fell asleep wrapped in each other's arms. I didn't care about the smell of sex, and I could no longer hear the calls of passion over the sound of his heart beating in his chest beneath my head.

I didn't see the missed call from Rhys until the morning.

CHAPTER 13

When I woke up hours later, I was alone. Demetrius was gone, and the message alert blinked on the phone next to the bed. I expected a text from him. He'd been so considerate before, so obviously I assumed it was a message letting me know where he was and when to expect him back.

There was a message from him, telling me he was getting things ready for checkout and the next part of our drive, but there was something else, something that made my stomach hurt. Two missed calls and a text from Rhys.

I saw I missed your call. Hope you're okay, and yes, we still need to talk. Let me know when you can.

Welcome back to the guilt tour. All the thoughts I'd been mulling over came back to my mind.

How could I do that to him? We should have left

the sex den. Why did I think I could handle being there after being on a sexual diet for so long? And what the hell was I going to do about Demetrius?

Things had just gotten a lot more complicated after the night we spent together. It wasn't just carnal desire. I couldn't lie to myself and pretend like it was. That wouldn't have allowed for the level of consideration he showed me. He confirmed I wanted him before we started. He used a condom. Hell, the man washed my hair in the shower!

The first whiff of sex hit me, and I got up. I had to get dressed and get the hell out of there. I could wait for Demetrius and Maggie outside if I needed to.

As I brushed my hair back into a low ponytail, I heard a small tapping knock on the door.

"Sy, girl, you up?" Maggie called from the other side of the door.

"Yeah, give me a moment." I finished my hair, then opened the door.

"Oh my god, you should have seen what I saw last night. Those people are freaky!" She laughed as she burst into the room. "I never could have imagined the shit I saw! I mean whips, chains. In one room, there was a wicker basket, a tennis racket, and a damn wax melting station!"

"Sounds interesting. I don't want to know what the basket was for."

"Well, they—" she stopped as she looked around the room and realized there was more action she missed out on.

"Oh, shit." Her eyes widened. "Did you?"

"Don't." I lifted my hand to avoid her question, but of course, that wouldn't stop her.

"Did you grab a little piece last night? Who was it?" She lifted the blanket from the bed as if she would find someone beneath it. "I'm surprised Demetrius didn't have a fit with you being right across the hall."

I didn't answer her. My cheeks warmed, and I tried to turn from her before she could see the spread of red flush across my face.

"Wait a damn minute!" She shuffled across the floor. "Are you saying it was Demetrius?"

I hadn't said a thing.

"Maggie."

"You and D? What happened to you not wanting him? What about Rhys? Did you talk to him? Is it over between you two?" She rambled.

"Do you need to make me feel worse than I do?" I

threw my hands up and flopped down onto the bed. "I don't know what happened. He showed up, knocking on the door. I opened the door, and the smell of sex and heat just took over."

"A siren without sex." She shook her head and sucked her teeth. "A full-powered one at that. This was a recipe for some sinful deliciousness."

"Maggie…" I sighed. "This is already hard, okay? You're not helping."

"Okay. Jokes aside, I'm being serious, Sy." She took a deep breath. "That's why you kept yourself isolated on that beach. Because of how strong you are and because you were afraid of what you would do. As if that's any life to live. Rhys gets to have normalcy while you stay locked up because he can't satisfy your appetite. If you ask me, I find nothing wrong with what happened here." She sat on the bed, then hopped up.

I raised a brow.

"Hey, just because I don't find it wrong doesn't mean I want to sit in it!" She laughed.

"I need to get out of here. They're still going at it." I shook my head. "The people here are animals. It's like I can feel it through the walls. I swear at one point it felt like they were climbing in the bed with me. "

"I know!" Maggie smiled. "They are another level of freaky. Apparently, it's like a convention or something."

"Wait, you said you saw something last night. What did you see?"

"I saw how freaky people can get when they know there are no limits. Man, this one couple had a mango, a jump rope, and a golf ball. When I tell you I did not know what they were going to do, but it didn't disappoint. See, the man took the mango and—"

I held my hand up to stop her. "I really don't want to know."

"Yeah, it's one of those things where it's better if you see it yourself." She grinned like a child with the greatest secret.

"Yeah, I bet." I sighed and looked at the phone again.

"They were swapping rooms too!" Maggie continued her report of the adventurous things she witnessed.

"What?"

"Yes! One man visited at least four different rooms last night. Like, how the hell do they keep going?"

"Some people have a bigger appetite than others." I shrugged. "Hell, I should know."

"Speaking of appetites, where's D?"

"He said he was handling some things and would get us all checked out. I guess we should get going. The faster I can get away from this place, the better."

I grabbed my phone and sent him a text saying we would wait outside. Luckily, he was already downstairs waiting.

Whenever you're ready. Head straight for the car. I just got back from getting gas. We're already checked out. Do you need me to come to walk down with you?

I smiled before responding.

No, Maggie is with me. I should be okay. Be there soon.

With Maggie holding my hand, we made a beeline for the exit. Instead of walking back down the hall where we could hear people in the hall, we took the stairs down. We made it outside with no issue, and Maggie jumped in the back seat, stretched out, and grinned. She was forcing me to sit up front with Demetrius.

It took twenty minutes for Demetrius to join us in the car. When he did, he shot me a quick glance that left everything to the imagination. I couldn't tell how he felt or what he was thinking. I expected him to bring it up, or to get clingy, but he didn't. He just started the car and got us back on the road.

Despite her pushing me to be next to him, Maggie

Maggie's laughter alerted me to their return. I glanced up to see the two headed back to the car. Quickly, I stuffed the necklace back in the bag and located the pills, which were in the next pocket I checked.

"Hey, they gave us extra fries and ice cream!" Maggie popped into the front seat.

"Oh, great," I said nervously.

"Here's your drink." Demetrius handed me a cup as he adjusted in his seat. "Did you find the pills okay?"

"Um, yeah, I did. Thanks." I grabbed the cup from him and occupied myself with opening the pill bottle. No, I didn't mention the necklace. What was I supposed to say?

"You know, I could drive. You need a break," I offered.

"You drive with the headache?" He laughed. "I don't think I want to risk my life like that."

"I could drive." Maggie popped her head up, two fries hanging from her mouth.

"You just enjoy the three burgers you got." He laughed. "You can hand me my fries now, though. I don't want you accidentally inhaling them with the rest of your food."

"How can you eat like that?" I asked as she

unwrapped a burger and shoved it into her mouth.

"Hey, don't hate on me for my good fortune." She grinned, a piece of burger stuck between her teeth. "I can't help it. I'm always hungry. This isn't for show. Besides, I never feel full, and I doubt I'll gain weight. It takes a lot to keep a body that really isn't alive going. More than just magic. I have to let this thing rest and rejuvenate. Besides, there are so many things I never got to experience: food, places, sex. The list goes on and on."

"You're not going out and having sex with some random person," I scolded her.

"Oh, so I guess the siren is the only one who gets to have any fun, huh?" She stuck her tongue out at me.

"I—" My face warmed, and Demetrius focused harder on the road, his grip tightening around the wheel.

"Oh shit." She slapped her hand over her mouth.

"Just finish your food." I waved her off.

The rest of the ride was long, awkward, but otherwise uneventful.

understood her assignment perfectly. She kept Demetrius busy, so I didn't have to talk to him. They discussed everything from food and art to politics and religion. The girl was much more well-read than I expected her to be, and she obviously impressed Demetrius.

Happy to be off the hook, I put my headphones in and stared out the window. The longer they talked about the world and all its many facets, the longer I could go without talking to him.

My phone buzzed. I looked down to see another text from Rhys.

Sy, are you okay?

"Fuck," I muttered. I'd forgotten to respond.

"Everything okay?" Demetrius asked, looking at me out of the corner of his eye.

"Yeah, I just forgot to do something. No biggie." It was, in fact, a huge deal.

I hesitated before texting Rhys back.

Yes, sorry it's been crazy. I'm okay.

Rhys: *Do you need anything?*

No, I'm okay. We're driving now. Will call you later. Stay safe.

I couldn't say anything else. I didn't have the words. How could I tell him what I'd done? It would break his heart. I accidentally invited Demetrius into our space, and he was so upset. This was no accident. Mind overtaken by sex or not, I consented to be with Demetrius. He didn't take advantage of a situation he so easily could have.

After receiving no other message from Rhys, I put my phone back in my pocket and returned to watching the passing fields until my mind drifted off, and I slept.

The hum of the engine pushed through my dream of Demetrius. This wasn't the man who spent the night with me. It was his other self. Demetrius stood in a field of red flowers in his demon form, body twice the size as his human with flesh darkened and tough like leather, and holding something in his clawed hand. As I tried to get closer, he only grew in size, getting so tall I could barely see his knee.

I called out to him, hoping he would answer me. I needed to see what was in his hand. Instead, he turned and walked away. Each massive step taking him a mile away from me. I ran through the field and tried to catch up to him, but I continued to shrink until even the blades of grass were gigantic in comparison.

"Syrinada." Maggie tapped my shoulder, waking me from the dream just as a massive ant nearly crushed me.

"Yes?" I sat up and rubbed the side of my face, which was cold from being pressed up against the window.

"We're stopping for food." She laughed. "Damn, you were getting some good sleep. You want anything to eat?"

"Uh, yeah." I looked out the window to check where we were. A simple diner sat next to the gas station. "Fries and a coke if they have it."

"Okay, I'll be right back." She nodded and hopped out of the car.

I rubbed my eyes again. The bright sun made them hurt. Sitting in the car alone, I looked out the window and saw a dark figure standing in the distance, watching me. I couldn't make out who it was, but something told me I knew them, or at least I should. No matter how hard I tried to focus, I couldn't get a clear view of them. I considered getting out of the car to approach the person, but the door opened.

I looked away from the mystery person to find Demetrius standing at the open door. He leaned in the car. "They don't have coke, Pepsi, okay?"

"Um, yeah, that's fine." I nodded.

He looked at me, brows furrowed. "Are you okay?"

"Yeah, just tired, I think." I rubbed my temple. "Do

you have anything for a headache?"

"Yeah, in the pocket on that bag." He pointed to the black bag on the back seat. "Help yourself."

"Thanks."

Demetrius closed the door, retreating into the diner to get the order of food. I returned my attention to the window, searching for the figure, but I couldn't find them. I shrugged, thinking my mind was just playing tricks on me, climbed into the back seat, and went to work searching for painkillers.

I grumbled as I realized just how many pockets the bag had. I could hear the pill bottle rattling, but I couldn't find it. While digging into the third pocket, I found not the bottle of relief, but something else. A small jewelry box. I should have minded my business, put the box back in the pocket, and continued my hunt for the pill bottle. I didn't do that.

I opened the box, and my heart stopped. Inside was a necklace, and hanging from the chain was a charm, just like the one Demetrius wore. Just like the one Malachi wore. A spelled peace meant to keep his darker half at bay. Demetrius still wore his. It hung around his neck, hidden beneath the shirt. Why did he have another one?

I inspected it. It wasn't Malachi's either. I was familiar with the blue charm with the black center that made it resemble an eye. Who was this one for?

Maggie's laughter alerted me to their return. I glanced up to see the two headed back to the car. Quickly, I stuffed the necklace back in the bag and located the pills, which were in the next pocket I checked.

"Hey, they gave us extra fries and ice cream!" Maggie popped into the front seat.

"Oh, great," I said nervously.

"Here's your drink." Demetrius handed me a cup as he adjusted in his seat. "Did you find the pills okay?"

"Um, yeah, I did. Thanks." I grabbed the cup from him and occupied myself with opening the pill bottle. No, I didn't mention the necklace. What was I supposed to say?

"You know, I could drive. You need a break," I offered.

"You drive with the headache?" He laughed. "I don't think I want to risk my life like that."

"I could drive." Maggie popped her head up, two fries hanging from her mouth.

"You just enjoy the three burgers you got." He laughed. "You can hand me my fries now, though. I don't want you accidentally inhaling them with the rest of your food."

"How can you eat like that?" I asked as she

unwrapped a burger and shoved it into her mouth.

"Hey, don't hate on me for my good fortune." She grinned, a piece of burger stuck between her teeth. "I can't help it. I'm always hungry. This isn't for show. Besides, I never feel full, and I doubt I'll gain weight. It takes a lot to keep a body that really isn't alive going. More than just magic. I have to let this thing rest and rejuvenate. Besides, there are so many things I never got to experience: food, places, sex. The list goes on and on."

"You're not going out and having sex with some random person," I scolded her.

"Oh, so I guess the siren is the only one who gets to have any fun, huh?" She stuck her tongue out at me.

"I—" My face warmed, and Demetrius focused harder on the road, his grip tightening around the wheel.

"Oh shit." She slapped her hand over her mouth.

"Just finish your food." I waved her off.

The rest of the ride was long, awkward, but otherwise uneventful.

CHAPTER 14

Eleven hours later, we were stopping in a small town with a large gold sign that said *Welcome to Belenutia, Montana*. I'd never heard of the place, and it didn't show on the map on my phone. When I asked Demetrius about it, he mumbled something about how the app needed to update, which was clearly a brush off.

Despite his efforts to ignore me, I couldn't help but continue to search for the town. There were no records of the place that had rows of brick houses and some of the best paved roads I'd ever seen. The oddest part about the town was the lack of people. We drove for ten minutes from the welcome sign and saw no one. The only evidence of life was the few lights that shone from within some homes.

The car came to a stop outside of the largest house we'd seen since entering the town, which made it feel more important than the others. While the other houses were single story brick and wood with simple finishes, this one had three floors and looked far more modern features, including large windows, grey stone finishing, and black fencing that matched the railing around the balcony that sat over the garage.

"Stay here, I need to make sure everything is in order before we go inside," he instructed us after parking the car.

"Yep." Maggie nodded.

As soon as his door closed, she turned around in her seat to look at me.

"Sy, I am so sorry. I really didn't mean to blurt that out. I just, my mouth gets away from me," she said, apologizing for words she absently spoken hours ago.

"It's fine. I mean, it sucked, and you really need to work on your timing, but it's fine." I looked to the porch where he disappeared. "It's going to blow up in my face, anyway."

"What do you mean?" She followed my line of sight.

"Maggie, I'm with Rhys. I chose him as my mate, and yet I still called Demetrius?" I dropped my head into my hands. "Not once but twice. I pulled that man to me. I can't blame him for what happened."

"What do you mean, you called him?" she asked. "You didn't tell me you asked him to come to our room."

"It wasn't like that. You were right, okay? My siren wants more than Rhys. It's been a struggle. Hell, it was a struggle before he left. I love him, but he isn't enough for me, you know." I gripped the seat and dropped my head back as the frustrated words poured from me. "Sexually, I'm starving, and I hide away in my little corner, hoping it will go away, but it doesn't. It just keeps getting worse every day."

"Have you told Rhys any of this?" Maggie asked, her voice gentle with pity.

"No, how can I? That would crush him." I hadn't told him anything because no matter how hard I tried, I couldn't get through to him. "It's not even me, you know. I mean, it is, but it's that part of me that should only want Rhys, and yet here I am, calling Demetrius."

"You can't deny this part of yourself, Syrinada. I mean, look at what just happened. As hard as you fought it, you still lost." She put her hand on my shoulder. "At some point, you're going to have to accept who you really are."

"I have,"

"No, you haven't, because if you had, you wouldn't have allowed this to go on," she spoke honestly. "You wouldn't be forcing yourself to live a life that has no chance of fulfilling you."

"But Rhys—" I started, but Maggie wasn't having it.

"Will have to understand that if he intends to spend his life with a siren, he is going to have to throw traditional ideas out the damn window. He may be enough for your heart, but there are other parts of you that need to be satisfied."

"You're right." I nodded. "I know you are. It just doesn't make this any easier."

"And I suggest you speak to him about it soon." She looked to the left of the car, and my eyes followed hers. "I don't think it's going to get any easier for you to contain your siren."

"Oh, my god." My mouth hung open. Thank God for tinted windows or the man approaching would have seen the way we were both gawking at him.

He had to be almost seven feet tall, and his body was muscle on top of muscle. Even with the windows closed, I could smell him. The sex of him, the musk. It was completely intoxicating, and if I hadn't been with Demetrius just the night before, I would have done a lot more to the man than gawk at him.

"Who the hell is that?" Maggie asked and took a long swig of her drink.

"I don't know, but I have a feeling we are going to find out."

The man climbed the stairs and went into the house.

"Wait, we're staying in this house, with a man who looks like that?" Maggie looked at me. "Are you going to be okay?"

"I don't think I have any other choice."

Maggie and I waited, not so patiently, in the car for Demetrius to return. We didn't see anyone else, though she kept her eyes open wide, hoping that another hunk would appear.

Demetrius returned with a woman by his side who was just as tall as the man we saw enter the home. She had short red hair and enormous eyes, and her skin reminded me of mahogany obsidian stone. Just like the man, she smelled of sex. I couldn't take my eyes off her.

"You ready?" Maggie pointed to Demetrius, who waved us forward.

"Again, I don't have a choice but to be," I huffed. "Time to see how much control I really have."

"Syrinada, Maggie, this is Nevay." Demetrius made the introductions as we jumped out of the car. "She has been so gracious as to welcome us into her home."

"It's nice to meet you." Maggie shook the giant

woman's hand.

"Yes, thank you so much for your hospitality." I reached out to shake her hand as well. When our skin touched, fire shot up my arm and back down in a bolt that passed from my hand to hers.

"You weren't lying about her, were you, Demetrius?" Nevay spoke with a sultry tone that teased my senses. I wasn't typically drawn to women, but there were exceptions. Nevay was one of them. "You're one powerful siren."

"Yes, I am, but what are you?" I looked at my hand when she released her hold on me. I didn't know a thing about Nevay, but I could tell she wasn't human.

"I am something that requires much more explanation." She nodded with a slight smile. "Perhaps we can do that inside. I know you all have had a long journey. You must be tired."

"Of course. Let me grab my bags." I looked back at the car.

"Oh, don't worry about that. The fray will get it." She waved her hand absentmindedly.

"The what?" I glanced at Maggie, who shrugged, not knowing what Nevay was talking about either.

"They're our servants." She paused, considering her words. "Working to pay off a debt, if you will."

"A debt?" Maggie asked.

"Yes." Nevay looked over her shoulder as she led us into her house. "A debt owed is one that must be paid."

"Right," Maggie responded, then looked at me from the corner of her eye.

Nevay ushered us inside a house that felt much more regal inside than it appeared outside. Just beyond the massive windows in the front of the house were two walls that blocked the view of the home from the outside. Beyond those walls to the right was a sitting room. To the left, a set of stairs, and ahead was a long hall that revealed the house was much larger than I originally thought.

Nevay gave us a quick tour, quickly pointing out where we could find the kitchen and bathrooms should we need them. She also pointed out the access to the back porch, where they would often have tea, and the patio that she said was great for getting a sun bath.

"Here are your rooms." She pointed out the doors to our selected rooms on the third floor of the home.

"How are the bags already here?" I looked at mine stacked neatly by the door.

"The fray are quick workers," Nevay said proudly. "Take your time to freshen up. We will have tea ready downstairs when you are ready."

"Thank you." I grabbed the bag on the top of the pile.

"You okay?" Demetrius asked as he opened his bedroom door. Maggie had already disappeared into hers.

"Yes, I'm fine. See you downstairs?"

"Yeah." He stepped inside the room and shut the door.

Uncomfortable standing in the hall alone, I picked up the rest of my bags and went inside the room. It wasn't anything special. A bed, desk, and dresser. A simple closet. I did the quick check and then sat on the bed. Maybe I could get a quick nap before I had to meet the others for what felt like a mandatory tea before dinner.

I almost fell on the floor because, as I was sitting, the ghostly form of Maggie walked through the wall.

"Hey, neighbor." She waved her fingers at me.

"Damn it, you scared me." I clutched my chest. "Don't do that!"

"This place gives you the heebie jeebies too, huh?" Maggie asked.

"Something like that." I steadied myself on the bed.

"Or a ghost just came through the damn wall."

"Look, I don't trust this place. Why would Demetrius want to bring us to such a creepy-ass home?" Maggie ignored my response and went right into her budding conspiracy theory. "It's all modern and chic in this weird little ass town, and it's on a farm! Nothing about that adds up!"

"I don't know, but he trusts them, and so far, I don't see any reason we shouldn't." Something about the home and its owner felt off, but Demetrius called them friends. Who was I to judge someone for their unconventional ways?

"No reason, huh? What about the invisible indentured servants?" Maggie pointed to the door where no one stood. "A debt is owed, and it must be paid, or whatever that creepy shit was."

"Maggie." I held up my hand to hush her. "We just got here, and we know nothing about these people or their servants. We can't jump to conclusions."

"You're right. Let me not make judgments before I even learn anything, but I'm telling you, Sy. Something isn't right here, and like you said earlier, it's going to blow up in our faces."

"We should get ready for tea." I tried to refocus her.

"Oh yes, teatime. I guess one good thing will come

of this." She winked.

"What's that?" I raised a brow, certain she was talking about the food.

"I get to get cute!" She smiled, then walked through the wall back to her room.

Though I really wanted to sleep, my mind wouldn't allow it. Not after Maggie's ghostly warning of our new host. She wasn't wrong. My intuition was doing double time as well. The house was creepy, and so were its inhabitants. I freshened up, taking a quick shower in the shared bathroom to wash the hours of driving off my body, and then put on a simple dress. Peach with white flowers. Fitting for tea.

I found my way downstairs to the back porch, where the others waited.

"Syrinada," Nevay welcomed me into the space with a warm smile. "I love that dress. It complements your skin beautifully. Oh, but the hair." She frowned.

"My hair?"

"Yes, why have it hidden?" She stepped over to me, and before I could tell her to keep her damn hands out of my hair, she unraveled my braid, and my hair fell around my face. "There. Ah, that's much better."

"Um…" I paused, considering cursing out the woman for putting her hands in my hair. We were guests in her home, but that didn't give her a right to touch me.

"Nevay, how many times do I have to remind you it is not polite to touch people without their permission?" the deep voice boomed.

"I was just," Nevay stopped. "I'm sorry, Syrinada. I didn't mean to invade your personal space."

"It's okay." I nodded.

"You're too polite," the voice spoke again as he came into view. This man whose skin radiated the warmth of the sun. Hell, he was so tall he probably absorbed the heat directly from it.

"I…" my eyes climbed the length of the russet skinned man.

"Hello, Syrinada. I'm Omar." He held his hand out to me. "It's a pleasure to meet you."

I placed my hand in his, experiencing the same burst of power as I did with Nevay. Only it softened beneath his kiss on the back of my hand.

"Wonderful." He smiled as he lifted his lips from my hand.

Demetrius entered the room behind Omar, and I could see him bristling at the sight of my hand clutched in Omar's.

"Demetrius, you held back." Omar looked over his shoulder at Demetrius.

"I beg your pardon?" Demetrius spoke through a tightened jaw.

'You didn't tell me how beautiful she is. This woman is magnetic. Did you plan to keep her all to yourself?"

"No." Demetrius shrugged. "I told you the details I thought were important for this trip, but yes, she is very beautiful."

"Thank you," I said. "But you two can stop referring to me as if I'm not in the room. If we are considering manners, that isn't very polite, now is it?"

"Ah, and she is a spitfire." Omar chuckled. "I like you."

"I'm glad you like me." I pulled my hand from him. "We'll see if I feel the same about you."

"We will." Omar flashed a smile, revealing perfect teeth beneath his full lips. He winked, and I noticed his long eyelashes over hazel eyes. The man was beautiful.

"So, what tea are we having today, sister?" he asked Nevay.

"Mango Passionfruit," she said proudly. "It's a new blend I'm in love with!"

"Another fruity concoction." Omar frowned. "Must we experiment every day?"

"Hey, Mr. All I Drink is Earl Grey, I'm sorry, but I like to mix things up." Nevay slapped her brother on the shoulder. "Loosen up, please."

While the two chattered about tea, I stepped away from them and moved closer to Demetrius.

"Who are these people?" I whispered. "It would be nice to know who we're bunking with."

"Yeah." Maggie popped her head from behind us, scaring me so badly I nearly peed myself.

"Please stop doing that," I fussed at her.

"My bad." She winked. "So, D, who are your friends?" she whispered.

"They are Giants," Demetrius answered, as if what he said didn't sound completely ridiculous.

"I mean, they're tall, but Giants?" I looked at the two, who were inexplicably still arguing about the merits of what qualified as tea.

"More accurately, they're the descendants of giants. The gene is there but has been diluted by years of breeding with humans. So, they're just abnormally tall, but they still possess the strength of their ancestors."

"Interesting." Maggie sucked her teeth. "I think Omar has a thing for Sy."

"What?" I nudged her in the side. "What are you talking about?"

"He does not." Demetrius frowned.

"You two can play dumb, but homeboy was sizing Sy up, and not because he liked the dress." She tapped Demetrius on the shoulder. "I wouldn't be surprised if he made a move on her."

"We won't be here long enough for that," Demetrius grunted. "I'll make sure of that."

CHAPTER 15

*O*ur tea time was cut short because Omar and Nevay couldn't come to terms with the choices of tea or the finger foods she suggested. None of us cared. I didn't even want tea, but they were so hung up on things being perfect that they refused to see that we were uninterested.

After we were done with tea, Maggie disappeared with a handful of finger sandwiches, and Demetrius left to make a few phone calls, which left me alone. I wandered the halls of the house, finding my way back to the study Nevay pointed out during our initial tour.

The room was all white with grey shelves that lined each wall. In the center of the room was a simple black desk and chair. They had an impressive collection of books that talked about the different supernatural beings and magic structures. It was information I wished I had my entire life.

"It's good to see you've settled in," Omar spoke from the door.

"Yes, well, again, I'm glad you've welcomed us here." I looked up from the book about giants. "I couldn't help myself. Your collection is amazing. There's so much here I don't know."

"Of course." He pointed at the book in my hands. "Also, reading up on your hosts. Good idea."

"Yes, well, Demetrius mentioned your lineage. I'm still so new to this world. All the reading I've done, and I still keep finding out new things." I closed the book. Rhys had provided me with books and information, but even they had their limits.

"There are many wonders in this world. Things we could never hope to understand." He crossed the room to pick up a book with a vibrant blue cover about drag-ons and handed it to me. "It's the thirst for knowledge that drives us to understand that which we do not, that keeps us going."

"Dragons?" I grabbed the book and ran my fingers across the image of the beast on the front of it. "Actual dragons."

"Yes, Demetrius mentioned you may be headed into dragon territories on your travel. I suggest you read up," he said.

"Thank you. I doubt I'll have enough time to read this. We're leaving in the morning, I believe." I placed the book down on the black desk with the glass top.

"Ah, that's right. What a shame it will be to see you go," Omar flirted.

"I should actually go to get some rest." I stood, intending to return the book about giants to its shelf.

Omar approached me from behind to assist as I struggled to reach the shelf I got it from. His hand reached over my head, grabbed the book, and easily slid it back into position on the shelf. I turned, expecting him to retreat. He didn't.

"You know, you really are beautiful," he breathed, and his chest rose in my face. "I don't say that just to flatter you."

"Thank you." I nodded. The man was so close that if I moved an inch, I'd be on him, and I couldn't let that happen, not with the way my body responded when he kissed my hand. "Excuse me."

"Yes, of course, sorry." He stepped aside. "Are you afraid?"

"Afraid?" I looked up at him, worried he could somehow read my mind and knew the thoughts I had about cheating on Rhys with yet another man who could likely satisfy my siren more than he could.

"Of the journey ahead of you. I can't claim to know all the details. That friend of yours keeps a lot of secrets, but I can tell from the way he is protective of you that this is more than a simple friend's trip," Omar spoke of Demetrius.

"I'm concerned, yes, but I wouldn't say afraid," I corrected him. "Things can quickly shift, I know how it goes."

"Beauty and bravery," he complimented me.

Omar stepped closer to me again, closing this space between our bodies, but something changed. His hazel eyes locked on to mine, and it was as if the pressure in the room changed. I could no longer feel my feet. It felt like I was floating. There was something deeper inside of me that responded to him deeper than even my siren.

As I stared into those eyes, my mind drifted away from the physical space. I had the same feeling of shifting to the metaphysical place that I created with Rhys, only this time, I didn't need his magic to blend with mine. I didn't even make the choice to go there.

"What is this?" I asked him. "How did you do that?"

"I didn't do this. You did." Omar reached for me, and as much as I felt I should coil from his touch, I did not. "This is what it is to give in to yourself, Syrinada."

"What do you mean? I did this?" I looked around the blank space. There was nothing but a soft blue light that flickered as my mind raced.

"There are things you do every day you don't realize. Ways you limit yourself. Tell me how amazing you would feel if you didn't have to do that, if you didn't have to keep yourself locked away." Omar's voice had a calming quality that eased the frantic pacing of my heart. "That part of you, that strong, beautiful, and magical part of you. What if you didn't have to hide her true potential simply to abide by the rules of the world you lived in?"

"I don't know what you're talking about."

Omar grabbed my hand, and I felt that spark of magic again. The trail of energy shot up my arm, but instead of returning to him, it kept going. It reached into my neck, down my spine, and shot off waves of cross-fire that reached all the way to my toes. This wasn't just sexual arousal, it was something deeper, and it made every part of me feel electric, and I wanted to explore it.

It was one of those moments where you know you should back away. You know that if you keep going, it's going to mean something terrible for you later, yet you still do it because it's intriguing. It's new and exciting. After everything I'd been through, after the drama with the brothers, and my failing relationship with Rhys, I wanted the excitement.

"You said you want to learn all the things this world offers you," Omar spoke as he examined my expression. "What if I said I could give it to you?"

"What do you mean?" I asked in a shaky tone as my body revved with unspoken energy.

"I can see what you're doing, even if you don't want to admit it. You limit yourself so you don't hurt the people around you." Omar pulled me closer to him, moving his hand from my arm to my waist. "And I know you realize that's exactly what you're doing. Don't you? You know there is more, that you have an untapped power inside of you that's just waiting to get out.

"Why not fully accept who you are and allow the people in your life to learn that part of you? You may not see it now, but you're hurting yourself and your friends because in the long run, it is that untapped version of yourself you're going to need. Whatever journey you're on right now, you will not be successful unless you learn to embrace who you really are."

"I can't do that. It would mean—" I scrambled to make sense of everything I'd been telling myself. The rules I couldn't break, the people it would hurt if I did.

"This is not a time for you to make promises to me or anyone else. You don't owe me an explanation for your decisions. I only tell you what I have observed." He looked into my eyes as he spoke, and if we weren't standing in a void, everything would have disappeared. "I, like everyone else around you, simply want the best for you because I see just how amazing you really are, but you are the one who has to decide what is best. No one else."

Staring into Omar's eyes, all I could think about were Maggie's words. Life was about discovery. It was about figuring out who you really were and what you really wanted out of your time in this world. At that moment, I wanted to remove myself from my reality as much as possible. I wanted to feel something that wasn't attached to the months of the trauma, of hurt, and struggle that got me there.

Omar laced his fingers with mine, reengaging the sparks, and he pulled me close to him. He understood where my mind was and what I wanted. This wasn't an act of sexual prowess. This wasn't my aligning with what he wanted me to do, it was simply discovery.

I stepped closer to him, eliminating the space between us. My chest pressed against his stomach, and he lowered his face to mine. Omar understood what I wanted, and he kissed me. At first it was good, it was new, and it felt even more amazing than the touch of his hand on my skin, but then it felt wrong. His lips transformed from the warm supple masses that tasted like honey, and instead, they were cold, dry, and tasted of death and decay, and I nearly gagged in his mouth.

I pulled away from him, stumbling from the imaginary world back into the white room lined with bookshelves.

"Are you okay?" Omar reached out to me.

"We shouldn't do this." I stepped back further, out of his reach. "This isn't right. There's just too much going on. I'm sorry."

"You're right." He nodded. "Perhaps there will be another time for us."

"Yeah maybe." I tried to keep the frown from my face. What did he mean by us? "I should really get some rest. We have a long drive ahead of us."

"Of course. Don't let me keep you awake." I turned to leave the room, but he called me. "Syrinada."

"Yes?" I turned back to him to see his arm outstretched to me with the blue book he took from the shelf in his hand.

"Take this book with you. I think you will need to know all you can about our dragon friends."

"Oh, I couldn't take your book." I shook my head. "I wouldn't feel right."

"Consider it a gift." He smiled. "Something to remember us by after you leave."

"Thank you." I took the book from him without further debate and left the study.

~*~

Instead of heading for my room, I made a detour past the door where Demetrius would sleep and headed for Maggie's room. I needed to talk to someone about what happened. There was no way I would tell him about his friend pressing up on me.

I stepped inside, closed the door behind me, and pressed my back against the door. I put my fingers to my lips, remembering the sweet taste of honey, and then frowned with the memory of the decay that followed it.

"Maggie?" I said her name as I fumbled around the darkness for the light.

Finding a small lamp on a table, I turned it on. When I turned around, I saw Maggie laying across the bed.

"How can you sleep so much?" I walked over to the bed and tapped her shoulder, but she didn't move. I stepped around the bed so I could look at her face, and instead of a peaceful sleeping girl, I found my friend, eyes rolled into the back of her head and blood dripping from her nose.

"Oh, my god." I lifted her from the bed. "Maggie, please wake up. Please."

"Sy?" she groaned.

"Yes, I'm here." I helped her sit up. "Are you okay? What the hell happened?"

"Shit, that one almost sent me back to the other side." She pressed her palm against her forehead.

"What? What did you do?" I found a towel, handing it to her so she could clean her nose.

"Nothing. I was just trying to do some digging. You know, find out some info on our hosts." Maggie shrugged.

"Are you serious?" I whispered. "Why would you do that?"

"Sy, something is up with these people. I know it." She put the towel on the bed. "I don't know what they're hiding, but I know it's something, and considering the level of security they have here, I'd say it's something big."

"Stop this. Okay?" I sat on the bed. "What if something would have happened to you? I need you here with me. This isn't worth it."

"They're hiding something here. I know it. I can feel it."

"Whatever it is, it's none of our business. Look, we're out of here tomorrow, okay? We won't even be around them. People are allowed their secrets, Maggie. Just stay out of trouble until then, please."

"Yeah, okay. Maybe you're right."

"I am." I smacked her leg. "Don't get so wrapped up in trying to have an adventure that you forget about why we're really here."

"Yes, Mom. Whatever you say." Maggie rolled her eyes and flopped back on the bed. "But who's to say their secrets aren't exactly why we're really here?"

CHAPTER 16

*"**A**re you sure you can't stay longer?"* I heard Nevay's voice as I descended the stairs.

"No, we really need to get back on the road," Demetrius responded. "We're on a tight timeline."

"Of course," Nevay said, her voice shifting from cheer to disappointment. "It's just I would love to have more time with Syrinada. Omar totally hogged her time last night."

"He did?" Demetrius asked. "I didn't know that."

"Good morning," I spoke, rounding the corner to see the tail end of Demetrius's frown.

"Syrinada. It's so good to see you." Nevay smiled, then the corners of her lips dropped as she examined my wardrobe. "Oh, jeans today, is it?"

"Yes, well, we're going to be in a car for hours." I shrugged under her judgmental glare.

"Right, of course." Nevay nodded. "I was just trying to convince Demetrius here to allow you to stay one more day."

"Oh." I raised a brow.

"I would love to get to know you," she added. "You know, have some girl time. I get so little of that around here."

"Maybe another time. We have a lot to do, and I have people who are waiting to see me." I pretended to want to return, because it was the polite thing to do.

"Oh? Who is that?" Nevay prodded.

"My, uh, my mate. Rhys." I don't know why I hesitated, but it didn't feel like I was telling the whole truth about Rhys.

"Rhys? Oh, I just assumed Demetrius was your mate." She pointed to Demetrius, who kept a straight face.

"No, I'm not," he said plainly.

"Sorry to stir up bad feelings." Nevay's eyes shifted between the two of us.

"No, it's fine," Demetrius responded, picking up a bag and tossing it over his shoulder. "Do you have your bags ready to go?"

"Yes, I'll grab them." I turned to head back up the steps, but Nevay stopped me.

"No worries! I'll get the fray to handle it." Nevay headed out of the room. "Just rest your mind, girl."

With Nevay headed off to issue her orders to the fray, beings I still hadn't seen, I followed Demetrius out to the car. He said nothing else to me as I watched him descend the porch steps and head to the vehicle, which appeared freshly washed. The fresh shine of wax, no doubt the work of the fray.

"Demetrius, are you okay?" I asked.

"Yes, why do you ask?" He loaded the bag into the trunk.

"Something is wrong. I know it is." I placed my hand on his arm as he shut the trunk, and he looked at me. "Tell me."

"There is just a lot on my mind." He sighed. "It's fine."

"Demetrius, it's not fine. Tell me what's going on," I urged him. "If we're going to work together, we have to be honest with each other, and I need to know what's going on inside your head."

"I uh…" He looked back at the house, chewed his lip, and huffed. "You want to take a walk?"

"Sure." I nodded. Whatever it was he needed to say, he clearly didn't feel comfortable saying it within earshot of our hosts, which didn't make me trust them anymore.

We were five minutes into a brisk walk that left us hidden in a grove of trees that stood east of Nevay and Omar's home. Demetrius checked over his shoulder so many times I started doing the same. Were we being watched or followed?

"What's on your mind?" I asked when he slowed his pace.

"It's difficult to say." He paused, dropped his shoulders, and then let his guard down. "Being back with you, out on this journey, it has brought up a lot of feelings and reminded me of all the times I've been trying to avoid thinking about."

"I know the feeling." I watched the limbs of the trees that moved above his head. "What thoughts have you been avoiding?"

"Verena," he spoke the name that broke my heart, but not nearly as much as I knew it did his.

"Oh?" I wasn't expecting him to say her name. There were so many other things I considered he would be worried about. The misbehaving werewolves, the hungry vampires, the hybrids, or even his missing brother, but not Verena.

"Yeah." He leaned against a tree and looked back toward the house. "I wish I could say I healed from the loss, but it's only been a few months, and how realistic is it I would come anywhere near healing? I could avoid thinking about her for a while, but now you're here, I'm reliving all of it. Every time I look at you, I replay those moments in my mind. Thinking of everything we've been through is hard enough, but then to hear you talk about Rhys, well, it makes it hurt so much more."

"You really loved her, didn't you?" I asked the question I knew I didn't want to know the genuine answer to because it would mean someone else held his heart. For the first time, I considered if I wanted that to happen.

"Yes, I did. I don't know if it was true love. You know, that kind of love that lasts forever. I wanted it to be." He paused, examining my response to his confession before continuing. "There was something else, something I never got confirmed."

"What?" My heart pounded in my chest, anticipating what he could say next.

"She was pregnant with my child." His deep voice broke with a level of sadness I'd never be able to comprehend. Demetrius wasn't just mourning a lover, he was mourning the loss of a potential child. A man who had only one other blood member of his family had possibly lost the chance to continue his bloodline.

"What?" I covered my mouth with my hand, not sure what words would ease his pain.

"Yes. The night before the battle with your father, she told me she suspected she might be. She should have stayed away, gone somewhere safe. I asked her to go, but she refused." He paused. "I mean, you knew we were together, right? I know we didn't make an official announcement, but we were."

"Yes, I knew." I nodded.

"In the short time while you were away with Rhys, before our bond ended." He punched the tree. "I keep thinking that's why this happened. Because I knew I bound myself to you. I chose you, but I was with her. But, yeah, I think she got pregnant. It wasn't the right thing to do, Syrinada. I know that. It's so hard because she loved me despite knowing I could never mate with her, that I could never bond with her how sirens do. Yet she was still there by my side, and I never got to show her just how much I loved and appreciated her for accepting even the limited version of me. The part of me I could give to her."

"Demetrius, I am so sorry."

"I keep telling you that you have nothing to

apologize to me for." Even in his pain, he tried to absolve me of my guilt.

"But I do. I bonded with you, knowing I didn't want that, and yeah, it was because I thought you were dead, and that it wouldn't really stick, but it was still a selfish choice. Instead of facing not feeling for Malachi what he wanted me to, I hid from it, and because of that, I made it impossible for you to know love outside of me. I took away your freedom to bond."

"You took nothing away from me," he said, and when I turned from him, he grabbed my wrist to pull me back. "Look at me. The thing you don't seem to understand is I bonded with the woman I wanted to be with. Everyone keeps making it sound like the bond between mates is solely on the woman, but that's not how it works. Just like my brother, I chose you, and yeah, I wish you choosing me back was a genuine choice, but at the end of the day, I still chose you. What I had with Verena wasn't secondary. It didn't lack because of the bond we have. I still loved her, and she loved me. This is not a unique situation. Not everyone gets to be with the mate they would have chosen."

"You could have had a child." I looked into his eyes, and I could see the sadness that was there.

"Yes, I could have, but maybe it wasn't time for me. Maybe it will never be time. I don't even know what a child born to a hybrid demon merman would be like, but I wanted to find out. I'm not going to lie about that. I wanted to know what fatherhood would be like.

"For so long, my brother and I, we've tried our best to keep the memory of our family alive. We've tried to sustain relics of what once was, but it would have been nice to add to that legacy. To build something fresh for us, to not feel like it all ends when we're no longer here.

"That's what all this is about, right? We're here to preserve something to continue the bloodline to build for the next generation, but what if there is no next generation? I struggle with that thought every damn day, Syrinada. What if the line ends here? What was it really for?"

"I really wish I knew what to say to you now." My thoughts raced around his words as I tried to make sense of the swell of emotions they caused within me. "I've been so busy trying to outrun the legacy of my father, I never thought of the next generation."

"There really isn't anything you can say. It's just good to get it off my chest. I would have loved to have talked to my brother about this, but he's nowhere to be found. I'm not even sure if he knew what I lost." Demetrius looked up at the sky and then back to me, and I wished I could transform into Malachi, if only to give him what he needed most. "He was so upset, and he had every right to be, but it would have been nice to have him there when I needed him."

"He'll come home. He just needs the same time we

all do. If it wasn't for all this shit going on, I wouldn't be here talking to you now. I'd still be hiding away from the world, trying to figure out how I feel about what I lost, trying to figure out what happens next for me in a world that doesn't want me here." I touched his beard covered chin and smiled softly. "If it weren't for a ghost stepping into my bedroom and ripping me out of my home, I'd still be just like Malachi, trying to understand what happened and where to go from here."

"Yeah, you're right. I guess that's how life works. It doesn't give you time to dig your way out of the shit before it throws the next steaming pile of bull your way." He smirked.

"No, it doesn't." I waited for a moment and looked at the man in front of me. His strong features softened with heartache. "Are you going to be okay, Demetrius? I mean, I know you want to help, but if it's going to do you more harm than good, maybe you need to step away. We can figure this out. You've already told us where we can find Imara."

"Do you really think I would just walk away from you now?" He turned serious again. "As if I would risk anything happening to you."

"No, I don't think you would do it on your own, but if I have to kick you in the ass to make you go take care of yourself, I will." I nudged his shoulder.

"You kick my ass?" He laughed, and a few locs fell

from the bun he usually kept them in.

"Yes." I held up my fists as if prepared to box him. "I'm scrappy when I need to be. I could take you on, no problem."

"Yeah, I'm sure. Can you see me just shaking in my boots over here?"

"Well, good. You should be afraid. Just know if I think you need to walk away, I'm going to make you."

"I appreciate your caring for me, but I'm okay. Really."

"Good." I put my hand on his shoulder. "Because I'm glad you're here, and I know it's been difficult, but I appreciate you for everything you've done."

"Thank you." Demetrius put his hand over mine and looked me in the eye. "For listening, it really means a lot to me."

The wind picked up, blowing strands of my hair into my face. Demetrius moved the hairs, tucked them behind my ear, and when his fingers lingered on my neck, my heart skipped a beat. I swallowed my nerves to respond. "Anytime."

By the time we made it back to the house, Maggie was getting in the car. Our bags were already loaded and ready to go. Demetrius headed into the house to say his last goodbyes, something I opted out of because I didn't want to see Omar again. After another ten minutes, we were on the road again.

"I'm glad to get the hell out of there." Maggie slouched in the back seat.

"Didn't like it?" Demetrius looked over his shoulder at her.

"No, as a matter of fact. I know they're your friends, but that Nevay gave me a bad feeling. I tried to look around, but there are voids all over the place." She rubbed her temples and groaned. "Something isn't right in there."

"Voids?" Demetrius asked, looking in the review mirror at her. "What do you mean?"

"Places I couldn't go to, even in my ghostly form, and when I tried, I walked away with a headache or worse."

"I saw her. It was bad," I confirmed. "Her nose was bleeding."

"Why would they need that?" Maggie asked. "Why booby trap the house if there is nothing to hide?"

"Maybe to keep out nosey ghosts?" He laughed.

"Yeah, right, or to hide their dirty secrets." She stuck her tongue out. "People who don't have big ass skeletons in their closets don't do that!"

"Well, we aren't there anymore. We don't have to worry about what secrets they have locked away in their closets." I looked back at her. "You can chill now. How far do we have to go?" I asked as he pulled onto the expressway.

"We should make it to Washington by nightfall." Demetrius double-checked the GPS. "Last leg, and I have booked another hotel in the area in case we need it. Confirmed not to be a secret sex den."

"Good, I can't do another long-ass car ride," Maggie commented.

"You ready to see your sister again?" Demetrius asked.

"I don't know how to answer that. We barely saw each other before, and then she was gone again. I don't even know her. To be honest, it feels weird even calling her my sister," I answered honestly. My relationship with Imara wasn't exactly one built on a foundation of lifelong love. I knew just about as much about my sister as anyone else. Maybe even less after all the detective work Demetrius had his men do.

"This could be an opportunity for you two to connect," he responded. "Build something you could have had all along."

"I thought of that, but how much time would we really have for bonding considering they want us to go hunting down other hybrids?" I tapped the non-existent watch on my wrist. "I mean, this will be dangerous. It won't be easy."

"Nothing worth it ever is." Demetrius tapped my leg.

"Who is it worth it for? Me? The covens? Who benefits from this?" I asked because I didn't know the answer. I was on some all-important mission, and no one had taken the time to explain why it was so important.

"The world?" He shrugged. "Isn't that what it's always about?"

"The world?" I shook my head. "You really think this will impact the entire world?"

"I mean, yeah, if the hybrids can do what your ancestors believe, it could mean bad times for the world. They could use their power to destroy everything. The balance between good and evil." He kept his eyes on the road. "If that falls out of whack, it's going to impact everything. Not just those of us with magic."

"That's real, huh?"

"Very real. To everything, there must be balance. We all walk a tightrope, and if it leans too far in any direction, we fall. We cannot allow the entire world to fall because what we have to do isn't easy." He sounded like a church elder or a monk. How could I debate him when he made so much sense?

"We can't allow?" I focused on his phrasing. "Are we in the position to allow anything?"

"If we do nothing, we allow it." He nodded. "It's like people who hate how things are going in their community but don't stand up to voice their opinions. Their silence is only equipping their opposition to continuing with their harmful actions. Our choice to do the hard work now is our voice being heard."

"You're wise, you know that?"

"I only pay attention when the old heads speak to me." He winked. "Besides, soon we'll have more help."

"That's if she is open to it," I corrected him.

"She will be." He reached over again and touched my leg, this time letting his hand linger on my thigh. "Keep a positive mindset. You saved her life back there. Your father would have used her power against her, just like he planned to do to you. If you hadn't done what you did, she wouldn't have her freedom now."

"When did you become so optimistic?"

"When I lost my life." He winked. "Clawing your way back from death, it does something to you. It makes you see the glass half full."

We had another uneventful drive, stopping only for

gas and food, and once for Maggie to relieve her bladder of the thirty-six ounces of raspberry slushy she guzzled down after inhaling another round of burgers and fries.

"Why don't you just go ghost mode and take care of that?" Demetrius teased her.

"The bladder is connected to the body. If I go ghost mode, your lovely leather interior will be ruined. Is that what you want?" Maggie threatened. "I'll do it if that's what you prefer."

"No, do not do that!" Demetrius frowned. "Pulling over now."

As soon as he pulled into the service station, Maggie flung the door open. I laughed so hard my side hurt and then even harder as Demetrius jumped to inspect the back seat.

"What are you doing?" I asked him between snorts of laughter.

"Hey, I gotta be sure. I don't want urine from the undead back here." He took out a flashlight to make sure he didn't miss a speck, and I smacked the dashboard as another fit of laughter started. "This isn't funny, Syrinada."

"That's your opinion." I pointed. "I think this is hilarious."

We got back on the road, and instead of heading to the hotel, Demetrius chose to first take us to the location where he was told my sister lived. I expected it to be something quaint and inconspicuous, but I couldn't have been more wrong. We pulled up to a massive, dark gray mansion, and my jaw dropped. The place looked like it could house one hundred people and had a large circular driveway that ended where a pair of tall iron gates stood, blocking access to the home.

"Wow, it looks like your sister is living the good life," Demetrius commented, impressed by the home.

"You think?" I nodded.

"Hell, she is a succubus. I wouldn't be surprised if she sucked the keys right out of that vampire's hands," Maggie said. "Put a little whammy on him."

"What?" I glanced back at her. "You think she seduced Straught?"

"You two are so much alike. You use sexual energy to get your men to do what you want. She does the same, except with a slight twist," Demetrius commented. "Where women want to kill you, they all want to bang her too. Equal opportunity sexual pull. Unfortunately, she has to feed herself from sex. For you, it's optional, but for her, it's a way of life. She can't survive long without it."

"What does that have to do with Straught lending

her his home?" I asked.

"Nothing, but doesn't it just make this even more interesting?" Maggie slapped my shoulder. "And it's amazing to think about the two of them together."

"Gross." I gagged.

"Hey, I'm not related to her." Maggie laughed.

"Whatever you say, but it brings up another point." I looked ahead at the house. "There is a lot I have a lot to learn about my sister."

"Yes, you do," Demetrius agreed.

"Do you think she's alone?" I leaned forward in my seat.

"I doubt it." Demetrius pointed to the driveway. "There are seven cars here, and none of them look like they belong here."

"I see." I peered at the vehicles and found a van and a few simple sedans, one even with rust on it, which meant visitors. Straught didn't loan them to her with the house. He would never own a car that had a bumper sticker that said honk if you like boats.

"Yes, so we need to be prepared for anything," he said.

"What do you suggest? Do we just walk up and

knock on the door?" Maggie leaned her head between our seat. "Or jus bust in guns blazing?"

"Guns?" I raised a brow. "And where are you getting these guns from?"

"Best approach is to knock unless you want to sneak in, and I'm not sure how smart that would be, considering what she is." Demetrius pushed Maggie back in her seat.

"Yeah, you're right. There may also be others like her in there," Maggie said. "Succubi ride together, watch each other's backs."

"So, knock on the door and ask for my sister, the succubus." I leaned back in my seat. "Simple enough."

"The best way I can think of."

"Great, let's go." I hopped out of the car.

We had to walk from the end of the driveway to the house, leaving the car parked on the curb. The gates wouldn't budge, but there was an entrance to the left, which made for easy access. I thought it was a dumb design but realized this place was for vampires who likely welcomed lost prey on their properties.

The music that blared from inside the house was so loud we had to bang on the door. It took a while, but finally, someone answered. The black door opened to reveal a tall, full-figured woman who immediately looked Demetrius up and down and licked her lips like she was staring at her next snack.

"Look what we have here. Someone's delivered new treats," she said in a low voice, looking only at the man of the group.

"Yeah, no." I stepped in front of Demetrius instinctually. "We're here for Imara." So much for pleasantries.

"Imara?" She looked at me for a moment, then took a deep breath and smiled. "You're the sister, right? Yeah, I see it. The resemblance. You have the same nose. Your sister isn't here, but she'll be back soon. You're welcome to come in and wait for her."

She pulled the door further opened and looked Demetrius in the eye before waving him forward and blowing him a kiss.

"We'll wait outside." I puffed up.

"Whatever you want." She closed the door, but not before winking at him.

"Can you believe her?" I huffed as I stomped away from the door.

"I can't believe you." Maggie smirked. "Ready to fight for what's yours?"

"I..." I hesitated.

"No point in denying it, woman. We all saw it." Maggie skipped ahead of me.

I looked back at Demetrius and felt my face warm with embarrassment. He didn't make me feel bad about it. He just shook his head at Maggie.

"That girl is a trip. It's not a problem. We can wait in the car." He nodded to the car.

Before we made it to the car, the iron gates groaned, opening to let an arriving vehicle enter. The black car pulled into the driveway, stopping just ahead of us.

"You think that's her?" I asked Demetrius who stiffened by my side, ready to protect me if things went left.

"Could be," he answered.

We waited for an unnerving amount of time before the passenger door opened, and she stepped out. I nervously stood there, waiting for her to acknowledge me, but then the second door opened, and my heart stopped. What was he doing there?

"Malachi?"

CHAPTER 17

I nearly choked when Malachi stepped out of the car. All this time Demetrius was looking for him, and there he was with my sister. They didn't see us at first, but when they did; the world froze. Malachi spotted his brother, then me, then he bristled. Anger flashed across his face before he looked away from us.

"Imara?" Maggie called out, oblivious to the awkward moment.

"Yes?" she answered and looked over at us. "Oh, my god."

"I think she remembers you." Maggie nudged me with her elbow.

"Yeah." I swallowed, eyes shifting between the two. What emotions was I supposed to deal with first?

Nothing could have prepared me to see Malachi.

I didn't even know how to feel about seeing Imara. Demetrius was just as tense next to me as his brother was. This was the first time he'd seen his brother in months, and after what he told me back at Nevay's place, I wasn't sure how he would respond.

"What is he doing here?" Demetrius asked, his voice much more strained than I was expecting.

"Hell if I know," I answered.

"How about we go on over and find out? This stare down is getting more awkward with each second." Maggie hopped off toward them.

"I guess we're going over." I followed her and heard Demetrius mumble something beneath his breath before he joined us.

"Syrinada, what are you doing here?" Imara asked as she walked around the car to meet us.

"It's a long story." I smiled.

"Whatever the story, it's good to see you." She paused, looking over my shoulder at the other Denali brother. "But something tells me you aren't here just for a friendly visit."

"I wish I could say I was." I shrugged. "We need to talk to you about something. There is some shit going down that we could really use your help with."

"Okay, let's go inside. It looks like rain soon. I know you love the water, but I could do without it." She laughed while kicking the car door closed. "I just got my hair to act right, and if it gets wet, these curls are going to shrink up like a damn sponge!"

"Nice ride," Maggie said, appreciating the sporty vehicle they arrived in.

"Thanks, a friend gave it to me." Imara looked back at her, then paused. "Wait, didn't you die?"

"Yes, in fact, I did." Maggie bounced forward. "But the powers that be gave me a second pass at this human life thing."

"Seriously? I didn't know that was possible." Imara gawked.

"No one did." Maggie beamed. "I'm kinda the first of my kind. At least I think I am. I didn't really think to ask before they kicked me out of the ghostly realm to come back here with Sy."

"How was it? You know, being dead?" Imara's eyes widened with curiosity.

"Girl, let me tell you!" Maggie linked her arm with Imara, and the two walked up the stairs, happily discussing life after death. You would think Maggie would get tired of explaining what it was like to be a ghost, but she did it with more enthusiasm each time.

Malachi entered the house after them, and I followed at the rear with Demetrius.

"You good?" I touched his forearm, causing him to look at me and not his brother, who walked ahead of us.

"Yeah," he gave the quick response.

"If you need to step away," I offered, and we stopped walking, falling further behind the others.

"Syrinada, I can handle myself. Yes, it's difficult seeing him, but this is important. Besides, I don't want to give him another chance to run off on me." He looked at the door to the house. "I can tell he's already thinking of it."

"You're right. I guess it's time for us to face our siblings." I followed his line of sight. "Any chance this won't be a total disaster?"

"At least yours doesn't look like she wants to rip your head off." He chuckled.

"Hey, what are brothers for?" I patted him on the back and laughed as we turned and made our way to enter the house.

Inside, the large woman welcomed us again, and just as she did the first time, she looked at Demetrius like he was a meal waiting to be plated. I couldn't help it. I bristled. Whatever it was inside of me that still felt connected to Demetrius wanted to poke her eyes right out of her head.

"Welcome back." She blew him a kiss, and I bristled at her blatant affection.

"Crissette, not now," Imara addressed the woman.

"Whatever you say." She winked at Demetrius, then looked at me with an expression that told me she knew exactly how much I hated her. "There will be plenty of time for us to get acquainted later."

"In your dreams," I muttered.

"Really?" Malachi shook his head, and I felt my face warm with embarrassment.

"Malachi," I started, but he walked away from me, following Imara and Maggie down the hall. "Shit."

"It's okay. He'll be okay. He's a big boy," Demetrius commented.

"I know, but I don't need to rub it in his face," I responded without considering what I was implying.

"What exactly do you think you're rubbing in his face?" Demetrius grabbed my arm and pulled me back to him.

"The…" I left the thought unspoken. This was not the time for me to admit there was still a bond between us. Yes, we both knew it, but it wasn't something that needed to be said just after Malachi walked back into our lives. "Nothing."

"You two coming?" Maggie called down the hall, interrupting the tense moment.

"Yes," I answered and hurried to join them, leaving Demetrius to follow.

"Don't take too long," Crissette called out, and I cursed her name beneath my breath.

At the back of the house was a grey room with a large round table positioned in the center. On the far wall was a large portrait of Straught and a drip chandelier hung over the table in the center of the room. The space looked to be set up for conferences, which was perfect for what we had to do. Imara had already sat down, and Maggie was joining her when I walked into the room. I took the empty chair across from Imara and waited for Demetrius to join us.

Malachi refused to sit at the table. Instead, he stood in the corner of the room behind Imara, which was about as far away from us as he could get. Imara threw a confused look over her shoulder at him, then followed his eyes to me. Her brow wrinkled, and my stomach knotted. This was going to be much more complicated than I had prepared for.

"What brings you here?" she asked, looking back at him once again before giving us her undivided attention.

"It's a long story." I straightened in my chair. "But to save time, I'll give you the short version. Thanks to some horrible works of magic, plans by our father, and other unknown entities, there are other hybrids. Beings like you and I that exist in the world, and right now, they pose a potential threat to the balance of things. We have been recruited," I pointed to Maggie and Demetrius, "to find the hybrids and stop them from doing anything that might threaten the balance of good and evil."

"What?" Her eyes widened.

"I know it sounds insane, but it's the truth. They want us to come together to stop whatever these people are planning. It doesn't look good." I paused, allowing her time to get what I was saying.

"Who recruited you?" she asked. "Why can't they stop this from happening?"

"The coven, well more accurately, the ancestors," Maggie explained. "And they can't do anything because they're spirits of the witches and warlocks who have already died. There's only so much they're allowed to do in the living world."

"You're telling me a bunch of dead witches came to you and asked you to stand and fight against a group of unknown hybrid beings to save the fate of the world?" Imara recounted.

"Yes, its sounds insane, but it's the truth." I nodded.

"And I take it you're here to ask me to join you?" Imara asked, throwing another quick glance at the stoic man behind her.

"Yes." Maggie grinned and clapped her hands. "Isn't it just a total mind fuck?"

"Like I said," I shot Maggie a questionable gaze, "the balance of the world is at stake," I said, then shook my head and laughed. "Wow, I sound like I'm in a comic book."

"Yeah, you do." Imara sat forward. "But keep going, I'm interested."

"There is a reason they want you with me. One that may or may not make all of this sound even more insane," I continued.

"And that is?"

"They believe we may have another sibling." I paused, looked between Maggie and Demetrius, then continued. "A dragon."

"A dragon?" She coughed. "You've got to be shitting me! Our twisted daddy hooked up with a dragon? I thought they went extinct centuries ago!"

"Yeah, apparently that is a common misconception, and well, they're still hanging around out there."

"Alright, so let me see if I have this all clear. You're

here, my long-lost sister, to ask that I join you in your plight to save the balance of the world by taking on evil hybrids. Oh, and one of them may be our sibling who is half-witch, half-dragon?"

"Yes," I answered.

"Sounds insane, right?" Maggie laughed.

"Okay." Imara shrugged. "Count me in."

"What?" Malachi spoke for the first time, clearly disappointed by her decision.

"I'll do it." She sat back in her chair. "Honestly, life around here has been pretty boring lately. I came here to get away from everything, to make sense of life. You know, find my purpose. What better purpose can a girl get than saving the world?"

"You aren't even going to talk to me about this first?" Malachi stepped to the table next to her.

"What exactly is there to talk about? My sister needs me. I'm here." She pointed to Demetrius. "Haven't you noticed your brother on the other side of this table as well? We have to help."

"I—" he started, but she cut him off.

"Look, I won't decide for you, but I'm going. You can do what you want to do." She stood from the table and turned to Malachi. "And let's get something straight.

I don't have to get your permission to do what I want. You can disagree with whatever choice I make, but it is my decision."

"Imara." Malachi frowned. "I really think we need to discuss this before—"

"I'm hungry. Does anyone else want something to eat?" she interrupted him again.

"I could eat," Maggie answered cheerfully, as if she hadn't just devoured two burgers an hour before we got there.

"Great, I'll get food. Syrinada, you mind filling me in on more of the details later? It's been a long day."

"Yeah, of course." I nodded.

Imara left the room with Maggie joining her. The two would spend the next hour giggling about food options, the limitations of ghosts, and the affairs Imara had inside the vampire's home.

"I expected more resistance than that, didn't you?" I looked at Demetrius.

"Yeah," He moved his chair back from the table. "Didn't think she would be so eager to join us, but I guess it's good we don't have to try that hard to convince her."

"Like she said, she's bored," Malachi huffed and pushed Imara's empty chair back to the table.

"What are you doing here?" Demetrius stood. "I looked everywhere for you. Where have you been?"

"I've been around, and I'm here because," he paused, "I'm with Imara now."

"With Imara?" I asked, shocked, disgusted, and on some level, jealous. No, I didn't have the right, but this was Malachi, a man I'd spent so many intimate moments with, and Imara was my sister.

"Yeah, is that a problem?" he asked, then looked at his brother beside me.

"I mean, no, I just, I'm shocked." Of course, he would respond that way. Here I was upset that he was with my sister while standing next to Demetrius. There was no difference.

"About as shocked as I am to come home and find you here with my brother." He put it out there, what everyone had clearly assumed.

"Malachi," Demetrius warned him not to continue.

"Look, it's all good." Malachi held up his hands and headed for the door. "You got the girl. I got my girl. We're good. And now we all get to go on a trip to save the world. Hooray."

"This isn't going to be easy." I tapped the table

nervously.

"You know," Demetrius grinned, "you keep saying that, and every time you do, shit gets a lot more difficult. Do me a favor. Let that be the last time."

CHAPTER 18

inner was a feast that none of us expected. The mansion had a massive kitchen equipped with a table large enough to fit twenty people. They covered the length of the table in food options supplied by a local caterer.

"You have all this food every night?" Demetrius pointed to the table.

"Not every night, but yeah." Imara shrugged. "People are very generous with us."

"Damn, steak, chicken, and fish." I looked over the meat options.

"We get a lot of guests. They all have different dietary needs." Crissette walked over to us, once again looking at Demetrius like he was one of the meat options on the table. "We aim to please in whatever way we can."

"Yeah, um…" Demetrius stepped back from her, walking around to the opposite side of the table. "I'll just help myself."

"You do that," she spoke to him but winked at me.

I was convinced the big bitch was doing anything she could at that point to get under my skin. Instead of cursing her out, I joined Demetrius and loaded my plate. Maggie, of course, was already sitting with two full plates in front of her.

Surrounding the table were a mixture of succubi and humans. There were three other succubi besides Imara and Crissette, who constantly shot hungry glances at Demetrius. The humans were all in varying states of arousal and infatuation with their supernatural hosts.

Despite the smell of arousal and the building sexual energy in the room, I remained calm throughout the dinner, and I couldn't help but feel it was because of the man chewing through a piece of steak next to me. Every time I felt myself getting revved up, Demetrius' leg would touch mine, or his shoulder would brush against me, and I would calm right back down.

"Should we say something about this?" I asked Demetrius under my breath.

"What's there to say?" he whispered.

"I mean, there are humans here. They're openly

feeding on them," I pointed out.

"Yes, they are allowed, within reason. As long as no one dies, and it doesn't bring attention from the human population."

"So, it's okay for them but not for sirens?"

"Hey, there are different rules for everyone," he explained between bites of steak. "Sirens had the same deal. They just went too far, so they put harsher rules in place."

While Demetrius continued his meal, I scanned the room and found Malachi at the opposite end of the table, effectively avoiding us, but it wasn't just us he avoided. Following his line of sight, I saw Imara sitting and chatting with Maggie. She'd completely dismissed his feelings in front of us, which I was sure was like pouring salt into an already bleeding wound.

Imara left the table to grab a bottle of wine off the counter, and Malachi followed her. Soon, the two were in a hushed argument that only looked to get more intense with each passing moment. I should have looked away, minded my own business, but I didn't, and when Imara looked over her shoulder, we were looking eye to eye. My sister threw her hands in the air, pushed Malachi aside, grabbed a bottle of wine, and stormed out of the kitchen.

Malachi stood by himself for a minute before he

also turned and left the room.

"You know what that's about, right?" Maggie pointed to the door where Malachi had left.

"What?" I asked.

"Imara knows Malachi is clearly still in love with you. It's not like he is doing anything to hide it. I mean, the man got visibly upset when he saw you with Demetrius, and every time you get heated over the giant succubus eyeing the big brother, he gets more upset. You think Imara is just sitting there happily unaware?"

"No." I stood from the table. "I need to go talk to him."

"You sure that's smart?" she asked. "I mean, you think he will take it well?"

"No," I looked across the room for the door again, "but there is no way we're gonna be able to work together if we don't discuss this now. It's going to suck, I know that, but what happened between us isn't just going to go away. Do you think we should just try to ignore it and let it blow up while we're potentially fighting dragons or who knows what else we're going to be up against out there?"

"No, you're right. Just be careful." Maggie bumped my shoulder with hers.

"Careful, Maggie, you're going to make me think

you care about me." I winked at her.

"Oh, stop it. You already know I care, but seriously, Sy, be careful. I know you're worried about hurting him, but consider yourself as well." She pulled me away from the table and the listening man at my side. "Like I said before, you're always so concerned with everyone else that you forget to consider yourself. I know how you feel about Malachi, and I know hurting him is going to hurt you, but you're right. You two need to face this now because it's not going away. Malachi needs to move on, even if it doesn't mean he gets to stay with your sister."

"I'm not trying to break them up," I insisted. "That's not what this is about."

"I know you're not, but the thing about facing the truth is it forces things to change. Maybe when Malachi faces his truth, he'll find that he can't be with Imara anymore."

"Yeah, I don't want to think about that. Just enjoy your food, and I will talk to you later."

"You don't have to tell me to enjoy my food. I'm definitely going to." Maggie grabbed the empty plate she'd left on the table and headed back to the end of the feast where most of the meat sat. Knowing her, she would clear that entire table by herself if they let her.

~*~

It wasn't hard to find Malachi. I followed his familiar scent of earthen musk to the small office on the opposite end of the house. It was one of the few in the house that didn't smell of sex. He stood looking out the large pane windows that opened to the wooded area behind the house.

"Malachi." I tapped on the door as I entered the room.

"Syrinada," he answered, back to me, staring out the window.

"Are you okay?" I asked. "You looked upset when you left. I just wanted to check on you."

"I'm fine," he responded, still with his back to me.

"Look, I just wanted to say—" I started, but he interrupted me.

"I know what you're here for, and don't bother." He held his hand up.

"What?"

"You want to make me feel better about you being with Demetrius." He laughed dryly. "I can't believe this shit."

"I'm not with Demetrius," I defended myself. "At

least not the way you think."

"You're bonded, I can tell." His shoulders flexed with unspoken rage. "Hell, the entire house can feel what's going on between you two."

"Yeah, well, I don't know what that's all about, but I'm still with Rhys," I reminded him of the decision I made before. "I chose Rhys."

"You did, and yet there is still something between the two of you." He took a deep breath, then it sounded as if he had to force the following words to flow out. "You've been together too."

"I—"

"Again, don't bother trying to deny it." He finally turned to me, face turned in a disgusted scowl. "I can smell him on you."

"What can I say?"

"There is nothing to be said, Sy." He softened. "It didn't work out. I got that. I accepted that, and I left you alone, and now you show up here asking for us all to go off to fight evil hybrids together."

"Technically, I came to ask Imara," I corrected him. "I didn't know you were here. None of us knew where you were."

"Even better," he sneered. "So you just want to rub

it in my face, then take off and leave me here."

"I didn't mean it that way. Of course, we want you to join us. We just didn't expect to find you here."

"As an afterthought. Of course, why would I think it would be any different from it has always been?"

"Malachi, that is not fair." I shook my head. "Your brother has been searching for you for months, and he came up empty. You know damn well you made yourself hard to find. If it wasn't for Straught telling us he let Imara stay in this house, we wouldn't have found her either."

"Look, it's okay. We'll do this, get it over with, and go our separate ways until the fate of the world is once again at risk. Does that sound good to you?"

"You aren't really being fair here. How can you be so upset? You left, remember?" I pointed the blame where it really belonged. Malachi was acting as if we shut him out when we hadn't. "When everything was said and done, you disappeared. What did you expect to happen?"

"I didn't expect you to jump in bed with my brother after you made such a big deal about being with Rhys!" he shouted, and I swore the entire house fell silent.

"That is not what happened!" I insisted.

"Then why do you smell like him?" He crossed the

room, stepping close to me, and looked me in the eye. "Why do you get so upset when Crissette flirts with him? Why are you so relaxed, so content next to him? Tell me, why is it that now you respond to him like you used to with me?"

"Things change," I said simply.

"Yeah, they do, and where is Rhys? Your chosen mate," Malachi accused me. "Why isn't he here to calm your primal urges."

"Don't go there," I warned him.

"Was he not good enough for you? Did you toss him aside like you did me?" Malachi's anger grew, and the air warmed.

"Stop." I said, afraid his demon half would emerge or my siren would snap from the feeling of being threatened. Neither would be good.

"No, tell me. Where is he?" Malachi spread his arms and waved to the room. "Where is the witch that was such a better match for you than I was?"

"He left me!" I screamed. "There, you happy? For months I've been alone while Rhys was out doing, I don't know what, and I'd still be alone, or worse, dead, if Ebon hadn't ripped me out of that solitude. While you were out here building a relationship with my sister, I was alone. Dealing with the guilt of having to kill my own father."

There it was, my pathetic truth, hanging between us like a neon sign that read, Sy's a sad siren. I was supposed to be one of the most powerful beings. At least, that was what everyone was so concerned about. Instead, I was living a life of a captive shark waiting for spectators to come by and tell me how scary I looked.

"Sy—"

"No, you act like we have done some huge injustice to you. You aren't the only one who went through shit! Your own brother needed you, and you left him to deal with all of it on his own while you went off to lick your wounds! You want to come at me for a bond I tried to get rid of while you are fucking my sister?" I pointed to the door as if our siblings were standing there and shook my head at him. "Here I am trying to comfort you, and you're being such a fucking hypocrite right now. Well, I'm done."

"I didn't mean—"

"What?" I snapped at him. "What didn't you mean?"

He said nothing.

"Look, I don't want to keep going over this. There is so much more we need to be concerned with. Life-threatening shit, so I'm done. Right now, I'm telling you

I'm done." I held my hands up in surrender. "Whatever happens between me and Rhys or me and Demetrius isn't any concern of yours. If you're coming with us, then do it for the right reasons. I only came to talk to you so we can bury this shit and move on."

"Right, considered it buried." He stepped around me and headed for the exit.

"Good, because I know Imara will be glad to know that as well." I shouldn't have said it, but I couldn't help it. Malachi was being a jerk, and I knew his actions would hurt my sister.

He left, closing the door behind him. A minute later, it opened again, and Maggie stepped in.

"Tell me, how awkward was that?" she whispered and shut the door behind her.

"Were you spying again?" I sighed. "You have to stop that."

"Me, spy, never." She pointed behind her. "Demetrius scolded me for being greedy, so I went to look around. You know, check out the mansion. It's some freaky shit going on in this place. That hotel sex den has nothing on the succubi orgies. You know, watching all the sex stuff was fun before. Here it's just sick."

"What do you mean?" I frowned.

"Some of these people are so bored with the act

of sex that they're doing some really kinky, borderline terrifying shit out there." She shuddered. "Like, how do they even come up with bringing a hot iron into the mix?"

"Hmm." I bit my lip, considering what they could use it for and if I would enjoy it.

"Earth to Sy!" Maggie snapped her fingers in front of my face. "You okay, girl? All the sexual energy here got you revved up?"

"Actually no. It's different." I abandoned the thoughts of the sexual deviants in the house. "There is definitely sexual energy here. Enough to get me aroused. I can taste it, but I'm not interested in it."

"Probably because you wouldn't be able to feed." Maggie nodded. "It would be like going to an all-meat buffet when you're a vegetarian."

"What?"

"A siren and a succubus, essentially the same thing. You get together, and you're both trying to feed. You just kinda cancel each other out. Unless one is exponentially stronger than the other." Maggie grinned with excitement. "Come to think of it, I bet you could take Crissette out."

"Yeah, well, that isn't a theory I'm trying to prove right now."

"Come on, just try it. Maybe then she'll back the hell off, Demetrius." Maggie winked.

"As tempting as that is, we have other things to worry about." It was tempting, but I didn't believe my sister would appreciate my attempting to end one of her friends.

"Gotcha." She leaned on the arm of the chair that sat next to the window. "What's the plan? We got the crew together."

"I was hoping you would know." This was the time that her all-knowing ghost powers were supposed to kick in. They'd done the research, figured out what we were up against. Wasn't that the point of Maggie being with me? "How are we supposed to track down a bunch of hybrid entities?"

"I may have the answer to that." Demetrius entered, holding up a piece of paper. "Sorry to eavesdrop, but I couldn't help over hearing what you were talking about."

"What's that?" I asked.

"Intel." He nodded. "We've been tracking people like Syrinada for a while."

"You have? Why?" I felt a little sting with the 'people like Syrinada' comment.

"The request came from the head of Deuterio."

Demetrius looked me in the eye to convey that this wasn't his idea. They were his boss, and he had to do as told. "They wanted to know if there were other threats."

"Threats." I sighed. "Right."

"Yes, well, we found nine." He handed me the paper.

"Nine?" I took the paper to read over the list.

"Honestly, I thought there would be more." Maggie looked over my shoulder at the list.

"There were. At least they were born. A lot of them died shortly after their birth, incompatibility of their parental genetics. Some were killed by their own people, and others just died in accidents, fights, or by natural causes. Nine remain."

"And those are ones we have to deal with." I read the list that had descriptions of multiple species crossbreeding. Not all were half-witch which meant it was a much bigger issue than we thought.

"Honestly, of the nine there are three I would be concerned with. They migrated, got together shortly after your existence came to light," Demetrius explained. "We believe the attacks the coven made inspired them to team up."

"I take it you have information on them?" I asked.

"I do." He pulled out another piece of paper from his jacket pocket and unfolded it.

"And that is?" Maggie asked.

"It's an overview of what we found. We have photos, locations, and more. I have more on my computer, but I figured we would go over all the details with Imara and Malachi." He paused. "Syrinada, there is something else you should know."

"And that is?"

"There is a dragon who we think is half-warlock." He all but confirmed what Ebon feared.

"Oh." I looked at Maggie, then back to Demetrius.

"If what Maggie said is true, you may have a brother." He nodded.

"And the family gets bigger," Maggie noted.

"And a lot more complicated." I ran my hand through my hair. "Where is Imara? We need to discuss this."

"Good luck with that. She locked herself up in her sex chambers." Maggie smirked.

"I'll go get her," I offered.

"You sure that's a good idea?" Demetrius asked.

"Yeah, I'm fine. We need to get this over with."

"Be careful in there," Maggie called after me, but I could hear the tinge of excitement in her voice.

CHAPTER 19

I could feel it pulsing down the hall, sexual energy like nothing I'd ever experienced before, even in the hotel full of orgies. This was something different, aided by magic and power. This was unnerving.

Imara had retreated into her room after leaving the kitchen. It wasn't difficult to understand why. Malachi. He looked at me with heartbreak in his eyes. Here he was, supposedly in a relationship with her, living a life together, and yet when he saw me with Demetrius, he looked like he would explode.

Imara and I didn't know each other, but we were sisters. That had to do something to her. I honestly didn't know how to approach the topic. What was I supposed to say to her? Hey, sorry for coming here, bringing news of this crazy-ass journey we need to go on. And oh, sorry about your guy brooding over me being with his brother.

It was an impossible situation. The more I thought about it, the more I wanted to run the other way. When I volunteered to retrieve her, I hadn't considered that Malachi might actually come up. She might want to discuss what once existed between him and me.

Could I tell her that Malachi helped me discover the siren inside of me? That we fucked, that he chose me as his mate, and I turned him down? Had he told her any of it? What if he kept it a secret, and I blurted out an apology for something she knew nothing about? That would only make things worse.

I couldn't run away, though. I had to face the music, and I had to make a genuine effort to get to know my sister. That was what really mattered. Not Malachi, not his feelings, at least not at that moment. The entire point of going there was to get to know Imara and build a relationship with her. We needed to work together if any of this was going to work.

My mother thought it would be perfect for us to get to bond and to build a sisterhood. If I was honest, my only concern was about survival. We needed to live through the bullshit. The sisterhood stuff could come later.

I stood outside the door, taking several deep breaths to balance my mind before entering. Sex, power, sex, power. It was like a rhythmic chant inside my head. Sex and power waited on the other side of that door, and I needed to be prepared to face them both. I couldn't let the siren take over. Lucky for me, she wasn't as hyper as she typically was. Maggie was right. There was a change.

I wouldn't lose myself. That wasn't an issue. I was aroused, but it was like before I found out about my siren. It didn't consume me. If I wanted to, I could push it out of my head.

Standing outside the door, I could tell there were more than succubus or incubus beings in the mansion. They had food, humans, vampires, and others, whose scents I wasn't familiar with. I could smell it on the waves of sexual aroma that flowed through the halls. It was those other odors, the ones of prey, I had to worry about. Still, I was okay. Being with Demetrius was different. It left me satisfied even days later.

"Get it over with," I mutter to myself.

I pushed the door opened, and my mouth fell open at the sight. Sex, power, and blood. Imara kneeled on a bed, with two vampires on either side of her. They bit into her neck while blood dripped down to her breast. They fed on her as she fed on them. What looked like smoke, the color of burning wood, lifted from the vampire's mouth and flowed into Imara.

As she inhaled their essence, the wounds left behind by their teeth healed. Imara bounced between two men, one biting her neck from behind, the other biting into her breast. She looked beautiful, in control, and powerful. She cried out in ecstasy before she turned to me and winked.

It was then that I realized there was a third lying beneath her. She rocked her hips and drew in his essence. This one was different. Instead of the dark red of the vampires, he was an earthy green. I narrowed my gaze at the third man and focused on his scent. Werewolf.

"Imara," I called her name and waited.

She looked at me but said nothing. Instead, she went back to her werewolf, biting into his shoulder as he held on to her.

"We need to talk," I said.

"Do we?" She looked up. "I can think of other things we need to do now."

"This is important."

"Yeah, and so is this." She stopped, and so did the men in her bed. "Join me, sister. I know you want to. I can feel your energy shifting."

"I—"

"You like the wolf, do you?" She looked down at the man beneath her. "Or perhaps vampires are your thing."

The door closed behind me, and I turned to see

two men, neither with a stitch of clothing on, standing there. Already aroused, they looked at me with hunger in their eyes. My mouth watered as I felt the energy of their arousal pressing against me.

"You're absolutely stunning," the first said. He was tall with brown skin and bright eyes that glowed like the sun.

"Just as beautiful as your sister," the other said. He was shorter, and his ivory skin stood in stark comparison to his friend's.

"Are you going to join us?" the brown-skinned vampire asked, his fangs flashing in his smile.

"I…" would I join them? Did I dare to allow vampires to do to me what I just saw them doing to my sister? "I'm here to talk with my sister. Not to join in on what you're doing here."

"Oh, Sy, give in," Imara called out behind me. "You know you want to."

When she spoke, I felt the words wrap around me. She might not have been a siren, but Imara had her own lure, and it enticed something more inside of me. I tried to fight against it, but it was powerful. When I turned to look at her, I saw the strands of energy she sent my way. She pushed the energy toward me. I opened my mouth, and the energy filled my mouth. It flooded my body, and I couldn't do anything to stop it. When she stopped, my body hummed with intensity.

"Please, say yes." The second vampire walked closer to me. "I would love to taste you."

"Yes, I imagine you are delicious."

"Well…" I looked around, my mind completely flooded by my sister's sexual energy. "I don't see what it would hurt."

The first vampire took that invitation and ran with it. He grabbed me by the neck and pulled me close to him, putting his lips against the bare flesh of my throat. He didn't bite me. Instead, he kissed me, gently at first, then with more aggression as his tongue joined in.

While he kissed my neck, his friend took to another task and removed my clothing. With vampire speed, he peeled away the layers that hid my body from them.

"Mmm," he moaned as he slipped my pants from my hips.

My senses became overwhelmed as their hands covered my body, cupping my ass and my breasts. It felt like they touched every bit of me at the same time. My pussy got wetter with each passing second, and the scent of my own arousal flooded the room, and when it did, the wolf howled.

I didn't remember moving, but in a flash I was on the empty bed in the room opposite from where Imara still enjoyed her sexual feast. They laid me on the bed and continued their intense foreplay.

"Can we taste you?" the brown-skinned vampire asked as he once again flashed his fangs.

"I…" I thought about it for a moment. A vampire had never bitten me. What did it feel like? Suddenly, as the juices flowed between my legs and the blood rushed in my veins, I wanted to know. "Yes."

They both moaned happily before biting into me. The first bite startled me. The second intrigued me, and by the time third pierced my flesh, it was erotic, adding to the thrill of the moment. I wanted more. More than kisses and nibbles.

Then I noticed her, my siren, rising to the surface, being called to action by what was happening in the exterior world. I let her free. I locked her away for so long, forced her to hide because I couldn't trust myself not to hurt anyone, but there, with the vampires, it was safe. I couldn't kill them.

Just as the vampire bit me again, I opened my mouth to announce another side of myself. The siren sang, and the vampires became more aggressive. The brown-skinned vampire lifted me from the bed and pulled me to his lap, quickly thrusting inside of me. I moaned as the strange sensation filled me. It was like icy-hot, cold at first, but then quickly warming.

I rocked my hips, riding him and enjoying every moment. His friend, the ivory vampire, joined in from behind, grabbing my breasts and teasing my nipples before he bit down on my neck again. Just as my sister did, I opened my mouth and pulled in their life force to replenish what they took from me.

Ivory wanted more of me. He pulled me from his friend's lap and bent me over, sliding deep inside. While he did, I took his brown-skinned friend into my mouth, sucking more of that life force through the tip of his dick.

It wasn't over.

The ivory man flipped me onto my back, then filled me again, putting his weight on top of me. The smile stretched across my face with excitement when brown-skinned entered ivory from behind. I'd never been involved in something so erotic, and yet I wanted more.

I locked eyes with ivory. "Fuck him harder. Let me feel you."

Ivory grinned hungrily and added more power to his thrust. Brown-skinned screamed in pleasure and bit down on Ivory's neck while I pulled more energy from Ivory.

A new pair of hands reached into the bed. A woman. She kissed brown-skin's neck and moved to me, but I wasn't interested in being with a woman. When I didn't give into her, she left our bed and crossed the room to where my sister still rode the wolf. She mounted the wolf's face and kissed Imara as I watched another man enter the room. A human.

He joined our trio, and as much as I enjoyed the vampires, the human tasted better. His kisses were fresher, his hands more eager. His touch was warm, while theirs left an icy feeling on the skin.

He was my focus, but they still worked. There was something in the back of my mind, some part of me that warned of what I was doing.

I came again and felt like I could keep going forever. Then I glimpsed myself in the mirror. My eyes glowed, and the men around me looked weak. When I looked at them, they were fine. Each one was healthy and as strong as when I first saw them, but when I looked back in the mirror, it was like ripping off a mask I didn't know was there. The image was one of horror, not ecstasy.

The vampires looked older, weaker, but the human. His muscles were gone, his hair was gray. If I kept going, he would die.

"Stop!" I pushed the vampire from me. He would be fine, but the human would not. "I'm so sorry!"

His eyes rolled back in his head, and his flesh paled. His chest struggled to rise and fall as he gasped for air. I leaned over him, focusing my energy toward him, and gave back to him what I took away. The soft essence flowed from me back into him.

"Imara," I called her name, and she looked at me, first with pleasure, then with annoyance. "We need to talk."

"Oh, okay." She pushed away one of her men who I could see looked similar to the ones in my bed. The vampires would heal on their own. She grabbed a robe, covering her body, and headed for the door. I turned to look back at the room. The vampires continued to fuck.

One looked at the human, and I knew he would soon become a meal of another kind.

~*~

Leaving the room, I couldn't find the words to say. I never imagined anything like that would happen. I pulled my clothes back on, hoping no one would see, but I knew even if they didn't see, they would know exactly what I did. Malachi would smell it on me, and Demetrius, if the bond existed between us like I thought it did, he would have felt it.

It was the same way it happened with Malachi. Whenever I was with someone else, he could feel it through whatever bond existed between as well.

I followed Imara down the hall from the room where the others continued fucking to another room. It was the only bedroom that didn't have a pre-marked smell of sex. She headed straight for the closet to change her clothes, and as I looked around, I realized that this was a private room.

Unlike the others, they set it up for comfort, not for sex, not for access to bodies. This was the world I expected my sister to have.

As Imara dressed, pulling a flowing summer dress over her body, I thought about what it would have been like to be with her growing up. Would we have shared each other clothes? Would we have told each other stories about the guys we almost sucked dry? Could we have bonded like my mother said, or would we have been rivals like some siblings were? We would never know what life could have been for us. All we had was the moment, and all we could do was build and go forward.

"Alright, you wanted to talk." Imara closed the door to her closet and sat on the bed next to the window. "Let's talk."

"Yes, we do. Obviously, we have to go back to the others and figure out our plan, but I wanted time for just us," I explained. "Before things get even more insane than they already are."

"I understand." She crossed her legs. "What do you want to talk about?"

"I don't have an agenda, Imara." I sat on the chair across from her bed. "This is strange. All of it. The drama, the sex, the—"

"Brothers," she finished my sentence.

"I…" I knew we would have to discuss it. It was the enormous elephant in the room we couldn't avoid. Malachi.

"Look, Malachi told me all about you two. I know what happened, and I'm okay with it." She leaned across the foot of the bed, bracing her head with her hand. "Yes, it sucks to see him so obviously still concerned with you, but I mean, it's nothing I can't deal with. I mean, that's life. He loved you, the kind of love that doesn't just vanish overnight."

"I really didn't mean to come back here to disturb anything between you. I didn't even know he was here."

"Like I said, I'm fine with it, and I'll tell you like I told him. I know there are things about sirens I will never understand. The bond you two had is something that is untouchable, and I'm not even going to sit here pretend like I care to compete with it. Malachi made a choice to be with me, and I chose to be with him, knowing full well what you meant to him, but I will not sit around and wait for him to decide again that he wants to be with me. You are my sister, and he's a guy. A guy I really care for, but not a guy I can't live without."

"That's the thing, isn't it? He wants someone who can't live without him." She put it in perfect words. Malachi wanted that magical bond that was promised to mermen. He wanted a woman who needed him to survive. I wasn't that woman, and apparently neither was my sister.

"Well, he should look somewhere other than these two sisters because we are strong, independent, and self-sufficient. We don't need him, and I don't know about you, but I'm not wasting a moment feeling bad about that."

"So, we're okay?" I asked because that was what I was really worried about. Not Malachi. I wanted a chance to have a sister, and if what existed between Malachi and me ruined that, I would never forgive myself.

"Were you concerned that we wouldn't be?" She smiled.

"Yeah, I mean, we don't know each other, and I'm here for like five minutes, and things are already complicated. I wouldn't have blamed you if you decided you wanted nothing to do with me."

"Girl, I am the daughter of a succubus and a warlock. Both of my parents didn't give a shit about me growing up. Hell, one of them tried to use me to enact some horrible plan of revenge against his own coven. I can handle a little drama. Meeting you is one of the most normal things to happen to me, and I'm excited that I get to know you now."

"You are?" I smiled.

"Oh yeah. I even went back to New Orleans after everything settled to see if I could find you, but no one knew where you were. That's when I ran into Malachi. At first, we bonded over our shared connection with you. He told me about what happened, and for that reason, I kept my distance from him, but I don't know, in time we moved past it. We created our own bond, and it was comfortable and sweet. But I went back there for you, not for him."

"You know, my mom said I should come here to try to build a relationship with you. She said it would be good if we could become family, you know, the bond of sisterhood."

"You think your mom thought our sister hood bonding would include a shared orgy?" Imara scoffed.

"I gotta say I don't think she did." We laughed together, and for the first time, I heard Imara's laugh, and it reminded me of my own. "What was that back there?"

"What do you mean?" she asked.

"How you persuaded me to join in on the action?" I clarified. "And why didn't I really see what was going on?"

"Oh shit, sorry about that. Once I get going, sometimes I lose myself to the moment. It's my allure, kind of like your siren's call. I use it to bring people to my bed. Or to just convince someone to give into what they really want."

"That's a powerful allure."

"Yeah, it comes in handy." She got up from the bed. "I guess we should get back to the others, huh?"

"Yeah, I think I want to take a shower before I go back down there. Get some of the sex off me." I sniffed my shirt and frowned.

"Not that it's going to help anything. I mean, even without the orgy, you reek of sex, but have at it." She pointed to the door at the back of the room. "We look about the same size, so if you find anything in the closet you want, go for it. I'll meet you downstairs."

CHAPTER 20

I showered and put on a pair of sweats and a loose tank top I found in Imara's closet. Most of her clothes were form fitting or airy. There was no in between. After dressing, I made my way back down the stairs to the large gray room, where we told Imara about what we needed to do. Everyone was there waiting for me.

"Feeling better?" Maggie leaned back in her seat to look at me.

"Yes." I pushed my damp hair over my shoulder.

"Good." Demetrius pulled out a chair for me next to him, and I sat.

"So, what do we have?" Imara asked.

"We believe we know where the hybrids are holding up," Demetrius began.

"Where is that?" Maggie asked.

"Anchorage," he answered.

"Alaska?" Malachi frowned.

"Yeah, I know how much you love it there," Demetrius joked, but Malachi didn't laugh.

"Care to fill us in?" Maggie asked.

"It's nothing," Malachi barked.

"Just that Malachi got his ass beat there by a couple of Bear shifters." Demetrius snickered.

"What?" I asked.

"I didn't." Malachi frowned. "It wasn't a fair fight."

"That's what happens when you get drunk and start flapping off at the mouth." Demetrius laughed.

"Anyway," Malachi huffed. "Can we stay on topic, please?"

"Of course." Demetrius flipped through the pages in front of him. "We've noted a new structure in the Denali mountains, one I doubt any local government has approved. It's protected by a spell. Took one powerful witch to find it."

"So, the hybrids are hiding in a spelled castle in the sky?" Maggie said excitedly.

"I didn't say it was a castle." Demetrius looked at her.

"Yeah, but that just sounds so much cooler, doesn't it?" She clapped.

"What about the dragon?" I asked.

"Yes, there is a dragon. We think he used his power to get this place up there."

"Who are the others?" Imara looked at the pages. "You said there were nine?"

"Yes." Demetrius spread out photos, some grainy and unfocused. "Wish we had better images, but these are the nine, ten now counting the dragon. Five are half witch, mixing with bear, wolf, and of course, dragon. The others, we're still trying to decipher."

"So, the cards are stacked against us." Imara nodded. "Great."

"Yes, we're going to need some help," Demetrius agreed.

"Have anyone in mind?" Malachi asked.

"We have some locals in the area I can call on, but I think it would be smart if we brought in others. If any of their powers are close to what Syrinada can do, it's going to take a lot more than just the five of us to get this done."

"I'll come along for the ride," Crissette spoke, leaning against the doorframe.

"What?" I leaned forward to look around Demetrius at her.

"Hell, I can't have my girl headed off to war without me." She pointed to Imara.

"Sure you don't need to stay here and hold down the fort?" I pointed out. "I'm sure there are lots of Succubi things to take care of around here."

"And miss out on the action?" Crissette winked at Demetrius. "No way."

"The more the merrier," Demetrius responded.

"Great," I muttered, and he stiffened by my side.

"Syrinada," he whispered. "You okay?"

I nodded and tapped my knee against his leg. He slid his hand beneath the table to squeeze my knee, and I calmed.

"When do we leave?" Malachi asked, once again displaying his irritation.

"Tomorrow. We could all use some rest," Demetrius answered, his hand still on my leg. "We'll regroup in the morning. I'll arrange transportation."

"Perfect." Malachi stood and left the room.

"Let me show you to your room," Crissette offered.

"We're not staying here," I snapped.

"We aren't?" Maggie asked. "I was sure we would stay in the lavish mansion tonight."

"No, Maggie." I frowned at her. "Demetrius got us a hotel. We're staying there."

"Oh, but we have so much room here," Crissette insisted, and Imara laughed.

"I'd rather not," I insisted.

"If you insist." She smiled, shot another flirty look at Demetrius, and then left the room.

"We should get going, since we aren't staying here." Demetrius stood.

"Yeah, gotta get our beauty rest, right, Sy?" Maggie held back laughter.

"Shut up." I punched her in the shoulder. "Let's go."

~*~

"You really were going to fight her if she got near him,

huh?" Maggie asked as we stood at the entrance to the small hotel.

"Maggie." I tried to brush her off, but I knew she wouldn't let it go.

"Girl, you know I gotta poke at you for it. Look at you all territorial about Demetrius. Not wanting someone to even flirt with him, meanwhile, you were just banging vamps."

"I know. It makes no sense. It's not even something I want to do." I sighed. "It's embarrassing to react like some love-sick girl, but it's like it's another part of me takes over, and when she flirts with him, I see red."

"Your siren." Maggie pointed to me. "It's her, claiming her man."

"Yeah." I shrugged. "I guess you're right."

"Does she get that way for Rhys?" Maggie asked as a couple holding hands slipped by us.

"What?" I asked.

"Rhys, you know, the guy you chose to be with." She raised a brow. "Does your siren get like that when someone flirts with Rhys?"

"Oh um…" I felt embarrassed. With everything going on, Rhys was the furthest thing from my mind. "No. I mean, I don't really know. I've never experienced that."

"Women don't flirt with him?"

"No. I mean, we've never been around other people together. It's always been us in hiding or me in hiding alone," I said. "I mean, I'd like to think I would be upset if someone flirted with him in front of me."

"I see." She looked back at Demetrius. "Have you talked to him?"

"Demetrius? About what?"

"Rhys, girl!" Maggie snapped her fingers in my face. "Have you talked to Rhys?"

"Oh, no." I pulled the phone from my pocket. "I should call him. Just tired of missed calls and texts."

"You do that. I'm going to make sure I have a room with a minibar, or at least get money to hit the vending machine." She smiled. "D can afford it, I'm sure!"

"Have fun." I looked at the phone in my hand.

With Maggie bouncing off inside the building, I sat on the bench next to the doors. I tapped the screen, found Rhys' number, and hit the call button. It rang four times, and just as I was about to hang up, the line clicked.

"Hello?" Rhys answered, voice dry as if just waking

from sleep.

"Rhys? Did I wake you?"

"Sy?" he groaned. "Is that you?"

"Yes, it's me." I frowned. I really wished he would stop calling me by the shortened version of my name. It used to make me so happy when he said my name, but it was yet another thing that had changed between us.

"Are you okay?" he asked.

"Yes, I just…" I paused. "Just wanted to talk."

"Oh,"

"If you're sleeping, we can talk later."

"No, it's okay. I should be up," he said. "I meant to take a quick nap, but you know how that goes."

"Where are you?" I asked.

"New York."

I checked the time. It was almost midnight, which meant it was almost three in the morning for him.

"It's the middle of the night. You should sleep. I'll talk to you later."

"Sy," he paused, "we can talk now."

"Okay."

"How are you?" he asked.

"I'm good. We're making progress. We found Imara," I gave him an update.

"Your sister, I didn't know you were going to find her," he reminded me I hadn't exactly told him what I was up to since leaving our home.

"That's right, we haven't really spoken. I just assumed the covens knew what was happening."

"I know Ebon reached out to you. That's all we know," he said.

"Yeah, well, she reached out and told me about the problem with the hybrids. The hybrids everyone seems to know about," I said, hoping he would deny any knowledge of them, but of course, he didn't. After a minute of silence, I continued. "And your silence suggests you knew as well."

"Yes, I did," he said.

"She asked that I put together a team. People who could come together to try to deal with the issue. Imara was, of course, top of the list."

"And Demetrius?"

"No, not specifically. They dropped Maggie and

I off in Chicago. We needed help, so we went to their house. I thought Malachi would be there, but he wasn't."

"So, it's you, Maggie, Imara, and Demetrius. That's the dream team?" he asked almost mockingly.

"And Malachi," I added.

"I thought you said he wasn't there." Rhys sounded more tense.

"He wasn't. Turns out he's been with Imara this whole time."

"Right."

"It's complicated," I said.

"I see," he said.

"Rhys, I didn't call you to tell you about a plot to face hybrids." I leaned back on the bench and stared at the dark sky above me.

"What did you call me to talk about?" he asked.

"Us. Obviously."

"Us."

"Yes, I mean, I haven't seen you in so long, and then, once again, my world gets flipped upside down. What happened with Demetrius wasn't supposed to happen."

"Yeah," he said.

"Can you say more than one and two word responses, please?"

"What do you want me to say, Sy?"

"Anything. Tell me how you feel. Tell me what's on your mind. Say anything. Dammit, I've been reaching out to you for days and hitting a wall."

"I've been busy," he gave the short explanation.

"Just like you've been busy since you left. What was supposed to be a few days turned to weeks and now months, Rhys."

"That's not my fault."

"I didn't say it was anyone's fault."

"Look, I get it. You're a siren. You have needs. Demetrius fills them. I'm not happy with it, but I'm trying to accept it. Besides, you're with him now and will be for I don't know how long. You went to him for help, Sy, not me."

"I didn't have a choice. I had no phone. I couldn't reach out to you."

"And what about having him in our space? That hurt me, you know."

"I know. It wasn't intentional."

"Right."

"Rhys."

"Look, I know you want me to say we're okay, but honestly, Sy, I don't know that we are. Our relationship was already strained before this. I want you to be okay, that's all I know. Outside of that, I don't really know what to say to you."

"Okay,"

"I really need to get back to work."

"Right."

"I'll talk to you later?"

"Yeah, okay."

I hung up the phone.

CHAPTER 21

I stood under the flow of water, allowing the trail of the shower to blend with the tears that fell down my face. What I had with Rhys was changing, and I didn't know what would happen between us. What was worse was I didn't know what I wanted to happen. I loved Rhys, but I couldn't figure out if I was still holding on to a version of him that no longer existed.

When we first met, he gave me butterflies, and through the weeks we spent training together, getting to know each other, that changed. He became my protector, but he was more than that. He was someone I looked to for genuine support. Rhys didn't have expectations for what I was supposed to be, or at least, he never told me about them if he did. He didn't pressure me into anything.

I thought we would be together. Mated, but something about it always felt lacking. It was what I was afraid to face with Demetrius. That missing piece, that hole I felt every day for months, suddenly wasn't there anymore. Not when I was with him, I was torn, and I didn't know what way to go.

I climbed from the shower, dressed in a loose shirt and a pair of boy shirts, and sat on the bed. It was late, and I should have been sleeping, but my mind was racing. My pulse flying. Sleep wouldn't be possible.

Just as I turned on the movie Pretty Woman, there was a knock on the door.

Looking through the peephole, I saw him, Demetrius.

"Is everything okay?" I asked after I opened the door.

"Yes, I…" He paused and frowned, staring at me. "Are you okay?"

"Yes, why?" I looked over his shoulder at the empty hall. "What happened?"

"Can I come in?" he asked.

"Oh, sure, come in." I stepped aside and let him into the room.

"I just felt like I needed to come here," he explained.

"Did I call you again? If I did, I didn't mean to,"

I apologized. I hadn't been aroused or even really thinking about him.

"No, call it intuition." He smiled. "I just felt I needed to be here with you."

"Oh."

"I can tell you're upset. If you don't want to talk about it or you don't want me to be here, just say the word, and I will go."

"No, if you feel you should be here, then you should." I closed the door. "Stay."

"What's on your mind?" he asked.

"You really want to know?" I smirked.

"Yes." He looked around the room, inspecting every corner. "I do."

"Rhys," I answered. "Rhys is on my mind."

"You talked to him?" Demetrius asked.

"I did," I admitted.

"How did it go?"

"About as good as can be expected." I sat on the bed.

Demetrius pointed to the bed beside me, a question

if he could join. I nodded.

"Tell me, what did he say?" Demetrius asked, placing his hand on my knee.

"He doesn't know what he wants. He's not sure if he wants to be with me or not, and I can't blame him. He wants me to be okay, but he is hurting."

"Understandable," Demetrius said. "I've been there."

"It would be great if I knew what to say to him. I wish there were magical words that could fix it all. I hate he feels this way, and I hate that I'm the one who made him feel it."

"You didn't intend to hurt him," Demetrius tried to comfort me.

"Intention is shit."

"How so?"

"Just because you don't intend something doesn't mean it doesn't hurt, and it doesn't invalidate the other person's feelings. I would never want to hurt Rhys. It's the last thing I would do after everything we've been through, but I did. Just like I hurt you, just like I hurt Malachi."

"Sy, we are all adults here. This is a shitty situation, everything from how your aunt raised you to how you found out about who you are. You're still unpacking all of that. People are bound to get hurt, and anyone who has voluntarily become a part of this, because I'll remind you that no one was forced, did so understanding that you still have a lot to figure out."

"I feel like I should be in therapy." I ran my hands through my hair. "Wonder how much it would cost to unpack all of this."

"Yeah, you probably should." He laughed. "Though I have had little luck with the paranormal therapist. Most of them are human who don't really understand what we're going through."

"Wait, there are really paranormal therapist?" I gawked. "Seriously?"

"Of course. Hell, we all have issues, Syrinada. Some people need help to figure their shit out. Maybe after all this is said and done, we can get you set up with someone," he offered. "Only the best."

"I'll definitely take you up on that." I leaned back on my elbows and dropped my head back. "Maybe someone else will have better luck clearing my brain up for me."

"What are you going to do about Rhys?" he asked.

"Give him his space," I said the only thing I could think of. "What more is there for me to do? He needs to figure things out on his end just as much as I do. I'll try to keep the lines of communication open as best as I can."

"Good. You should do that." He turned to the television and smiled. "You know I always loved this movie."

"Yeah? Me too." I laughed. "It's probably a bad thing, but I connected so much with Julia Roberts. This is the first time I saw her on film, and I felt so connected with her."

"Makes sense. She's a siren." He pointed to the actress on the screen.

"What?" I leaned forward. "Be for real."

"Yeah, never got her stone, though. As alluring as she already is, could you imagine what she would be like with her full power?"

"Wait, you can't just coast past that fact. She's a siren!" I laughed. "I don't know why, but I never assumed there would be others just walking around out there."

"Yeah, a lot of the celebrities you love are supernatural." He nodded. "Most of the A-list stars, in fact. They work together, help each other level up."

"Like who?" I perked up, ready for him to spill the tea.

"You ever seen the show Simply Seductress?" Demetrius spoke of the show I'd devoured countless times.

"Yes." I clapped. "The show about the supernatural detectives."

"I'd say seventy-five percent of that cast were actual supernatural, including the producer."

"That's insane. I loved that show." I sighed. "There definitely should have been more seasons."

"Too bad they got shut down. I think it was the Succubi who called for it." Demetrius laughed. "They didn't like the way there were being portrayed, even though it looked spot on to me."

"What?"

"Oh yes, it was a ton of drama surrounding it." He adjusted the volume on the television. "There usually is anytime there is a piece of media that touches so closely to home."

Demetrius spent the next hour distracting me from my thoughts and gossiping with me about the supernatural celebrity news. He shared a website with me that explained while most humans thought it was satire, it was actual news. Things about shifters, magic portals, the works. They got tired of trying to hide things, so they added humor to it. Most people read it for entertainment, not realizing it was actual news about things happening in the world.

"It's late," Demetrius said as the credits rolled. "I should go."

"Oh, yeah. I guess so."

"I could stay if you would like."

"No, it's fine."

"Syrinada." He looked into my eyes. "Do I have to remind you I can feel what you feel?"

"Yeah." I thought about it. What would it mean if he stayed?

"You know, my staying doesn't mean anything has to happen between us."

"It doesn't," I repeated.

"No." He nodded. "Nothing at all."

"Stay?" I asked.

"Of course." He nodded. "Whatever you need."

Demetrius pulled the covers back for me to climb beneath, then sat on top of the covers next to me.

"You should sleep." He yawned.

"You too." I touched his chest.

"Okay." He reached over and pulled me close to him. "We'll both sleep."

He fell asleep before me, and I laughed. Demetrius was a talker. Soft mumbles about trees and honey crossed his lips between snores. I fell asleep, wrapped in the comfort of his warmth and listening to the hum in his chest.

~*~

The next morning, I woke up in his arms, and it felt amazing. I got used to waking up alone. Even when I wasn't alone when I went to bed, but he was still there, arms still wrapped around me in an embrace I never wanted to get away from.

His breathing shifted from the calm of sleep to the controlled breathing of consciousness, and I knew he was awake. He didn't move, kept his arm around me, and allowed me to remain where I was, unmoved. I thought of staying that way. How long could I stretch the moment?

For the first time, I was happy when I woke up. My mind didn't immediately start racing about trying to figure out things I had no answers for. I wanted to be there with him, never leaving his side, and it made me feel good to have a clear head, but then the phone rang.

Demetrius's phone buzzed on the nightstand, and he attempted to ignore it. It stopped, but then immediately began again.

"You going to get that?" I asked, nuzzling closer to him.

"I didn't want to wake you." He brushed my hair from my face.

"I've been awake for a while. Just comfortable." I yawned.

"You keep comfortable. The call can wait."

"Can it?" I looked up at him.

He glanced at the phone, which lay face up so he could see the screen, then frowned. "Maybe not."

"Get it." I nudged his side. "It's okay."

"Yeah, I think I will. Sorry."

I waved off his apology as he answered the phone.

"Yeah?" he answered.

The muffled sound of a man's voice came across the line. I couldn't make out what he said, but whatever it was, it got Demetrius tense. He shifted his weight beneath me, and I knew our sweet moment was over.

"Yeah, I'm on it. Make sure he doesn't know we're on to him. I'm trying to figure this shit out." He hung up the phone and groaned.

"I take it that wasn't the best news," I said against his chest.

"No, it wasn't," he confirmed.

"Sorry to hear that." I sat up.

"It's okay." He touched my arm, sending a chill through me.

"Anything I can help with?"

"Nope." He got up from the bed. "We need to get back over to the mansion. Gotta regroup with the others."

"Demetrius."

"Yeah?" He looked back at me.

"You know how you said you can feel what I feel?" I lead. "That you know what I'm going through?"

"Yeah,"

"It goes both ways." I looked him in the eyes. I could feel how upset he was. "Maybe you don't want to talk about it now, but just like you were here for me, I'm there for you."

"I will be okay, Syrinada. I promise." He grabbed my hand, pressed his lips gently against my palm, then turned and headed for the door.

Two hours later, we were pulling up to Imara's borrowed house. There were fewer cars in the driveway, meaning their guests had left. Crissette stood on the steps waving at our car.

"Oh look, it's your favorite succubus," Maggie joked from the back seat.

"How great," I responded sarcastically.

"Good morning, Demetrius," she spoke only to him as we all get out of the car.

"I guess she doesn't see us standing here?" I frowned, and Maggie poke me in the side.

"You know she's only doing that because she knows it gets under your skin," she whispered. "Maybe if you ignore it, she will stop."

"Yeah, well, she might want to be worried about something getting under her skin if she doesn't stop."

"Okay, I see you're issuing threats now. Fight for your man, girl." Maggie pointed at Demetrius, who was already walking into the house.

"Just shut up." I chuckled.

"It's good to see this side of you. It makes you more human." Maggie pushed me forward. "Good morning, Crissette!" she called out.

"Oh, hi." The big bitch gave us a small wave, then followed Demetrius into the house.

I growled, and Maggie laughed. "Down, girl!"

The inside of the house was different. There was no longer the overwhelming feeling of sex. Windows were open letting fresh air flow, and I could tell there were fewer people there.

"Everyone bounced already?" I asked Imara as she approached, coming down the stairs.

"Yes, as a matter of fact." She looked around. "This isn't my house. As much as I wish it were. I didn't want to leave it full of sex crazed maniacs. These people can get out of hand if left unchecked."

"I see."

"So, do we have a plan?" she asked.

"Malachi and Demetrius are in the back waiting for us," Crissette announced.

"Thanks," Imara answered and turned to head that way. She paused, looking over her shoulder at me. "You coming?"

"Yeah, I am."

We met in the same room as before. This time, Demetrius took charge of the room. He handed us all envelopes.

"You all will take a direct private flight into Anchorage."

"You're not coming with us?" Crissette pouted, and I clinched my fist at my side.

"No." He gave a small awkward smile. "I need to go take care of some things and gather more help for us. Once that is done, I'll join you with the second team. You have lodging arranged for the first night. Cornel will meet you when you get off the plane. He is our point man. He will then take you up into the mountains. You need to be careful. The place is heavily protected.

"Sy and Maggie, you'll need to come up with a spell to break through. Reach out to the coven if you have to. Maybe Roxanne can help you figure out a way to get through the protection spell. Your folder has everything we've found out about it."

"Okay." I nodded and tried to hide how awkward the idea of talking to Roxanne made me feel. Yeah, just calling to ask about barrier spells, let's ignore the fact that I cheated on your son, and he dumped my ass.

Easy.

Demetrius finished giving us our orders. The hope was to have a careful conversation but to be prepared for anything but that. When he finished, Maggie went in search of food while the others left to finish packing and loading their car.

"What are you thinking?" Demetrius sat beside me.

"I'm thinking that all of this is insane, and I don't want to reach out to my almost-ex boyfriend's mom for help."

"I know. I'm sorry." He put his arm around me. "If there were another way, I would propose it, but there still aren't many witches willing to work with you."

"I know." I leaned my head back on his arm. "Let's make a deal now."

"What's that?"

"We never say sorry again, at least not for things we can't change or that aren't our fault." I looked him in the eye. "I'm tired of apologizing, Demetrius."

"Okay, that sounds good to me." He smiled.

"You're leaving me to travel with this group?" I poked him in the side.

"You can handle it." He laughed, rubbing the spot

where I poked.

"Oh yeah, tension like this is nothing I can't take."

"It might be good for you all. Therapeutic."

"Right. You know, when they asked me to put together a team, I didn't think it meant dealing with old trauma. For once, could a plight to save the world come with a new cast of characters that don't have a horrible history?" I straightened.

"I wouldn't say the history is horrible, just complicated." Demetrius sighed.

"Why is it you get to escape your complicated history while I have to face mine?"

"Hey, I'm just doing what's necessary here."

"Right, and you can't organize a team over the phone?"

He chuckled. "Alright, you got me. I'm just not ready to deal with my little brother. Besides, there are other unrelated things I need to look into."

"Just make sure you hurry and meet us there." I stood from my seat and stretched my arms over my head.

"I will." He looked up at me, and there was something there, something I couldn't place.

I don't know why I did it, but I gave in to my impulse, and I kissed him. I placed my hands on either side of his face and pressed my lips against his. It was soft, intimate, and what I needed.

"We're ready to go." Malachi cleared his throat, and we both looked up at him. Two thieves caught red-handed.

"We'll be right there," Demetrius answered.

"Great." I sighed. "Yeah, you better hurry the hell up."

CHAPTER 22

I'd never been on a private plane before, but the experience was one I could definitely do again. No assigned seating or being forced to sit in front of a kid who obviously missed their calling as a soccer star. No waiting in a crowded terminal with people who smelled of an odd mixture of sex and death. We drove straight to the plane, got on, and took off.

"You know, I never asked. Just how rich are the Denalis because damn!" Maggie looked around the plane with wide eyes.

"I never thought about it." I shrugged.

It wasn't like I asked Malachi for their tax statements. I always knew Demetrius did good for himself. Malachi only ever said his brother worked in the private sector. What that meant, I didn't really care to know.

"Maybe you can ask him at your next sleepover,"

she teased.

"What?" I looked at her with wide eyes.

"I know he spent the night in your room. Mine was right next to yours, remember?" she pointed out. "For a hotel equipped to have different guests, they have really thin walls. Unfortunately, no one was having any real fun."

"Oh."

"I didn't go ghost and peek in!" She slapped my arm. "But I heard you two laughing and talking."

"Yeah, he came to talk." I nodded. "It may have been just what I needed after all this."

"And he stayed, but you did nothing else." She nodded.

"No, we just slept." The small smile lifted the corners of my mouth. "He talks in his sleep."

"Interesting." She sat back in her seat.

"What?" I raised a brow.

"I don't know. Things on the rocks with Rhys. You're getting closer to Demetrius."

"Can we please focus on something else?" I shook my head because I didn't want to think about the rocky status of my relationships with the men in my life.

"Like the brooding brother on the other side of the plane?" She shot a look at Malachi, who sat staring out the window.

"Or the hybrids we're supposed to be finding." I turned the conversation to something more important. "I swear I don't know if you're here to help with this problem or to set me up with Demetrius."

"I'm just being an observant friend. I care about you, Syrinada. All this hybrid stuff is secondary for me." She shrugged.

"Well, for me, right now, it's the priority, and I'd rather avoid any further discussion about all the male driven confusion in my life right now." I pulled out my earbuds that Demetrius provided, opened the streaming app on my phone to play calming music, and tuned out the rest of the world.

The ride was smooth, and like any other time I'd ever been on a plane, I passed out the second the plane reached its peak altitude and leveled out, which I was thankful for because I didn't want to have to think about interacting with Crissette, who made inappropriate comments about Demetrius, and I wanted to avoid Malachi at all costs.

He hadn't said another word to me or his brother after catching us kissing. As if things weren't awkward enough, the moment he witnessed was intimate and personal, and after we told him there was nothing between us, he saw with his eyes that there was. It was one thing for his gut to tell him that something was there. It was another thing for him to witness it play out in real time.

As I drifted to sleep, Maggie and Imara chattered on about things that Maggie would miss after she would have to leave this world again, and I was happy she had someone else to talk to. Don't get me wrong, I loved Maggie, but my mind was tired, and she only brought up things I didn't want to think about.

I didn't want to think about Rhys. I didn't want to consider having to call Roxanne or any of the other the complicated facets of relationships I didn't even understand for myself. When Ebon pulled me from my home, she told me I needed to deal with hybrids. The goal was to protect the balance between good and evil. This was not supposed to be some emotional trip down memory lane, and it damn sure wasn't supposed to have me facing all the things I wanted to avoid.

Four hours later, I woke up when the plane landed. The touchdown shook the plane and ripped me from a sweet dream of having tea with my mother. I wondered where she was and wished I could call her and find out. She'd be happy to know I was with Imara.

Twenty minutes later, our group was jumping out of the plane into a small field where four trucks waited. I was the last to climb out and saw Malachi shaking hands with a man who had shoulders as wide as a door.

"Syrinada, I presume?" The man looked up at me.

"Yes," I said as I walked down the steps to join them on the ground.

"Even more beautiful than your pictures." He smiled a crooked grin. "I'm Cornell. Demetrius asked that I take good care of you."

"Of course, he did," Malachi smirked.

Cornell shot him a questioning gaze and then turned back to me. "Once we get your bags loaded, we'll hit the road."

"Thank you." I shook his hand and watched as mine disappeared into his massive hold.

Cornell was a bear shifter. He wasn't particularly tall and had a dad bod. Stomach pudge and all, but there was something about him that just oozed sex. He was one of those men who was so confident they could wear rags from the trash and somehow make it look sexy. What made Cornell that much more attractive was that I knew his confident wasn't ill-founded. He could back it up.

"Dibs on the big bear!" Imara whispered in my ear as we watched the guys load the trunks with our luggage.

"He's all yours." I shrugged. "Trust me, I have way too much drama on my hands as it is with the male population."

"More for me." She put her arm around my shoulder.

"What about Malachi?" I glanced at the brother who helped with loading the bags.

"What about him? He knows who I am. I will not limit myself to just one man. It would mean death for both of us." She licked her lips and air humped in the crudest way before turning and going to the car, shifting her aggressive display to a sensuous walk when Cornell turned to look at her.

We loaded into three different cars, each driven by a bear. Close to where we landed was their campsite. A wooded area that comprised a collection of log cabins. Some of them looked like they built them before the invention of electricity, while others were far more modern. Luckily, they set us up in one with more modern amenities.

Unfortunately, we were all assigned to stay in the same cabin, which meant I got to sleep in the same place with two people who, at the moment, were clearly not the biggest fans of me. Crissette only wanted to push my buttons, and everything I did pushed Malachi.

"Oh, the merman returns!" a boisterous voice called out as we unloaded the trucks.

"Fuck," Malachi muttered under his breath. "This just keeps getting better."

"Back for a second round?" the bear shifter with red hair jogged over to the line of vehicles.

"Nate." Malachi turned and forced a smile onto his face. "I'm just here to handle some business, man."

"Oh, come on, don't be so tense. Shit happens when we get a little too intoxicated," he joked. "You remember, don't you?"

"Yeah, it does." Malachi gave a tight nod. "That's not gonna happen this time around."

"What happened?" Imara asked.

"Oh, just Malachi thinking he could take on two bears while pissy drunk is all." He slapped Malachi on the shirt. "Hell, he might have stood a chance if he didn't trip and fall into that pig shit!"

"Pig shit?" Imara gasped.

"Can we please drop it?" Malachi grunted.

"Yes, we can," Cornell returned. "Y'all get settled. Dinner will be ready soon." He pointed to a large cabin that stood across from ours. "That's my place. Come on over when you're ready. We have a few things to cover before we call it a night. Need to make sure everyone is on the same page before we head out in the morning."

"I love it when you Denalis come around." Nate grinned. "We always get to get into some action."

"Oh, so you're joining us?" Imara asked with a seductive grin on her face.

"You damn right I am!" Nate flashed another enormous smile at her.

"Great." Malachi threw the bag over his shoulder and headed inside.

The dinner was delicious. Cornell was an excellent chef, serving up steak, potatoes, and veggies. A hearty meal before a day of climbing a mountain. We all sat around his kitchen table, devoured the food in silence, and then went out behind his cabin where there was a fire pit.

The fire crackled, and the air smelled of the hemlock, spruce trees, and other plants in the area. The sounds of animals scurrying through the woods added to the ambiance. My thoughts drifted to him, and I wished his arm was around me again, and his lips were on my cheek. It would have been a great moment to share. My phone buzzed in my pocket, and I took it out to see the message from him.

You okay, those bears treating you right?

Yes.

I wish I were there with you. I'll be there soon.

Hurry.

I turned the screen off and slipped the phone back into my pocket as that pang of guilt returned because it wasn't Rhys I was talking to. I had to make a decision, and it was one I didn't want to make.

"We're going to need to head out early in the morning if we're going to make time. Make sure you get some rest tonight." Cornell handed Imara a beer as he sat in the lawn chair next to her. "The climb will take us about a day, so we'll make camp tomorrow night when we reach our stopping point. The plan is for us to push on and reach the barrier in time for Demetrius and the others to get here."

"Are you sure he will be here by then?" I asked.

"Yes, according to our last conversation." Cornell sipped from his beer. "He's gathering up a team of people, making a pit stop in New York, and then heading here."

"Why is he stopping there?" Malachi tensed up when he asked the question.

"I don't really ask the big man what he's up to. I just do as I'm told." Cornell tipped his beer to Malachi.

"Right." Still riddled with tension, Malachi stood from his seat and turned to go into the cabin. "I'm gonna get some sleep."

"I guess the festivities are over." Imara looked at the departing man.

"I guess so," Cornell agreed.

"Well, I'm beat." Maggie followed Malachi's lead and headed for the cabin. "Thanks for the grub," she called over her shoulder.

Crissette was already inside. After dinner, she disappeared saying she didn't need to hear all the details of our trip. We just needed to let her know what to do when the time came, which left me sitting alone with Imara and Cornell, both of who looked at me like they wanted me to get the hell out of there.

"Think I'm just going to take a quick walk before going to bed." I stood with an awkward chuckle. "Still have some energy to burn off."

"You and me both, sister." Imara winked at me, and as I got up from my seat, she turned her focus on Cornell.

I didn't know what those two got up to that night, but I knew Imara did not sleep in our cabin.

CHAPTER
23

W*e met in the morning as planned.* Three other bears and a jaguar shifter joined us for the journey up the mountain. As they gathered their things, I pulled out my phone to dial a number Demetrius programmed in it for me.

I couldn't put off the call any longer because Cornell explained that once we got going up the mountain, I would lose service. It rang three times before she answered.

"Hello?" her voice was just as warm and mothering as I remembered.

"Hi, is this Roxanne?"

"Yes, it is." She paused. "Oh, Syrinada, is that you?"

"Yes, it is," I answered nervously, not sure if she would welcome a call from me.

"It's so good to hear from you. I was just talking to your mother the other day," she exclaimed. "She'll be so glad to know you're alright."

"My mom?"

"Yes, she came to me worried. Said your home was destroyed in a storm, and you weren't there. I did a soft tracking spell to let her know you were still alive," Roxanne explained. "Told her it would be good for her to invest in a phone, but she didn't go for it."

I chuckled because it was a conversation I'd already had with her. My mother was anti-technology. "Is she okay?"

"Yes, she was worried, but she is okay," Roxanne reported. "How can I help you? I take it you have a reason for calling me and not my son."

"Yes, actually. We're tracking down hybrids, and we believe we found them, but they're using a barrier spell."

"Oh, what kind?" she asked.

I sent her a picture of Demetrius' notes. "You should get a picture now."

"Oh, okay. I see." She paused as she reviewed the images I sent over. "Are you alone, or is there another witch around?"

"Maggie is here as well as Imara."

"Maggie, the one who died?" she said with far less surprise than I felt was warranted.

"Yes, and my sister. She is a half-witch like me."

"Oh right, the succubus who hasn't been tested," she muttered.

"Tested?" I frowned as Imara walked by me. "She has to be tested? Like I was with the spirits?"

"Never mind. Give me a few minutes, and I'll text you the spell. Does that work?" Roxanne brushed off my concerns.

"Um, yes. I think we still have about an hour before we head out."

"Perfect. I'll get it to you by then. This spell isn't that complex. The three of you should be able to break it with ease."

"Thank you."

"Is there anything else?" she asked.

"Yes, um," I hesitated because I wasn't sure how much she knew about the dynamic of my relationship with her son. "Have you talked to Rhys?"

"Not for a few days now, but he should be back

here soon."

"Okay, thanks."

I hung up the phone and returned to the group.

"She give you a spell?" Imara approached me with a satisfied grin on her face.

"Not yet, but she will send one over." I waved the phone at her. "Told her we have about an hour before we head up the mountain."

"It's weird that Maggie couldn't just tap into those ghosts buddies of hers to get one, right?" Imara asked.

"They don't really like to interfere." Maggie joined us and damn near scared me out of my skin.

"I didn't mean—" Imara was clearly surprised by Maggie's sudden arrival.

"No, it's fine, but yeah, as much as I would love to just tag them in, I can't. I've tried." Maggie shrugged.

"You have?" I asked. "When did you try?"

"Yeah, when we were in the giant's house. I tried reaching out to them for answers, and I hit a wall. While I'm here, I'm just like any other witch. Gotta figure shit out on my own."

"What the hell good is that?" Imara scoffed.

"They can't interfere. It's all about the balance. If they put their hand in the cookie jar, it will skew things," I gave the explanation Ebon and Demetrius drilled into my mind. "We can't shift too far in either direction, good or bad."

"Why did I not understand that we would walk up the mountain?" Maggie complained.

"Hey, at least you have the option of just going ghost," I pointed out her advantage. "Save the leg strength and just float your ass on up there."

"I wouldn't do that. Besides, If I do, then I lose everything I'm carrying. Factory reset, remember?"

"Oh, right."

"Did Roxanne text you?"

"Not yet. Hopefully she does before we get too high up." I looked at my phone.

Almost an hour later, as the crew gathered, ready to start our trek, my phone buzzed in my pocket. Thinking it was going to be from Roxanne, I eagerly took it out to receive our instructions. It wasn't her.

Rhys: I know we aren't talking. But please stay safe.

Seconds later, he sent another message.

Rhys: If you're up to it, I'd like to work things out.

I opened the message with every intention of replying to him, but my phone buzzed again.

Demetrius: I know you're headed out soon. Stay safe. I'll see you tomorrow.

I chewed my lip, unsure of whom to respond to and just decided not to reply to either of them. Putting the phone in my back pocket, I joined the others on the trail that led from the back of the cabins up into the mountain.

"Do you guys own these mountains?" Maggie asked Malachi. "I mean, they're named after you."

"I doubt that," Malachi answered. "These mountains predate my bloodline, but as far as I know, there is no connection."

"It's weird though, right? That this takes place here," Maggie pointed out. "Trekking up the Denali Mountain with the Denali brothers on a journey to save the world."

"I have recognized the irony." Malachi nodded.

"I don't think it's a coincidence," Maggie continued. "I no longer believe in those. Everything happens for a reason. There is a significant purpose behind every event. Even the ones that go unnoticed."

"I take it they aren't at the top of the mountains?" Crissette paused, looking up at the peak. "I don't see any castle up there."

"No, they aren't, but it's still going to be a challenge to get to where they are," Nate answered. "Luckily, we have ways to traverse the mountain faster."

"Oh?" Maggie chimed in.

"We like to stay away from the human trails, which means dealing with the worst the mountains have to offer," Cornell explained. "But there are passageways powered by magic that allow for a faster route. What would take days will take hours with using the connected portals."

"This ought to be fun." Maggie clapped.

"It can be, but it can also make you horribly sick," Nate joked.

"Oh, a wonderful surprise." I frowned. The last thing I wanted was to be throwing up my breakfast.

We started up the mountain and quickly hit the rough terrain Cornell talked about. By an hour in, my legs were burning, and my stomach was cramping, making me regret the extra helping of eggs I'd scarfed down at the breakfast table. Maggie, who complained in advance about the hike, was actually doing well with the activity. She bounced ahead of me, smiling and snacking on a jerky stick.

"You're strangely athletic."

"Maybe my ghostliness means I don't get as

fatigued as you?" She shrugged. "Which is strange because I was seriously exhausted last night."

"What happened to those magical portals we were supposed to be using?" I called out, and Cornell, who was at the head of the group, turned to me.

"Funny you should mention that. We've reached the first one." He pointed ahead to where an out of place circular structure stood between two trees. It clearly didn't belong there, but if he hadn't pointed it out, I was not sure I would have noticed it.

Cornell and Nate stepped to the ring and ran their hands along the length of each side. When they were done, the ring came to life, and where we could see clearly through it before, we could no longer. It was an unbroken wall of light.

"I never thought I'd be able to go through one of these." Maggie popped the last bite of her jerky into her mouth.

"You know about them?" I asked.

"Yeah, you know Menaria?"

"That strange vampire that helped us in New Orleans?" I thought of the woman who literally unhinged her jaw and devoured a demon in front of me. "How could I forget?"

"These contraptions are her people's doing,"

Maggie explained. "She told me about them a couple of times, but I never got to try it out."

With their instructions, the group stepped through the portal one by one. Cornell went through first. I was behind Imara in line, with Maggie behind me.

The experience of walking through the light felt much like crossing over into Deuterio, the siren realm underneath the sea. It was shocking at first, then it calmed, but the difference was, when I stepped on the other side, my head spun, and I very nearly lost all the food in my stomach.

Imara stood ahead of me, gasping for air, equally messed up by the experience. Maggie bounced through the opening, shouting and waving her hands like she'd just got off the best ride at the amusement park.

"That was awesome!" she boasted. "When can we do it again?"

"You really are a strange one." Cornell chuckled.

"That's an understatement." I rolled my eyes.

"It's okay, Sy. I'm sure you'll do better on the next one." Maggie patted my shoulder and walked ahead of me.

An hour later, we were passing through another portal, and I, in fact, did not do better with that one.

By the time the sun left the sky and we were setting up our camping site, I still hadn't heard from Roxanne. Checking my phone, I realized the odds of her getting through to me were slim. I barely had one bar on the service icon, and even that flickered in and out.

With the camp set up and food in our stomachs, everyone settled in for the night. Malachi walked off alone, and Imara was still hanging out with Cornell. I followed Malachi and found him standing and looking out into the mountain range.

"Did you need something?" he asked.

"No, sorry. We just haven't really talked, and I was concerned about you being out here by yourself," I admitted as I stepped to his side.

"I have a lot on my mind." Malachi stared into the distance.

"Oh, I can leave. Didn't mean to interrupt." I stepped back.

"Sy, what do you want?" His shoulders dropped.

"Excuse me?"

"You're here. You didn't just come to turn and go back."

"I just wanted to see if you were okay. Things are awkward as hell with you right now," I explained. "I'm just concerned about you, that's all."

"Should I apologize for that?" He looked over his shoulder at me.

"Did I ask for an apology?" I snapped. "You don't have to be a dick to me right now. Excuse me for checking in on you after watching Imara with Cornell. I thought you might be upset."

"I'm used to it." He turned. "I've accepted Imara for who she is. Same way I accepted you."

"Did you really?" I shook my head. "Doesn't feel like you did."

"Excuse me?"

"All this time, I wonder if you ever actually accepted me or if you just gave up on trying to change me," I voiced the feelings I'd been swallowing for over a year.

"Wow." He threw his hands up. "I don't even know what to say to that, Sy."

"No, I'm being real. This is not me trying to start a fight with you," I said calmly. "I've never been exactly what you wanted me to be."

"Great way to not start a fight, accuse me of trying to change who you are."

"How else do you expect me to think about this?

You said you were okay with us not being together and now look how you treat me."

"I said I was okay with your decision to be with Rhys." He pointed at me. "He was who you loved, and yet, are you with him?"

"No, because he abandoned me," I said through tight lips. "But I guess you knew that, right? Or did you just assume that all this time I've been with your brother?"

"What?"

"Yeah, work was more important, and if it wasn't for this hybrid shit, I would still be alone, Malachi. Demetrius has done nothing but be nice to me. He welcomed me and this bullshit back into his world even though he is hurting from losing you, Verena, and his child!"

"His what?" Malachi's jaw dropped. "What did you say?"

"Shit." I shook my head. "It wasn't my place to say that."

"What child?"

"He doesn't know for sure, but Verena might have been pregnant when she died. He was going to be a father, and yet when all that shit blew up, where were you? He needed you, but you left, and I have been blaming myself for that. Blaming myself for you needing to go off and heal, but I refuse to take the blame anymore, Malachi."

"I never asked you to take the blame."

"All you've done since we got here is sulk and try to make everyone else feel like shit. When does it end? Me and you aren't together, I get that, but it's not like things are peachy for any of us. I'm struggling to process all of this, to deal with having to potentially kill another one of my family members. Do you see me making everyone else feel like shit because of it?"

"You want a reward for your maturity?" he asked sarcastically.

"I want you to stop acting like a total asshole. I want us to get through this without all this drama. That is what I want. I want to feel like you won't be a liability when we get up there."

"A liability?"

"Your emotions cloud your judgment."

"I'm confused. You wanted to make sure I'm okay. I'm okay. That's enough. I don't need your criticism any more than you need my sulking, so how about we make a deal? I'll smile and get through this, and when it's over, I'll leave. You can do whatever the hell you want, with whoever you want, and you won't have to worry about me again."

"You're just going to run away again?"

"It's what I do best, apparently." Malachi pushed by me and headed back for the campsite.

"Great." I kicked a rock and watched it tumble down the mountain side.

~*~

The next day, we were back on the trail and passed through two more portals before we reached our stopping point.

"This is where we wait," Cornell announced, and Imara and I clung to each other for dear life.

"I need to have sex. Now," Imara huffed. "I think those damn things are sucking the chi right out of me."

"Is that what this is?" I clutched my knees and thought of the one person who could help me feel steady. "When will he be here?"

"I'm not sure," Cornell answered. "We're actually running behind now. He should have been here already."

"How much time do we have before we need to move?" Malachi asked. "I'm assuming my brother had a time set for all this to go down."

"A few hours. Our intel says they're usually calm until then," Cornell confirmed.

"Good." Malachi nodded. "Hopefully he gets here before then."

"Yeah, because we can't go any further." Cornell pointed ahead. "We're just about five yards from their parameter."

The barrier was just ahead of us. Invisible, but the energy it put off was strong. Nate tossed a rock at it, and the damn thing bounced back with such force it almost took his head off.

"No way we're getting through that without a spell." Nate pointed at the invisible wall.

"I still haven't heard from Roxanne." I looked at my phone. "How the hell are we going to get through that thing?"

"I don't think we will have to worry about that." Maggie pointed to the sky, and we all watched as a green projectile that left a trail of yellow smoke behind it slammed into the barrier wall.

The impact was so strong that it shook the

mountain, and we all struggled to keep our feet as the barrier solidified, then fell to the ground around us in large shards of glass that we moved to avoid. I dived to the ground away from the others and looked back when I heard screams of pain.

Mark, a bear shifter, took a cut on the arm after he went left when he should have gone right. His arm bled, and Nate worked quickly, wrapping the wound in a bandage.

After the barrier fell, there was silence, and then three more projectiles struck the ground.

"Move in!" Cornell commanded, and we all ran forward, crossing the rough terrain until we saw the building in the picture Demetrius gave us.

Behind the structure, two massive gray wings lifted in the sky. My eyes followed the being whose shadow cast a massive shadow across the ground. I wanted to get closer, but just then, something hard smacked the back of my head.

I ran forward, catching sight of Malachi, and followed his path, despite the pain in my head. I followed him into the building as more explosions hit. We barely made it inside when the walls crumbled around us.

CHAPTER 24

My head spun as my eyes fluttered, struggling to open against the bright lights. The sterile ceiling above my head moved in waves before settling. I waited, hoping the feeling of internal terror would pass, but it didn't. The longer I lay there, the more intense it felt until I felt like I would vomit.

My thoughts ran wild. That wasn't the first time I'd woken up in a mysterious location, strapped to a bed with no recollection of how I got there. The memories of that moment, of being trapped with a monster, flashed across my mind, and I panicked. Checking my arms and legs, I found that there were no restraints, so I sat up.

The feeling of confusion and nausea got that much worse the moment my head lifted from the pillow. My mouth fell open as I took the massive wall of water in that stood in front of me. The darkness stretched out infinitely. As if that didn't freak me out enough, my lungs seized when the dark, massive body swam past the window.

The massive eye, a yellow and red orb, stared through the window. It stopped, hanging there as if calculating a way to get into the room. My gut told me that if given a chance, the damn thing would swallow me whole. If it could, it would eat me. I stared, didn't move, and hoped like hell it didn't ram into the window. That, for sure, would break it. My heart raced as I recounted scenes from movies of underwater labs and beasts banging against the glass to swallow its inhabitants. Would that be my fate?

Eventually, the massive spectator grew bored with the display and swam on. I didn't know why, but I counted how long it took for it to pass. Sixteen seconds. It took sixteen seconds for the entire body to swim by the window, and when the tip of its gigantic tail passed, I could finally breathe again, and my mind returned to the bigger question. Where the hell was I, and who was responsible?

The nauseous feeling didn't pass. What had they done to me? The last thing I could remember clearly was standing inside the building where the hybrids were. We'd barely made it to them after the barrier came crashing down. We were so close to being done with all of this. So close to understanding what they wanted, and yet, here I was, back at the beginning. Stuck in a point of confusion.

Of course, I had none of my belongings. They dressed me in pale pink sweatpants and a matching sweatshirt. No pockets, and as I looked around the room, the walls were flat. No closet where I might find my stuff.

"Think, girl!" I muttered to myself.

The only thing I could think to do was to reach with my mind, but to who? Rhys had already blocked me, and I was no longer connected to Malachi. I'd never tried to do it with Demetrius, but I pulled him into my dream world. I also apparently called him to my bedroom. If my unconscious mind could do it, then my conscious one had to be able to do it as well.

After several deep breaths, I did the same thing I'd done with Malachi before. Stretched the reaches of my mind, focusing on the man I wanted to speak to. I thought of his voice, his touch, the feeling of calm that came over me whenever we were together, and I pushed my mind to him. I could feel it working, being lifted from my physical form.

And I was foolish enough to think it might actually work. I thought he might answer me, but I felt a hard slam. A wall shot up. Something was stopping me. Demetrius wasn't there. No matter how many times I tried, I met the same resistance. Where was he? What if he was searching for me, hoping to find me and coming up empty?

Giving up on reaching out, I concluded that I was on my own. First, I had to figure out where the hell I was, then I had to free myself.

Everything in the room was white. It felt like being inside a hospital room, which made sense considering the hospital bed I lay in. Again, I took account of everything around me. There was a desk and a chair to my right, and a door to my left. Nothing else. I heard the humming of electricity I assumed was coming from devices left unseen.

Despite the sickening feeling in my stomach, I tried to keep my mind clear and focus on the task at hand. I had to get free. There was a small drawer on the desk. Though I doubted there was anything in it to help me, it was the only option I had.

I swung my legs over the edge of the bed, took a deep breath to calm the urge to empty my stomach on the floor, and hopped off the bed. I fell flat on my fucking face.

"What the hell?" I tried to get up, but my legs felt heavy. I looked down to find that my legs weren't there at all. Instead, my tail, the unique form of red and gold, laid beneath me. "Shit."

I didn't know what the hell was going on, but I knew if whoever held me there found my ass on the floor, they would make sure I couldn't figure it out. I struggled to climb back into the bed, and the second my tail lifted from the floor, my lower half returned to two legs.

"What the fuck?" I asked no one at all.

How was I supposed to get out of there without the use of my legs?

I waited a few moments and tried it again, and again, I fell flat on my face and had to struggle with the weight of my drying tail to pull myself back into the bed. I might have tried again. I was stubborn that way, but I heard approaching footsteps outside my door.

I lay back in the bed, trying to catch my breath. Something in my gut told me the people I heard were coming for me. I needed to appear as normal as a captive siren could.

The steps paused just outside of my door, and voices spoke in a low whisper. One male, one female. When the whispers stopped, one set of footsteps continued down the hall while the doorknob turned. Someone was coming inside.

"Hello, Syrinada," the soft voice spoke as a short woman with light skin and lilac colored hair cut into a bob entered the room. "It's great to see you're awake finally. It's been a few days. We were getting concerned about you."

I looked at her with a blank stare. "Where am I?" I

asked.

"You're in a safe environment."

"That doesn't answer my question." I paused. "Wait, did you say days?"

"Yes, four days, to be exact. Sometimes those guys can get a little heavy-handed with the sedatives. I don't know how many times we have to tell them that one shot is enough. I mean, it's enough to take down two elephants. Why they think more than that is necessary is beyond me. We pulled three needles out of you. To be honest, I didn't know if you would survive or not."

"Who are you?" I asked.

"Who I am is really no concern. My job is to make sure you are okay, keep you safe, and prepare you for what is coming."

"And what's that?" I asked, but she ignored me. I snatched her arm and pulled her closer to me. "Answer my question."

"Ask questions I'm allowed to answer, and I will." She pulled away from me and straightened her jacket, pulling the sleeve down over a small silver bracelet with Greek lettering on it.

"Where the hell am I? What have you done to me? Why can't I get out of this bed?"

"You are in a safe place, as I stated. A facility meant to help strengthen and restore unique beings such as yourself." A practiced smile stretched across her face. "And your legs, well, dear, you see, we must take precautions to protect you at all costs. We can't have you running around and hurting yourself. We have to keep you safe."

"Safe, my ass," I huffed. "Call it what it is, lockdown. As if this isn't really some underwater prison."

"Now, how are you feeling today?" She went on with her task.

"Are you fucking kidding me? You kidnapped me, drugged me, and dumped my ass in an underwater room. How the fuck do you think I'm feeling?"

"Stressed, got it." She pulled out a small tablet and stylus and scribbled notes on the screen.

"Stressed." I rolled my eyes. "That's one way to put it."

"Are you hungry? What would you like to eat?"

My stomach growled at the sound of food, but I didn't answer. Despite the protest from my stomach, I wouldn't be eating anything the woman brought me. If she wanted to pump more poison into me, I would not make it any easier for her.

"I'll send in the salmon. It was fresh today," she

continued when I didn't respond. "I think you will like it. Our notes state you are a fan of fresh seafood."

"Of course, you have notes about me." I chuckled. "This is sick."

"We take pride in understanding our patients as best as we can."

"Patient?"

She tapped the wall behind the bed, and it lit up starting a screen I didn't know was there. I looked over my shoulder to see the numbers and weird symbols, words in languages I didn't understand.

"Your vitals are looking good. Your blood pressure is a tad elevated. It would do you some good to relax, but so far, everything else is in perfect order," she rattled off the information as if I weren't there against my will.

Again, I didn't respond. That cheery airhead wasn't listening to me, and I wouldn't keep wasting my breath.

She did more writing on the pocket tablet and asked me a series of questions about my preferences in food, clothing, and even beverages. All of which I left unanswered. If she wanted the information, she would have to review whatever notes they had about me, and when she was done, she left, the same empty smile plastered across her face.

I lay there in the bed and stared at the ceiling again.

What the hell was I going to do?

Again, I contemplated taking my chances on the floor, but there were footsteps outside the door. This time, they passed by, and a few moments later, I heard another door open and close not far from me. There were other rooms, just like my own. Maybe whoever else they locked away in the so-called safe space could join me in trying to get the hell out of there.

That became the plan. Get to the other mystery guests. To do that meant I had to get out of the room through a door with no knob and without functioning legs. How else was I meant to contact them?

I noticed then that the chair at the desk had wheels. If I could make it to the chair, I could use it to move around. It wouldn't be easy, but it would be better than trying to drag my tail across the floor. All I could hope was that there wasn't a lock on the door. They made it impossible for me to walk. Why would they need a lock on the door?

I waited to see if I heard anymore other movement, when I didn't, I made my move. The first step was throwing myself onto the floor and landing as close to the chair as possible so I wouldn't have to drag my heavy tail far. By the time I climbed into the chair, sweat covered my face and soaked my armpits.

Once in the chair, I lifted my tail from the floor long enough for my legs to return. I almost flipped out of the damn thing, but it worked. I carefully placed my feet on the base of the chair and started the awkward process of pushing myself across the room.

After a few minutes of uncoordinated sliding, I made it to the door. I paused there, waiting to catch my breath before continuing.

"You got this," I tried to motivate myself to continue.

I placed my hand against the part of the door where I saw the nurse touch and held it there, hoping something would happen. Instead of opening like it had for her, the damn thing shocked me. My hand pulled back and cursed the door until I heard footsteps again. I hurried to push myself back across the room to the bed.

Climbing from the chair wasn't as easy as I thought it would be, but I did so without touching the ground again. As soon as I was stable, I kicked the chair, pushing it back across the room to the desk. If anyone saw it out of place, it might alert them to what I was trying to do.

The door opened, and this time, a man entered, pushing a small metal food cart. The smell of salmon filled the room. He didn't speak to me, though he looked like he wanted to. Instead, he went to work transferring the food from the cart to the table that pulled out from the bottom of the bed.

His sleeve lifted, and I saw it. The same small bracelet with Geek lettering just like the one the bubble-headed nurse wore. Was it some welcome tag? The lettering on his was different. Maybe it worked to tell them apart. I imagined he was an aide like in hospitals, whose job it was to dole out food and toiletries.

The silent man laid the food out, straightened the covers on my bed, and fluffed the pillow behind my head. He paused, looking at me closely before opening another hidden compartment and pulling out a towel. He dabbed the sweat from my brow, smiled as if satisfied with my appearance, and then tapped the wall. A thermometer appeared, and he adjusted the temperature. Finished with the job, he went to leave the room but noticed the chair was out of place. Of course, he fixed it and then headed out of the room.

I observed him and tried to hide the shock that filled me when I witnessed how he opened the door. He shook his hand, dropping the bracelet to the base of his wrist, and a knob appeared. When his hand contacted the knob, the bracelet lit up, and there was a faint beeping noise, and then the lock opened. The damn bracelet was a key.

My mind raced. I had to get that damn bracelet. It would be my only chance of breaking free.

Again, I heard the door open at the other end of the hall, and when it did, a deep and angry voice called out. I should have been concerned, but the sound made me happy. My stomach flipped with flutters of butterflies in the recognition of that voice.

Malachi.

CHAPTER 25

Malachi was there, in the underwater prison. That knowledge was the hope I needed. I immediately tried to reach out to him. Using my mind, stretching my energy to him. I knew he was there. All I had to do was reach out to him. I tried for hours to connect with him, but the link between us was severed. I would have to find another way to reach him.

My mind was heavy with exhaustion from trying to leave and from hours of unsuccessfully reaching out to Malachi. I fell asleep hopeful that with a fresh mind I could come up with another plan.

When I woke up, the wall of water was lighter. I took it to mean the sun was up. The smell of fish still lingered in the air from the uneaten meal. I pushed the tray away, accidentally knocking it on the floor, and it only made the smell worse. I groaned and fell back onto the bed.

The sound of footsteps rang out again, and I waited to find out which room they would enter. As the doorknob to my room turned, I had a brilliant thought. If I could hear him, maybe he could hear me. The moment the door opened I hopped up.

"Malachi!" I screamed out. "I'm here, Malachi, it's me—" I couldn't finish because the nurse, whose hair was now a bright shade of pink, slammed the door behind her.

She turned to me, a scowl in place of that odd smile she wore before. Hopefully, he heard me because the usually bubbly woman turned mean.

"Don't do that again. I would hate to have to punish you," she said as she approached me. She stopped and stared at the mess on the floor. "I take it you didn't like the salmon."

"Not particularly." I frowned.

"I'll have Mac clean that up." She pulled out her tablet and tapped away on the screen. "Would you like another meal to replace this one?"

"Keep your fishy meals," I snapped.

"Very well."

She tapped a new area of the wall, and a drawer popped out. Inside, I saw a row of torture tools. She lifted a muzzle from the drawer and laid it on the meal table. A warning, but her threat to me also confirmed what I thought. Malachi was in there. Why else would she want to keep me from calling out his name unless he could hear me?

That was all I needed to know. I let her finish her routine visit in peace. Her questions were still unanswered, and again, she promised to send food I didn't want.

"Try not to get it on the floor next time," she said and stepped around the mess as she headed for the exit.

This routine continued three more times. Three days I sat in the bed trying to figure out what I could do to get to Malachi. I didn't want to call out to him again for fear that the bitch might actually muzzle me. It was hard enough being stripped of my ability to walk. On the third day, as I lay in bed ignoring another plate of food and trying not to go insane with worry, I heard him.

"Sy!" Malachi called my name.

I sat up in bed, but before I could respond, there was the sound of chaos. A battle I hoped would end in our favor, but when the hall outside my door quieted, his door slammed shut, and the footfalls of the aides rang out. They stopped just outside my door.

"We're going to have to move him. It's too risky having them this close," a deep voice spoke.

"I'll put in the request," a fairylike trill answered him.

My heart sank into my stomach. They were going to remove him. If they did, we would lose any hope of getting out alive. Things were tough between Malachi and me, but we worked well together. When shit hit the fan, we put our difficulties aside and got the job done. I needed to get to him before they did.

The man returned with my food. His visits kept me going as I pulled energy from him. I couldn't take much because it might blow my cover. Just enough to keep my mind fresh despite the emptiness in my stomach from not eating.

His routine was the same. Just like the others. He moved like a robot. Entered the door, quick peek out the window, adjust the tray, and place the food. Look around the room for anything that may be out of place, fix things, and leave. This time, my pillow was out of place. I dropped it to the floor just to the left of the bed.

He rounded the bed after placing my food to pick it up, and when he bent over, I had my moment. As soon as he lifted the pillow, I grabbed him. Pulled him to the bed and pressed my lips firmly against his. Humming my siren song, I filled his mind with my will. He gave in as my lips pressed against his, and I pulled more from him. Eyes wide with fear, he softened as his body went limp across the bed. I'd taken just enough to subdue, not to kill. It would keep the man unconscious, hopefully long enough for me to escape.

I had little time to get this done. It took some effort to get the bracelet off his wrist, but when I did, I moved quickly. Again, reaching the chair was a struggle, but thanks to the energy I pulled from Mac, it was a lot easier to accomplish than before. I hopped from the bed to the chair, scooted across the room, and held the bracelet up to the door.

It didn't work initially, and I thought my plan had failed, but I tried again, this time slipping the bracelet over my wrist, and it worked.

I took a deep breath before opening the door and hoped I could make it to Malachi.

Opening the door, I realized my mistake. I assumed his door would be the only other one, but there were five others, two to the left and three to the right. From the sound of footsteps, I knew he was to the right. I had a one in three chance of getting it right.

The hall was empty, so I took the chance and moved. I didn't know how long it would be until they realized Mac was no longer handling his duties. They ran a tight ship, so I was sure they expected him somewhere else. I didn't know what would happen after I made it to Malachi's room, but I knew we would come up with something together.

I scooted the chair down the hall, being careful not to let my feet touch the floor, which was hard considering the walls were flat. I ping-ponged back and forth across the space and took a chance. Something about the second door felt right. It felt familiar. When I made it, I took a deep breath, lifted my hand to the doorknob, and turned.

The door opened, and I looked over my shoulder to make sure I was still safe before struggling to pull myself and the chair through the door. The room was dark, but unlike mine, all four walls were solid. I carefully entered.

I struggled to see in the darkness. There were shadows, but nothing I could make out. Running my hand along the wall, I failed to find a light to turn on. Still, I felt I was in the right place. The sense of familiarity grew the longer I was in the room.

"Malachi? Are you here?" I whispered into the darkness, hoping for a response.

Though there was no response, there was a change. In the back corner of the room, I saw eyes, glowing red hot. It was him. I knew it. Just as I found him before in Xylon, this was Malachi.

The eyes moved, and with the movement came the sound of chains rattling, dragging against the floor. They had him chained like an animal. I continued searching for a light, sliding the chair further into the room as my hand felt for a switch.

I hit gold when the bracelet lit up and engaged a panel. On the screen was a lightbulb. I pressed it, and the room filled with light and revealed Malachi in his demon form. I sat there, waiting for him to react, and when his lips lifted into a scowl, my heart raced with fear. He didn't recognize me.

Malachi growled and charged at me. I pushed against the wall, sending the chair sliding back, and barely made it out of his reach. Still, he tried everything he could to get to me. His claws tore into the floor as he tried to pull himself closer.

"Malachi," I spoke his name. "It's me, Syrinada."

I hoped the sound of my voice would help, but he still didn't recognize me.

"Please." I lifted my hand to him but flinched when he snarled and swiped at me. "Remember me. I need you to know who I am. It's the only way we're going to make it out of this alive."

Carefully, I reached out again, locking eyes with him, and hoped he wouldn't attack me. He allowed me to place my hand on his face, and when I did, Malachi relaxed into me. I took this as a win. He knew who I was, and we would make it out together. I was wrong.

A second after I let my guard down, his large hand wrapped around my wrist and dragged me out of the chair. I lurched forward and fell on my face. Instinct told me to get away, try to crawl out of his reach again, but the moment my feet hit the ground, my legs shifted to tail, and I was too heavy for a quick escape.

Malachi jumped back from me, shaking his head in confusion as he looked at me. He focused on my tail. There was the recognition I wanted. He reached out, touching the tip of my tail, which sparked, and he retreated again.

"Sy?" the distorted voice spoke my name.

"Malachi." I looked up at him from the floor.

"What the hell?"

"Help me. Please." I reached out to him, and he hesitated for a moment before walking over to me.

Malachi lifted me into his arms, and as soon as I was off the ground, my tail shifted back to my legs.

"What's happening?" He stared at my legs and then looked me in the eye. "Sy, this is you, right? Am I losing my mind?"

"No, you aren't. It's me." I sighed. "I don't know how to explain it, but whatever this place is, it's disrupting our magic. We need to get out of here."

"I don't feel good." Even with his distorted features, I could see the worry in his expression. Malachi was afraid.

"Me neither." I looked at the bed. "You can sit me down. As long as my feet don't touch the ground, I'm okay."

"How did we get here?" he asked after placing me on the bed. "What the hell is this? Who did this to us?" Malachi asked questions I didn't have the answers for.

"I wish I knew. I really do, but I don't. Right now, the important part is how we're getting out."

"Where is Demetrius, Imara?" he asked about our siblings, and my heart melted again, remembering that I tried to reach out to his brother and failed.

"I wish I knew, but I hope they're far away from here." My shoulders slumped. "I tried reaching Demetrius the same way I used to reach out to you, but I hit a wall, like there is something keeping me from him and from you."

"I heard you." He touched the sides of his head. "I thought I was dreaming, or my mind was playing games on me, but I heard you calling out to me. It was you, wasn't it?"

"It was, yes." I nodded. "I would have tried again, but that bitch threatened to muzzle me if I did."

"You're alive." Malachi touched my leg, still trying to make sense of my being there.

"Yes, I am."

"They told me..." He slumped next to me on the bed and sobbed.

"Malachi, what's wrong?" I lifted his face. "Tell me."

"They told me you died." He shook his head. "After I heard your voice, I wanted to get to you, but they told me I was wrong, that I could never find you again because you didn't make it out of there."

"I'm here," I confirmed. "A little backward in the tail department, but I'm here."

"What's that about? Why did your tail shift?"

"I don't know. It's been that way since I got here. I'm assuming you've been in your demon form as well?"

"Yes, I don't know where my charm is." He lifted his hand to the empty spot on his chest where the small piece that resembled an eye usually hung. The magic piece that kept his darker side at bay. "Tylia is going to kick my ass if I have to get another one made."

"I think she will be more concerned about your making it out of here alive."

"I hope you're right." He chuckled.

"How do you feel, outside of being unable to turn back?" I touched his face again and really felt the toughness of his skin and the raised areas of flesh. "It's still so strange to see you like this."

"Trust me, this has been me my entire life, and it's not easy for me to look at myself like this either." He placed his hand on top of mind. "I'm okay, a little sick to my stomach. It's been the same way since I got here."

"Have you eaten anything?"

"No, I rather starve to death." He pointed to the tray beside his bed. "They keep bringing me food, but I'll be damn if I volunteer for poisoning."

"Same." I smirked. "Salmon. Every day they bring me salmon, and it sits there stinking up the place."

"When we get out of here, we can get actual food." He paused. "Do you have a plan for that?"

"I hadn't thought that far ahead," I admitted. "I just wanted to know you were here, that I wasn't alone."

"It's time we came up with one." He looked at the door. "They're pretty routine here. It won't be long until they come to check in on us."

"Yeah, soon they're going to realize I'm gone. The guy I knocked out in my room will probably wake up soon."

"Your room."

"Yes, it's just down the hall. Different from this

one."

"How so?" He frowned. "Wait, you knocked a guy out?"

"Actually, I pulled some of his energy. Just enough to give me the strength to get here," I said proudly. "He will be fine, and my room isn't like yours. There is a large window that opens up to the ocean. Did you know we were underwater?"

"I didn't, but that makes sense. The way I feel."

"What do you mean?"

"It's like my legs ache. My tail can sense where we are. It is trying to break free. Maybe that's why yours appears when you touch the ground. There is something really fucked up going on here."

"Yeah, well, hopefully we get out before we find out what the hell they're doing here. I know whatever it is, it's not good."

"Maybe we can break it." Malachi looked hopeful.

"What?"

"You said there is a window in your room. What if we can break through? Did you try?"

"How do you expect to break through a window?"

He looked at his hand. "You shocked me before. Your power is still there. Do you think you can do that trick with your tail?"

"I don't know. It really wasn't my plan to do that. It just happened because I was afraid you were going to kill me."

"Channel that fear, because these people might just try to do that if they catch us."

"Okay, but you're going to have to carry me back to my room. If I touch the ground, I'm useless."

"I think I can handle that." He stood and held his hands out to me. "Wait my chains."

"Oh, put me on the floor?" I asked.

When he did, I turned, focused on my thoughts as my tail reappeared, pointed the tip of my tail to the chains, and it worked. A pop of power, and the chains fell away.

I climbed back into his arms, and he carried me to the door. We paused, listening to see if anyone was approaching, and we heard nothing. In the hall, I pointed to my door, and he quickly carried me over. Once inside, we both took a deep breath. Mac was still on the floor, snoring.

"You really put on in on him, huh?"

"I did what I had to do." I shrugged.

"I'm going to sit you down now. Okay?"

"Yep."

He lowered me to the floor and again my tail appeared.

"Wait." Malachi lifted the desk, carrying it across the room, and jammed it against the door. "Okay, it won't do much, but it may buy us a few more seconds."

"Right."

"Whenever you're ready." He pointed to the window. "Aim and fire."

I closed my eyes, focusing and hoping my magic would work again. The first try created a few sparks but nothing major. I looked at Malachi, who watched me with hopeful eyes. I tried again, pushing my power through the length of my tail, and the second time it worked.

A strong flash of magic shot out of the tip and smacked the glass. It made a small impression but not much.

"Keep aiming for that spot. It will weaken," Malachi ordered.

Three more times, and the fissure spread. On the

fourth time, it opened, and water spilled through, and I felt hope.

I did it again, and this time, the power broke through the glass. When it did, my mind rang with noise as I had a flash feeling of being connected to the outside world. I thought of Demetrius and Rhys, and for a moment, I could feel them both. With the reconnection came something else. The ill-feeling that had my stomach in knots faded.

"You feel that?" I asked Malachi.

"Yeah, I do. It's working." He walked over to the window and touched it with his hand. "Again!"

I did it again, forcing the power to flow from me, and just as I thought it would lead to our freedom, we heard banging on the door. We were running out of time.

"Again, Sy." Malachi pounded the glass with his fist. "Hit it again."

"I'm tired."

"Fuck." He dropped to the floor beside me. "Feed, pull your strength from me."

"I can't. You're just as weak as I am."

"Yeah, but I don't have a powerful tail to break us out, and that damn desk will not hold for long."

"Okay." I nodded, and he kissed me. The dark energy of his demon filled my body and left my head spinning for a moment. I took a deep breath and gave it everything I had left in me.

The sound was explosive. The glass finally broke, and water flooded into the room.

"Yes!" Malachi cheered, preparing to escape.

"Malachi." While he celebrated; my heart filled with terror.

He punched the glass, and it broke further. "One more, and we're out of here."

"Malachi!" I called his name, forcing him to turn his attention to me.

"What is it?"

I pointed to my lower half, where I no longer had a tail. When the water touched me, my legs reappeared.

"How is this possible?"

"It has to be whatever they did to me. I can't swim. I won't survive out there."

"We can make it."

"There was an enormous whale, shark, whatever, outside my window! There is no way I'm going to outswim something like that without my tail."

"Then I'm just going to have to swim for both of us." He punched the glass. "Think you can get another blast off?"

"Not with my tail." I struggled to stand. My legs felt like the water I stood in. I lifted my hands now, using them to channel the energy I needed to break free. There was more to me than my siren half. I was a witch from a powerful bloodline. I needed to use that. Another blast ripped from my palms and slammed into the glass. That was it. That was what we needed.

But it was too late. Before the glass gave in, before Malachi could pull me into his arms, the door burst open, and two massive men tackled Malachi. He fought, but more came in, and as the room flooded with water, the now yellow-haired nursed entered. Anger on her face, she lifted her hand to the window, and the damage reversed.

I felt it again, that connection sharp in the back of my mind, and I screamed out with my mind. This was the only chance I would have to connect with him. I hoped like hell he would hear me, and he could find me. Mentally I screamed out to the only person I felt could help us.

Just as they pulled me from the room, and before the window sealed shut, I heard him respond.

"I'm coming."

CHAPTER 26

I laid in the new room, this time tied to the bed. They weren't taking any chances. I fought. I tried my best to stay with Malachi, but they pulled us in two different directions. A bag slid over my head, and all I could do was listen as he struggled to fight for freedom.

This time, I was in an unfamiliar room. There were no windows, and it had the powerful scent of cleaning solution. Someone else was in the room. I could hear the clamoring of tools and the clinking of glasses they moved around.

I looked to the left to see the back of someone's head. Long orange braids fell down their back, clashing against the same white outfit the others wore. It was hard to see. My head spun again, and I saw the tubes connected to the bag hanging above my head.

"You're an interesting specimen. The first one to

even come close to escaping." He turned around. "It surprised me to see that, but it makes for substantial data collection."

He walked over to me, and I could see the rainbows in his eyes. Bright orbs of light danced behind his iris, and I warmed. What was this effect he had on me? My panic subsided, and I sank, heavy like a boulder, into the bed. Something inside told me to fight, to resist his touch, but I couldn't.

"Syrinada, such a pretty name." His voice was a warm breeze caressing against my soul. A verbal tranquilizer. When he spoke, my eyelids felt heavy, and a yawn crept up my throat.

"Who are you?" I said drowsily.

"You ask the wrong questions, dear," he said, sounding eerily similar to the bubble headed nurse.

"Why am I here?" I changed my question.

"Yes, better question indeed. Why?" He turned from me and moved around a few more items on the table. "We should always ask why. Not enough people are concerned with the why. They only want to know what and how, but never why. Imagine, living a life, toddling along, and not understanding the purpose of what you're doing. People should never be so content with their ignorance."

"What do you want from me?" I asked another question I feared he wouldn't actually answer.

"And we get closer to gold." He smiled. "I say, if you keep this up, you just might ask the right one."

"You're avoiding. Answer my questions."

"Observant as well." He smiled, and there was a light behind his eyes that grew with intensity. "In time, but for now, you need to rest. There is much that needs to be done."

I didn't know how long it was that I went in and out of consciousness, but the feeling of intense warmth that covered my body whenever I would wake coddled me and pushed me back into a deep slumber. That was also the first time in a while I didn't have actual dreams. It wasn't the recounting of the past or the imaginings of the future. It was icy darkness, emptiness, a void that no matter how hard I tried, I couldn't escape.

Every time my eyes opened he was there. Still messing about with things on the table. He did nothing with the tools. I wondered if they were just props, something for him to do with his hands while he worked his magic on me.

It was in his eyes. I came to realize that hypnotic rainbow with the strange warm back light. It worked on me every time I would wake. I struggled to ask questions he would never answer. He only rambled on about what was and wasn't the right thing for me to ask but never actually gave me information when I posed a question he thought poignant. And then that voice would turn on me. It shifted from normalcy to the melody that reached into my heart and made me feel whole and relaxed.

It felt like at least three days before I got out of the bed again. It was hard to tell without the window opening up to the sea to showcase the change of lighting. Unlike my former caretaker, he did not offer me food. He didn't pretend it was necessary for my survival.

He spoke about human behavior and how times were soon to change. We were supposed to navigate the world with questions to understand our purpose. It became a broken record playing over and over in my mind until I would fall asleep again.

"Please stop this." I shook away the clouds from my mind when his voice once again became the changed sound meant to subdue me.

"I'm sorry?"

"Stop this," I repeated. "Get out of my head."

"I am not in your head."

"I feel you, your energy. You're trying to put me back to sleep. Stop it."

He paused, looking down at me pensively before

responding. "There is more work to be done, but this will pass soon enough."

I continued to go in and out of consciousness until finally I woke alone. There was no tinkering man, moving around tools he never used. The heaviness was gone from my brain. I sat up in the bed, no longer strapped down by restraints. The lights above my head were brighter, giving me an instant headache. My legs ached, and I rubbed them.

"You can get up if you like." He came around the corner.

"Yeah right and fall flat on my ass when my legs turn into a tail again."

"Oh, we've fixed that. It was supposed to be a precautionary measure, but it appears we underestimated your power. Both unsettling and exciting." He looked at me like I was a piece of clay fit for molding. Or one he'd just taken out of the kiln. Either way, I didn't like it.

I looked at the floor like they made it of lava. Did I trust him? I couldn't tell if it was a smart move or not, but what else was I supposed to do? Despite what he wanted I was still going to find a way out of that place. I slowly put my legs over the edge of the bed and dropped to the floor.

My feet touched the floor, and I frowned, waiting for the shift that would land me on my face again. When my legs remained, my shoulders relaxed. My legs hurt, perhaps from lack of use, perhaps from something else they'd done to me.

"Explore your new room," he suggested. "It's not much to it, but it's better than what you had before."

"No ocean view?" I joked.

"Not a mistake we're willing to make twice."

I walked around, just enjoying having legs again. The room was no better, blank, except there was another door, a bathroom.

"You can take a shower," he happily offered. "It's been a while for you, hasn't it?"

"You would know better than I do. I don't even know how long I've been here."

"Seventeen days."

"What?"

"You've been here, at our facilities, for seventeen days." He checked his notes. "Yes, seventeen days."

"In the facilities you won't tell me the purpose of."

"You never asked the purpose of these facilities. You only asked why you were here."

"Fine." I took a deep breath to cool my attitude.

"What are the purposes of these facilities?"

"Ah, an answer I can provide." He smiled. "Our purpose at Xenco is to perform genetic testing on supernatural beings."

"Genetic testing?" I frowned.

"Yes, it's actually quite fascinating. We have so many subjects of blended species. Some are not as successful as other, but you, oh you were something like we've never seen before."

"I bet."

"Honestly, you're the one we've been waiting to bring in. Able to fully possess the powers of both sides of your lineage and develop new ones we couldn't have imagined. The seeds you will carry to fruition will be magnificent. We just have to find the right paring."

"Excuse me? Seeds?" I stepped back. "What the hell do you mean seeds?"

"Yes, of course. Reproduction has always been our goal." He sat down. "The point of this is to breed vessels strong enough not only to do wonderful things but to possess a power this world has only seen once before. We aim to bring that power back here, but we need vessels strong enough."

"Yeah, I'm not having any babies." I shook my head. "You can get that out of your head."

"Oh, but you will." He smiled.

"What is this power?" I tried to redirect him from thoughts of impregnating me.

"I really shouldn't tell you." He shook waved a thin finger at me. "Secrets and all."

"Hey, you want me to pop out a child so you can infuse it with some power I don't know. Tell me. It's not like I can swim out of here, right? You made sure of that."

He looked around, paranoid, then lowered his voice. "Alright, I just have to talk about this with someone else."

"Okay." I stepped forward.

"We're bringing them back." The smile stretched across his thin face, and even though I didn't know who he was talking about, it made the hair stand on the back of my neck.

"Bringing who back?"

"The titans, of course." His eyes widened with excitement. "We want to bring them back. They belong here. Something big is going to happen soon, and if they aren't here, we will have no way of stopping it."

"You can't be serious." The only titans I knew of were buried in the depth of hell and put there by a powerful god, and if I hadn't lived through some seriously freaky shit, I would have questioned this man's sanity for thinking any of it was real.

"Oh, but I am." He grinned. "Years of research and development, and we're almost there!"

"You expect me to believe you want to bring back centuries old power and put inside of me?"

"It's a little more complicated than that. We need to dig them up from the earth. We know the locations, but they can be tricky to get to. Once they're here, they need a vessel. The ones we've found haven't lasted very long at all. Trolls and Giants seem to withstand the pressure the best. This is the only way we are going to bring them back. Creating a vessel genetically prepared to hold their power. The gods are trying to come back to earth, and if that happens, they will rain fire on all the world. The Titans are our only way to stop that from happening."

"You know how insane this sounds, right?" I searched the room for anything I could use as a weapon should he attack, but of course, there was nothing.

"Yes, I do, but that doesn't make it any less true. This organization has been working for decades to make this happen. Doing research and bringing the information needed to get this together. Now that you are here, we finally have the right combination."

"You didn't make me. My sick father did."

"Yes, and how do you think he got the idea for it?"

"I…"

"Yes, it was us. We fed him the delusions of grandeur. It's typically enough to make the power-hungry man of any species act. It took a lot of time to figure out that this was the combination of power we needed. You can feed off the life force of anyone and give it back. Not all sirens can do that. You're also able to use the natural powers of the world around you, further adding to your strength. This is what we need. You will produce babies so strong they will contain the souls of the returning titans. It's a precaution in case their bodies break down when we wake them."

"You're doing all of this, and you don't even know if it's necessary?"

"Well, no, but we have proof."

"Proof?"

"Yes, some that have returned already, and their bodies, their vessels, aren't able to contain them. To avoid this, I believe we must extract the titans' souls. We haven't figured out how to keep them intact. Such a tricky thing this all is. It's going to be a wonderful thing you will be a part of."

"I am not doing this."

"Oh, dear. I'm sorry, but you don't have a choice.

This is what we made you for, and the testing shows we finally got it right." He turned from me. "This must happen soon. We won't be able to keep their energy on this plane for much longer without a proper vessel. If we fail, it will mean so many years of work lost. People have lost their lives for this."

"I don't give a damn about who lost their lives."

"Oh, but you will."

"You want me to have babies you can put titan souls in?"

"Well, yes. We just need to get the right mate for you, and I'm sure he'll be here soon. You reached out to him, yes?"

"What?"

"Your mate." He nodded. "When the glass broke."

"Demetrius," I said his name, horrified.

"Yes, that's the one. Strong. Even came back from the dead to be with you."

"What?"

"Oh yes, he died but fought his way back from the depths of hell to return to you. Have you not had that conversation yet? It was quite a show to witness."

"You're lying. Demetrius didn't die. He survived."

"He told you that, did he?"

"He—"

"That is a conversation the two of you will have to have. For now, you really should get rest."

I felt him in my head again, that heavy fog that took over. "No, don't do this again."

"I'm sorry, but there really is no other way."

I felt his arms catch me as the floor disappeared beneath my feet, and he carried me back to the bed.

CHAPTER 27

DEMETRIUS

We'd just made it to Denali when we saw it. The explosion that shook the mountain. As quickly as we raced through the portals to reach the top, we weren't fast enough. Crossing the last one, the team came out just as the rest of the building crumbled.

"Search every fucking inch!" I ordered the team. "Find them!"

It was like walking into a war zone. Someone had attacked the hybrids' hold, but who? Who else was looking for this place? Who else knew the hybrids existed?

"Demetrius." Cornell approached me, dirty and grime covering every inch of his body.

"Did you find her?" I asked. "Is she okay?"

He shook his head. "We've tried. She isn't here."

"Keep looking," I ordered. "I'm not leaving here without her."

Syrinada was gone. We looked everywhere, turned every stone, but there was no sign of her.

Ash covered every inch of the mountainside. I did not know what happened, and I still tried to make sense of it. We accounted for most of the team that went up the mountain. Everyone except Malachi, Syrinada, and Imara. Where the hell were they?

I looked at the damage when Nate approached me. Crissette was right by his side.

"What happened here?" I asked. "Tell me everything."

"Man, we did everything you said. We were waiting for you to get here. Syrinada and Maggie were trying to figure out how to get through that barrier because they had received no help from the witch, but then everything went to shit. We looked up, saw the first strike, and then just chaos."

"Who was it?" I asked.

"I have no idea, D. That thing was like an aircraft, but it looked alien, fluid. I could barely get my eyes to focus on it, but it hit again and again and then claws ripped creatures up from the ground."

"They came for the hybrids." I examined the scene again. "They're the only ones missing."

"We can't find the others," Crissette offered. "Not one person who should have been in there."

"If they hoped to get the hybrids, we delivered three powerful ones right to them." I kicked the brick next to me. "Fuck! They knew we were coming."

"Who?" Nate asked. "Who could have done this?"

"I don't know, but I'm going to find out."

"What do you want us to do?" Cornell walked up again. "Everyone's gathered, ready to proceed however you see fit."

"Keep looking. We're not leaving here until I know more. I refuse to believe this was a random attack by an unknown entity. They did everything they could to destroy this place. They did that for a reason. We need to find out what they were trying to cover up."

I pulled the phone from my pocket. The screen was lit with the message icon. I tapped it to find her name. There was one message, typed with errors.

Something's wrong.

That was all she said. Something was wrong. She didn't have enough time to understand what was going on. Knowing her, she raced in to help without thinking about how it might hurt her.

Not everyone survived what happened. Hours into scouring the land, we pulled up bodies. Nate sobbed over Deek, his long-time friend, a panther shifter who didn't make it out of the blast alive. It was hard to watch as we tried to pull ourselves together.

"I think I found something." Cornell ran up to me, wiping ash from his face.

"What is it?" I turned to him, hopeful whatever it was would lead us to the missing members of our team.

"It's a laptop, pretty beat up, but maybe we can get something off it." Cornell handed the black computer to me. "There isn't much tech here, so this stands out to me."

"Are you sure it's not one of ours?" I examined the charred casing carefully.

"No, it was behind the walls." He pointed to the broken structure. "Only ones that made it in before it collapsed were Syrinada, Malachi, and Imara."

"Maggie." I thought of the sarcastic girl with the insatiable appetite.

"What?" he asked.

"Where is Maggie?" I looked up from the computer in my hands. "Has anyone seen her?"

"The ghost chick?"

"Yes." I frowned. "The ghost chick."

"No one has seen her since the first blast. Maybe it took her out. What happens to someone who is already dead when they get blown up?"

"Seriously?"

"Sorry." He shrugged. "It was a genuine question."

"Finish cleaning the area. We need to get out of here. I need to find them."

I knew it was a long shot, but I called her. I dialed the number of the phone I'd given to Syrinada, but it went straight to voicemail. Malachi's number also took me straight to voicemail, but that had been the case for months. Couldn't be sure he ever unblocked me.

I looked around. There had to be something. Something we were missing. The laptop was a good lead, but we needed more. How long would it take to get anything valuable from it, if there was anything there at all? As I walked around, kicking the rubble aside, I heard her. A small cough followed by a soft moan of pain.

I lifted the fallen debris. The closer to the center of the building, the worse it was. I threw brick and rubble to the side and nearly gave up, but I saw her hand sticking out beneath another plank. I pulled it up, and there was Imara.

"Shit." I pulled her into my arms. "Are you—"

I wanted to ask if she was okay, but the woman latched onto me and instantly fed. I watched my energy pull from my mouth in a flow that filled her body. Her eyes lit up a cool blue as she took only what she needed to, maybe a little more. I fell back, still holding her in my arms as she finished her feed.

"Demetrius?" She looked up at me as that cool light faded from her eyes. "What are you doing here?"

"Someone attacked. We didn't get her in time to help. Are you okay?" I breathed deeply to push away the dizziness caused by her feed.

"She pushed me out of the way. They almost took me, but she saved me." She coughed, throat still dry from ash and dust.

"What?" I knew who she was talking about, her sister.

"Sy, they took her?" She looked around. "Demetrius, did they take her?"

"I don't know. We're still trying to figure it out. There are a lot of people hurt, but we haven't found Malachi or Syrinada. I was worried you were lost, too." I stood and held my hand out to her. "Did you see anything at all?"

"I don't know." She grabbed my hand, and when she was on her feet, she continued. "Wait, there were people. They appeared out of nowhere. Big as hell, too. They had to be like seven feet tall. We couldn't see them at first, you know. We tried, but they were wearing some weird suits. It made them look blurry. I could feel them though, you know?"

"Are you sure?"

"Yes, and they came in here. It was all a trap. Those hybrids, the ones they sent us here to talk to. They weren't even alive. Most of them are already dead. They were bait. I think they thought they were here to do something more. I don't know what to think. It's all jumbled."

"Calm down. We need to get you out of here. You need to save your strength. We can talk about this when we get somewhere safe. Something tells me they're not done with this place."

The men did more searching, hunting through the broken building, hoping to find anything. It would be days before we excavated it all, and even then, we may still never know what the truth was. By the time we made it back to the campsite, they'd found two more computers and a small metal box. We tried to open it, but magic sealed it.

"How the hell are you going to get that thing open?" Cornell pointed to the box and handed me a cold beer.

"I don't know, but I'm sure I know someone who does." I accepted the offered drink.

"Be careful. I don't know what that was, but it was like nothing we've ever seen before," he noted.

"I'll keep that in mind." I watched over my team, who loaded the vehicles that would carry our crew to the plane.

"If you need anything," Cornell offered, as always.

"Take care of your people. You've already lost so much." I touched his shoulder. "I'll handle it from here."

"We're leaving?" Imara asked, returning from her shower. Her short hair was clean from the dirt and hung loosely around her face. She looked like her sister.

"Yes, I think we got all we're going to get from here. The men will keep digging for information. If they find anything, they'll send it our way." I handed her a new jacket to wear. "How are you feeling?"

"I'm okay. Sore as hell, but I'll recover." She rolled her shoulder.

"Do you need to feed?" I asked and thought of how many times I'd wondered the same thing about Syrinada. Was she okay? Did she need to feed?

"Your friend helped me out." She winked at Cornell.

"Glad he could assist you." I nodded because, as much as I cared about her safety, I didn't want to feed her again. It was wrong on so many levels.

"Where exactly are we headed?" Imara asked.

"One of your favorite places, New Orleans."

"Oh sweet, I could use some good beignets!"

All I knew was Syrinada was missing, so was my brother, and the one person I needed to talk to was one I wanted nothing to do with. Rhys.

~*~

"Are you feeling better now?" I watched Imara climb down the steps of the plane, wiping her lips.

"Yes, thank you." She looked back over her shoulder at the door. "I'm sorry to use so many of them."

"None of them looked like they were unhappy about it." On the long plane ride from Alaska to New Orleans, she'd fed on every man in the vessel beside me and the pilot. As soon as the plane touched down, she went for him.

She left my men exhausted but alive. Most would

recover soon. One, however, would need about a week. It was safe to say she liked the werewolf from Maine.

"I guess not." She smiled. "I feel great, though. Ready to go kick some sister stealing asses!"

"Great, now that you're restored, you think you can fill me in on what happened?" I opened the car door for her, walked around, and jumped into the driver's seat. "Every account I've gotten has been from the outside. What happened in there?"

"Well, you know what happened leading up. The barrier breaking and the attack. Malachi ran in, and Syrinada and Maggie followed. So did I. The others were scrambling to take cover. The further we ran the more blasts came. Then there was the smell of death, like stomach turning decay. There was no way that was fresh, you know?"

"You think they were dead before you got there?"

"Not everyone, but someone was." She nodded. "When we got close enough, Maggie went in, all ghostly, and came back to tell us what she saw."

"And that was?"

"Those hybrids were already half dead. Most of them were dead. Something bad happened to them. Here's the weird part. The blasts that broke the barrier didn't touch the building. They were strategic, hitting the outer walls, but the interior was fine. That was, until we went inside to investigate."

"What did you find?"

"We only found one person who was still alive. A dragon, I think. She had scaled skin, but it looked like she was struggling to shift. Her stomach was ripped open, like an alien had come out of her."

"Did she say anything?"

"Only things she said was to run. She told us to run and hide." Imara took a deep breath. "Demetrius, this was a trap. Whoever took Syrinada and Malachi knew we were coming. Anyone they wanted from that place they'd already taken, and the rest, they'd killed."

"What the hell is going on?" I put the key in the ignition and started the engine.

"I have no idea, but it's sick. The next thing we knew, bombs were going off. Maggie disappeared, like something ripped her from this world. I looked up as Sy pushed me out of the way and half the building came falling down on top of me. The next thing I remember was you standing above me. Sorry I pulled from you."

"Don't worry about it," I reassured her. "You needed to feed. I'm just glad I found you in time."

"Yeah, but I know how my sister feels about you. Just make sure there is no misunderstanding."

"Hmm." She knew how Syrinada felt about me. Funny, because I didn't.

"What?" she asked.

"Nothing." I kept my thoughts to myself. It would have been inappropriate to use that moment to find out what she knew about Syrinada's feelings toward me.

"What are we going to do? I mean, they're gone, aren't they?" Imara stared out the window, the same pensive expression I'd seen on her sister's face many times before. "Where are they?"

"I don't know, but I know how we can find them. We're going to have to talk to Rhys." I gripped the steering wheel tighter, having said his name aloud.

"Rhys, the one she chose over both of you." Imara wasn't one for tact.

"Yes." I couldn't mask the hurt in my response. My jaw tightened, and my heart ached. She'd chosen him, a witch, over me. I'd never said how much it hurt me, but it did.

"And somehow she is still mated to you?" Imara spoke to what everyone so clearly observed.

"Yes." I nodded. "I'm not sure how it's possible, but she is. Despite the ritual to break our bond."

"You know, you guys have some complicated shit. I

used to think my life was a shit show, you know, trying not to kill people with sex." She leaned back in her seat. "After I managed that, it was all pretty smooth, but I'll take that over this shit any day of the week."

"It must be hard, being with Malachi and knowing all of this." I wondered how she was handling her side of the messy scenario.

"At first, yes, but hell, I'm not a one-man kind of woman either. I really care for Malachi, but even he isn't enough for me, and I can tell he hates that about me."

"Yeah, my brother is a monogamy kind of guy." I chuckled.

"And what about you?" She turned in her seat to look me in the face. "What kind of guy are you? You're mated to her. She is in love with him."

"I'm, well, I don't know what I am anymore. That changed. A lot about me has changed."

"Is it a change you want, or is it one you're giving into for her?"

"I wish I could tell you." I shifted the gear, and the car lurched forward.

"Something tells me you better figure it out before you face her witchy beau."

"That gives me approximately two hours. I'll see if

I can make that happen."

CHAPTER 28

DEMETRIUS

Even sitting in the car with the windows up, the smell of Roxanne's food had my stomach growling. No doubt she knew we were coming long before we headed her way. Even so, she didn't come out of the house to greet us. A careful move to allow for pensive planning and nervous reconsideration of our visit.

"Do you plan to sit out here all day, or are we going to go inside?" Imara asked. "I know you smell that food. Sex is a substantial meal, but ya girl is starving for something real, like beignets."

"How do you know she made beignets?"

"Hey, this is Roxanne we're talking about. She knows what I like." Imara tapped the door handle.

"Does she?" I looked at her from the corner of my eye. "I didn't realize you two were so close."

"Yes, Malachi and I kinda stayed with her a bit when we were here." She shrugged. "The woman is truly hospitable."

"Right." I looked at the welcoming doorway. "Alright, let's get this over with."

We exited the car, checking our surroundings once more before climbing the stairs. I'd knocked exactly once before the door swung open.

"Demetrius, how good to see you here." Roxanne stood with a warm smile and knowing eyes.

"Hello, Roxanne, may we come in?" I asked as we met her on the porch.

"Of course. Oh, it's you." She looked at Imara. "Back for more beignets, I imagine."

"You remembered!" Imara smiled and winked at me. "I mean, if you have any on hand."

"Of course, I do." Roxanne pointed to the kitchen. "Got some fresh in the kitchen cooling off now."

"Oh, you are the best!" Imara clapped. That time, her actions reminded me of Maggie. The girl we hadn't heard from since shit went haywire.

Roxanne stepped back, opening the door wider so we could enter the home. Just as it did the last time I'd visited the witch's home, the relaxing sensation, the homey embrace, washed over me, and suddenly, I wanted to take a long nap.

"What brings you here?" our host asked as she took the lead, rounding the corner to enter the small sitting room.

"We need to talk to Rhys," I answered as I took the seat she pointed out to me.

"He isn't here, but he's headed home." She glanced at the clock that hung on the wall behind me. "Shouldn't be long until he gets here, but I have food ready, and you two make yourselves at home."

"How are things with the coven?" I asked, making small talk, but the answer really concerned me. The things I'd learned about the vampires raised more interest in what was happening within the covens. I knew she wouldn't tell me too much, though.

"Things are good, finally. Hasn't been this way in a long time. That's a big part of what Rhys has been doing. I know he hates to be away from Syrinada so much, but the balance of our people was off in a big way." A proud expression touched her face. "He's played a big part in putting that back right."

"I'm sure he has." I dropped my eyes to the carpeted floor.

"Wait, is something wrong with Syrinada?"

Roxanne asked. "Is that why you're here?"

"She is missing," Imara admitted.

"Missing?" Roxanne's eyes widened. "I assumed she was with your brother, but—"

"She is. At least we think she is. Either way, I need your son's help to find her."

"Well, hell, what he is doing can wait." She walked out of the room and called Rhys. Moments later, after the sound of rushing air, he came walking through the front door and storming down the hall.

"Where is she? What's wrong?" Rhys asked with panicked eyes.

"Hello, Rhys," I greeted him.

"Where is Syrinada?" he asked again, looking at me as if I had kidnapped her myself.

"Don't be rude." Roxane popped him on the shoulder. "That's not the way we greet guests in this home."

"Hello, Demetrius," he huffed. "Where is she?"

"We don't know. That's why we're here. There was an attack in the mountains, and she, along with my brother, was taken," I reported. "I'm hoping you can help track her down with that dream space of yours."

"Why do you need me for that? You were there." Rhys looked at me like he wanted to put his fist through my face, and I couldn't blame him for it. He had every right to hate me.

"Not by choice and not by hers, either. It was a freak accident." That was about as much explanation as I was willing to give him about what happened. "That is a space you created with her. I cannot access it. It has to be you."

"Fuck." Rhys pressed his fist against the wall, clearly stifling the urge to punch it out of respect for his mother's home.

"What's wrong?" Roxanne asked.

"I destroyed it," he revealed.

"What?" I jumped from my seat. "What do you mean you destroyed it?"

"When I saw you there with her." He looked at me. "I unraveled the thread. It took both of our magic to build that bridge."

"So, we can't find her?" Imara spoke for the first time since Rhys' arrival.

"Not like that, no," Rhys answered her.

"There has to be another way," Imara said, and her cool demeanor finally cracked.

"I'm sure there is." Roxanne crossed the room to comfort Imara. "And we'll find it, but first, you all need to eat. This isn't the type of work to be done on empty stomachs."

"Right," Imara agreed.

"Let's go give these two a moment to cool their jets." Roxanne led Imara out of the room and called back to us. "I suggest you two put your differences aside now."

Roxanne intended for us to talk, but where there was a lot that needed to be discussed, and neither of us cared to. Our focus was on Syrinada, and even though he had his jaw set as tight as a vice grip, I knew Rhys was on the same page. We could never be friends. We could never simply overlook the uncomfortable feeling of loving someone who wasn't completely yours.

"Are we really going to talk about this?" Rhys asked, looking at the doorway where his mother left.

"Is there really anything to say?" I looked him in the eye when he turned back to me.

"I guess there isn't." He inhaled. "Look, I just want to make sure she is safe. That's all. Anything outside of that isn't my business."

"What is that supposed to mean?"

"I'm sure she told you I wanted to end things."

I didn't respond.

"I don't know that I can do this. Be on the other side of you." Rhys pointed at me. "But I love her, and I want her to be okay."

"That feeling is mutual," I responded.

"So, we get her back, and everything else is mute until she is safe," Rhys issued the truce.

"Agreed," I accepted it.

BREAK

"Can you reach her?" Imara rationed the last of the beignets, putting small pieces in her mouth to savor the flavor.

"What?"

"If Rhys can't, maybe you can." She pointed to me. "Don't you have your own sort of psychic connection to here? At least, that's what Malachi said it was. He tried once to connect with her, but it didn't work. Said the bond was broken. But you two—"

She stopped, finally noticing how Rhys' face turned red.

"Oh, shit, sorry," she apologized to him.

"No, you're right. There is a bond. If we can use it

in our favor, then we should." He turned to me. "You should try it."

"Okay." I put my cup of sweet tea down on the table. "I'll try."

I didn't tell them I'd been trying to reach Syrinada through our bond since the moment she disappeared. Every time I did, I hit an invisible wall that bounced my emotional outcry back to me, but I tried again. I closed my eyes, took deep breaths, and reached with my mind to the woman I once felt on the other side of a faint connection, and again, I hit that wall.

"It's like something is keeping me out," I said. "It just pushes me away from her."

"What?" Rhys asked. "What exactly are you feeling?"

"Wherever she is, it's protected by powerful magic. I can feel her there. I just can't get through," I explained.

"So, she is still alive," Imara said with hope. "That's good, right?"

"You'll have to keep trying," Rhys urged.

"Of course, I will," I answered and tried to keep my annoyance out of my tone. Obviously, I would keep trying.

I spent the next four days of trying to reach her to no avail while Rhys and Roxanne repaired the bond between them. Just as Rhys said, without Syrinada's energy, there was no way to recreate the space the two once shared with each other.

On the fifth day, Roxanne sat at the head of the dinner table looking at three worried faces.

"I've put a call out to Deuterio," she announced.

"What?" I looked at her, shocked that she hadn't discussed the decision with me. "When?"

"This morning," she said plainly. "What we're doing here isn't working, and we don't know how much time we have left. Siliya needs to be here with us. She has a connection to her daughter, and I'm hoping she'll be able to strengthen what we're trying to accomplish here."

"Is it safe?" Rhys asked. "Things between the covens and the sirens are still on rough terms."

"We have a shared interest here," Roxanne explained. "Whatever is happening with Syrinada is going to impact all of us. Not just the sirens or the witches."

"Have you heard anything back?" I asked, skeptical that they heard her message.

"Yes, Siliya is heading here soon," Roxanne

answered.

"What about the council?" I asked. "What are they going to do?"

"I'm not sure," she answered. "I didn't ask for any council. I asked for Siliya."

"Is this going to be a problem?" Imara asked, pushing her food around her plate just as she had been doing for the past five minutes.

"It might. I hadn't reported any of this to the council."

"Why?" Rhys asked.

"They are looking for any reason to hurt Syrinada. If they think for a moment that something has corrupted her, they won't hesitate to strike."

"How is that fair?" Imara straightened. "Someone kidnaps her and does who knows what to her, and they're blaming her?"

"They're afraid of her," Roxanne said. "Always have been."

"She did nothing wrong!" Imara smacked the table.

"No one here believes she did," Rhys said, placing his hand on her shoulder. "We're on her side, and we're going to make sure she is safe."

The next morning, Siliya arrived, but she wasn't alone. Three others joined her. Two men and a woman. The men I knew. Miguel was a merman older that I was, but not as strong. He had white hair that hung down his caramel skin in loose braids. Keon, another who was younger but eager and kept close to Siliya. He flowed with her like the currents of the sea. He had a bald head, dark skin, and a wide nose that wrinkled when he smiled. Something he did every time Siliya spoke.

"What's going on there?" Imara whispered in my ear after noticing the vibe between the Siliya and her companion.

"I don't know, and I'm not asking questions." I chuckled.

The third, a woman, was someone I'd never encountered. She was full figured and had breasts the size of my head. A fact I tried hard not to focus on. This was made difficult because they practically waved at me every time she spoke. When she mentioned having a twin sister, I wondered if they shared those assets. I forced the creep thoughts from my mind as she held her hand out to me.

"Demetrius Denali, I've heard so much about you." She placed her hand in mind and shook. "I'm Lafe. Nice to meet you."

"You as well." I smiled, noting the faint discoloring of a scar that stretched across her face. The horizontal mark lay just beneath her eyes, reaching from one side of her face to the other.

An hour later, we were all sitting around the dinner table again. Roxanne quickly produced a meal that had to be aided by magic. The feast was so much there was barely room on the table for our plates. Lafe took the chair to the right of me, while Imara claimed the one to the left. Rhys squeezed in between Miguel and Keon, who still looked at Siliya like she was the air he needed to breathe.

While Roxanne filled the table with another delicious meal, Rhys and I reported what happened to Siliya.

"So, my daughter ran into a castle on the side of a mountain and was abducted?" Siliya looked across the table at us.

"Yes," Rhys answered.

"And neither of you, her mates, can reach her?"

"Yes," I groaned because I hated being lumped in with Rhys. "We've been trying for days."

"So that leaves us here," Roxanne said as she sat down. "Trying to figure out a way to repair the connections. I hoped your bond with your daughter would help us."

"I wish I could say it would," Siliya said, near tears. "But since her father died, the connection between us isn't the same."

"So, we're screwed then?" Imara leaned back in her seat. "This is ridiculous."

I wanted to say something to comfort her, but as I began, my heart raced, and my head felt like it was being ripped from my shoulders. I clutched the edge of the table as a surge of energy ripped through me and screamed.

"What's wrong?" Imara touched my shoulder, then jumped back when the connection shocked her. "Dammit, what was that?"

"It's her," I said through gritted teeth. "I can feel her!"

My fingers dug into the table, leaving an impression in the wood as my own name rang in my head. My name spoken in her voice. Syrinada was trying to reach out to me, and it filled me with conflicting emotions. Rage because I could tell she was hurting, and relief because I knew she was alive.

All I could say was, "I'm coming," and then the wall slammed back in place. I hoped she heard me on the other side before we were cut off.

"It's gone." I fell back into the chair. "She's gone."

"Are you sure it was her?" Siliya rushed to my side. "Was it Syrinada?"

"Yes, it was her. She was afraid. There was a struggle. I don't know."

"Think!" Rhys clutched his drink, his face telling his frustration. "There has to be more. What did you see? Did you feel anything?"

I closed my eyes and focused on the experience. There was more than just her voice. There were flashes in between the intense moments and sounds. A white room, men struggling, a large window broken, and leaking water into the room.

"She's under water," I said.

"What?" Siliya asked. "Where?"

"Some strange room, under water, there was a large window. She broke through it, but they stopped her."

"Who stopped her?" Imara asked.

"I don't know." I shook my head. "There was a struggle, a lot of bodies moving around."

"I need to get to my daughter," she said. "Keep

trying. If she is under water, I think there is a way to find her, but I can't do it here."

An hour later, we waved goodbye to Siliya and her companions. She'd explained to us she intended to return to Deuterio and enlist the help of a few of her friends. Since Syrinada was underwater, the best bet would be to leverage her network in the sea. Someone had to know something about the underwater structure.

"She's fighting." Rhys sat down on the sofa in the living room.

"Of course, she is," I said, my chest swelling with pride, taking the armchair across from him.

"Maybe you can get through now," Imara suggested to Roxanne. The two of them stood in the center of the room, discussing our options.

"I'll need a link to her power." Roxanne thought about what Imara suggested.

"Wait," Imara brightened.

"What?" Roxanne asked.

"I know very little about this magic thing, but can't you use Demetrius?" Imara pointed to me.

"What?" Rhys straightened.

"You need a connection to her. Demetrius has a mental connection. We have proof that it's still there. Can you build on that?" Imara continued.

"You know, you might be on to something." Roxanne wagged her finger as she thought through Imara's suggestion.

"You think we can do this?" I asked.

"Absolutely, but we're going to need help," Roxanne said.

"Who could possibly help with this?" Rhys asked.

"Celia, oh and your aunt," Roxanne spoke of the witch and the siren.

"You want to bring Tylia to the bayou?" I asked. "You sure about that?"

"Yes, something tells me we're going to need a strong siren, and Siliya already has her part to play in this. While she is working her angle, we must explore ours. Tylia is the next best thing."

"Okay, I'll call her," I agreed.

CHAPTER 29

DEMETRIUS

"**Well, look at you,**" Tylia called out as we piled out of the car at the edge of the bayou. "My boy, just as handsome as ever."

The small woman was just as big in personality as ever, and her curls bounced around her full face like punctuations to her words. I expected the woman to have the rest of her boys along for the ride. They were other supernatural men she'd adopted as her sons, but she stood there alone.

"Tylia." I approached the woman with open arms. "Where are the boys?"

.   "Didn't think there would be room for them on that dinky little boat. Besides, I have them working on some things for me. Are you okay?" She looked at me after a quick hug. "Your eyes. They're telling me a story I don't think I like."

"I'm okay, thank you," I assured the woman who felt more like a mother to me than the woman who gave birth to me. "Just want to get this done."

"We're going to get your brother back and Syrinada." She touched my forehead. "Ease your mind and your heart."

"I hope so." I placed my hand over hers and welcomed the comfort of her touch.

"Are we good to go?" Rhys asked as he headed for the small boat roped to the pier.

"Yeah, we're all here." I let Imara and Roxanne pass me before following Tylia. "We're good to go."

After stepping into the boat, I removed the rope that tied it to the pier and kicked us off. The ride was eerie as always when floating through predator filled waters. I tried not to think of the last time I guided the boat to Celia's home. Malachi and I were fighting, and Syrinada looked as though she would jump from the boat every time another alligator's head broke the surface of the murky water.

Tylia and Roxanne chattered about spells and techniques that could help us find Syrinada. Tylia spoke of the task she'd sent the boys on. A scavenger hunt to find special herbs and tools she would need for the magic she hoped to work. Everyone worked toward a common goal.

We pulled up close to the home and carefully crossed from the boat to the house. The alligators were calm but still made their presence known as they floated nearby and peered at us from the murky waters.

"It's about time you got here." Celia poked her head out from the doorway. She'd changed her hair, braiding in spots of colored yarn in with her own, but still dressed like a hippie.

"Of course, you were expecting us." I waved to her and caught the scent of weed wafting out from the inside of the house.

"Yeah, well, that's the thing about being able to see into the future. You always have a vague idea of what will come next." She winked at me and waved the others forward. "Come on in. Let's get this over with."

I was the last to leave the boat. I had to make sure the others got out safely and avoided the waters. It was also a reason to linger before entering Celia's home. At first, I thought I felt someone watching us, but after scanning the area, it was clear it was my paranoia getting to me. It wasn't a hidden spy making me feel uneasy. It was my fear that I'd made the wrong decision to let her go alone. I wanted to be followed, because it would mean I could catch the asshole who'd taken them away.

"Glad to have you back here, boy." Celia smiled as I entered the bead hung doorway.

"Thank you for helping, Celia." I nodded. "I wish we could meet under better circumstances."

"This is better than a virtual trip to bring you back from hell," she whispered before addressing the room. "Alright. We have a lot to do. The last time this boy visited me, I created a binding. One that linked Demetrius to his brother and the siren. That bind is still in place. We will use it to locate the others."

"Will that work?" Rhys asked. "Everything else has failed."

"Without a doubt," Celia said with confidence. "And I assumed you came here because you tried other avenues that didn't work the way you hoped they would. I am always the last result, child."

"How does it work?" Roxanne asked, intrigued by Celia's method. She stood in the corner next to Tylia, who carefully considered every herb, bobble, and jar in the room.

"I will need blood from Demetrius and," she lifted her finger and drew a line in the air from me to Imara, "you. The siren's sister. That will work."

"Me? Why?" Imara shot a questioning glance at me.

"You're her blood. I can tap into the binding of your heritage. It is a powerful magic, after all." Celia swayed like she was dancing to a song only she could hear. "Whatever is blocking your sister, it's strong, so we have to use everything we have to break through."

"Is this safe?" Imara asked me, but Celia answered before I could say a word.

"Would he have brought you here if it wasn't?" Celia sucked her teeth and turned her soulful eyes on me. "Keep bringing me these hardheaded women."

"Celia," I pleaded.

"We must wait until things are in place." Celia waved me off and continued her swayed dance around the room. "Only when the time is right can we do what needs to be done. It should be soon."

"What things?" Rhys asked.

"I've spoken to the girl's mother. The siren. Such a beauty she is," Celia answered. "She is in Deuterio. We believe the child is underwater now, so we must tie into the powers of the ocean. It's going to help us."

Celia pulled out a small copper chalice. Wrapped around the stem was a braid. She ran her finger across the lip of the cup before placing it down on the small altar in the center of the floor. After another moment of her swayed dance, she sat, crossed-legged, in front of it.

"How will we know when it's time?" Roxanne stepped away from the corner just long enough to look into the chalice and inspect the herbs at the bottom of the cup.

"The braid will unravel. We start as soon as it does. Unfortunately, the connection will end as soon as the braid is undone." Celia pointed to the hair. "It's a pretty long piece, so we should have an adequate amount of time to get things done. If you all are careful with how you use it."

"Imara, sit." She pointed to the floor to the right of her. "Rhys is in the middle. Demetrius, to my left, please."

"Now what?" Imara asked after we each took the seats she pointed out to us.

"Now I need your blood." Celia held her hand out to Imara. "It will only take a moment, and you'll hardly even feel the pain."

"I'm sure," Imara huffed but gave her hand to the seer.

"Rhys, Demetrius, hold your hands out above the cup," Celia instructed.

She stacked our hands, palms facing left, and waited. Then the room filled with the smell of the ocean, like the magic transported us from the swamps to the ocean side. I could hear the waves crashing and feel the breeze on my neck and then, in one swift motion, Celia sliced her blade through each of our palms.

I didn't feel the pain or see what happened in the room after the blade cut through my flesh.

I saw them. Together in their world, but I was only a spectator. Rhys stood with Syrinada in the same space before. Repaired by magic. The bed where they'd spent their time apart together stood behind them.

"Sy?" Rhys spoke to her, but Syrinada looked confused.

"Rhys?" She ran to him. "Tell me this is real. Tell me this isn't some messed up dream."

"It's real. I'm here." He pulled her into his arms. "We're coming for you. We just need to know where you are."

It hurt to see her in his arms, but the sound of her voice, and the feeling of her life, was better than anything I'd ever experienced before. She was okay. I still had time to make it right.

I couldn't hear the rest of their conversation. Instead, my mind rushed through a flash of images I'd never seen before. It was like watching someone else's memories. A cold sterile room, a large window that looked out into the dark waters. A massive whale swam by.

Then, in a flash, I was outside of the structure. An underwater lab. Large, white, and surrounded by sharks and other creatures. Another flash, a beach. They transferred me from a plane into a boat, but they restrained my body, submerged in water inside of a capsule.

A flash, and I was on top of a mountain. I looked up just intime to see the explosion. These memories were not my own. They were hers. Locked away in her subconscious. Syrinada knew the way, and she painted me a map.

"I know where they are," I announced as my mind snapped back to the present. The small room with the hippie seer reappeared just as the last of the braid unraveled around the stem of the cup.

"Good," Rhys muttered. "Can we go now?"

"As far as I'm concerned." Celia leaned back with a satisfied look on her face and winked at me. "I've done my job. Now, if you don't mind, I'd like to get back to my session."

~&~

"What did you see?" Tylia asked as we drove in her sedan, away from the swamp and toward Roxanne's home. We followed closely behind the others, who Rhys drove.

"The directions to Syrinada," I answered.

"I know, my boy. I can tell there was more than a list of directions," Tylia spoke in that nurturing tone that made it hard for me to keep anything from her. "What did you see?"

"She was with him. Rhys," I said. "In that space they used their magic to create. She ran into his arms."

"Didn't like that?" She nudged my arm.

"Not particularly, no," I admitted. "But there was more. I saw how they took her, how they trapped her before moving her to that underwater building. She was out of it, but somehow, I saw it all as if I was looking through her eyes."

"Demetrius Denali," she said my full name, and I knew she meant business.

"I'm focused. Promise," I assured her. "It's just not what I was expecting. Didn't think I'd see it all like that and feel it. She was numb inside, like they broke her."

"What about Malachi?" she asked. "Was he there? Is he okay?"

"I felt him, but I didn't see him." I turned the car to follow Rhys down the main road. "He's alive. Weak but alive."

"Good." She paused. "You wanted to ask Celia about the child, didn't you?"

"Yes, but this wasn't the time. Also—"

"Better not to know for sure?" she read my mind like she often did.

"It might destroy me if I do." I glanced at the soft face of the woman who was, in every sense of the word, my mother. "I can push through a lot. You know? I'm built strong, but that, if I knew it was true, it would break me in a way I'm afraid I can't come back from."

"I understand." She held her hand out to me, and I laced my fingers with hers. "My boys. Always in such trouble, but still, your heart is just as strong as the day I took you in."

"Thank you."

The drive to Roxanne's home was uneventful. We pulled up outside the house, and Tylia hopped out quickly to join Roxanne and Imara inside. Rhys remained in his car, and so did I. Both of us clearly had a lot on our mind. As much as I preferred to avoid the man and his emotions, there was a nagging feeling that it wouldn't benefit us if we did. Rhys must have come to the same conclusion because the moment I opened my door, so did he.

"Rhys," I addressed him.

"Demetrius," he said my name like he wanted to punch me.

"What's on your mind?" I asked, trying to keep my tone and temper calm despite the negative energy I felt coming from him.

"She doesn't want you to come," Rhys blurted out, then turned to look at the distant trees.

"What?" I asked. "What do you mean she doesn't want me to come?"

"Sy asked me to make sure you stay away from that place." He clenched his jaw before continuing. "Said it's not safe for you."

"And you're mad because of that?" I scoffed. "You've got to be kidding me with this."

"She cares about you." Rhys looked at me with a hard expression. "She wants to make sure you don't get hurt."

"So the fuck what?" I laughed in his face. "You're upset now because you realize Syrinada cares about me? Where have you been for the last year, Rhys? After everything we've been through together, you're shocked she cares? The woman was my mate! But she chose you. So suck it up and get over it like I did."

"Forget it." Rhys turned his back on me and headed for the house.

"Look, we're all pissy in this. You, me, and Malachi. This situation is messy as hell, but you need to get your head out of your ass. Decide if you're in this or not because it will not get any easier. Right now, I'm not concerned about anything but getting Syrinada and my brother back from the monsters who took them."

"Well, it must be nice to be so level-headed." He looked over his shoulder at me.

"Funny, I thought that was what she liked about you." I walked by him, looking straight ahead. "Guess she was wrong."

CHAPTER 30

RHYS

Demetrius left me standing outside my home *looking at a closed door, and I thought about jumping back in the car and driving away.* Hell, I knew what he said was right. I needed to get out of my head and get my emotions in check. Just because it made sense logically didn't mean I could make it happen.

Maybe he was used to the heartbreak. Used to her doing what she wanted despite his feelings, but I wasn't. I knew things between Syrinada and I had gotten difficult, but I didn't think that was enough for her to turn her back on what we built together. I talked to my mother and to friends about her. About how shitty it felt to leave her alone, but I guess it was my fault for never saying it to her.

The truth was I was afraid. Afraid that if I admitted it out loud I couldn't give her everything she needed, she'd take that and run. That my truth would give her the out she needed, the permission to walk away from me without guilt. Maybe that said more about me than her that I wanted her to feel like she needed to be around me, but I needed her to need me.

The crazy part was I intended to tell her that things had to change. That she couldn't stay locked up away from the world because I saw what it was doing to her. I wanted to talk to her, but every time I opened my mouth, it turned into an argument, and she didn't want words in the little time we had to spend together. She wanted action, so I gave her what she wanted, or at least I told myself that was what I was doing. In reality, I was just giving myself an out. A way not to face the difficult conversation I felt would end in her leaving me.

Funny how my fight to keep her was what pushed her away.

I couldn't go in the house where the others waited to talk about our plans to rush into the oceans and save Syrinada. I couldn't fathom sitting across from him. The man I knew she belonged with. The man I knew she never got out of her system no matter how much she insisted she was over him.

I didn't want to look into that man's eyes and see the pieces of her that he held. I didn't want to feel the bond that still existed between the two of them. That was the weird thing about being bonded to a siren that no one told you about before you took the plunge. No one could have prepared me for that, but I felt everything she did.

Demetrius thought my show of emotions were a petty display about her caring for him, but what he didn't understand was that I felt that care. I felt that concern, and it wasn't just a friend being worried for a friend. It was love. It was something deep inside of her that wanted to protect this man in the way I wanted her to care for and protect me.

It was petty on my part to say those words out loud. It was weak for me to stand across from him and say, "You have a piece of the woman I want entirely for myself, and it pisses me off."

I kept those thoughts to myself.

I gave myself ten minutes. Ten minutes to feel what I had to feel. To work through the emotions and clear my mind. Ten minutes to get myself together mentally and emotionally before I walked through the door and faced him and the rest of the team of people who'd come together to try to save a lost siren.

~*~

My mother wasted no time in laying out the food we would gather around. By the time I made it into the house, they were already digging into helpings of shrimp and grits, beignets, which she kept on hand because of how long they took to make, and whatever else my mother could whip up. She saved a seat for me right next to her knowing I would need her support. No matter what happened, I knew she would be there for me. She always was.

"Now that we're all here, we need to get down to business." My mother took control of the conversation when no one else did. "We're going to need a lot of power to pull this off, and that means we need to get that ghost girl back here."

"Ghost girl?" Tylia looked around the table, landing on Demetrius. "What ghost girl?"

"She's talking about Maggie." Imara popped another piece of food into her mouth and chased it with a gulp of sweet tea.

"The one who died out in that field?" Tylia pointed out the window and to the back of our house where Maggie sacrificed her mortal self to save Syrinada's mother.

"Yes, hence the term ghost." My mother laughed at the woman who'd become a regular around our home since the battle with Alderic and his demons. "I believe she's back with the ancestors now. They let her come here. Think of it as a temporary loan to help us clear this mess up, but I haven't felt her presence in the land of the living since Syrinada and the others were taken. My hope is that we can bring her back because we're going to need her."

"What do we do if they don't let her come back?" Imara asked. "What if they say no?"

"We'll figure that out if it happens," my mother answered then addressed Demetrius and me. "Maggie has a connection to Syrinada that none of you do by blood, love, or whatever. When she made that sacrifice, she gave a piece of herself to that girl. I felt it happen. Never felt something so strong before, and even before that she let Syrinada cypher her magic so many times that it left more of her magic with the siren each time. In a way, they share that magic now. I think that is why she was sent back to the spirit room."

"Sent back?" Demetrius leaned forward, intrigued by the premise. "What do you mean she was sent back?"

"Maggie's job here wasn't done. When she agreed to come, she entered a contract with the other side. She didn't fulfill the terms of that contract, so it wasn't our ancestors who took her away," she explained her theory. Though she spoke it as fact, I knew my mother couldn't know for sure what happened to Maggie. "Someone pushed her out of this realm, and I intend to pull her right back."

"Alright so let's get it done. What do you need?" Tylia leaned back in her chair.

"This is something that only us witches can do." My mother placed her hand on mine and squeezed it. "I just need my son and some peace and quiet. The rest of you find a room and rest up because soon we're gonna have to get on the move."

"You know, technically speaking, I'm a witch too," Imara offered.

"A hybrid witch who hasn't been trialed by the ancestors," my mother said softly. "I'm sorry, but they haven't accepted you yet, and they won't answer a call if you're on the other end of it."

"Ouch." Imara kicked out from the table and picked up the basket with the remaining beignets. "I'm just going to take the rest of these beignets and go eat my emotions."

"I'll go talk to her." Demetrius nodded at my mother then followed Imara out of the room.

After she showed Tylia the room she could use to rest, I followed my mother into her alter room. It was the one space in our home that she would allow no one into because she used the room to communicate with the ancestors, which meant the space had to remain clear of any unwanted energy.

She was so careful about keeping the room clear of negative vibration that she lit and waved the cleansing stick around herself before turning to me. Even I would not be allowed inside until she was sure I wouldn't bring any bad energy with me.

After she cleaned me, I was allowed to walk inside, but she stopped me after closing the door behind me.

"Before we start, you're gonna have to cleanse your heart too." She poked me in the chest with her finger. "I feel the confliction inside of you."

"I'm fine, mother. Really." I looked down at the woman who twisted her lips at me.

"Are you really gonna stand there and lie to me?" She sucked her teeth. "I raised you to be an honest man."

"Mom," I spoke but she grabbed my lips pinching them between her fingers and refusing me the ability to speak.

"Look, boy, I know what you've been going through. Trust me, this is not something I ever would have wanted for you." She let me lips go. "You fell in love with a siren, and I've seen what that does to people. Alderic was one of them. No matter how tough that man thought he was, he fell for a siren, and it wasn't the one we thought. He loved Syrinada's auntie. The one who drove herself nuts trying to prove it to him. I saw it in his eyes, but it ate away at him, and I don't want to see the same thing happen to you."

"I love her, Mom." My shoulders slumped because she saw right through me, and there was no sense trying to hide from it anymore. "I really do, but I don't think I can give her what she wants. I don't even know if I'm what she wants anymore."

"I hate to be the one to tell you, but that's something you're gonna have to become okay with." She lifted her hand to my chin. "It happens to us all. We change over time. Have you ever considered that maybe she isn't what you want anymore? You made a big promise to someone you knew for a very short time, and it was a promise you couldn't have had any way of understanding the weight of. Now, I love Syrinada like she was my own, and I love her mother, and I'll do anything to make sure they're both safe, but you are my priority."

"You think I rushed into this with her."

"I think you made the best decision for you at the time, but right now, times are different. You are different, and so is she." The smokes from the cleansing stick danced around us as she spoke. "That girl was in the middle of figuring out who she was, and I don't even think she's done yet. Both of you have a long way to go. Son, I love you both dearly, but if this relationship needs to end, then you let it end because I am not gonna lose you to the love of a siren like I lost my best friend."

"I'm nothing like Alderic, Mom., I defended myself. Yes, I loved Syrinada, but I could never go as far as he did to keep her.

"Oh, I know you're not, and don't get me wrong, I don't think the boy I raised could ever do the type of evil that man did, but you are a man, and despite how tough y'all want to pretend to be, you're all just as fragile as the flowers that grow in my garden." She laughed and wiped the sweat from her brow. "You rise and bloom, and you reach for the sun. Right now, Syrinada is your sun. At least you want her to be, but that sun is moving further and further away, and I don't want to see my child wither away because he's still reaching for something that is so far outside of his grasp."

"She still loves him," I admitted then swallowed the foul taste it left in my mouth to say those words aloud. "I thought it would be Malachi. I told myself she'd love Malachi, and I could contend with that because I knew she loved me more, but that's not what I'm up against here, Mom. She cares for Malachi, but he's just a friend to her. Demetrius is so much more. That man is a part of her, and I don't know if I can compete that."

"Tell me something." She looked at me, and my heart felt lighter, but then her words sent it crashing back down with the weight of the world. "Why would you ever want to put yourself in a position where you feel you need to compete? The woman who holds your heart should want you and nothing more. Because that's the kind of man you are. Again, I ask you to consider that just because you made this commitment doesn't mean that she's the one for you."

"I know you're right, I do, but it's gonna take me a lot longer to get there."

"I understand. I really do." She winked. "Your

momma has had her fair share of heartbreaks. Believe me."

"Mom, my heart and my mind is clear. Yes, I still have some confusion, but that's something I can't get rid of right now."

"Alright. Well, that's good enough for me. Let's get this done."

We walked over to the center of the room where the altar stood and washed our hands in the cleansing water before beginning. My mother lit the ancestor candle, and we held hands, standing on either side of the altar. There were no words to speak, no incantations. We spoke with our hearts not with our minds. In an instant, we were taken from the altar room and into the realm of ghosts.

I thought we would see Maggie. Despite how much she got into my skin when she was alive, I had been looking forward to seeing the woman again. My mom was right, Maggie had a piece of Syrinada with her. Knowing that gave me an odd sense of hope. If Maggie came back, maybe it would bring back something I felt I'd been missing. That piece of the siren that at one time belonged to me but I'd obviously lost.

But Maggie wasn't the ghost we met when we made it to the ancestral realm. Instead, we saw Amelia. The spirit I only recognized because of Syrinada's description. She was everything Syrinada said she was. Right down to the large eyes, the color of cognac, and the calming warmth of her presence. She had a bald head and large gold earrings that dangled above her shoulders. She stood in a field of grass, tall enough to come up to her knees, and the gown she wore danced in colors of cream and gold and gave her an angelic look.

"Roxanne, it's good to see you," Amelia spoke, and I felt like my heart would cry. All the emotions I tried to swallow swelled to the brim.

"Amelia, thank you for seeing us," my mother responded.

"You look disappointed." Amelia smiled. "What's the matter, Roxanne?"

"I was just expecting to see Ebon when we arrived," my mother admitted.

"Ah. Yes, I know, but she's busy right now," Amelia explained the small ghost's absence. "There are pressing matters to tend to."

"Well, then, I won't keep you here long." My mother nodded. "We're here about Margaret. We need her back with us in the land of the living. Someone has taken Syrinada and the boy, Malachi. I believe we can use Margaret's connection to Syrinada to help us free them from their captors."

"I'm aware of your plan, Roxanne," Amelia said in a way that told she wouldn't be giving my mother what she wanted.

"But you're here to tell me no. Is that you're here instead of Ebon?" My mother came to the same conclusion as I had.

"You always wear a brilliant woman." Amelia smiled, and a warm breeze washed over us, and I knew it was for my mother. That calming sensation. She tried to tame my mother's fiery spirit. "While your plan would work, we cannot allow Margaret to come back to Earth. Not right now. There are bigger entities at play, powers that are greater than our own, and we must approach this with care."

"What powers?" I asked, and for the first time, Amelia looked at me. I swallowed the sudden lump of nerves that formed in my throat. Had I spoken out of turn? Would I be kicked out of the spirit realm for doing so?

"The Titans," Amelia responded cooly before she returned her attention to my mother.

"I'm sorry what?" my mother asked. "Titans?"

"Yes, we considered revealing this information to you sooner, but thought we could avoid it if Syrinada and the others were successful in their task. What we didn't consider was that we were playing right into their game. We gave them what they wanted."

"Titans wanted Syrinada? I'm confused," I spoke out of turn again. This time, Amelia didn't address me. She continued speaking directly to my mother.

"There are people who are trying to bring the Titans back," Amelia explained. "Two have returned, but the bodies they inhabit are dying. They are not strong enough to contain the beings. These people who work to bring them back think they can change the course of history, or at least create a new path forward."

"I don't know much about the Titans, but I thought they were all dead," my mother addressed Amelia. "You tellin' me they're trying to resurrect the dead?"

"Those powerful beings were never destroyed, not in the way that people wanted them to be," Amelia addressed her confusion. "They were simply put to rest, and now they seek a way back. They think they can do that with the powers that Syrinada and others like her possess."

"The hybrids." My mother sighed. "So, you weren't afraid of what she would do with her powers but of what other people would do."

"Exactly." Amelia smiled. "We know Syrinada's heart. She is a good person, but her intentions mean nothing in the greater scheme of things. If they can find a way to use her power to harm the rest of the world, Syrinada will be exactly the threat so many people feared she would become."

"Why does this affect Margaret or her ability to return to earth?" my mother asked as another warm breeze passed across the field.

"You said it yourself when you soke to the others. Margaret is a part of Syrinada, but she is also a part of this realm. If the Titans were to get ahold of her, they would be able to use Margaret to access this plane. That is not something we can allow no matter what is happening with the land of the living. It's best that you all figure out how to get Syrinada back without her help. Because if they get access to our world here, then there is nothing stopping them from doing exactly what they want to do."

"What do they want to do?" I asked.

"What does any god ever want to do?" my mother spoke with understanding, but Amelia provided the full explanation.

"They want to remake the earth in their image. Think about how they didn't get the chance before, how stronger beings came and took that opportunity away from them. A lot of people talk about the Titans as if they were these benevolent beings, but the only reason they didn't look like monsters was because there were more horrific beings at the time. So, they came out looking like the good guys in the end." Amelia's dress danced more violently in the rising wind. "Right now, I'm telling you they are the bad guys. They want to change the world, and they want to sever any connection that reaches to something with the potential to threaten their power."

"They want to sever our connection to our ancestors?"

"Yes, and that is why we cannot allow Margaret to return until we know it is safe for her. No ghost, no matter how powerful or how old, will be allowed to step foot back on that side of the veil until this is done."

"Does that mean you're going to leave us alone?" I asked. "Isn't that just giving them exactly what they want? To sever our connection to the ancestors will make us weaker."

"We are not leaving you without help. It just won't be as direct anymore." Amelia still looked at me with soft eyes despite my repeated outburst. I could feel her understanding. She knew the struggle that went on inside my heart. "Now, time is running out, and soon the Titans will have exactly what they want. I suspect you might want to get a move on. I wish I could give you more help apart from this general guidance, but for now, that's all I can do."

Amelia's voice lingered a while after her body faded away. I thought we'd be kicked out of the spirit realm, but it was more of a gentle push. Something held us there. I watched as the edges of what I could see slowly broke apart. Just as we were about to be taken away from the ghostly realm, we heard a familiar voice calling out to us.

"Wait, please." Maggie ran over to us. Despite her presence, the space around us continued to dissolve, which meant she wasn't strong enough to sustain it on her own. We only had a little time left to speak to her.

"Maggie," I called her name. "It's so good to see you."

"Roxanne, I need to talk to you." She waved to me but spoke to my mother, and it felt good to know that she was still the same woman we knew before she died.

"What is it that you're risking punishment for?" my mother asked, and I followed the quick glance to the edge of the space.

"She's not telling you everything. The Titans aren't just looking for a way back. They have it. Syrinada is a vessel for them." She peered at my mother, hoping she would understand her meaning.

"How is Syrinada a vessel?" I asked because I didn't understand, but Maggie looked at my mother more intensely.

"Oh no. They want to impregnate her?"

"Yes, they think she can give them a child, that they can then transpose a Titan spirit into. They aren't just trying to wake the Titans; they are literally trying to have them be reborn on Earth, and they want to use Syrinada to do it."

"Hell no!" I yelled. "How do we stop that from happening?"

"Syrinada isn't the only powerful hybrid on Earth" Maggie looked between my mother and me. "She has a sister. One that they haven't factored her into their equation yet."

"Imara?" my mother said the name of the woman who was in our home.

"If Syrinada is the one to solve their problem. Imara is the one to break it."

"How?"

"I haven't quite figured that part out yet, but Syrinada becomes something different when she's with her sister. I've seen it. Tell her she needs to get her sister's side and use her unique power to fix this."

"Wait." I had more questions to ask. I wanted to know what Maggie knew about Syrinada and her sister. I wanted her to tell me something to make me believe we would come out of this alive, but our time was up. Maggie's body trembled, and then something powerful and angry pulled her away from us. Then that same entity kicked my mother and I out of the realm of ghost and back to the troubled earth.

CHAPTER 31

RHYS

There was no gentle return to our bodies. I damn near fell on my ass, but my mother's hold on my hands was firm and kept me upright. While I felt like I would shatter, she opened her eyes calmly. The only evidence of what she'd been through was presented by the soft sheen of sweat on her forehead.

"So, no Maggie," I huffed. "What are we going to do?"

"Find another way. That's all we can do." She smiled, but there was an undeniable sorrow in her eyes.

"Mom, what's wrong?" I asked as she let go of me.

"I'm just exhausted, and I hoped I could bring something to help you."

"It's not your fault," I tried to comfort her. "There was no way you could have known that it was the ancestors who took Maggie away."

"I know, but that doesn't change the fact that you're going to go in there without them by your side. Our magic, our connection to our ancestors, is what makes us strong. Without that, the risk you take if you go after them will be far greater."

"I'll be okay, Mom. I'm strong enough. Besides, it's not like I can't use my magic at all."

"True." She placed her hand on my cheek. "Just promise me if it comes down to it, you make sure you come home to me."

"Mom."

"I'm serious Rhys," she said, tears in her eyes. "You're all I got left in this world."

We left the altar room intending to round up everyone so we could discuss what happened, but despite my mother's instructions to rest, they were already gathered in the living room. How could anyone rest when things were so messed up? Demetrius stood by the window, looking out with a conflicted expression on his face. I wondered what troubled the man who seemed to have it all together.

Imara sat with Tylia on the couch speaking in low tones about something I couldn't hear. It felt too intimate to pry.

"Oh, you're back. How did it go? Is Maggie coming back?" Imara looked at us then around us when we came in the room. "Is she coming later?"

"Unfortunately, no. The ancestors will not allow Maggie to come back," my mother answered her question. "Things are a lot more complicated than we thought. If she comes back to earth, it could be too dangerous for her and a lot of other people."

"More complicated how?" Tylia asked. "What are we up against?"

"According to the ancestors, this isn't just another witch we're dealing with. We're up against Titans. Beings who are thought to be like a step away from a god. The people who took Syrinada want to use her as a tool to bring them back."

"What do you mean they want to use Syrinada?" Imara asked. "Use her how?"

"They want her to be the vessel for these new beings," my mother answered her. "They want her to give birth to babies that will then be possessed by the Titans. I'm not sure exactly the science or magic behind it, but that's basically what we're looking at."

"You've gotta be kidding me?" Tylia straightened. "That's unnatural."

"I don't think these people care about the laws of

nature." I shoved my hands into my pockets to keep from punching the wall. I didn't care what the situation was, if I did that, my mother would knock me upside my head.

"They were looking for other hybrids," my mother continued her explanation as she moved to sit in the armchair across from Imara and Tylia. "We're not sure if they found others, but Syrinada is apparently exactly what they were looking for."

"What's so special about her?" Imara asked. "Why do they want her?"

"We haven't quite figured that out yet," my mother said. "If we knew, maybe we could figure out how to save her, or at least get some understanding on how to protect her in the future."

"I know what it is," Demetrius spoke but didn't turn from the window. Still, I heard it in his voice. Pain and regret, the markers of a man who felt like he failed.

"You do?" Tylia asked. "What is it?"

"It's a reason so many people were terrified or her. It's not just because she is a hybrid. We've seen hybrids before. Hell, I'm a hybrid. There is something special about her." He turned from the window, rubbing the back of his neck as he continued. "Syrinada comes from a very powerful bloodline. One that goes all the way back to the titans."

"You've got to be kidding me." My mother's mouth fell open. "How have I never known this?"

"It's not something that is freely shared, for obvious reasons, but it is true. Syrinada is a direct descendant of the Titan, Tethys. It's why my brother and I were responsible for keeping her safe," he continued. "It wasn't a request from the sirens. It was a request from hell. Protect her at all costs."

"Wait, are you saying your demon daddy asked you to keep an eye on my sister?" Imara blurted out. "Well, fuck."

"There are a lot of people who have an interest in using Syrinada's power for their own advantages, but more who want to stop that from happening. They know what will happen if the wrong people gain access to her."

"That sheds some light on things, but it doesn't change the fact that we need to get her back before they do what they want." My mother looked around the room at the worried faces, including my own. "So, for now, we have to come up with a new plan. One I believe is going to mean you all have to go to Deuterio."

"What? I haven't been there in a long time, and I don't plan on going back," Tylia said. "I'll help you as much as I can until you leave."

"Tylia, I hate to ask you." Demetrius walked over

to the woman who looked at him like she had already given in to his request before he could ask it. "I know you don't like our home, and you have every right to feel that way, but I need you and your power. It's Malachi, even if you don't care to save Syrinada as much as the rest of us do, Malachi is out there too. He needs us."

"Well..." She took a deep breath then threw her hands up in the air, giving in to him just as I imagined she would. "I guess I've been away from home long enough. I'll survive one visit."

"Thank you." Demetrius pulled her hand into his. "I really appreciate it."

"Alright. We got some preparations to make." Tylia turned her attention to my mother. "We should be able to create a portal right here that will take us straight to Deuterio."

"You can do that?" My mother rubbed her chin. "I thought you had to be in the ocean for that to work."

"Syrinada isn't the only siren who ever got her stone. I'm a fully powered siren, and I'm fully pissed off, so yeah, I can do that. So long as I get a little help from a witch."

"Whatever you need." My mother nodded, and when Tylia stood and headed out of the room, so did she.

With no desire to have another awkward conversation with Demetrius or engage in small talk with Imara, I excused myself. There was something I needed to do before we left. My mother was right, I had to clear my head and my heart. I had to prepare myself for the chance that Syrinada and I would no longer be together when everything was said and done.

~*~

While Tylia and my mother worked on the portal that would take us from New Orleans straight into the siren's underwater world, I decided that the best use of my time was to center myself. There were a lot of emotions inside of me that I hadn't dealt with, and I knew better than most that walking into any sort of battle with conflicting emotions was a bad idea.

In my bedroom, I lit the incense that brought me the most peace. Black Copal. I sat in the center of the floor, took several cleansing breaths, and as much as I wanted to avoid ever feeling the way I felt the last time I saw her, I meditated. Just as I knew it would, it took me right back to the moment that broke my heart.

"Sy?" I saw her the moment I stepped into the space, but she looked around, confused.

"Rhys?" She ran to me and wrapped her arms around my neck, and my heart smiled from her touch. "Tell me this is real. Tell me this isn't some messed up dream."

"It's real. I'm here." Arms around her waist, I pulled her closer to me. I buried my face in her hair and inhaled the smell of the ocean. "We're coming for you. We just need to know where you are."

"I'm here. It's hard." She leaned back to look at me but squinted as if trying to clear her vision.

"What is?" I touched her face, hoping that feeling my hand would help steady her mind.

"They drugged me. My mind is heavy," she said, and I could hear the effects of the medication in her voice.

"Who drugged you? Sy, I need to know where you are." I tried to nudge her gently, but we needed information. "What's happening to you?"

"Underwater. They have me underwater. I don't know where. It's Omar."

"Omar?" I had no idea who she spoke of. "Who is Omar? I need you to focus, Sy."

"Don't let Demetrius come here. Please." There it was. The moment his name slipped past her lips I felt it. The crack in my heart, that pain I tried to ignore, it split further, and the tear burned in my chest."

"Sy, I'm worried about you. I need to find you." I rubbed her face again to bring her thoughts back to me. "Give me something I can work with."

"Sharks. Big sharks. Bigger than anything I've seen. Their eyes are huge. I saw them outside my window, green and yellow with sparks of red. I can't get out. My tail won't work in the water anymore," she rambled, and I struggled to keep up with her.

"How is that possible?" I looked down at her legs. "What do you mean it won't work?"

"Whatever they drugged me with. It stops me from being able to shift, Rhys. I've tried so many times, and nothing happens."

"I'm going to find you. Just please hang on." I pulled her closer to me again and pressed my lips to her forehead because I couldn't bear the thought of kissing her lips.

"I'm so sorry, Rhys," she apologized. "I'm so sorry."

Before I could tell her she owed me no apology, the vision ended.

I came out of the meditation, heart somehow heavier and lighter than before. I still hadn't come to terms with my changing relationship, but I had something else. A new clarity of what she said to me. Details I didn't remember before.

"Dammit." I jumped up from the floor and ran down the hall to Demetrius' room. The door stood open, so I rushed in. "I remembered something."

"What?" He looked up from the bed where he sat.

"Something Syrinada said to me before when we met in our dream space," I explained. "I guess I was too focused on my own feelings to remember it before."

"Okay. What did she say?" Demetrius stood from the bed, now more alert.

"She's trapped, underwater," I repeated what I remembered.

"Well yeah, we know that." Demetrius frowned. "Anything else, or are you just going to tell me that the Titans have her?"

"Something about large sharks, and her tail not working." I dug for the details that were already fading from my mind. "Oh, and someone named Omar drugged her. Whatever they gave her, it's stopping her from being able to shift."

"Omar?" Demetrius stepped closer to me and pulled his dreadlocks up into a bun behind his head. "Are you sure she said Omar?"

"Yes. I thought it was the drugs messing with her mind because I don't know any Omar." I paused then recognized the guilty look on his face. "I take it you know who this Omar is?"

"Yeah, he's a giant. Or at least a descendent of one. He helped us." Demetrius kicked the leg of the bed.

"Dammit."

"Well, looks like your friend wasn't your friend at all." I leaned against the desk.

"Anything else?" Demetrius pulled a phone from his pocket.

"No. Just large sharks, bigger than she's seen before." I thought of the other details she gave me.

"There has to be more."

"Not unless the sharks eye color makes a different. She is drugged. Whatever they've done to her, I could barely see her or hear her voice. She went on about green eyes with yellow and—"

"Sparks of red?" The man looked at me like that small detail had ruined his entire month.

"Yes." I nodded. "That's exactly what she said."

"I know where she is." He sighed. "Dammit."

"I take it we aren't happy about her location?"

"What she described is the Munra shark. They only exist in one area of Deuterio." He sighed. "Just happens to be the most dangerous area."

"And that's where we're headed?" I rubbed the bridge of my nose with my fingers.

"Of course, it is." Demetrius slapped me on the shoulder as he passed me to exit the bedroom.

CHAPTER
32

DEMETRIUS

There was only one place we would find the Munra shark, and that was on the cusp. Right at the edge of Deuterio where the siren world blended with something darker. The edge of another realm we called the Bane. It was where the darkest beings dwelled. Where those of us who sought danger roamed. It was where my mother met my father.

I'd only been there once before. When I fought my way back from hell.

"They're at the cusp," I told Tylia when she returned from her work with Roxanne to prepare the portal.

"Are you sure?" The color drained from her face leaving her brown skin looking damn near grey for a moment. "That can't be right."

"Rhys remembered more of what Syrinada told him. She described seeing the Munra shark."

"Well, I'll be damned." She scratched her head. "Well, I guess we know where we're going now. Not that I'm all that pleased about it."

"Trust me, you aren't the only one."

"I know how you feel about the place." She placed her hand on my arm. "They're going to be okay, Demetrius. We'll get them back."

"Tylia, that place. You don't know what it does to us. Depending on where they are, how close they are to the edge, Malachi may not be himself when we get there. It messed my head up being that close to hell."

"But you were on the other side, Demetrius. Let's just hope he isn't there. We know where he is. We know how to get there. We're going to bring him back, and both of you are going to be okay."

"I hope you're right." I placed my hand on hers and could feel the magic she worked on me to calm my spirit.

"Are you absolutely certain this is what we're up against? I mean, there's no reason for us to go there if there's a chance it could be wrong."

"There's no question about it." I closed my eyes and saw the flashes of Syrinada's memories again. "I saw it in my own eyes, even though I wanted it to be wrong. That's where they are which means we're gonna need a lot more backup when we go in there. This isn't going to be easy, not that I thought it would be, but whoever we're up against is going to put up one hell of a fight."

"They would need to be pretty fearsome to establish any sort of sustainable presence at the cusp, wouldn't they?"

"Fearsome and fearless, considering the kind of beings that threaten those waters." I nodded.

Tylia was right. Anything capable of not only surviving at the cusp but of establishing a functioning ecosystem there, was something that was going to take a lot to bring down, and that was what we had to do. It wouldn't be as simple as rescuing Syrinada and Malachi. We needed to shut the entire operation down and make sure they couldn't continue their efforts.

I could tell Roxanne and Rhys didn't truly understand what would happen if the titans were allowed to return to earth. It wouldn't end with them. It would mean more damage, more beings who were forced to live in hell or wherever their souls were banished, would seek to return and with the titans in charge, that would be much easier to accomplish.

They wouldn't stop with cutting the covens off from their ancestors. They would continue, severing whatever connections they could, which would inevitably mean cutting Deuterio off from the human world as well.

"You look like you just found out some really bad

news." Imara rounded the corner into the living room where I stood with Tylia.

"Nothing we can't handle." I nodded. "Enjoy your nap?"

"As if I was actually able to sleep." She stretched her arms above her head before digging her hands into her hair and shaking the curls. "I'm hungry."

"Again?" Tylia laughed.

"Well, honestly, I need something a little stronger than beignets." She winked. "If you get what I mean."

"Can't help you there." Tylia shrugged. "Sorry, sista."

"I'll survive." Imara yawned. "So, are we ready to go? I have to admit, I'm pretty excited about the opportunity to see this underwater world."

"That's entirely up to Tylia." I looked at the older woman. "Is the portal ready?"

"Yeah, now that we know exactly where to aim it. We might as well get going. No sense in holding off any longer."

"Lead the way." Imara grinned.

"We're all set up in the basement," Roxanne chimed in from behind Imara.

Tylia and Roxanne had worked for hours creating the portal that would allow us to cut out the trip to the ocean before we could leave the human realm. They used a variety of herbs and materials I would never understand, but what I did gather was the key ingredient was water straight from Deuterio. For a woman who swore she never wanted to return home, Tylia sure kept a sizeable collection of the water from our world in her possession.

It was true the water held magical properties that the oceans and seas of earth could never hope to replicate, but I believed it was a more sentimental reason behind her choice. Tylia missed Deuterio, even though she would never admit it. We all did.

The problem was our home wasn't exactly the most welcoming place, especially to those who chose to leave it all behind. Though Tylia led a quiet life, there were people in Deuterio who would blame her just as much as anyone else for the bad shit that went down at home. There were stories about how open and carefree our people were at one point. That was not the case. There was too much suspicion and bad blood making the waters murky.

We didn't know what would happen once we stepped across the portal. It didn't matter what backlash we would face. We had to go. This was so much bigger than we ever thought it was and a hell of a lot more dangerous. Not only was Syrinada's life in danger, but so was Malachi, and by an extension of what the Titans planned to do, so was the rest of the world.

After Rhys joined us, we all went down to the basement. It was a small space, but it was large enough for what we needed to do. The only one who wouldn't be crossing the portal was Roxanne, and she had a look on her face that made my heart ache. It was a look of a mother worried for her child. In the lack of a leader concerned for her people.

I often forgot that Roxanne wasn't just Rhys's mother. She was the new leader of the New Orleans coven of witches. There were hundreds, if not thousands, of lives that counted on the decision she'd made. To send her son across a portal into a realm that she'd never been to was a huge risk for the High Priestess.

Though it wasn't promised, her role and responsibility to her people could potentially pass down through her bloodline, and as far as I knew, her family tree ended with him. How would the members of her coven respond if they found out she very well could have sent off their next leader to his death? Would they trust her to continue in her role? Would they seek to push her out? I knew the weight of responsibility, but I could never fathom what she carried.

It was supposed to be easier. At least, that was what I told myself. I wanted us to be able to walk into Deuterio, grab my brother and my mate, and walk right back out. I wanted to reassure Roxanne that I would bring her son back unharmed, even though he wasn't my favorite person by any measurement. I wanted to protect Imara, who was so ready to jump into this to save her sister but had very little understanding of what existed beyond the realm of humans.

There were so many things I'd seen and done. Battles I'd faced that I doubted Imara or Rhys could ever consider. I'd become accustomed to it, though. Since I was a boy, it'd been my job to protect others. Before my mother died, and long after she was gone, I had the echoes of her voice in my mind telling me I was meant to be a hero.

That was why I couldn't just stand by and wait for someone else to get the job done. It was why I was preparing to go to the cusp, even though Syrinada sent the message that I shouldn't. She didn't want me to risk going there because there was a threat on my life. That much was obvious, especially since Omar was there, but no matter the risk for me, I had to go. To save her and to save my brother, because if I didn't, there was no way they were going to make it out alive.

I recognized how destructive it could be to always load my shoulders with the weight of that much responsibility, but I wasn't the person to put it there. It was the truth given to me when I thought I lost my life and when I woke up in Hell. Those were the words burned into my memory and repeated to me when I fought to find my way back home. It was what I heard just before the clutches of evil let me free. I had to protect my brother, and I had to protect my mate. Nothing else in the world mattered if I couldn't keep them safe.

In the center of the basement floor was the marker for the portal. To me it looked like a bunch of twigs and branches, but I knew there was more to go along with it. I'd studied what I could of the magic of the covens, but very little of it ever made sense to me. There was a semi-circle of wax poured around the outer ring of the marker. The four of us who would cross the portal stood in front of the open end of the wax.

"Alright we have to hold hands and run for it." Tylia stood in front of us. "The portal technically should only allow two people to go through, but if we are quick, we should be able to make it work, but let go, and you get left behind because it will close as soon as the energy connection breaks."

"Is this really safe?" Imara looked at me then back at Tylia. "Not to be rude, but I'm not trying to get an arm chopped off because this thing decided to close before I could make it all the way through."

"Theoretically, yes." Tylia scratched her chin. "Though that would be an interesting thing to see."

"Right." Imara turned to me and mouthed the words, is she out of her mind?

I just laughed because I had the same thought

plenty of times before. Tylia wasn't the type to play it by the book. She preferred to create her own rules. It was one of the biggest reasons she left Deuterio to begin with. She didn't agree with the laws being put in place and refused to bend to them.

"I will go through first," Tylia continued. "Demetrius will be the last. That is the strongest connection we can create. Rhys and Imara, take a good breath before you cross, and as soon as you're on the other side of that barrier, you need to put up your protection for air. We won't be able to breathe for you once we're underwater."

"We're good." Rhys looked at Imara. "I will do the spell. Your internal magic will sustain it for as long as we need to be underwater."

"Thanks for that because drowning two seconds into the trip would suck." She playfully winked at him.

Roxanne moved around the marker to Rhys. She looked at her son, and I could see the tears she held back. The moment felt too intimate to witness, and as she pulled him into her arms, I looked away. Though I couldn't see their embrace, I heard the whispers of a silent prayer. She laid a cover of protection over her son.

"You remember what I told you, right? Make sure you come back to me." Her voice trembled with unspoken fear.

"I will," Rhys responded then said something I

couldn't make out before he whispered, "Thank you."

I looked back up when I heard Roxanne's careful steps that placed her back on the other side of the portal marker. Tylia, looked back at me for confirmation that we were good to go. When I nodded, she reached into her pocket and pulled out what looked like a small blue orb.

She rolled it around her fingers, pressed it to her lips, then tossed it in front of her into the center of the marker. The small orb spun, and as it did, it lit up. A moment later, a light, born of pure energy, shone from the center of the orb. Then it stretched. The orb became a disk, the disk became a panel, the panel became a doorway of water that blocked out the witch who stood on the other side of the portal.

I could feel the magic radiating from the wall of water that stood before us. It was familiar. It felt like home. My home. Deuterio. The energy that came from it was hectic, but the longer it stood the more stable it became. As soon as I felt it level out, Tylia turned to us.

"Let's go."

She held her hand out Rhys who wrapped his hand around hers. Imara clutched his other hand and held hers out to me. I took a deep breath, grabbed hold of the Imara's hand, and then we ran for it.

CHAPTER 33

DEMETRIUS

No one lost an arm, but I did get my tail back.

And it felt damn good to have it. There was no denying the freedom a tail provided as opposed to legs. With legs, you're limited to the available pathways available on land, but with a tail, underwater was limitless. You can make your own path.

It was more than being directionally free. I had three physical modes. Humanoid, Merman, and Demon. Three side of myself all with varying levels of power. Human being the weakest, of course, though I was still far stronger than any normal human man.

My demon, still bound to two legs, was strong as hell, but oftentimes it felt unruly like it would consume me if I let it. No matter what, whenever I set it free, I had to maintain some sense of control. If not, I risked losing myself to him, because in some sense, he was a person all on his own. Another mentality trapped inside me.

That wasn't the case with my merman. It was strength, agility, freedom, and all me. I never felt more relaxed than when I was swimming through the waters of Deuterio, no matter how many potential threats it presented. When I was with my tail, I could truly let my guard down.

I looked down to see the dark blue hues of my scales as they shimmered in the underwater light. That was the thing about Deuterio. It wasn't dark and gloomy like you would think a city at the bottom of the ocean would be. It had its own source of light that rose and fell just like the sun on earth.

Ahead of me, Tylia swam in happy circles using her tail to push and pull her, and I could see her joy as much as I felt my own. I had no idea how long it'd been since she was in our waters or felt the magic that came with it. What I witnessed was more than a siren coming home, it was a woman healing. Deuterio welcomed her, even if the people there wouldn't be as kind.

Rhys and Imara swam close to me. Just as he promised, the moment they were through, he cast the spell that acclimated them to the waters. Rhys was accustomed to the changes of his body, the webbing between his fingers and toes in the pocket of air that wrapped around his face. He'd been to Deuterio before and had some idea of what to expect.

This was a completely new experience for Imara. Watching her was like witnessing a child learn to walk for the first time. Her eyes were wide as she looked over her body. She wiggled her hands in front of her face and swam in tight circles as she tested out the changes to her body.

"Is this really happening?" She stopped and slapped her hand over her mouth. "Oh, oh shit! I can actually talk underwater! This is a total mind fuck."

"Yeah, as long as the spell is in place, you will be fine." Rhys laughed at her. "I remember my first time doing it. Just make sure you remember to breath. Sometimes I would suddenly feel like I was drowning because I absentmindedly held my breath."

"Right. How long does this last?" she asked and swam in another circle.

"As long as we need it to," Rhys answered her question before he turned to me. "What's the plan from here?"

"Oh shit! Look at your tail!" Imara blurted out before I could answer Rhys. "You really are a merman!"

"Well, yes." I laughed then pointed at Tylia. "And she is a siren, or mermaid, if you will."

"I don't know what I expected to happen, but you have a tail and everything!" She swam closer to me then paused. "Is it okay if I touch it? I don't want to be rude."

"Go ahead." I couldn't help laughing at her again.

When she touched me, I expected to feel just a normal hand on my tail. Like a someone petting their puppy, but it was nothing like that. At first, I felt her hand, followed by a familiar sensation that I'd only ever felt when I was with Syrinada. A charge of magic and power I thought was unique to the siren.

And then, there was arousal so intense that if I had my legs, I would have had to hide my bulge. The immediate and intense arousal lasted a moment before the succubus sucked away my power. It was like standing in front of an oven. The heat brushed across my body as I felt my energy move to the point of contact and leave transfer from me to her.

"This is insane." Imara ran her fingers along my tail, completely unaware of what was happening at first, but when she realized what was going on, and she pulled her hand back. "Oh shit! Did I just?"

"What?" Tylia returned to us. "What happened?"

"I think I just succubused him." Imara held her hand to her chest. "I didn't mean to do that. I promise. It was just one touch."

"You pulled unintentionally and absorbed his energy?" Tylia asked. "You really are a lot like your sister, you know that?"

"That has never happened to me before. I'm sorry, D," Imara apologized again and pushed the wild halo of hair from her face. "Usually, I have to control it. I haven't felt like that since I was in college."

"Maybe your powers are different here." Rhys looked at her like she was something to study. "You might want to keep your hands to yourself for a while."

"Of course." She turned another pitiful look on me. "I'm so sorry."

"You don't have to keep apologizing." I shook off the feeling, and in a few moments, I was fine again. "I'm okay. Besides, it's a good thing we found this out before we got you near the rest of the population."

"Keeping my hands to myself." She tucked her hands under her armpits. "That should be easy enough, right? I mean it's not like people are just jumping at the chance to be touched by a stranger."

"What's the plan now?" Rhys chimed in. "Imara will not touch anyone, cool, but I'm assuming we're going to be recruiting more help, right?"

"Actually, Syrinada's mother has already done most of the work. In a moment, someone will come get us to escort us to the meeting point," I reported what information I had. "I'm not sure who she was able to gather, but I have my own people here as well who have reported back to me her progress. We should have a sizable group to go with us."

"That's reassuring." Tylia nodded. "Because I damn sure have no allies here anymore."

"Sylia has planned the rest of the trip. She has a very strategic mindset." I couldn't help but to be impressed by the siren who'd spent over twenty years frozen in ice and came out of it swinging. Not only had she already reestablished her position in the community, but she spent her time advocating for her daughter and other beings like her.

As if they were waiting for my explanation to finish, the moment I stopped talking, the welcoming party swam up to us. Four men and two women led by a person I'd worked with many times before.

"Demetrius." His voice was just as loud as ever. I often joked that without the cushion of water, listening to the man speak would result in a ruptured eardrum.

"Boyd," I greeted him. "Thank you for coming."

"Good to see you." Boyd tilted his head, arm over his chest. He looked over our crew, and his green tail flickered when he laid eyes on Imara. "Wish it was under better circumstances."

"Yeah, I wish it were too. It would be nice to come

home just for a simple visit." I chuckled.

"Maybe you can plan for that when this is done." Ayla, a siren swam up to me with the same formal greeting. "That's if the world isn't already in danger again."

"Isn't it always?" Tylia smirked and the two women laughed.

"I heard your brother is caught up as well. Is that true?" Boyd asked.

"Unfortunately, yes." I nodded. "Which is why this is a very sensitive matter for me."

"Damn, well let's not waste any more time." Boyd straightened his shoulders and puffed out his chest, back to business. "Everyone's gathered and ready to go. They're just waiting on you."

"In that case, lead the way."

Boyd swam ahead of our group and led us from our point of entry to the outer edges of the city, Mioku. Mioku was one of the smaller cities, but it was one of the most beautiful. Every time I visited, I found myself wanting to extend my stay. The people of Mioku were focused on beauty. That applied to not only their personal appearance but also their city.

Their buildings were pristine, constructed with only the best materials and with dedicated crews who were paid top dollar to keep the structures clean. They were so clean that the light bounced off the buildings, making them shine like jewels.

It was fitting for the people who took great care of their hair and skin. Every person wore braids, and the styles told of their status. Those who wore their hair adorned with seashells and other gems were of higher statue than others who typically wore plain braids.

Where we were going, they wouldn't see more than the outer edge of the city and a few people who were only being nosey about the group that gathered, but still I watched Imara. Her reaction to the world, to seeing the people and the life that existed under the sea was fascinating.

She held in her comments, but I could see her eyes bulge and her hands clasp together. I heard the soft gasps of excitement, and wished I could experience the world for the first time again.

As we got closer, I had to switch my frame of thinking. Even with everything that had happened, there were still a lot of people who didn't trust Syrinada, and a lot more who would refuse to fight on her side. As far as they were concerned, Syrinada was evil and deserved whatever bad fortune came her way.

Luckily, there were people who remembered Sylia. They remembered she was a good and fair woman. Even more, they remembered the sacrifices she and the people in her family made to make sure our people would survive. Theirs was a bloodline that stood the test of time. Sure, she faced judgment for her involvement with the warlock, but it appeared she'd already earned their forgiveness for that. Still, she fought for that same grace for Syrinada, who'd made no choice to be born what she was.

We swam inside the structure on the edge of the city that had been designated as our meeting quarters. It was a simple building covered in strategically placed coral and teeming with fish. The kind that didn't fear us. While they were beautiful, they tasted like rubber bands.

While the others swam ahead, I fell back to do a sweep of the area. I trusted Boyd and his team, but I had to be sure we weren't being followed. Besides, I was less familiar with the area, and it was a personal preference to get the lay of the land for myself.

Mioku was chosen because it was the territory where we would receive the least backlash. That didn't mean it was without enemies. Whenever you did anything that went against the norm, you could be sure there would be people who opposed your efforts. I was not foolish to think there were people in Mioku who would prefer we not be doing what we intended.

Not only that, but I suspected there were those of our population who were likely working with the organization established at the cusp, which meant they understood what we were trying to prevent from happening. It was the only explanation that explained how it was possible for an entire compound to be built without anyone knowing about it.

That was the part that bothered me the most, the question that lingered on a constant loop in my mind. How did it get there? Even though the general consensus was to stay as far away from the cusp as possible, there were still teams put in place who were responsible for monitoring the area. Because we knew the potential dangers that could access the dark corner and use it to cross over from other realms, we had to be sure Deuterio was safe.

Despite the protocols put in place, they still managed to build a structure the size of a small city. Not only that, but they transported beings in and out of that compound from other worlds, completely undetected. When I realized where Syrinada and Malachi were, I had my men do some digging. Not one report was ever filed about the compound.

Not a single red flag for the elders to investigate. If any word of the compound was reported, there was no doubt my team would have been alerted. They would have had me bring in the best to investigate and eliminate the threat. I knew Sylia's focus was on getting to the cusp and bringing back our people, but I had to consider other things, like who the hell allowed it to happen, and if they were pretending to be on our side.

As I watched more people swim into the building, I also had to consider that maybe to some of the people inside, I was a possible traitor. Just as I contemplated who our allies were, I knew there were those who questioned me. It wasn't outside of the realm of possibilities that I would be working with some darker entities. Afterall, I was a half demon hybrid who everyone believed to have died. Stories of how I'd clawed my way from hell, though born mostly of fictional speculation and not of factual information, ran rampant the moment everyone found out I was alive.

Since my return, despite my position, there'd been a break down in the chain of communication with home. I found myself having to jump through far too many loops to get information which had been freely provided to me before. I brushed it off, told myself that they were just being careful and wanted to make sure they could trust me.

As I swam around the edge of Mioku, I had to consider if the powers that be had realized something was wrong, and if they were pointing the blame at me. It wouldn't be the first time our people decided that someone was unworthy of trust without any real evidence of the matter.

Satisfied with my search of the area, I ended my own internal speculation and headed inside to join the others. Besides, I didn't want to leave Imara alone for too long. Even with Rhys and Tylia with her, there was no telling what the succubus was capable of. I hadn't ever heard of another succubus visiting Deuterio before.

Knowing Tylia, she was already making mental notes about the effects it had on Imara. The question then would be, did it affect her because she was a succubus or because she was a hybrid? Would it have the same effect on all other succubi who came there? Those were questions that would have to wait to be answered.

Inside the simple building was a simple setup. It was built for entertainment, operas and plays. I imagined that was before the city's center shifted and left the relic on the border's edge. Syrinada's mother stood at the head of a large room on a wide stage. Inside, there were about one hundred people, which was about eighty more than I honestly expected to find.

As I looked at the woman who stood ready to address the crowd, I was reminded of the Influence Sylia held. She wasn't just a beautiful face. She wasn't just a powerful siren, she was a royal in Deuterio, the head of one of the original bloodlines, and even though she had much to repair for her family's legacy, there were people who would always show her the respect she deserved, and they would fight for her when she asked.

"I want to thank you all for being here today despite the uncertainty we face at this time," Sylia, who looked so much like the woman we aimed to save, addressed the room as I entered, and everyone came to attention. I took several deep breaths to calm the noise inside my mind, the cacophony of screams of Syrinada's name.

"I know for most of you, this was a difficult choice to make," she continued. "You don't know who to trust, but you have put your faith in me, and I cannot even begin to express to you my gratitude for that faith. Right now, my daughter's life is at risk, and while that is more than enough for me to swim into battle, I can appreciate that it may not be enough for you all to want to put your lives on the line.

"What I hope to impress upon you now is the understanding that this far surpasses the life of just one siren, no matter how much I value that life. What is happening at the cusp will affect all of us. There is no doubt in my mind. We are not just going there to save one siren anymore."

As the hushed whispers washed over the crowd, a large merman I didn't know swam out with a massive board, and on it was a diagram. It illustrated the structure I'd seen in my vision. The compound at the cusp.

"This is where we're headed." Sylia pointed to the diagram. "A facility that exists at the cusp that no one has explanation for. We have little information about this place, but we do know there are beings being held there against their will. They are being experimented on. We cannot allow that to happen in Deuterio. Furthermore, we know for a fact that at least four of the people inside the facility are merpeople.

"There isn't much time for us to do what needs to be done. Typically, I'd hoped to give you all time to rest and wrap your minds around the information. As it stands, they are getting closer and closer to completing what they have set out to do, and we simply cannot allow it."

"What are they trying to do?" someone called out from the front of the room.

"I'm glad you asked." Sylia smiled, and I could feel the warmth all the way at the back of the room. "Let me shed some light on things for those of you who are unaware. We all know about the Titans. It's something we're taught about from a very early age for an important reason. Those beings? Those ones who the humans at one point in history celebrated. They are trying to come back to Earth.

"If they succeed, they will take over that world, and we know what happens when they get their hands on one. They come for all. The problem also lies in the fact that the titans won't come alone. If we allow them to return to Earth, they will awaken the others. Their presence alone will be powerful enough to pull back the gods and the monsters they once commanded.

"Those that we have fought for centuries to quiet.

I'll remind you that it wasn't just our people standing in that fight but supernatural beings from this realm into the next and far beyond that. We fought to get to a place where we can live our lives without constant fear.

"I won't stand here and pretend we have ever known true peace. After all these years, I'm no longer convinced it's an obtainable thing. There will always be conflicts, whether external or internal, but what I do know is that the hell our people experienced under the thumbs of the titans and the gods is not one we ever want to return to.

"So again, I thank you for coming here to help me get my daughter back, but I want to remind you of what is truly at stake. My daughter, the one you feared so much, is not the enemy. She is not the one that is threatening us right now despite the power she possesses.

"It is the people who captured her who wish to use her power to bring something far darker than she could ever do on her own. We will go to the cusp, and we will destroy that facility and the people who seek to do evil. We will tear them down, and we'll bring every lost soul inside back home."

When she finished speaking, the room was still. Everyone quietly reflected on what Sylia said to them. I'd expected immediate cheering and war cries but realized this was better. Sylia looked proud as she watched the people carefully consider the message she delivered.

These weren't people blindly following a name. These were well informed minds with a common goal who were deciding their stance, and then it happened.

One by one, they lit up with something I doubted I would ever be able to effectively replicate. It was something beyond an admiration. It was a light fed by Sylia, and I understood more than ever as I watched her mother address the crowd, where Syrinada got her presence from. The impact that woman had on my heart, my soul, my mind, even when she was nowhere near me, was a direct result of the magic she inherited from her mother.

A moment later, they stood, and they cheered. Ready to run into battle.

Sylia watched the reaction for only a moment before she left the stage. I watched her, expecting her to personally greet the people in the room. Instead, she made a direct line for me, and it felt like my heart jumped up my throat.

"Demetrius." She smiled, and my heart calmed. "It's good to see you again."

"You as well, Sylia," I greeted her, hand over my chest.

"I think the two of us need to talk." She glanced to the left at the woman I hadn't realized was next to me. Imara waved back nervously. "Do you think we can have a moment alone?"

"Of course," I agreed, and Imara pouted but swam back to join Rhys with Tylia.

CHAPTER 34

SYRINADA

It happened. It really happened. It wasn't a dream that I made-up in my mind. I felt him. He was real. I didn't know how he did it, but somehow, Rhys repaired the space we built together. Our rendezvous, and it felt amazing to be back there. It felt whole again, and yes, I felt better knowing that he still cared.

His message renewed my hope. He and the others were coming for us. We weren't on our own. Even though I told him to tell Demetrius to stay back, I knew the Denali brother would never take a back seat. He would come with the others because he felt it was his duty to do so.

Despite the renewed hope, I still had a problem I needed to solve. Thanks to the medication they injected into my veins, I was still unable to control my shit. Water or not, I had no access to my tail. They made sure of it and even allowed me to bathe in the ocean water to prove it wouldn't work. The man who revealed their horrible plan to me still held power over me. He was in control as long as they kept me drugged up.

They weren't taking any more chances that I wouldn't eat the food. Even with me being able to get up and move around. The drugs and whatever nutrients they deemed necessary were being pumped directly into my arm.

I tried to be the compliant patient. Obviously, it would work in my favor if I did, but I couldn't help myself. Something inside me screamed to be free because I wasn't meant to be someone's captive. Even after the man was oddly sweet to me, I fought because I didn't want to be held against my will. I didn't want to be used as something to be experimented on. I didn't belong there. Neither did Malachi.

After I spoke to Rhys, I lay in the stiff clinic bed trying to hold on to the echoes of that connection. I could still feel it there, but I knew he wasn't on the other side anymore. All I could do was wait and hope he was successful in his attempt. Then I had an idea, and with it came the racing of my heart and my mind. What if I could use the residual energy, the fading connection, to reach out to someone else?

Rhys was no longer there, but I still felt the outside world. I would only have one shot, one opportunity to reach out to someone. Anyone who could help us. There was only one person I could think of. I closed my eyes and pictured her face. The woman who looked like an older version of myself. Her eyes were my own, wide, and brown, though her nose was thinner. She had a smile that made me feel whole and a heart big enough to love the entire world. My mother.

I whispered her name to myself and let it play on a loop in my mind. I could only hope she would hear my call and that the connection would last long enough for her to answer. A few moments later, the familiar voice responded. The nurturing tone bounced around my mind the same way it had many times before I knew her.

"Syrinada? Baby, is that you?" Though I wished I could see her face, her voice was comfort enough.

"Mom? Oh, thank God it worked," I spoke with my inner voice because I was afraid someone would hear me.

"Oh, thank God, it's so good to hear your voice." I felt the love in her voice, and my heart felt whole again. "I've been trying so long to find a way to reach you, but I kept hitting a wall. I started to fear the worst."

"I'm here, I'm alive, but I'm scared. I was starting to think I wouldn't make it out of here, but Rhys contacted me."

"We're coming for you, baby. All of us."

"You cannot let Demetrius come here." It was a long

shot, but I hoped my mother would be able to convince the man to stay back. "It's not safe. If you're with him, please try to tell him not to come. I told Rhys, but he's not going to listen to him. I know he won't."

"They got through to you?"

"Yes, they did, but whatever they did, it's fading fast. Please, Mom. Don't let him come here. That's exactly what they want."

"Syrinada, you know as well I do that nothing is going to stop that man from coming to find you. Just make sure you're ready when we get there."

"I don't think I have much time. Whatever they did is fading. I can feel the connection weakening. I don't want that to happen. How do I fix it? How do I? What do I do?"

"Oh, let's not waste anytime then. You need to get up. You need to fight."

"I can't shift, Mom. I can't use my tail."

"Calm down and tell me what's happening? What do you mean you can't use your tail?"

"This drug they've given me, it altered my abilities," I explained. "It's like a wall between me and my siren, and I can't get past it."

"They've drugged you. No wonder we couldn't get

through to you."

"Yea, and no matter what I do, I cannot use my tail. I haven't been sitting here just waiting aimlessly for someone to come save me. I fought, Mom, I promise I did, and I almost got out, but the second the water touched my tail, it vanished. If I leave this compound, I'll drown. After that, I think they changed the drug because I can't access my tail at all anymore."

"That is a problem, but it is not without a solution. What about your other abilities?"

"What do you mean?"

"Baby, you're not just a siren. You have other powers, remember? Your dad was not the greatest man, I get that, but you inherited a lot of power from him. Have you tried to tap into that magic?"

"No, I—" I could have kicked my own ass at that point because at not one point did it occur to me that the other magic available to me would work. I just assumed if I couldn't use my tail, I couldn't use any of my powers. Because I was underwater, it was like the only thing I could think about was swimming away. "I can't believe I didn't think of that. I feel like such an idiot."

"You just needed guidance. Now that you have it, tap into that side of yourself. Let it bring you to safety. There is strength there, and you have access to it all. Why do you think everyone is so afraid of you? They know what you are capable of, even if you do not. Take this time and commune with your mothers. Ask them, and they will help you."

"I love you." I could feel her leaving, and I needed to say the words.

"I love you too, my sweet daughter. I'll see you again soon."

My mother's voice faded from my mind, and I lay there, eyes still closed and holding on to her words like they were a blanket I could wrap around myself. My story wouldn't end as some science experiment for a crazed man. I would be free. If only I could figure out how to tap into my magic.

I opened my eyes to stare at the white ceiling above my head. She said I needed to commune with my mothers, but what did that mean? She was my mother, but I had others, grandmothers, ancestors no longer in the realm of the living. They were still there, I knew it, I'd seen evidence of the spirits who watched from across the veil.

Maggie.

I thought of my friend. No one had mentioned her to me. Was she okay? Was she still in the land of the living, or had they forced her to return to the spirit realm after we failed to do what they wanted?

My thoughts remained with Maggie. I couldn't think of anything else but the girl who, when we first met, attacked and kidnapped me. I thought of her energy and of her infectious spirit. I thought of bravery and her sacrifice. Maggie would never give up. She would fight until her last breath.

I'd been to the realm. With her and Ebon. I'd stepped on the other side of the veil once. What was there to say I couldn't do it again? Even on my own. I took several calming breaths and then told myself I would do whatever it took to get there. The first thing I had to do was relax, not that it was hard to do with the drugs still flowing through my veins.

I brought to mind the image of the location where I last saw Ebon. The ghostly planes where the others were. It was a blur at first, like a memory from childhood, but the more I reminded myself of the details, the clearer the image became.

The small house barely big enough for two. The porch with two seats and a table for tea. The wild field of grass. Every detail came back to me slowly until I could almost feel the ghostly air on my skin. And then I did as my mother suggested, with my heart and mind, I asked my mothers for help. I asked that they guide me and show me how to reconnect with the power inside me.

"I thought you'd get here a lot sooner." Ebon, the small ghostly girl, appeared on the porch in front of me. She wore a simple white dress, black Mary Janes, and ruffle socks, like she was on her way to church.

"Ebon?" I realized then that my visualization had transformed into something tangible. I'd crossed over from the living world to the ancestral plane.

"It's about time you figured out that we were still here by your side, girl." Ebon waved her hand and a cup of tea appeared. She sipped it slowly and glanced at the seat next to her.

"I know, I feel like a complete idiot right now." I took the seat and waited for her to finish savoring the beverage.

"What good does it do any of us for you to be sitting around feeling sorry for yourself?" Ebon placed the cup down on the small table between us. "The important thing is that you're here now, and we can work on getting you out of this mess."

"So, it's true? I can use my magic to get me out of that place?" The possibility had me sitting on the edge of my seat. There was a way I could get myself free. My mother was right.

"Of course, you can." She smiled, and the breeze picked up bringing the scent of freshly cut grass with it. "It's a good thing you've never made a show of the magic you have. They might have taken precautions to keep that side of you in check as well, but you lean into that siren side a lot more."

"Can you tell me how to do it?" My nerves were at an all-time high. For all I knew, Ebon was about to go cryptic and tell me the best thing was for me to figure it out myself, and if that were the case, I was screwed. "I know I should have figured this out by now, but I really don't feel that connected to that side of myself."

"That's not entirely your fault." Ebon suddenly wore a guilty expression. "We may have put in a fail safe."

"You did what?" I scooted back in my seat, pushing the whisps of hair from my face. "What does that mean? A fail safe?"

"You remember when we first met?" She picked up the teacup again, but this time, she only held it between her hands in her lap.

"Yes, how could I forget?" I was chained to a wall, force fed a hallucinogenic, and damn near scared to death when she appeared to me.

"I fought for your freedom, Syrinada." Ebon's voice was soft as she spoke. Often, her presence made me forget that when she died, she was just a child. "There were others, ones you haven't met and likely never will, who thought it best to end your life. They thought the threat was too great, but I didn't believe that. I saw the good in you. There were others on my side as well. With their support, ultimately, the decision made was to let you live freely, but to put in an insurance package."

"You're losing me." I sighed. "Can you just be straight with me here? What did you do?"

"We weren't sure if you could handle the power you inherited from your father, Syrinada. The reason those people can't sense your true strength is because we've hidden it. We put a block in place, one that limited your access to your ancestral magic. It's sort of like what they did to the sirens. Put their powers in a stone that they have to retrieve."

"From the top of a damn volcano. You want me to do that again?" I laughed hysterically before the panic set in. "I don't have time for this. We're going to die in that damn place because everyone is constantly testing me. Why do I have to keep proving I'm not a monster?"

"I know, it's not fair, but you don't have to do anything as drastic as the Naiad's walk."

"Damnit." I leaned back into the seat. "I guess I should thank you for at least standing up for me."

"You're welcome." Ebon smiled. "Now, as for the people who captured you, they know your father was a warlock. They know you are half witch, but what they don't know is just how strong your bloodline is."

"It is?"

"Yes, and it's about damn time you learned yet another secret about yourself that was kept from you.

There are people on this side who would prefer I didn't tell you, but we can't keep these secrets anymore. I don't think there is a chance in hell you're going to survive any of this if we don't be honest with you."

"Okay, I think I'm ready to hear another life altering secret about myself." I wished I had a cup of the tea she drank, and one appeared in front of me. I hesitated to take it, but when she nodded, I picked it up and sipped it as she began.

"On your mother side, you are the direct descendent of a titan," she explained and already I could feel my blood pressure rising. "That side of your bloodline is what makes you an ideal candidate for what those people are trying to accomplish, but there's something more to it, and it may not be the greatest thing, but it's something powerful."

"What is it?" The hairs on the back of my neck stood up, which meant whatever she had to say wasn't good.

"Syrinada, on your father's side, your bloodline stretches back to something that more would believe is darkness than light. I choose to believe that people make the choice of how to use to their magic and that determines if its good or bad."

"But?" I asked and sipped the tea again because it was the only thing I could think to do to keep myself from running away.

"Well, if I'm honest then I have to admit that this is one case where I'm not so sure." She paused, only briefly, and as the cool breeze came in again, she continued. "You are the descendant of one of the darkest warlocks our world has ever known. A man who borrowed magic from the devil himself. Or at least that's what everyone believes."

"You've got to be kidding me."

"I wish I were. From what I've heard, the man never even knew he has decedents. They say he came into town once, had a fling that went too far and resulted in a bloodline full of powerful witches and warlocks, most of whom turned dark. That is why the covens fear you. They think you will be just like your father. They think you will turn dark, and if that happens, with your siren abilities, they're afraid they won't stand a chance in hell at stopping you."

"Who was the warlock?" I pictured a man who looked like my father, a man who shared my nose and the random dark thoughts that passed through my mind. Had I inherited it all from him?

"His name is Daegal. Never heard of a last name for him."

"That's a strange name." I chose to focus on the mundane because what she said was far too heavy for me to unpack.

"From what I heard he made it up himself. I wish I could give you more information, but no one knows anything else about his family tree. All I've ever heard is that the man appeared one day, drunk and yelling about genies. He had sex with one of the witches then checked out never to be seen again. Some people still think he's out there using the borrowed magic to keep him alive."

"You mean you don't know? Isn't there some ghostly registry or something?" It was what I imagined death would be like. You cross over to the other side, sign in, and get your how-to-ghost handbook.

"We're not all connected like that. He isn't a part of our coven, even if his children were, but he has to be dead. I mean, the man is older than I am. He's older than any of the witches on this side of the veil, but I haven't seen him over here, which I guess could mean he is still somewhere with the living, unless he found himself somewhere in a darker place than we can imagine, but that's not the point."

"It isn't?"

"No, of course not. I'm not here to give you a history lesson on that man. What I'm here to do is tell you that you are powerful. You need to tap into that power, Syrinada, because if you don't, those people will break you. It's what they're trying to do. You're a siren, and you have to choose to become pregnant. They can't just wait for you to ovulate. That's what those drugs are meant to do.

"Those drugs they're pumping into your veins are meant to weaken your resolve and make you more impressionable. They think they're working. It's good you've been pretending to be so compliant. It bought you more time. The calvary is coming, Syrinada, but they can't do it on their own. I don't care how strong they think they are. You have to fight, just like your Mama told you. And yes, I heard the conversation."

"How do I connect with it? I mean, you're telling me I have this great power inside of me, but I haven't felt it this entire time."

"First, you need to understand what it is before you can connect to it. It's that darkness inside of you, that part of yourself you have been suppressing ever since you found out who you are. You feel it, and I'm telling you that it wasn't just your daddy making you feel it. It is a part of you. Now typically I wouldn't tell you to go tapping into darkness, but in this situation, I think it's fitting. You cannot let them do what they want to do."

"Tap into the darkness?" I couldn't help the laugh that came out of me. "You have all been telling me to leave that part of myself alone. Literally chained me up because you were afraid I would go dark, and now you're telling me to just go ahead and let it happen?"

"Yes. Tap in, but just don't let it consume you. Hope

like hell you don't lose yourself within it." Ebon pulled my hand into hers. "When you leave this plane, the barrier we put in place to shield you from that magic will no longer be there. Once we remove it, we cannot put it back up, so you need to decide if this is really what you want to do."

"Tap into darkness or become some freaky titan incubator?" Again, I laughed to keep from crying. "What choice do I really have here? Do it."

I expected more of a show. Some big ceremony where Ebon would say a spell over my body and I would feel the barrier they implanted break down. It wasn't nearly as dramatic. Instead, I drifted away from the ancestral plane like a leaf in the wind and landed gently back in my body.

With the first conscious breath I took, I felt the difference. My body, the energy inside, and the feel of the world around me, it had all changed. The darkness that existed inside of me, the magic Ebon spoke of, it was there. In a way I never felt it before. The alarming part of it was how it felt… like that part of me celebrated. As if that magic was a person all its own, and it heard what Ebon said to me. It knew what I had to do.

I hesitated. Ebon said they wouldn't be able to put the barrier back up. Did that mean if I embraced it, even for a moment, I would risk losing myself completely? Could I ever pull back from it? Suddenly, I was terrified because all that time I thought I had it in check, when really, I barely knew what it was.

I was terrified because I knew that despite my worry, I had to do it. Ebon and my mother were right. If I had the power to free myself, to save me and my friends, I had to do so.

Even after I returned to my body, I laid there with my eyes closed because I didn't know what was coming next, but I could feel everything around me. The cold sterile room where they left me alone. The firm mattress beneath my back. The instruments he used to perform his tests. The buzzing of equipment in nearby rooms. I felt the entire structure of the building around me and the dark, vast of water outside its walls. I felt it all. How could I have changed so much already? How could I feel this powerful even before I made the commitment in my mind and heart?

I held my breath and gave myself one more moment to reconsider, but there was no point in it. My mind was made up, regardless of the consequences. Whatever the outcome, I'd deal with it later. Survival was all that mattered.

When I released the breath, I accepted all that darkness that lingered in the background and the recesses of my mind. I embraced the dark hold, felt the cold of its power stretch across my body. That sticky feeling that pushed through my veins. This was the power the covens feared. This was the Magic the sirens thought I would use against them. This was the power my father wanted to use for his benefit.

By the time I drew my next breath, I was someone completely different.

After it was done, I had one thought. Find Malachi and get the hell out of there. I opened my eyes, sat up, and threw my feet over the edge of the bed. I took one step toward the door.

Then the building shook. At first, I only felt the rumbles, but then I heard them. Explosions. The compound was under attack.

CHAPTER 35

There were two more explosions further away from me. I waited for a third, but nothing happened. When it didn't, I made my move. I could only hope the sounds were of someone coming to rescue us and not to make thing worse for us.

The door was the same as before, locked with a key I had no access to, but I didn't need it. All I had to do was trust in my power. I held my palm over the lock and felt the surge of energy pulse from within me. It passed through my palm and into the panel. A moment later, I heard the clicking of the mechanism that kept it secure, and the door popped open.

I stepped out into the hallway prepared to defend myself against whatever orderly came at me. They wouldn't allow me to just walk out without a fight, but there was no one. I could hear the screams of people in the distance, and I felt the panic they felt. Their fear felt like a drug to me. Powerful and intoxicating.

As tempting as it was to follow the sounds of terror, I knew that wasn't the way for me. Somewhere in the compound, Malachi was still locked up. I had to get him out, and I could feel him. He wasn't in the area where the people battled.

I stood in the white hall and blocked everything from my mind except Malachi. I needed to find him, and like a beacon, I felt his energy pulsing from the opposite direction. Though I felt him, I couldn't get a clear vision of where they kept him.

Despite the battle that went on in the building, I knew it was still too dangerous to call out to Malachi. The best thing I could do was keep a low profile and avoid conflict for as long as possible.

Instead of calling out, I tried to use that internal voice to reach him. With my power restored, even if it wasn't my siren side, it should have worked. With a calm mind, I thought of my friend. I remembered the way I heard his voice in my head before. The feeling of our connection. I found it inside my heart and pieced it back together. It was still there. It would always be there.

First my heart warmed, then my mind tingled, and I knew it worked. The connection was restored.

Malachi? Please tell me you can hear me. I spoke with

my inner voice and waited for him to answer me, but nothing happened. Three more times I tried before I got a response, but it wasn't from the man I thought it would be from.

"Syrinada?" His voice was deep, smooth, and warm like a fresh cup of coffee. It gave me the same energy boost as the caffeinated beverage did.

"Demetrius?" Though he wasn't who I thought I would reach, hearing his voice excited me.

"Sy, where are you?" he asked. *"I'm here. Tell me how to get to you."*

"Demetrius? No, you can't be here. It's a trap. I told them not to let you come."

"I know it's a trap, and I don't give a damn. You're my mate, and there was no way I was going to stay behind and risk losing you."

I said nothing back because my mind was still trying to wrap around the fact that he called me his mate. Demetrius came to save his mate. Me. Would he still feel the same after learning what I did to get free? That I embraced the darkness.

"Where are you?" he repeated his question. *"Come on, tell me something I can use."*

"I'm trying to find Malachi. He is here too. They trapped him, but I don't know where. We found each other and were

trying to escape, but they stopped us."

"We have people here helping. Just stay safe. Describe your surroundings."

"I'm in a long hall, lots of doors with no handles." I did my best to describe the blank slate in front of me. *"I can feel Malachi. He is on a lower level. I'm going to find him."*

"I know I can't stop you or convince you to wait for me? Just please be safe."

I stepped to the door closest to me. I knew it wasn't Malachi, but there was someone on the other side. Someone strong. I could have opened the door, but I didn't because I couldn't be sure whoever it was would be on my side.

"I will, but there are more people here. I can feel them. They're locked away just like I was. They're going to experiment on all these people."

"We know, and we're going to get everyone out. Right now, we have to focus on you. No one else."

"I have to find Malachi."

"I understand. Again, be safe."

Demetrius' voice left my mind, but I could still feel the connection there. As I headed down the hall, I couldn't help but think about what he said. He called me his mate, and even though it shocked me to hear it,

I couldn't deny it. There wasn't one part of me that felt like he was wrong. I couldn't explain it, but even though I'd chosen to be with Rhys, Demetrius was still my mate. Reaching the end of the hallway, I reminded myself of my current task. Find Malachi.

There had to be a way to connect with him. I could feel his energy in the building though it felt hard to lock on to.

"Use the magic," I whispered to myself then closed my eyes and focused on what I felt was Malachi's energy. "Please show me the way."

First felt the beacon. It was a pulsing energy that hooked into my core and pulled me forward. When I opened my eyes, I saw it. Whisps of grey that floated in the air and headed off to the left. At the end of the hall was a door marked as a stairway.

"Yes," I celebrated as I followed the path laid out to me.

I knew it was the right way because when I touched the door, I felt his energy grow. The further I went through the maze of hallways and staircases, it continued to get stronger. Each time I reached a door that wouldn't open, I used my magic to break the lock. I went down two flights of stairs before I found the floor where his energy felt the strongest.

The moment I stepped into the hallway, even

before the whisps showed me the way, I knew he was there. I could feel him, that dark energy of his demon. It had to be him. Eager to get him out of whatever lockup they had him in, I ran to the door, and without question, placed my hand on the panel. It wasn't until after I heard the door unlock that I questioned if I'd made the right choice.

I tapped the door to open it but then backed up. It slowly swung open revealing the dark interior of the room. It was the same as when I first found him. Odd to say I took comfort in the darkness, but I told myself it meant he had to be inside. Malachi's demon preferred the dark.

"Malachi, are you there?" I called out to him and hoped the sound of my voice would soothe the beast. "It's me, Syrinada. I'm going to get us out of here."

I stood in the hallway, waiting for a response. Anything that told me there was life inside the darkness, but there was nothing. Maybe it wasn't enough just to call out to him.

"Shit," I said because I didn't want to do what I felt I needed to. I took a step forward with every intention of going into the darkness and pulling my friend out, but before my foot hit the floor, I heard it. The deep growl. The anger. The evil. Whatever was hidden in the shadowed room was not Malachi.

I slowly backed away from the door but kept my

eyes focused ahead of me. Something was inside, and I could hear it moving. To turn before I knew what I was up against would be a mistake. On my third step, I heard another growl and the sound of furniture being tossed around. On my fourth step the small metal chair came flying out of the room. I ducked just before it took my head off. By the fifth step I could see the eyes staring back at me.

Bright yellow eyes locked in on me and tracked me like a predator hunting its prey. I still couldn't see the beast, but I knew I had to get out of there. Careful steps were not enough. I needed to put as much space between me and it as possible. I took a deep breath for courage and then turned and bolted down the hallway. If I could make it back to the stairwell, I might be able to get away.

Not only could I hear the thing chasing me, but I also felt it. Every step it took made the floor beneath my feet tremble. Then there were the growls, the deep roars and the sounds of hard hits against the wall. As I turned the corner, I glanced back to see what was after me. This was not a demon.

If it was, it was nothing like the ones I'd seen before. I wasn't sure what it was, but it was ugly as hell. It had grey skin with yellow stripes around its shoulder and down the enormous arms that ended with massive, clawed hands. Its eyes were massive and yellow, its nose inset, and it had rows of teeth that were set outside its lips.

It roared as it ran down the hall, its large body knocking into the walls and sharp claws ripped into them and left huge gashes in the white surface. Despite its size and apparent disorientation, it was moving fast. As I continued running, I heard it getting closer. It was going to get me.

When I reached the end of the hall, I realized my mistake. I turned the wrong way. Instead of reaching the doorway that led to the stairs, I hit a dead end.

"Fuck!" I called out. As I watched the monster get closer to me, I realized I wouldn't be able to run away. I had to stand and fight, or that thing was going to chew my head off.

"Use your magic," I hyped myself up. The magic was mine, the power that came with it. I just had to believe it would do what I needed it to.

Just as it lunged for me, I dropped back holding both palms out and felt the heat as a burst of energy shot out of my hands. It hit the thing in the center of its wide chest and knocked the beast over. It fell backward, clawing up the wall as it did, but I knew it wasn't enough. The thing got back up and came at me again. I shot it again, but it was smart enough to realize what I was doing and dodged the second blow.

It ran for me, and though I wanted to act, I panicked

again, and I froze. The beast slammed the back of its hand into my chest and knocked me off my feet. My vision blurred, and the back of my head stung from the impact against the wall. When I looked up, it towered over me, claws ready to rip me apart, and just as I thought I would die, something powerful blasted it from the left, knocking it into the wall.

"Sy." The hand stuck out to me, and I looked up to find Rhys standing next to me.

"Rhys!" I took his hand, and he pulled me to my feet.

"Are you hurt?" He tried to examine me, but I wrapped my arms around his neck to hug him.

"No, I'm okay," I said into his shoulder. "I'm so happy to see you."

"What the hell is that thing?" Rhys pushed me behind him, and we backed away from the beast as it stirred.

"I don't know. I thought it was Malachi, but when I opened the door, that came out."

"Dammit." Rhys glanced over his shoulder at me. "That should have taken that thing out for good."

It got back up, and Rhys tried to fight it. He shot it with wave after wave of his power, but it wasn't enough. Each hit was less effective as the monster adapted to

Rhy's ability. When it got within range, it hit him with the same backhand that knocked me over before.

I thought it might come after me, but it kept its focus on Rhys, and it looked like it was going to kill him. There was no way I could let that happen. The anger I felt, watching that thing look down on Rhys like he was nothing, was enough to give me what I needed to tap further into my internal darkness.

"Hey!" I called out, and the beast looked at me. "Bring your ugly ass over here!"

The damn thing actually looked offended by my comment. Its face snarled, and it grunted before rubbing its massive paw across its face. Then it ran for me. That time, I didn't try to blast it with power, it would be expecting that, so I had to do something different. Instead, I let the magic guide me, and it did something unexpected.

That dark energy tapped into the power around me and linked directly to the electricity that ran through the walls. Above my head, the lights flickered, and the power surged through me. It built inside my chest, and for a moment, I thought I'd made the wrong move, but then it hit the beast from every angle. It shot out from the walls, not me. The shocking display of light wrapped around the thing like a net, and when it ended, the beast was shriveled up on the floor like a raisin.

"Woah." Rhys got back to his feet and stood over

the twisted body of the beast.

"Yeah." I kicked its leg just to be sure it was really dead. "Are you okay?"

"I'm fine." Rhys rubbed the back of his neck. "How did you do that? What did they do to you?"

"It's a long story." I avoided a direct answer to his question because it wasn't the time to get into it.

"Whatever the story is, tell it later." Imara ran into the hallway from the stairwell behind us. "We got company."

CHAPTER 36

"What?" Rhys poke pressed his ear against the door to the stairwell. "Dammit."

"Those damn zombie orderlies are headed this way," Imara reported before she gave me a quick hug. "I'm glad you're still alive."

"So am I." I chuckled nervously. While it was good to see her, we were in a bad spot.

"Let's get the hell out of here." She pointed down the hall that led back to where I opened the door I thought was Malachi's. "There's another stairwell. Hopefully we can avoid them by going that way."

We ran down the hall, but we didn't make it far before four people, all dressed in white, came running into the hallway after us. I couldn't understand it at first. They felt different. A strange energy vibrated from each one and tickled the back of my mind. These weren't ordinary people. They each had powers of their own.

We skidded to a halt when the first one, a tall blonde man, flashed by us and cut off our path. Rhys, ever the protector, defended us with his magic. He trapped the man's ankles with an invisible barrier which quickly anchored him to the ground. As clever as the move was, it landed him on the short woman's bad side.

I felt her power before it worked on him and turned in time to see her focused expression. Eyes squinted, and mouth scowled. With her mind, she grabbed hold of Rhys.

"See how you like it." She smirked, and then Rhys' body lifted in the air, and he slammed face first into the ceiling before he dropped like a concrete brink to the floor. He gasped for air but couldn't catch his breath before she did it again. The second time he hit the floor, blood spilled from his lip.

"No!" I screamed, and the short woman fell on her ass though I'd done nothing but use my voice.

When I lifted my hands with every intention of tapping into that power inside of me, something changed. My vision rushed in a blur of colors, and then suddenly, I wasn't in the hallway anymore. Instead, I stood in a field of grass and wild flowers. In the distance there was a line of trees and a man standing beneath them.

"No, this isn't right." I shook my head to clear the delusion. "I've been here before. This isn't real!"

Quickly realizing someone else controlled my mind, I fought against the vision. "Give me back my mind!" When I screamed, the projected vision flickered, and for a moment, I was back in the hallway, but it snapped back into focus again.

Repeatedly, I pushed my mind back to reality, but whoever held my vision was strong. One moment I would be back in that field where I saw the Denali brother before my challenge, and the next I was in the hallway, watching my sister defend us alone, and there was nothing I could do.

"Sy!" she called out, but again, I couldn't do anything because my mind was ripped away. When I came back to. I watched as Imara ran across the hall, mouth open, and planted a kiss on the small guy who stood alone.

He resisted for only a moment, but then he gave into her, and she took everything from him. As his eyes closed, I felt my mind return to me, and it was just in time. The short woman turned her mind on Imara, and her body seized, but this time, I got the shot off.

The blast knocked her square in the side of the head, and when she fell, she cracked her skull against the wall. Imara had already taken out two of the others. All that was left was the quick guy, and when I turned my sights on him, he cowered, still anchored by Rhys' magic.

"What do we do about him?" Imara pointed to the man strapped to the floor.

"Something tells me he's not that big of a threat. He's just fast." I shrugged.

"Not anymore." Imara winked and flipped her curly hair from her face. "It really is good to see you. I was worried there for a minute."

"Me to." I didn't know what took over me, but I hugged her. I pulled her into my arms and held her as tightly as I could.

"Well, that's unexpected," she whispered but hugged me back.

"We still need to find Malachi." I refocused our goal when I let her go. "I thought I found him before, but I was seriously wrong."

"We're supposed to get you back to the others." Rhys coughed as he got back to his feet, and more blood dripped from his lip.

"Are you okay?" I asked.

"I'm fine, but we need to go now."

"I'm not going anywhere without Malachi," I said firmly. "No one is getting left behind here."

"You're damn straight," Imara agreed. "But we better get moving because you can bet your ass more or those henchmen are going to come running down here."

"You should go back to the others." I turned to Rhys. "We can handle this."

"What are you talking about?" He clutched his side. "I'm fine. Already healing. I'm not leaving you."

"You're clearly hurt, and we don't know what we're going into," I reasoned. "Whoever is coming, they're not looking for you, they're looking for me. I don't want you to be in their path."

"Sy, I don't think that's the smartest thing to do," he said. "I can protect you."

"I hate to say it, but I agree with her," Imara said.

"Seriously?" He looked at Imara and huffed. "I can't believe this."

"Look, I get the macho protector thing all you men seem to have going on but think about this logically." Imara pointed at his side. "You're going to slow us down, and we need to get in and out quickly."

"Fine." He threw his hands up in the air. "Whatever you say."

"I'm sorry." I reached out to him, but he pulled away.

"Don't be." Rhys turned and headed for the stairwell.

"You think he'll be okay?" Imara asked.

"I have no idea." I shrugged. "But this was the right choice.

We continued for the opposite stairwell, and I refocused my mind to find Malachi's energy signature. I found one, reddish brown whisps floated in front of me, leading the way. I could only hope this one was the right one. Imara kept up with me easily and watched my back whenever I worked my magic to clear our path.

I could feel Malachi's energy getting stronger, so I followed it and refocused my power each time I felt it increase. We couldn't afford to make another mistake. By the time we made it to the last doorway, I felt certain I was on the right path.

"He's just around that corner." I pointed ahead of us, and Imara nodded.

"Good job." She held her fist out, and I bumped it with my own.

Imara ran ahead of me, but when she rounded the corner, she came to a halt. My heart dropped because I thought we'd taken the wrong path again, but when I caught up with her, I realized we hadn't. Standing at the opposite end of the end of the hall was a giant woman

I'd met once before, and she had two others by her side. These weren't like the orderlies we dealt with before. They were dressed head to toe in black, and their faces were completely covered.

There was no denying the two were strong, I could feel the energy that came off them. It was dark but also different than anything I'd felt before. For one thing, it didn't belong to them. This power was much older than the two faceless beings, but at the same time, it felt like whatever they'd done only created a weak connection to what fed them their power. If we had to fight them, we could win simply by waiting it out because it wasn't strong enough to sustain it.

"Nevay?" I called out her name. "You were a part of this all along. I knew something was up with you!"

"Should have gone with that gut feeling, but you were too busy making googly eyes at my brother." Nevay dropped her hip and crossed her arms over her chest. "Still don't understand why he was so fascinated with you."

"Sounds like someone is jealous," Imara whispered. "Can you say incest?"

I chuckled at my sister's comment then called out to the giant at the end of the hall. "What are you doing here?"

"Making sure you don't ruin our plan." Nevay

rolled her eyes as if bored with our conversation. "Seriously, sometimes it's like talking to a wall with you."

"Our plan?" I asked. "You're not working alone?"

"God, I'm sick of this weak body!" she screamed then shook her head. "Of course, I'm not working alone."

"What do you mean you're sick of your body?" Imara asked then raised her brow at me.

"A giant is supposed to be stronger than this," Nevay continued to complain. "He swore this one would be better than the last."

"What's up with this chick?" Imara whispered to me.

"I have no idea." I shrugged.

"How is it you still haven't figured it out?" Nevay pointed at me with a scowl. "I mean, after all this time. It's so damn obvious I could hit you over the head with it. You know, he really had high hopes for you. He kept going on and on about how smart you were because he found you with that damn book. You're so smart, and yet here you still unable to figure out who we really are."

"Let's just say we're both morons and you tell us who you are and save us some time," Imara called out. "I'd really like to get this over with, and I'm not the kind of girl who likes to work out riddles."

"Fine. If you want to take the fun out of everything."

She ran her hand across her face, and for a moment, it changed, like her flesh ripped away, and before it could repair itself, we saw her true face. Honey colored skin with ice blue eyes and hair of gold.

"My name is Mnemosyne." She smiled wickedly. "That fast enough for you?"

"Mnemosyne, as in the titan?" I gawked at her. "You've got to be kidding me."

"Yes, so as you can see, I have a personal investment in you and your ability to produce strong babies. I need a new body. One that won't fall apart after a measly few years." She stepped forward, and the two guards moved with her like they were chained to her. "You know that's how long it took us to find you. Five long years I've been trapped inside this ridiculous body, and we almost gave up. We were days away from going back to the other side and waiting for another opportunity. It would have taken us another eon to come back, but then the siren woke up. Didn't she?"

"I take it she's talking about you?" Imara asked.

"Yeah." I swallowed the lump in my throat.

"We felt it. The moment you took your first life, that energy, that darkness. It was exactly what we needed, but still, we couldn't find you. It gave my brilliant brother an idea, though. We could simply look for others like you, and there were plenty to choose from. This place is full of hybrids just like you and your sister and those boys who love you so much. The youth, you're a special breed, aren't you? The magic of a witch, the power of a siren, and the bloodline of a titan." She damn near cheered. "And then that man, oh that beautiful man. He brought you right to us. Told us all your plans. All we had to do was sit and wait. How lucky could we get?"

"I'd say pretty damn lucky," I called back. "But I have a feeling your luck is about to run out."

"Big words from a girl who can't even access her tail."

"I don't need my tail to beat you. Like you said, there's a lot more to me than my siren, and your mad scientist only thought to suppress one side of me."

"A witch? So what?"

Tired of the conversation, I chose to use action over words and forced a blast at her. It knocked her back into the wall, and her face, still half masked, dripped blood.

"Get them!" she ordered the two men who stood guard with her.

As commanded, the two ran down the hall. They split their efforts. One came for me while the other attacked Imara. Funny she should speak down on witches, but her two guards wielded magic the same as I did. Only they were far more skilled than I was. Even after restoring the connection to my ancestral magic, without adequate training and practice, my skills were still shaky at best. All I could do was use my instincts.

I got one good shot off before they were on top of us, but the hit did enough damage. I felt their connection to whatever aided their magic weaken. Unfortunately, it was the only direct hit I would get as the one who charged me went blow for blow. Everything I shot at them, they blocked. Because I was a quick study, I realized the technique they used to block my hits. Grounded feet, centered, and arms crossed over the chest. When they shot their magic at me, a blast of air that would have collapsed my chest, I did the same block, and it worked.

I couldn't help but worry about my sister. She was strong, but she was also a witch. I could only assume that, just like me, the ancestors had cut off her access to her power, which meant she wouldn't be able to use it to defend herself, but every time I looked over to see Imara, she was holding her own. I realized him that I had to focus on my own enemy because if I let myself get distracted, it would hurt our cause, and it was exactly what happened.

I took one last glance to see if my sister was okay, and that was when the blow landed. It wasn't enough to kill me, but it was enough to knock me on my ass. My failure distracted Imara, and a moment later, she suffered her own devastating blow. They stood over her, ready to end her life, but I refused to let that happen. There was no way I was just going to lay there and watch my sister die. We had only just begun to get to know each other. No one would take that away from me.

Remembering Rhys' training, I centered myself in the time it took to take my next breath. There was power inside me, and by the way Ebon spoke of it, it was more than enough to take these assholes out. I thought of her words, of the bloodline that flowed all the way back to the Warlock who made a deal with the devil. I prepared for that evil to take over me, but instead, I felt something familiar. Something safer. It felt like being wrapped in a rainbow and then dunked into a cup of Sprite. Maggie.

I felt her power, but I knew she wasn't there. If she was, she'd have some smartass comment to make about me being on my ass and not on my feet. She wasn't there, but her magic was, and instead of going dark, I used the magic Maggie lent me and turned that into a wave of power. On my third breath, I sent that magic out from me, every bit that I could muster.

Everything went silent. For a moment, I heard nothing, I saw nothing, I felt nothing, and then it was like thunder. The wave passed through the hall with so much pressure that the walls rippled. The two who attacked us were caught in the flow, and both of their heads exploded from the pressure. They fell, and their blood spilled across the floor.

It wasn't what I expected. Their death was so gruesome, but there wasn't time to feel guilt or mourn them. The blast also knocked Mnemosyne over, but she wouldn't stay down for long.

Mnemosyne was dying. Even from the other end of the hall, I could feel her body breaking down. It didn't matter. She was still strong, and if we weren't smart, she would win the fight.

"You ready?" Imara stood next to me.

"Never thought I'd take on a titan." I got up from the floor and quickly put my hair up into a messy bun.

"Shit, never thought I'd be fighting in an underwater lair in the mermaid realm." Imara wiped blood from her lip. "But here we are."

"Here we are." I caught my breath.

"You're going to have to teach me that head explosion trick." She laughed. "Brutal but effective."

"Of course, as soon as we make it back on land." I winked at her.

"You bitch!" Mnemosyne yelled at us from across the hall. "How dare you!"

"Oh, sorry about your friends," I taunted her.

"I'll kill you!" she yelled and then the titan trapped

in a giant charged us.

When she charged, so did we. We split, running down either side of the hall and let her choose who to take on first. She came for me. I wasn't sure what to expect from a titan, but her body limited her power. The witches were an extension of herself, but without them, she could do little more than box us, and that was what she did. The first blow landed square on my jaw, and I fell back by at least four feet.

Imara was next. She dodged two hits before Mnemosyne knocked her down. We performed that dance in sequence again and again. Landing no hits of our own but taking them from the giant. Mnemosyne was a lot stronger than I thought, even in her weakened state, and for a giant in the small space, she was a lot more agile than I expected she would be.

Each punch landed harder than the one before.

"Okay, this isn't working." Imara landed next to me and spit blood on the floor. "I don't know how much longer I can keep this up."

"A succubus and a witch." Mnemosyne laughed. "As if the two of you could take me on."

"That's it." I smacked the floor.

"What?" Imara said. "Am I missing something."

"Why aren't we fighting like what we are?" I lowered my voice while Mnemosyne continued her rant about how weak we were. The woman loved to hear herself speak.

"Huh?"

"We're a succubus and a witch," I whispered. "We're trying to fight on her terms. Let's change the fucking terms."

Imara's eyes brightened as she caught my meaning. "I like the way you think, sister."

Despite the obvious pain she had to be in, Imara got up and ran for Mnemosyne. As the titan tried to defend herself, I sent a wave of power that knocked her feet from under her. She fell forward, and her face landed in between Imara's hands a second before she locked lips with the succubus. Imara sucked the life force from the titan as long as she could, but Mnemosyne knocked her away. Then I hit.

Blast after blast of energy and shocks of electricity went through the woman before Imara caught her lips again, pulling more energy from her. When she hit Imara the second time, my sister fell just beyond me. I moved into action and got two blasts off, but the titan dodged them and hit me. The blow was stronger than I thought it would be, and I fell into the wall, twisting my neck. The impact left me disoriented.

"Enough of this!" Mnemosyne yelled and stomped toward me.

I scooted back, sending weak blasts from one hand as I reached my sister.

Imara grabbed my wrist, and I thought she would pull me away from the titan. Instead, she pushed her energy into me. I felt it flow from her hand through my wrist and up my arm. Imara gave me the energy she took from Mnemosyne, and when she did, it didn't just heal the injury I sustained. It fixed something deep inside me.

I felt her awaken. That beautiful creature their drugs cut me off from. Her voice rang out. At first it was an internal cry, but then my lips parted, and my siren song filled the hallway.

When the Mnemosyne heard my song, the titan gave in to me like she was no better than the mortals she looked down on. She lost her fight and stood there looking at me like she wanted to give me anything I could ever ask of her.

Song still flowing, I stood and walked over to the woman who towered over me.

"Kneel," I said, and she did as I asked.

Then I planted my lips on hers, and just as my sister had before, I pulled the life from within her. The woman clung to me like I was the air she needed to breathe, but as I pulled from her and tasted that eternal life, felt it flow through me and tingle beneath my flesh, I knew I could never really take everything from her, so I had to make it impossible for her to remain.

While she kissed me, fed me her life, I placed my hands on either side of her face, gently caressing her to ease any lingering concern for her safety. Then, when I felt her body relax, her shoulders dropped, and she moaned into my mouth, I grabbed both sides of her torn mask and pulled. With the power given to me by my father's blood, I ripped away the shell of the giant's body, leaving it hanging on either side.

"Imara." I only said my sister's name once before she jumped into action.

Mnemosyne was still in my trance when Imara grabbed one half of the body, and I took the other. Together, we pulled, ripping the giant shell in two. By the time the titan realized what we'd done, it was too late.

I expected her to curse, scream about betrayal, and fight back, but she didn't. Mnemosyne lingered for a moment. Her energy floated above the remains of the body she'd stolen with a satisfied look on her face.

"He was right about you." She smiled with tears flowing down her face, and then she vanished.

CHAPTER 37

"*Woah, that was intense.*" I watched the last flicker of the titan disappear before I felt relief.

"Yeah." Imara dropped the flesh she still held in her hands. "And gross."

I stared at my sister because she looked different to me. I could feel the energy of the titan that linger inside her. Would it stay there forever? Would it stay inside me like Maggie's clearly had? Her body looked stronger; her wounds completely healed already.

"We need to get moving." I looked at the door Mnemosyne and her puppets guarded.

"Is he in there?" Imara turned to look at the door. "Malachi?"

"Yeah, at least I hope so." I shrugged. "I was wrong

before."

Imara walked over to the door and placed her hand on it. She took a deep breath then turned to me with a smile on her face. "It's him. I can feel him."

"What?" I joined her by the door. "You can?"

"You don't forget energy like that." She rubbed her hand on the door affirming her feeling. "It's definitely him."

"Good." I nodded but felt an internal doubt bubbling in my stomach. How could she be so sure when I wasn't. Was it my fear of making another mistake that stifled my confidence? "Well, I better unlock it."

Imara stepped aside, and I placed my hand on the panel, and like the others before it, it unlocked. I pushed the door open, and as expected, it was dark inside. My doubt was instantly erased with the air that came from the room. The deep earthy scent, with an edge of hellfire. Like the scent of coals left burning after the cookout. It was definitely Malachi.

Then a deep voice called out from the darkness. It spoke a name, and my heart broke with the sound.

"Imara?" Malachi took a step forward, but he was still out of view.

"It's me," she answered him. "I'm here, baby."

Malachi stepped forward, and just as he was before, he was in his demon form. That red skin lit up in the light as he reached for her. I thought she would be afraid of him, cower away from his dark form, but Imara embraced him. There was no fear. She wrapped her arms around his neck and kissed him.

"I know you don't typically need this, but considering what they did to you," Imara released her hold on him an pulled the familiar charm from her pocket. It was the piece he usually wore to keep his demon at bay. She placed necklace over his head, and when the charm touched his chest, the demon turned back into the man.

"Thank you." He looked at her with love and pulled her hand to his lips to kiss. "It's so good to see you."

I stood aside and watched them embrace and tried not to feel anger. I had no right to be upset by their display of intimacy, but it was there. All that time I wanted Malachi to get over me, but the moment it looked like he had, I felt jealous.

"Sy," Malachi acknowledge me.

"Malachi." I waved from the doorway.

"You did it." He looked grateful, relieved, but it was different. Something about him changed.

"Looks like it." I forced a smile because I didn't

want either of them to know how I really felt. "We should really get back to the others. I know they will need our help."

"You okay?" Malachi frowned.

"I'm fine," I lied and stepped further into the hallway. "Just tired, and I know our fight isn't over."

"You're right," he said. "I can feel it."

"What's the fastest way back?" I asked Imara.

"This way." Imara led the way back to the staircase we came from. "These stairs lead right up to the main floor. That's where I left Demetrius and the others."

"My brother is here?" Malachi asked.

"Of course, he is." She laughed and pointed at me. "Like he'd let us come to save that one without him."

"Lead the way," he said, and Imara took off running. Malachi was right behind her, and I followed behind him.

We were seven levels below the main floor. After we passed the third, two men entered the stairwell ahead of us and instantly attacked. They were both witches. I centered myself and prepared to battle them, but I didn't have to lift a finger.

Malachi was strong even without his demon. He

leapt over Imara's head and kicked the first guy in the side of the head, sending him flying over the railing. As he dropped, his head smacked the wall, and I heard the bone snap. Malachi then grabbed the other by the face. His hand crushed the man's skull like it was a plastic bottle. He sent that guy over the rail after his friend.

"Well, damn." I looked up at Malachi, and Imara laughed.

"I was not expecting that." She looked back at me. "Seems like they were experimenting on both of y'all."

"I don't know what happened. It's like I can still use my full demon strength even when I'm not turned."

"That's handy." Imara stepped up to him and squeezed his bicep.

"Yeah, it is. We're going to need your strength." I looked over the railing again at the limp bodies on the bottom level. "We should keep moving."

The door to the top floor swung open to a massive white room. One wall was made completely of glass, while the opposite, white just like every other wall in the compound, was splattered with blood. Dead bodies, people dressed in all white, littered the floor. The battle was over, but where were our allies?

"Syrinada?" her voice called from the opposite end of the room, and I turned to see my mother turning the corner and entering the room. "There you are!"

She ran for me, and I met her halfway, slamming into her hold. She ran her hands across my head and back. "You're safe."

"I am." I buried my head in her shoulder and inhaled her sweet scent. "You shouldn't be here."

"Shh," she hushed me. "I'm a fighter just like you. Where do you think you get it from?"

"Where are the others?" I asked just before a group of people entered the room from the same hall my mother had.

"They're coming," she answered.

"We need to get out of here," Imara said. "This isn't over. There are more people here."

"She's right." I nodded. "I can feel them."

"The others are working to free as many of the captives as possible."

"Not all of them are friendly," I said, thinking of the large beast we fought in the hallway.

"Syrinada." Demetrius pushed passed the group of men who entered ahead of him.

The sound of my name across his lips sent my heart

soaring. This man. Even at a time when my thoughts should have been pure, he had me ready to risk it all. All I could think about was how he called me his mate, and how I wanted to make him feel how I felt when he said it.

My mother stepped away from me a moment before he reached me. I expected him to say something or tell me how much he missed me. He wasted no time with words. Demetrius pulled me into his arms and kissed me, and I melted into him.

"I thought I'd never get to do that again," he said against my lips, and I smiled.

When he pulled away, that moment of happiness shattered as I saw Rhys enter the room over his shoulder. How could I forget he was there? How could I get so wrapped up in the moment? He looked so angry, but he said nothing. I wanted to address it, but it wasn't the time. A fact only made truer when the door behind us burst opened.

I heard their growls before I saw them, and I knew exactly what was coming. More of the beast, like that ugly grey and yellow thing it took two of us to kill, came into the room, but they didn't attack. The lined up and stood watching us, like they were soldiers waiting for orders.

"What the hell is this?" Demetrius said and pushed me behind him.

"What a wonderful reunion." The giant man clapped as he walked into the room behind his wall of monsters.

"Omar, you bastard," Demetrius cursed.

"Oh, you know, I think we should use my real name, no? Don't you think?" He bowed. "Allow me to introduce myself. My name is Oceanus."

"I don't give a fuck what your name is." Malachi stood next to his brother and pushed Imara behind him.

My sister bumped her arm against mine and whispered, "Are you okay?"

I nodded to her, but before I could speak, Oceanus called out my name.

"Syrinada." He peeked around the brothers who blocked his direct view of me. "Just as amazing as I thought you were. You defeated my sister, didn't you? I told her not to underestimate you."

"A lot of people tend to make that mistake." Demetrius glanced over his shoulder at me.

"I knew you were special. Flying colors on every test," Oceanus continued as if Demetrius had said nothing. "Now to just finish this up. You have a duty to fulfill, dear."

"That's never going to happen." Malachi was the

one to speak.

"Looks like I have to get rid of your fan club first." Oceanus smiled. "No worries, I came prepared. I knew he'd never give you up without a fight."

Oceanus stepped back to lean against the wall, then whistled. The sound signaled the line of beast, and without hesitation, they attacked.

As they charged forward, more people ran into the room. Allies. They formed a line in front of us, and Demetrius tried to push me further back, but I refused. There was no way I was going to sit out the fight. We outnumbered the monsters, but they were strong and relentless in their attack.

Imara and my mother were right by my side as I ran forward to aid in the fight. These beasts were brutal and would not give up. They flung mermen left and right and dealt far more damage than they took. Without our help, they would lose.

"Imara, tag team." I signaled my sister and pointed to the monster closet to us.

"This is going to taste nasty." She frowned then ran and jumped over the head of a mermaid who stabbed the beast in the arm with a spear. It caught her in midair, but Imara had already engaged her power. She sucked the life out of the monster until it released her. When she fell out of its hold, I channeled my energy in each hand

and expanded it out. The extensions formed invisible walls on each side of the beast. Imara rolled out of the way, pulling the mermaid with her. When I clapped my hands, the beast was crushed between the invisible barriers.

"How many more tricks like that do you have?" Imara ran up to me, spitting out the taste in her mouth.

"No clue." I shrugged. "I'm just going with the flow."

"Well, keep it up." My mother threw a spear that pierced the chest of another beast.

It fell but didn't die. Annoyed by the injury, the thing charged right for us. We braced ourselves, but before it could reach us, Demetrius slammed into its side sending it into the wall. He ran after it giving me a moment to look around.

We were losing the fight.

The first three beasts went down easily, but the others were more resilient. They adapted to the attacks easily and attacked with more force.

During the chaos, Oceanus hadn't moved. Unlike his sister, he didn't yell and scream. He barely seemed to pay attention at all. He leaned against the wall watching the bloodshed. When he glanced to the massive window, I followed his line of sight. That was when I saw the battle outside the window. Merpeople fought in the water against the underwater creatures. He knew exactly what he was doing.

"You can't just keep going at them like that," I told Demetrius after he knocked another beast to the ground. "They learn and adapt, and if you don't kill them on the first hit, you might as well not even waste your time."

"So, what do we do?" Demetrius asked.

Imara yelled across the room. "Tag team!"

"What does that mean?" I watched as she worked with Malachi to suck another one dry, and he ripped its head off.

"It means I go high, and you go low." I winked and ran off.

Demetrius was right by my side. I pointed to my target, and he ran ahead of me. He stopped and held his hands clasped together as a base. I ran, jumped into his hands, and he catapulted me across the room. I landed on the back on the beast, and as soon as I touched it, I pulled its life into me. It fell to its knees, and when it did, Demetrius, in his own demon form, followed his brother's example and ripped the head off.

My mother was already ahead of us. She used her siren song on one of the beasts. It swayed, enchanted by her song, and the distraction gave Rhys the opportunity to use his own magic. He sent a blast so powerful it ripped right through the things chest and left a gaping hole.

Just as it looked like the tide had turned in our favor. More of the ugly creatures entered the room, and as they did, Oceanus pushed more of his own strength to the beasts. I saw the strings of his energy, a deep blue essence that shot from him to each of the beasts. With each step they grew in size until they were at least twice the size of any other person in the room.

If he wasn't going to play fair, neither would I.

"Imara, get to Rhys now!" I called out.

My sister once again reacted like she could hear my thoughts. She ran to Rhys just before I turned my power to the large glass wall. Something told me those beasts weren't adept to swimming. The first blast cracked the thick glass. The second shattered it, and water rushed into the building.

I was right. The creatures panicked as soon as the water touched them. They shrieked like cats being forced into a bathtub, and as the room filled, they were sucked out into the ocean and ripped apart by the sea monsters who weren't picky about their meals.

Disoriented at first. I saw my mother with Imara and Rhys outside the room. They navigated the ocean, swimming to safety away from the sea monsters before they finished their free meal. Malachi joined them, holding another person in his arms as he swam.

Demetrius remained in the room with me. I locked eyes on him as he swam to me. At first, he looked relieved to see me, but then his eyes widened, and he swam fast.

"Move!" he called out.

I was too slow to react. The massive hand wrapped around my wrist, and I looked back to see Oceanus. I tried to get away from him, but he held firm. As Demetrius neared us, Oceanus waved his hand send a current into his chest that pulled him out of the window.

A white light wrapped around us, and as Demetrius called out my name, the titan transported me away from the ocean.

CHAPTER 38

There was warmth. Heat that lay over me like a blanket that stretched from my toes up my belly, but my chest and shoulders were cool. Then there was the breeze that carried salty air, and the sound of water. Waves crashing against the shore. My mind was at peace. I opened my eyes, and I was back at my beach house.

My head felt fuzzy like the static between stations on a radio. Was it all a dream? Did I seriously fall asleep watching television and dream that I had to take on a titan?

The curtains to the window were open. I couldn't remember if I closed them the night before, but when the uneven tan came in, I would regret it. I rubbed the back of my neck where there was a tightness the stretched down into my shoulders.

"Get up, girl," I fussed at myself because I couldn't stay in bed. Not that I had much to do around the house, but the unsettling dream made me want to move. Maybe movement would make it all feel less real.

I headed for the kitchen. Tea would calm my mind. Everything looked the same. The natural light came filtered through soft white curtains made of sheer fabric that hung at every window. The cool colors that felt like am extension of the beach and the waters outside of the home, it was all the same. As I moved through the house, I reminded myself to be grounded in the moment. I was okay. The house hadn't been smashed under a massive tide. This was my home. Rhys would return soon, and we would go on with our lives.

That thought made my stomach hurt. We would go on, as if nothing happened. Did I want that? Even if it was an elaborate dream, I still felt changed by it. It had revealed so much to me about who I was and how I'd been limiting myself to fit into someone else's choices. How would I explain that to Rhys without making him worry?

The one benefit of the dream was that I hadn't hurt him. He hadn't seen me with Demetrius, twice. I hadn't broken his heart, yet.

In the kitchen, I paused. I remembered leaving the tea set on the counter to dry, but it wasn't there. I searched through the cabinets, and each time I came up empty, my panic grew. It was a gift from my mother.

How could it be missing? I was so busy slamming the cabinet doors and tossing around the dishes that I hadn't heard him enter, but I froze when he called out to me.

"Sy," he called out to me. "What the hell are you doing in there?"

I turned around and dropped the glass cup in my hand, and it shattered at my feet. "Demetrius?"

"You look like you just saw a ghost." He crossed the room to pick up the shards of glass then looked up at me. "Are you okay?"

"What are you doing here?" I looked down at the man who stared at me like I'd lost my mind.

"What do you mean?" When he stood, the loose bun he had his dreadlocks in dropped, and his hair fell around his face. "Dammit, broke another one."

"Wait a minute." I walked away from him.

"Sy, your foot is bleeding." He pulled out a chair. "Sit down, please."

"Why are you calling me that?" I frowned when he spoke my name again.

"What?" He grabbed a towel and pressed it to the cut on my foot.

"You called me..." I stopped talking as my mind

rushed with a blend of fuzzy memories. My head spun as I remembered two truths. The one where I was with Rhys. I chose him over the Denali brothers. I severed my bond Demetrius so I could be with Rhys.

Then there was another timeline. One where I chose to remain with Demetrius. We defeated my father, and I left to be with him. We shared the beach house together. He was home with me most nights, and I never starved for him physically. I didn't keep myself locked away in the house because I wasn't afraid of what I might do.

My heart ached with confliction because while the history with Rhys felt realer, I wanted the one with Demetrius to be the truth. I wanted the love and freedom I felt. The way he looked at me while he cared for my foot knowing I would heal on my own. I wanted him.

"Are you okay?" He touched my face, bringing me out of the momentary shock. "Sy, I'm worried about you. What's going on?"

"Just a weird dream, and now my head is all messed up." I place my hand over his and leaned into the warmth of his touch.

"A dream that bad it has you tearing up the kitchen?"

"I was looking for the tea set. The one my mom gave me. I swore I left it on the counter."

"That tea set?" He pointed to the counter behind me, and when I turned, it was there. Sitting on the drying rack just as I remembered.

"I—" I rubbed my head. "I swear that was not there a moment ago."

"Sounds like you need to rest. Are you sure you're not getting sick?" He stood in front of me. "I shouldn't have left you alone last night."

"No, I mean, I don't feel sick." I touched my stomach. "I feel fine. Just a little off."

"Still, I'd feel better if you lay down. I will make the tea for you."

"Are you sure?"

"Of course." He held his hand out for me to help me up from the chair.

"Thank you."

"Anything for you, you know that." Demetrius kissed my forehead as I walked past him, and my stomach jumped.

It wasn't in the way of butterflies inspired by anticipation. This was something else. Something urgent like a warning. I looked at him and shook my head. Maybe he was right. Maybe I was getting sick. Served me right for sleeping with the windows open.

I made it back to my bed and climbed under the covers. The sun still warmed the bed, and as I snuggled deeper under the blanket, I wondered how I could have gotten so mixed up. Did I still have guilt over leaving Rhys? How long had it been since I last saw him? My mind spun out more questions than I had answers, and just as the panic felt like it would choke me, Demetrius entered the room carrying a tray with a tea, crackers, and fruit.

"I thought maybe you could also use a snack." He placed the tray on the nightstand next to me then moved to sit on the end of the bed. "Are you sure you're okay? I'm worried."

"Yes, I'm okay," I tried to reassure him, but I wasn't so sure myself if that was the truth. I wanted to be okay but couldn't shake the feeling that something wasn't right.

"What's on your mind, Sy? I know something is bothering you." He placed his hand on my leg and rubbed me through the covers.

Relaxed by his touch, I told him the truth. "Rhys."

"Rhys?" His jaw tightened for a moment then relaxed. I considered not saying anything else about it, but I wouldn't be able to escape the thoughts if I didn't.

"Yes, the dream I had." I touched my forehead where it ached. "I hurt him so much. I chose him and then I left him for you."

"So, I still win in the end?" He smiled and twisted his face like a cartoon character wining an unimportant trophy.

"Be serious, please." I laughed at his goofy expression.

"Okay, tell me more." He squeezed my leg gently. "What happened in the dream."

"I wanted to be with him, but he wasn't enough," I admitted what felt more like the truth than I was prepared for. "It didn't work. No matter how hard I tried. I felt stifled with him, and I just had to get away."

"That doesn't sound that bad," he said calmly. "You tried to work it out with him. It didn't work. Relationships fail, Sy. It sucks when they do, but it's not the end of the world."

"I know you're right." I grabbed the cup of tea. "I must sound ridiculous going on about a fictional relationship."

"You sound like someone who cares about how she impacts the people around her. I don't think that's ridiculous at all."

"Maybe you're right." I leaned back against the headboard and sipped the tea.

"I am. Just like I'm right about you needing to rest." The wide smile stretched across his face.

"Will you lay with me?" I pouted, and he groaned.

"You know I can never say no to that face." He kicked his shoes off and climbed into the bed beside me. "I'm glad you chose me. In this reality and in your dreams."

"Me too." I placed the cup back on the tray then turned to lay my head on his chest.

We lay there together, and Demetrius rubbed his hands through my hair while I continued telling him about my dream. He pulled me tighter when I spoke to the dangerous parts and kissed the top of my head when I remembered the sad things, like losing Maggie again.

Our conversation shifted from talks about the dream to hopes for our future. Demetrius wanted a life together, one where we explored the world, and every word he said spoke to my heart. Like he'd read my diary.

"I'll give you all of that and more," he whispered in my ear.

"More?" I looked up at him. "What more could there be?"

He placed his hand on my belly. "There's a lot more, Sy."

I glanced down at his hand on my stomach, and that urgent sensation was there again. This time, it edged into the realm of panic. I understood what he meant, but I was in no way ready to have that conversation with him. Not after what I dreamt.

"You can't mean."

"I do." He kissed my neck. "I want to have every experience with you."

"We have plenty of time for that." I sighed as his lips slid from my neck across my collar bone.

"Yes, we do." He stopped. "Would you have babies with me?"

"Huh?" My mind raced as his touch awakened my siren.

"Sy, would you have babies with me?" he repeated his question as he pulled the sheer top from my shoulders, and his lips found the top of my breast.

"Why do you keep calling me that?" I couldn't understand my own question, but I knew each time he called me by the shortened version of my name it felt weird. Had the dream really left that much of an impression on me?

"Just relax." He continued to kiss and caress me, and I allowed it. I slid down in the bed so my head could lay on the pillow while he undressed me, following the work his hands did with gentle kisses.

With my shorts removed, he placed his head between my legs and first kissed my lips. He danced around the outside and teased my clit with short blows of warm air. I gripped the sheet with the anticipation. I wanted him to taste me. I wanted to cum all over his face.

After more of his teasing, I couldn't take it anymore. I grabbed him by his locs and shoved his face into me. Demetrius chuckled and then he enjoyed his meal. His tongue played with my clit, making messy circles before he slid his fingers into me, and his lips wrapped around my clit to suck. He continued this until my first orgasm soaked his face.

Then he flipped me over and continued his feast. With my face planted into the pillow, he slipped a finger into my ass, and I couldn't help it, I came again.

"Dammit!" I cried out as he replaced the fingers in my pussy with his dick and slipped his thumb into my asshole.

Demetrius felt different from my dream. Longer, not as wide, but still good. He pounded me from behind, pushing my face deeper into the pillow as he did.

"Yeah baby, take that dick," he called out, and just before I came again, he stopped and flipped me over. He straddled my face. "Suck that dick."

And I did. I filled my mouth and throat with his length and gagged when he thrust his hips forward, sending himself further down my throat. After three pumps, he stopped, climbed down my body, and shoved his dick into my ass. Face to face he thrust over and over.

I was enjoying myself. Every moment of it. Until he kissed me.

With his lips came the taste of death and decay. The same I'd tasted only once before. When he kissed me in the study. I fought the bile that threatened to spew from my face into his.

He continued to fuck me while my mind raced. Overlapping thoughts and theories. The man inside me wasn't who I thought he was. I wanted to scream, fight, push him off me, but a deeper survival instinct told me that was the wrong thing to do.

I had the upper hand. I let out soft moans and closed my eyes so he couldn't see the disgust I felt. As he kissed my neck again, I calculated my options. This was not Demetrius. This was Omar or Oceanus, whatever name he chose to use. He planned to impregnate me with is child. He wanted to finish his plan. I understood.

If I pushed him away, I couldn't be sure he wouldn't kill me for it. Instead, I decided to do what my people were punished for. I let my siren take over.

The song bubbled up my throat, and my song filled

the air.

"Yes, please, sing for me baby." He bit into my shoulder and fucked me harder.

I relaxed my body, taking everything, he could give me, and then it happened. His energy slipped from him and into me. I fed from the titan, and it made me feel fuzzy again. I didn't know how much more I could take of him, but I would keep going because it felt like the only thing I could do. He was so happy with the thought that he was getting what he wanted that he didn't think to question my pull.

"More. Take more of me," he cried out as his hips moved faster. Then he pulled from me, flipped me on my stomach and kept going. I allowed it.

It felt good, and my siren continued to take from him. I felt it happen. The shift when the man who fucked me grew weaker. That was my moment. I pushed my hips back, reached behind me, and pulled him forward. He flipped over on his back, and I straddled him. His hands immediately grabbed my hips to pull me down on top of him harder. Each stroke, he weakened, but his mind flooded with the song that still passed through my lips. To him, he was in control.

And then I pulled from him. His energy slipped from his lips a dark blue and poured into me. The more I fed, the more the facade changed. The man beneath me changed from Demetrius, to Omar, to someone I'd never seen before. Someone ancient, powerful, but barely holding on to the human world. Oceanus.

I kept going. Because despite the strength of the titan inside, the human shell was only so strong. As I took more from him, more changed. Flashes of an underwater battle behind his head. The feel of air turned to the cool touch of water as I rocked my hips. The fake world he'd created and implanted in my mind was broke down.

I saw them, just outside a boundary of light. Rhys and Demetrius pounded their fists against the barrier and called my name. I couldn't stop. Not yet. I had to keep taking, I needed him as weak as I could get him.

The body between my legs withered, and it was then that the titan realized his mistake.

"No!" he screamed, and he tried to pull away from me, but as the fake image, the beach house by the ocean, disappeared, my tail reappeared.

I wrapped my tail around his waist, refusing to let him go, and pulled his lips closer to mine, pulling with more urgency. I couldn't let him get away.

He tried to push me off. He punched me and scratched at my flesh, but I refused. The wall of light that kept Demetrius and Rhys away flickered. I was almost there. I could keep going. My body felt full, like it would burst from the energy, but I kept going.

As soon as the barrier fell, Demetrius swam toward me, but he was stopped by my mother. She placed a hands on each of his shoulders and pushed him back.

"I have to help her," he insisted and tried to get around her, but my mother kept up with him.

"No! Not yet." She held her hand out to him then turned to me. "She has to release him first. You know that. Think, Demetrius!"

"Dammit." He looked over her at me, and though I saw him, my thoughts were consumed with the man I fed from.

My mother turned to look at me, and I saw the concern. She was worried for me, but she wasn't afraid. She called out to me, but still I fed, and when I refused to answer her, she spoke to me with her mind instead of her voice.

"Baby, let go." The words came in a gentle tone that filled my mind. "You have to let him go, Syrinada."

"No," I refused. "Not yet. I have to end him."

"It's too much. You know that. You can't consume it all. Let go."

"He will hurt you," I tried to reason with her. "If I let go, he will hurt them all."

"He can't hurt anyone anymore. Look at him," she spoke with more urgency. "Open your eyes and see the man you're feeding from. Look at what you're doing."

For the first time since the facade failed, I looked down again at the man I held onto, and my stomach turned when I saw the way his body had withered. His eyes were glossy and gray. The man wasn't even fighting anymore. The body was done, the power I fed on was the titan inside.

"Oh god." I relaxed my hold on the withered body, and he fell away.

I had a moment of panic when I witnessed the recovery happening. Almost instantly, Oceanus' energy began healing the body. I reached for him, prepared to pull from him again, for as long as it took, but before I got too him, Demetrius and Rhys were there. One took the arms while the other took the legs, and they pulled. The body tore apart like a sheet of paper, and the spirit of the titan jittered in the water, like a chaotic ball of energy, before it vanished.

"You're okay." My mother pulled me into her arms.

"What happened?" I sobbed because I finally felt able to release the emotions I'd bottled up inside. "Why did I do that? I've never… I learned to stop."

"You almost lost yourself." My mother touched my cheek. "But I'm here."

She guided me back into the building where the others waited. There was work to be done. Once inside, Rhys used his magic to repair the glass and pushed the rest of the water out. The compound had nearly flooded, but there were areas that were still untouched.

While they worked to save the other test subjects and deal with any of the people who worked with the titans, I sat alone in the large room looking out into the ocean. The strange beasts still swam outside. From time to time, one would stop and look into the room. There was one who kept returning.

I recognized him by the scar above his eye. Imagined it was from a fight with another creature. The fourth time he returned, I walked over to the glass to get a better look, and he swam closer. We stared at each other; two creatures feared for their nature. My heart ached. I felt something there, the darkness.

"I'm losing myself," I spoke to the creature. "I don't know what I'm going to do."

"You're not losing yourself," the voice of a friend spoke from behind, and when I saw her reflection in the glass, my mood soared to a new height.

"Maggie?" I turned to face her.

"Got yourself a new friend I see." She pointed to the glass where the creature still swam, looking inside.

"I guess so." I looked back over my shoulder, and I could have sworn he winked at me before turning to swim away.

"You know, if you asked me, I would say you've finally found yourself," she boasted. "And it's about damn time."

"I don't know about that. I feel more confused now than ever."

"Still letting those boys get in your head?" She nudged my shoulder.

"Never," I lied. "Where the hell have you been?"

"Back in the ghostly realm." She rolled her eyes. "It was so ridiculous. They didn't want me here in case you failed."

"What?" I felt hurt by their assumption. "They thought we would fail?"

"Ebon said it was something about my presence allowing the titans access to their realm." She sighed. "So maybe it was less about you not being able to get the job done and more of a security threat."

"Right." I leaned against the glass. "What happens now? Do you go back to the ghost realm for good?"

"No, apparently our job isn't done."

"It's not? The Hybrids are all either dead or locked up here. The threat of the titans returning is not an issue anymore. I mean, not that I'm not happy to be able to spend more time with you, but what more is there?" I asked.

"Well, the titans are gone, and if we're lucky, they won't be back for another thousand years or until someone else is crazy enough to try to resurrect them. Why anyone would want to bring a titan back to earth, I have no idea." Maggie shrugged. "But Ebon wants us to figure that out."

"So, someone else is behind this. It doesn't just end with them. Someone started this. Who?"

"One theory was your father," she answered bluntly.

"What?" I moved away from the glass. "What do you mean my father?"

"Your father created you and others like you. We saw that it was a design. They have all his notes. At first it was like a puzzle with missing pieces, but it came together. You and your sister and the others were supposed to be these powerful anchors. That's why they wanted you. They would have taken Imara too had you not pushed her out of the way. The others were too weak, but you two, you both harnessed the essence of a titan, and you still stand strong. The others, the ones you found, and the ones trapped here, they weren't strong enough."

"That doesn't explain why they think my father had anything to do with this."

"Ebon thinks he wanted to use the powers of the titans. He had some sort of plan to trap them, but honestly, we'll probably never know."

"This is too much." I shook my head.

"Tell me about it." Maggie placed her hand on my shoulder. "That's not all, though. They want us to find whoever else was collaborating with your father. According to his notes, he had partners."

"Great."

"But for now, we help with the clean-up of this place and make sure none of these experiments go off and create havoc elsewhere."

"Is that our job now?"

"Honestly, I think so." Maggie threw her hand over my shoulder. "Hey, look at it this way, as long as there is freaky shit going on, you and I will never be apart. I'll be your haunting bestie forever!"

CHAPTER 39

emetrius took control of the cleanup detail. I helped swim a few people to safety, but that was all he allowed. To be honest, I was grateful for the excuse not to hang around and risk bumping into Rhys again. It took seven hours to evacuate the building. I didn't see what they did with the bad guys, but I couldn't imagine it would be good. Maggie joked about the Denali brothers using their demon half to take them all to hell. That wasn't something I wanted to imagine.

Twenty-four hours after Oceanus disappeared, we were sitting at a beach house, looking out onto the ocean.

"Everyone's coming." Maggie appeared between my mother and me. "Should be here soon."

"Thank you." I touched her hand. "I'm so glad you get to stay."

"Hey, I've pretty much earned an all-access pass for the foreseeable future." Maggie plopped down in the seat next to me on the patio. "I can tell you there are some spirits on the other side who are pissed about it."

"Really, why?" My mother leaned forward in her seat like she was getting inside tips on the other world.

"Spirits aren't really allowed to just hang out on earth. Something about upsetting the balance." Maggie stole the bowl of fruit I had been nibbling on before he arrival. "But I made the case that I'm a part of this team, and I help keep Sy leveled. She needs me."

"You're right." I laughed when she stuffed a handful of grapes in her mouth. "I really do need you here."

"It's a good thing ghosts can live underwater then." My mother smiled.

"Why is that?" I turned to her.

"After everything that happened, after you defeated two titans, the council has decided that you belong with us in Deuterio. They are welcoming you home, Syrinada."

"Woah." Maggie gasped. "That's major news."

"Yeah, it is," I chewed my bottom lip as I thought about what she said.

"But?" my mother asked as the breeze picked up

and tussled her hair.

"I don't want to live in Deuterio," I rushed to speak. "I mean, it's cool that they are accepting of me now, but I just got my life back on earth. There are things I want to do, experiences I want to have. There's Imara."

"Your sister." She smiled and patted my hand. "This is good."

"Yeah, you were right." I relaxed when I realized she wouldn't be upset with me for deciding not to go back to Deuterio. "All that time I spent couped up and hiding away from the world, I should have been with her. Mom, there is a connection between us. I felt it when we fought together. I'm hoping its more than a mutual appreciation for destroying evil guys."

"That's good." She chuckled. "And I'm sure the two of you have a lot more in common than that."

"But I will visit. I mean, I can do that now, right?" I asked. "They won't turn me away or send those weird sharks after me if I do?"

"Of course, you can." She laughed. "No one's sending any shark after my baby, and now that things are settled, I can come and see you."

The staticky sound turned our heads to the end of the white patio. Neither of us moved because we knew what it was. A moment later, where we once saw the edge of the sandy path that led to the ocean, the air rippled, and a portal to the underwater world appeared. The group of four, led by Tylia, came through the opening before it shut.

Rhys, Malachi, Tylia, and Imara stood in front of us, magically dried by their trip and standing on solid legs.

"I will never get over that!" Imara clapped her hands. "We should be able to travel everywhere like that. Do you know how much time that would save?"

"I think I prefer slower method." Malachi shook his head. The man looked green in the face, like he was seconds from losing all the contents in his stomach.

"Where's D?" Maggie jumped from her seat.

I hadn't put it together that the eldest Denali brother wasn't there. I was too focused on the man who stood at the back of their group avoiding eye contact with me. My mouth felt dry as I contemplated what I could possibly say to him to bridge the gap.

I didn't want to make it about me. He was the one hurting in the situation. He deserved for me to allow him space to process the inevitable changes in our relationship and talk to him or listen. Only he could say what was best for me to do.

"There he is." Malachi pointed to the water where the dark-skinned man with dreadlocks that hung to his waist climbed from the ocean.

I had to stop myself from gawking at him like some horny teenager, but the man looked amazing. Demetrius had three others with him as he approached the patio where we sat.

"Brother," Demetrius greeted Malachi before the rest of us. "It's good to see you're all here, safe and sound." He scanned the group and lingered when he saw me. His features softened slightly, but it was enough to make my heart skip a beat.

"Beat you!" Imara pointed at him. "Told you there was no way you'd get here before we did."

"You're right." Demetrius held his hands up in defeat. "Still, we made pretty good timing."

"Everything all set?" Malachi asked as Imara stepped to his side. He put his arm around her. I expected to feel that same sense of territorial anger as I had before, but it wasn't there.

"Yes. The beasts are delt with. Anyone who worked with the titans are locked up and awaiting questioning. We'll figure out who is really behind this. I doubt we caught them."

"What about the other hybrids?" I asked. "What did you do with them?"

"They are safe." He smiled at me. "They won't be punished for what they are. Hell, if they are, then we would be too, but we will monitor them for the foreseeable future. Make sure they stay in line. There is still the question of how so many hybrids will impact the balance of nature. So far, we have no real reason to believe it will have any negative effect."

"Good." I nodded. "This is good."

"Does that mean we can actually relax?" Maggie asked. "I mean, not that I need any more time to relax."

"I think so." Demetrius pulled up the seat next to her and across from me. "If nothing else, it will give us time to reset. Figure out what's next."

"What's next is for me to go home. I know my boys are missing me," Tylia commented. "Rhys here is going to take me."

"Yes, I am." Rhys nodded.

"Wait." I stood. "Rhys, can we talk?"

"Yeah." He looked around the group. Everyone averted their eyes. "Sure."

We headed inside the house for privacy. The beach house looked at lot like the one we shared together, complete with the sandy color scheme. I sat on the white sofa and waited for him to join me.

"You wanted to talk?" Rhys stood next to the sofa, refusing to sit.

"Yes." I stood because I was uncomfortable sitting when he was standing. "I wanted to talk about us."

"Is there really anything to talk about?"

"Rhys."

"I know what you're going to say, Sy." His jaw clenched, and he took a deep breath before continuing. "You don't want to be with me anymore."

"That's not true."

"It's not?"

"No. I want you, Rhys. Just—"

"Not in the way I want you to want me?"

"No." I glanced out the window to the ocean because it was too hard to say what I needed to and look him in the eye. "I tried. I really did. You know, I thought it would be easy to ignore that side of myself. I could be the perfect mate to you, but it just wasn't enough for me. I don't know that it ever will be."

"I never asked you to ignore that side of you."

"No, you didn't, but we both know you can't handle it if I embrace it, either."

"Sy."

"Honestly, Rhys. Could you be okay with me going off to be with other men? Because that is what it would take. I need to feed, and it is so weird saying that, but I do. I need sex to sustain who I am. Even more now that the spirits have removed the block between me and my magic. If I don't be true to who I am, I'm afraid I will turn dark. I don't want that."

"I don't want that for you either." He stepped closer to me. "But you're right. I wouldn't be able to handle it. I thought it was just the Denali brothers, but the thought of you with anyone but me, I can't handle that. Not when you're supposed to be mine."

"I'm sorry."

"Don't be." He pulled me into his arms, and I laid my head on his shoulder. "What we had; it was real. It was love. It just wasn't the kind of love that's built to last."

"I still love you, Rhys." I looked into his face. "I always will."

"Good." He kissed my forehead. "Because there is no way I'm ever going to get over you."

~*~

Rhys stayed with me for a few minutes longer, then he left with Tylia. I stayed inside because I didn't want to face anyone else, and they respected my space, even Maggie, who I expected to pop in and tell me to get my ass up. I sat on that white sofa alone and stared out at the ocean until the blue water turned dark.

The cool breeze of night brushed across my skin, and I turned to the open door where Demetrius stood.

"Is everything okay?" I moved to get up, but he held his hand out to stop me.

"Everything is fine." He closed the door behind him. "Everyone is gone."

"What?" I frowned. "Why?"

"Because you need time away from them, and they all have work to do. This isn't over." Demetrius sat on the sofa next to me. "How are you feeling, Syrinada?"

I said nothing, just smiled at the man.

"Why are looking at me like that?"

"I really like the way you say my name. My whole name."

"Syrinada," he said it once more to make me smile, and it worked. "Answer my question, please. How are you feeling?"

"Sad, relieved, confused, worried." I shrugged. "It's a lot going on in my head and heart right now."

"How can I support you while you sort through it all?"

"When I figure that out, I'll let you know."

"Great, for now we can just sit here together." He grabbed my waist and pulled me over to him, and I laid my head on his shoulder.

"You're my mate. Aren't you?" I looked up at him.

"Yes." He nodded. "I am. I tried to find the answer, why our bond never broke, but I came up empty."

"Do you wish it had?" I asked because I needed to know, even if his answer hurt.

"Why do you ask that?"

"Come on, we both know this would have been a lot easier on you if the bond between us didn't exist."

"Do we?"

"Isn't it true?"

"I don't know that it is." He brushed his fingers across my cheek. "Even before we were mated, I was yours. You really don't know the effect you have on people. Why do you think they fight so hard for you. My brother, Rhys. They would do anything for you."

"Well, not your brother anymore."

"What do you mean?"

"Something changed down there. Whatever they did to him or me, it broke the bond I had with him. I don't feel him at all anymore."

"Hmm." Demetrius rubbed his chin. "He didn't mention it, but I'm not going to pretend to be sad about it. Not like I want my brother pining for the woman I love."

"You love me?"

"Isn't it obvious?"

"Nothing is obvious."

"Let me make it clear." He turned so we were face to face. "Syrinada Alia Sania, there hasn't been a moment in my life since you first looked at me that I haven't loved you. You are the essence of who I am. Long before you chose me, I chose you, and I still choose you. I choose to support you, love you, and embrace you in all facets."

"Wow." My breath caught in my chest. "I—"

"You will not say it back right now. That's not what this is."

"Demetrius."

"Syrinada, you just went through hell. Your relationship with Rhys is freshly ended, and you're still trying to figure out what's next in your life. I'm not going to be the next thing that keeps you from doing that." He pulled my hand to his lips and kissed it. "Take your time. I'm here. I'm not going anywhere. When you tell me you love me, that will be when it begins for us."

"I don't deserve you."

"You deserve everything your heart desires and things you can't even begin to fathom. It is my intention to make sure you have all of it and more."

"You really mean it, don't you?"

"You damn straight I do." I smiled.

"Demetrius?" I pulled his dreadlocks into my hand and felt the siren awaken inside me.

"Yes, Syrinada?" His grin turned devious as he felt the change within me.

"Kiss me."

He did. He pulled me into his arms and kissed me in a way that felt consuming and yet freeing. This man was mine, and I was his. As the waves crashed outside the window, I let his love wash over me, as I would forever…

ABOUT THE AUTHOR

Jessica Cage is an International Award Winning, and USA Today Best-Selling Author. Born and raised in Chicago, IL, writing has always been a passion for her. She dabbles in artistic creations of all sorts, but it's the pen that her hand itches to hold. Jessica had never considered following her dream to be a writer because she was told far too often "There is no money in writing." So she chose the path most often traveled. During pregnancy, she asked herself an important question. How would she be able to inspire her unborn son to follow his dreams and reach for the stars, if she never had the guts to do it herself? Jessica took a risk and unleash the plethora of characters and their crazy adventurous worlds that had previously existed only in her mind into the realm of readers. She did this with hopes to inspire not only her son but herself. Inviting the world to tag along on her journey to become the writer she has always wanted to be. She hopes to continue writing and bringing her signature Caged Fantasies to readers everywhere.